DON'T LOOK BACK

SEAN SCOTT GRIFFIN

REBEL
YEAH!

First Edition, 2025

*First published in the United Kingdom in 2025 by Rebel Yeah Ltd.
www.rebelyeah.co.uk*

*Copyright © 2025 Sean Scott Griffin
Cover design by Fabiana Borsari © 2025 Rebel Yeah!*

The moral right of the author has been asserted in accordance with the Copyright, Designs and Patents Act 1988.

All rights reserved.

No part of this publication may be reproduced, distributed, or transmitted in any form or by any means, including photocopying, recording, or other electronic or mechanical methods, without the prior written permission of the publisher, except as permitted by UK copyright law.

For permission requests, contact Rebel Yeah!: rebelsales@rebelyeah.co.uk

The story, all names, characters, and incidents portrayed in this novel are fictitious. No identification with actual persons (living or deceased), places, buildings, and products is intended or should be inferred. Any references to musical artists, songs, or albums are used for cultural commentary and fair use purposes.

*ISBN: 978-1-9191828-0-3
A CIP catalogue record for this book is available from the British Library*

For Margie, Cathy and Nico

CHAPTER 1
LIAM

DAY 1

Sitting on a cluttered tabletop, a dull silver CD with faded handwriting clicks into a Sony Discman D-99, circa mid-'90s, but it could well be older.

I mean, it was bought in the mid-'90s, but who the fuck knows, right? Who can remember back that far? Anyway, this Discman ain't just any cheap shitty Discman, it's a beast of a portable music playing machine, about 15cm x 15cm and the width of a fag packet, jet black, with quality silver buttons and a wicked little LCD on the bottom left. It's not one of those basic bitch ten quid CD "discmans" you got from Argos or Littlewoods or wherever you got your cheap shitty portable off-brand CD players from back in the day—the ones that skipped if you just looked at them, the ones that came with a laser so weak it could barely read the songs half the time because a speck of dust may have landed on it. No, this is a stone-cold classic—a piece of technical artistry made by a Japanese workforce so goddamn committed that to this very day it's still going strong and has outlived every cheap Chinese knock-off that has littered the planet since. This Sony Discman-D99 was a gift. This was a gift to Liam from his mum, and with God as my witness, it will outlive the lot of us.

Before the clamshell closes, the faded handwriting is just visible:

LeeLee & Sal's Mixtape
Classics & Tunes Only

The play button engages with that satisfying mechanical click that nobody born after 1999 properly understands.

First, silence. Then that guitar. *That guitar.* The strum of those few chords that send chills down the spine—A, B, D, G sharp—or whatever. I dunno, I'm not a musician. But when Thom Yorke starts singing about imminent death and fading out, it doesn't matter that you've heard "Street Spirit" ten thousand times before; it always has the uncanny ability to crawl inside your skull and make you take notice.

Four minutes and fourteen seconds of depressing bliss.

Those spine-tingling chords and Thom's falsetto drift into the empty space between the clutter of Liam's council flat. Which tells a story all of its own, but only if you know how to read it. Everything inside these concrete walls is a museum of someone else's taste. His mum's cheap pine units and flat-pack Ikea furniture, circa 2005, were never in fashion, and the overloaded shelves are fighting a losing battle with gravity. A dozen framed photos capture moments from before everything went wrong. Before... before... wai! We'll get into all that... first, let's talk about Liam.

Liam's in his late thirties, though I'm not even sure he realises this himself. The braids peeking out from under his bucket hat haven't been properly maintained in a long while, and his threadbare sky blue Adidas tracksuit—the same style he's worn since Tony Blair was in Downing Street—has seen better decades. He looks like he's stepped straight out of a '90s time capsule, which isn't far from the truth. In Liam's world, time stopped somewhere around 1996, and he's never quite figured out how to get it going again. Mixed race and mild-mannered, he's the kind of guy who still uses a CD Discman and can tell you *exactly* why modern music isn't as good as it used to be, even though nobody's asking. For all his optimism about life, he hasn't done much with it.

From the way the golden sun strikes the room at a perfect angle, it's morning, around 6 am, maybe 7. Long shadows hit the cheap furniture and unfashionable home decor. But Liam himself casts no shadow at all. He hasn't for years. With no means to escape or parents to show him the way, this boy is truly stuck. He does this a lot, sitting up all night waiting for the sun to rise and a new day to waste... or maybe for his mum to walk back in through the door. Today is Saturday. And Liam doesn't know it yet, but today will be the last day of his life.

~ 1996 ~

First, let's just skip back a few years. To the summer of 1996, to be exact.

The Digsbys live in a modest Victorian terrace on Lyndhurst Grove that's stood largely unchanged for a hundred odd years, yet today, the world around it thrums with an energy unique to this year. The wide street echoes with the sound of kids playing football, their shoes scuffing against the pavement, the ball bouncing off the walls as they argue over whether England will finally win something again at Euro '96. Spoiler alert, they didn't.

Inside homes across the country TVs flicker with images of Tony Blair, the fresh-faced leader of 'New Labour,' who just a year before swept to power on a promise that "Things Can Only Get Better", leading to a wave of mid-'90s optimism that, honestly, you just can't describe. Things got better for a bit, but the anointed one took a dark turn at the beginning of the new century, and, well, things have not gotten better since.

But it was the music spilling from the country's open windows that tells the true story of Britain, of its unfolding cultural revolution. This was the year after *Oasis v Blur*, aka 'The Battle of Britpop'. Their rivalry captivated the nation and split friends and families in a way that wouldn't be seen again until Brexit (just without the shame and economic decline).

Things changed after the 'Battle of Britpop'. 1996 became the year the Spice Girls countered the toxic machismo that the *Oasis v Blur* thing exemplified. 'Girl Power' was not just about music—it was a full-blown cultural shift where girls and women around the world fought back against the bucket hats, parkas and jingly jangly guitars.

But Britpop wasn't dead. Far from it. Pulp, Ocean Colour Scene, Suede, The Bluetones, Dodgy, Sleeper, The Charlatans, Mansun, Kula Shaker, Echobelly, Supergrass and Elastica, to name but a few, all had their moment. This list is not exhaustive, by the way; more came before and more came after. But this was 1996.

Aged around ten at the time, Liam's favourite band, Oasis, released "Don't Look Back In Anger" from *(What's the Story) Morning Glory?* They would have been gearing up to play Knebworth very soon. Not that our Liam's going. He never goes anywhere. Mum says they're always too skint and there's so much to see and do in London, that "every day is like a holiday." But he would like a trip to the seaside. Just once. His mate Steve goes to his grandparents' caravan in Great Yarmouth every summer, and Liam often dreams of the exotic climes and the yellow sandy beach he's seen in Steve's holiday photos.

From the top floor of the house, you can just make out the distant silhouette of Canary Wharf, its newly completed tower a symbol of the changing city and time. Outside, the sound of a car stereo carries on the hazy breeze, mixing Britpop anthems with the latest dance tracks, while somewhere, a church bell tolls the hour, just as it has done for over two hundred years.

The streets themselves tell a story of radical change. Corner shops now stock imported American breakfast cereals and ADHD-inducing candy alongside good ol' PG Tips. The video store windows are plastered with posters for Danny Boyle's 'Trainspotting,' Baz Luhrmann's 'Romeo+Juliet' and the Coen Brothers' 'Fargo', alongside 'Independence Day', 'Mission Impossible' and 'Twister'—and if you ask nicely, the video shop owner may just give you an old poster. The pub on the corner now serves cappuccinos for a quid, but these regulars still stick to their usual pints of bitter, even at 10 am. Market stalls sell plantains and scotch bonnets next to the traditional pie and mash shops, and pirate radio antennas illegally transmit UK Garage to the masses. On every lamppost, advertising board and closed-down shop are posters for trance nights happening somewhere, at some time.

This is Peckham, 1996—still rough around the edges, but feeling alive with an energy not felt in a long time. Where the Del Boys of the world hang with the Delroys, and where posters of Ian Wright and Bob Marley hang side by side. It's not all rose-tinted though; the threat of being stabbed or robbed is still very real. Crack will do that to a community. And gang culture thrives with fights between themselves as vicious as the fights with the neo-Nazis and football 'firms'.

But in this particular abode, there's a sense of possibility in the air. The house has seen over a century of London life pass by its windows, with countless families sharing the space between the walls—but even so, this year feels different. There's an unmistakable optimism, a feeling that Britain, and this family, are on the cusp of something new.

This is one of those older Victorian homes with the bathroom still downstairs next to the kitchen, allowing for a third bedroom upstairs. It's homely, with its woodchip wallpaper slightly peeling and a spiral-patterned carpet throughout that was already ancient when they moved in.

The living room is filled with the smell of chicken curry wafting from the kitchen, where Sally, experimenting with those new Chicken Tonight sauces, has left a pot on the hob. A hefty Ferguson TV sits in the corner, complete with a built-in VHS player—still blinking 12:00 because no one's quite figured out how to set the clock. There's a drawer underneath stuffed with recorded episodes of 'Bottom' and 'The Word', labels written in Sally's quite beautiful cursive handwriting. Liam's grey Game Boy sits idly on the edge of the tape drawer, ready to fall with the slightest of nudges. This is a place where things like falling Game Boys can happen, and no one gets shouted at, not by Sally anyway.

And on the wall is a "politely asked for" dog-eared poster of 'Pulp Fiction'. Mrs. Mia Wallace, aka Uma Thurman, looks effortlessly cool with her jet black bob, cigarette in hand, and gun lying in front of her.

Underneath the poster, the borrowed stereo stack system dominates—a high tower of black separate components with Sally, hidden behind, fiddling with the cables, trying and failing to get it to connect together. Her sweaty fingers and frustrated temperament are not helping the situation.

The summer heat refuses to relent; it must be 30 degrees outside, and being inside is no picnic. Even so, this is home. Not fancy, not flash, but warm, lived-in, and for most of the time, it's joyful and exuberant. The kind of place where time moves in sync with the rest of the world, not yet frozen, not yet broken.

"How do you know which songs to choose for a mixtape, Mumma?" Little Liam asks, sitting cross-legged in the middle of the carpet, watching his mum struggle, but not really wanting to help as he scans through a pile of CDs borrowed that morning from the local library. Fair enough, really, to any ten-year-old, the CDs are a lot more interesting than putting together a complicated stack system.

Sally pops her head up from behind the stereo. Early to mid-thirties, she's a petite woman who carries herself with purpose and pride. Her blonde bob is streaked with electric blue that catches the sunlight as she moves, and her high-waisted Levi's paired with a light blue Oasis *Definitely Maybe* tee instantly mark her as one of the *cool mums*. But beneath the attitude, she carries a fragility, which she fights hard to hide. Deeper still is the fierce protectiveness of a lioness—especially when it comes to her kids. This is Sally. Complex, often erratic, but always loving.

"What d'you say, LeeLee?" she sighs.

"How do you know which songs to choose? For a mixtape?" he repeats.

"Oh, that's easy love." She stops fussing with the equipment, taps ash from her cigarette into an empty Lilt can and shuffles under the table on her knees over to Little Liam. She gently puts both her hands on his little shoulders and smiles warmly. To this day, he can still remember the sweet citrus smell of her CK One perfume mixed with the disgusting aroma of her Marlboro Light ciggies. A heady, toxic mix of happy nostalgia and pain.

"Pick songs that mean something to you, babe. That speak to who you are inside."

Little Liam pays attention.

"Don't let anyone tell you different." She winks.

"Then... throw in a few surprises. Couple of slow jams to slow your brain down. And make sure you have a couple of big tunes. No one wants a who's who of B-sides."

"What's a B-side?" Little Liam asks innocently, as he picks up his new CD Discman D-99, still fresh in its cardboard box.

DAY 1

They say that great art is never finished, only abandoned. Four minutes fourteen seconds seems a short time to abandon a masterpiece like "Street Spirit", but what the fuck do I know, I'm not Thom Yorke. I'm just a sad mid-to-late-thirties, unemployed, wanker on the scrapheap who's watched too many episodes of 'Top of The Pops' and 'Friends', all of which lulled me into a false sense of security that the world was a bright and joyous place. An unwanted child of Thatcher's Britain, raised on Blair's broken promises and left to rot in the ruins of Cameron and Osborne's "austerity." Thanks chaps. I'm a living, breathing case study of generational decline. Because, ladies and gentlemen... I am a Millennial.

"My name is Liam Digsby and I am a Millennial."

We should have support groups or something, meet in church halls and drink shit coffee from poly cups. "Hi, I'm Liam, and it's been six years since I last thought I could afford a mortgage." Everyone else: "Hi, Liam." Wait, isn't that what Facebook and X are for—Millennials slagging off their station in life? I wouldn't know, I don't partake. No phone, no laptop, no social media. I am strictly offline.

CDs—thousands of.

NMEs—towering stacks of.

DVDs—thousands of.

VHS—hundreds of.

Vinyl—whatever I can afford.

Girlfriends—none.

Surprised?

I live in my mum's council flat and I wear the same clothes I've had since I was twenty. Adidas tracksuits. Exclusively. In an assortment of colours. But mostly light blue. Since my bed caved in, I've had to sleep on my mum's old bed, but it's okay because she's dead. I think. Along with my dad. Which I know for a fact, as I have his urn on the windowsill. Er, anything else? White mum. Black dad. In case you were wondering. If you need any more exposition, just ask.

Thirty days in **BIG RED LETTERS** it says. Thirty days to pack up a lifetime's worth of memories and vacate. Thirty days till the wrecking balls come to make me homeless.

Thirty. Fucking. Days.

I swear I got a letter about this flash new development three years ago—you know—the one I won't be a part of. Has three years really gone by just like that? Like a snap of the fingers.

Time's a funny thing, ain't it? How it runs different for different people. You see, time's relative. Einstein was onto something there. Might run slow as fuck for one person:

tick...

tock...

tick...

tock.

Or fast as lightning for another:

ticktockticktockticktockticktockticktockticktock

And sometimes, like for me, the clock just stops altogether. Getting it going again—well, that's the hard part.

Liam's got two watches in this flat. Dad's Seiko (broken) and a plastic Casio that tells perfect time... but he never wears it, because, what's the point? The Sony Discman D-99 still works though. Track one always plays without fail. And every time it does, Thom Yorke always sounds like he's singing about the end of the world.

Maybe he is. The demolition notice taped to Liam's door certainly thinks so.

From his footstool in the middle of the room, Liam can see everything exactly as she left it. The door she walked out of. The cheap digital wall clock from Dixons that stopped working the day she left. The half-drunk cup of tea on the counter she never came back to finish. Okay, he washed that out eventually—even time has its limits. But everything else? Preserved like a museum exhibit: 'The Life and Times of Sally Digsby, circa 2010'. Come see our special display on 'Things My Mum Never Came Back For', including one 'pre-loved grieving son'.

4 minutes and 14 seconds of genius perfection is nearly up, and right now, Liam cuts a lonely figure... in a lonely place... at a lonely time.

Outside the window, the world spins on. The only other tenant left on the block, childhood friend Steve-O, walks his three-legged Staffy past at precisely 8:17 every morning—and Liam would know that if he ever bothered to wear the plastic Casio watch.

The demolition crews inch closer and closer every day, home by home, memory by memory. Some days he thinks about moving the footstool, maybe rearranging the furniture. But what's the point? The wrecking balls are coming anyway. Besides, from this spot he can see both the front door and his CD collection. Everything that matters, really.

Thirty days. How to fill the time? He reorganises those CDs again. This is something he does in times of emotional distress, which means approximately twice daily. This morning's system: in the order of how each album makes him feel shit about himself. Radiohead's *The Bends* goes straight to the top, featuring none other than "Street Spirit" itself. Track one, side one of the CD mixtape they made together that summer. The summer of '96. When everything still made sense.

𝄞

Thom's "Street Spirit" has finally faded out and another day is beginning. Liam grabs his golf club, his Sony Discman and locks up the flat, though why bother when the estate is a ghost town. He heads down the walkway, where, rather depressingly, every door is boarded up with steel shutters—except for one small ray of light—Steve-O's, at the far end. One more holdout.

Despite the distinct lack of people on the estate these days, at least it no longer smells of fresh piss. Just stale piss.

A massive billboard looms over: LUXURY URBAN LIVING STARTING FROM £550,000. The glossy CGI rendering shows gleaming glass balconies, a rooftop garden, and young professionals sipping coffee at ground-floor boutiques. Some artist's fever dream of the future built on the sweat and blood of the people who invested in this town, the same people who will never get to reap the rewards—well that's what Liam thought to himself as he glanced at the poster, which to him is more like a CAPITALISED death warrant than an advert for a better future.

Steve-O's three-legged Staffy, Tyson, spots Liam first and bounds over, tail wagging, remembering better days when the estate was full of life and everyone stopped to talk to each other. Steve-O, a rather wiry man about Liam's age, always sporting a Chelsea baseball cap, tugs at the lead, avoiding eye contact.

"Alright, Steve?" Liam calls out. "Just us left now innit?"

Steve-O glances up at the billboard, then back at Liam, sheepishly. "I've taken their offer. I'm moving to Herne Bay next week."

Liam hides it well, but this is a stab to the gut.

"Some of us have to move on mate, can't all live forever in the past."

Liam forces a smile, but this stab went right to the heart. "Yeah, well, at least the rent's cheap."

Steve-O pulls Tyson away. "Wake up bruv. Time waits for no man."

Liam watches them disappear around the corner, past the construction fencing and bulldozers. His Discman whirs as it loads the next track—"Born Slippy" by Underworld. The perfect soundtrack for another day pretending that everything is in its right place and moving on schedule. He slips the headphones over his ears just as those first haunting synths kick in. The world around him fades away; the warning signs about asbestos, the half-demolished buildings, the empty windows like dead eyes staring down at him—all of it disappears under the pulsing rhythm. His footsteps unconsciously match the beat as he weaves between piles of rubble, abandoned scaffolding and the diggers waiting to tear down his home. By the time the vocals begin their hypnotic chant, he's fully gone, lost in his own private rave in this concrete ghost town. In his head, he's back in '96. Back when time still moved forward.

His car is parked a little walk away in the gentrified terrace of Lyndhurst Grove, where the Digsbys used to call home. Under the streetlights, taking up two spaces, because that's what you do with a car this special. DayGlo orange paintwork gleaming especially bright under today's morning sun, GTI badge proudly displayed, with aftermarket alloy wheels that cost more than the car itself. Lowered suspension, upgraded sound system and a dump valve. Yes, a Golf GTI Mk 2 with a dump valve. Built in 1984, but you'd never know it. Every panel has been replaced, every component upgraded. The ultimate continuation model. It's a bit like that philosophy question about the axe that's had three new heads and four new handles—is it still the same axe? Liam wouldn't know—he's never owned an axe—but he does have a banging boy racer Golf GTI! Though he's never been to a car meet, he's way too embarrassed by all those manchildren fawning over their cars.

Liam slides into the driver's seat and melts into the original worn leather as he turns the key. The engine coughs but refuses to catch. He tries again.

"Come on, Ol' Girl, don't do this to me."

Nothing but another false start.

Third time's the charm as the engine roars to life with a growl that would wake the dead; as it happens, it just annoys the young couple looking from the windows of his old house. The dump valve hisses as Liam over-revs it, just to make sure she's ready for the road today.

But wait. What's that? Is that a parking ticket on the windscreen?

Of course it is. Liam rips it off in full view of the warden, who's already ticketing a BMW parked on the pavement.

"Sir, you can't park here overnight!"

"Oh, really?" Liam calls back. "Cos I've been parking here for the last fifteen years and, er..."

The warden starts walking over, with his handheld misery box already typing in Liam's number plate. Liam takes his cue. He drops the Golf into first and pulls away nice and slow—no point giving the "man" another reason to raid his bank account.

There's something about driving this car that makes Liam feel so good, an intoxication that Liam's never been able to put his finger on. Yes, the car is banging. Yes, the stereo's bass can be felt a half mile away. ~~Yes, it's a babe magnet.~~ Yes, he could use it to pick up chicks if he wanted to. But he doesn't. Something about this car makes him feel—at home.

A brand new orange Tesla blocks the narrow street by the park entrance, its owner—a dweeby tech bro in a Patagonia gilet, takes photos of it for Instagram or whatever. "Nice colour, mate," Liam says as he squeezes past with inches to spare. The tech bro sneers back as Liam takes his cue and floors it through the entrance to the park.

"Can't beat the classics though," Liam shouts behind him.

Club in one hand, Discman in the other, headphones on, Liam strides through the park to his usual spot at the top of the hill overlooking the city. The Saturday morning sun's already burnt off the dew, and today promises to be another scorcher. The park is busy with kids on their school holidays, mums doing yoga and bodybuilders making use of the al fresco gym equipment—Peckham's very own muscle beach, this is not.

A young family sets up for a picnic at the top of the hill, complete with fancy M&S paper plates and proper glass champagne flutes. Dad's looking well-chuffed with himself as he pours what's probably top-whack Prosecco, and Mum artfully arranges croissants on a gingham tablecloth, while their "free-range" toddler is left to roam the park at will. A picture of Millennial middle-class contentment if ever there was. Oh wait—Mum's got the phone out—snap—one more for the Insta—snap. Fuck it if she never looks at that photo ever again, so long as she keeps up the pretence that their life is so much better than yours, who cares where the fuck the photos go? Some data server on Mars for all she cares. For now, it's all about #mumlife.

That's when Liam stops and gives them a long, hard look, almost making them feel uncomfortable.

"Good for you, what a lovely picnic," Liam states, and he means it. Causing confusion with the "admire, but don't talk to me" modern-day gentri-Millennial Londoner. You know the ones, the ones that have EVERYTHING you don't. As proven on Insta.

There's no point in Liam being bitter just because some people's clocks tick the right way round. Besides, the toddler's got chocolate spread all down its designer romper suit now. Or is that dog shit? Mum wouldn't know, she's too engaged with her social media accounts, waiting for strangers to validate her life choices with little heart-shaped lies.

Liam can't help but think to himself. Why have a picnic in this park? This is the kind of park where people like Steve-O take their dogs to take a dump and not clear up. Don't see the gentri-Millennials taking photos of that. Hampstead Heath, this ain't. But he keeps it to himself and avoids the little shit-covered toddler as he makes a beeline for his favourite teeing off spot.

God, it's fucking hot already, it's only 9.30 and it must be thirty degrees in the shade. Good thing I chose the top of this hill to practice my tee-off, where there's absolutely-no-fucking-shade-whatsoever. Liam thinks to himself as he peels off his track top, tying it around his waist. Still, need to practice, he thinks as he takes a golfing stance, readying his swing.

"Exercise. Good for the body. Good for the mind." The same mantra he repeats every time he puts the ball on the tee.

The picnic family give him the oddest look. Well, Mum's still on her phone, but Dad's starting to look concerned, probably wondering if he should pack up their artisanal sourdough and make a run for it.

Liam eyes his target, the duck pond. The place where a thousand Sports Direct golf balls have gone to die.

"FOOOOORRRRREEEEEE."

Liam swings... he slices... he grimaces. The ball flies in a graceful arc before disappearing into the morning haze. Perfect shot—if he'd been aiming for the outdoor gym equipment on the other side of the park. Which he definitely wasn't.

"OOOOWWWW." Echoes across the park, so loud, even the toddler stops to look up.

At Peckham's Muscle Beach—a rather large bodybuilder, shirtless and hairy, rubs his very bald head, his set of pull-ups very rudely interrupted. He looks around with furious anger, then spots Liam up on the hill waving his golf club. "Sorry mate!" Liam calls out. "My bad!" Then he shouts those words that every kid from every corner of the country has had to say at least five hundred times in their childhood: "CAN I GET MY BALL BACK PLEASE?" Which enrages the bodybuilder, who sets off across the park at blistering pace. Who thought guys with legs the size of tree trunks could move so quickly... not Liam, who backs down the hill in a comfortable jog to his car, thinking that the bodybuilder is way too big and slow to ever catch up to him.

Wrong. Because the bodybuilder is upon his car just as he slams the door shut.

"Oh no, shit, I'm sorry mate," Liam says, quickly locking the door.

"Ya little shit. I 'ave a competition tomorrow and now it looks like I have an egg growing out me head," shouts the bodybuilder, while rattling the door handle.

Liam looks at the bodybuilder's head. It is indeed bulging, and it is indeed the size of an egg.

"Maybe you can tell them you found a new muscle?" Liam says half-heartedly, further enraging the 6'7" beast who proceeds to smack his window in an effort to get inside. Changing tack, the gorilla-esque man begins to pull the lining of the cabriolet roof. "No, please don't!" But too late, he's torn a hole in the corner, just enough to get his hand inside to grab Liam's shoulder.

Liam sparks up the Golf and floors it. He exits the park into the street, mounting the curb to get past the orange Tesla. Looking back in the rearview mirror, he sees the raging bodybuilder, pumped on adrenaline and fuelled by steroids, sprinting down the street after him, while the Tesla bro stands back and films it all on his phone. Twat.

𝄞

"Pump numero seven, please," says Liam to the petrol station server, who absentmindedly just slaps the card machine in front of him.

Instead, Liam empties a few notes and lots of coins onto the counter, a depressing collection of silvers and coppers that scatter across the surface. A few escape and roll away, forcing him to chase after them on his hands and knees. The server watches quite indifferently to Liam's shenanigans as the queue behind quickly builds up.

"That's it, you've robbed my last forty-four pounds and twelve pence—for half a tank," Liam says, trying to maintain some dignity as he retrieves a two-pence piece from under the coffee station.

The server just shrugs. Yep. That's the price of inflation, and a 1984 gas guzzler.

Through the windows, the forecourt shimmers in the heat. At one of the pumps, a stressed-out mum leans against her well-driven Vauxhall Zafira with her head buried in her hands. Her cardigan has clearly seen better days, much like her car, where in the back, her kids wage civil war. Their screams can be heard through the open windows, and their wild gesturing suggests a dispute over territory, or sweets, or whose go on the Nintendo Switch it is—probably sweets. It's always about sweets.

The mum quickly wipes her eyes with her sleeve when she catches Liam staring, but there's no shame in her posture as she straightens up. Just bone-deep exhaustion and something else—a quiet dignity that catches Liam off guard.

"Apparently, there's no greater love than that of a mother," she says with a raw honesty that doesn't quite match her tired smile. "But honestly, I could just walk right now and never look back. Think I should?"

The question hangs heavy in the air between them.

Then, cutting through the moment, the youngest starts screaming, sounding more like a nuclear meltdown siren than a three-year-old. While the other kids continue to squabble, the mum just closes her eyes. Where she's going, who knows, but it's not a petrol station in

Peckham during a heatwave, that's for sure. Maybe Marbella. Maybe the Maldives. Anywhere but here.

Liam thinks fast, he grabs a bunch of forecourt-flowers. "From them," he says, super-chipper, missing the point entirely as he hands her the bunch.

Maybe she won't leave her kids, he hopes. Kids need their mums, he thinks.

The mum smiles and rolls her eyes at the gift. For a moment, there's genuine appreciation in her face before reality crashes back with another chorus of screams from the back seat. She pokes her head inside the car and screams at the top of her lungs. "SHUT IT OR NO MACCY D'S FOR LUNCH." Aaaaaaaaaaand silence.

When her Zafira pulls away, the flowers sail out the window, landing in the gutter where they'll no doubt wilt under today's merciless sun. But Liam's none the wiser, probably thinking he's just made someone's day better and saved those kids a lifetime of misery. He's good at that. Fooling himself.

"You have to pay for them," says the voice of God, booming over the forecourt.

Considering what he heard was more a statement than a direct command, Liam quickly walks to his car.

"Pump number seven, *you* have to *pay* for the *flowers*."

Thick exhaust fumes choke the air as the Golf sputters and stalls on the forecourt. Liam continues to ignore the voice of God, instead opting for a quick-ish getaway, if his Golf will allow it. It chugs and sputters again. No joy.

"*You* have to *pay* for those *flowers*, number seven, yes, *you* in the bright orange Golf."

But there's something in Liam's mirror that's caught his attention —enough to really choke the ignition. The enraged bodybuilder's reflection grows larger by the second, his thunder-thighs eating up the distance between them at an alarming rate.

"Come on, Ol' Girl, come on, come on," utters Liam to himself, while closing his eyes, hoping this minor hiccup will somehow resolve itself.

Nope.

BANG.

The bodybuilder's meaty fist slams against Liam's car with enough force to rock the whole chassis. "Gonna teach you some respect you dopey bastard..."

Liam grips his steering wheel for dear life. "Look mate, I said I was sorry about your head," he gestures to the egg-shaped lump on the bodybuilder's skull, which by now angrily throbs with a touch of sunburn.

The door flies open with enough force to make the hinges scream, and suddenly, Liam's being yanked from the sanctuary of his Golf back into the forecourt. To be fair, Liam is six foot himself and not a pushover by most people's standards. But to this guy, he may as well be a Stretch Armstrong. That's when Liam does something strange. No fighting stance, no attempt to run, none of the usual fight or flight scenarios. Instead, he goes limp as the bodybuilder rips off his bucket hat and puts him in a headlock, screaming obscenities that bounce off Liam's resignation.

The bodybuilder's massive arm draws back, his muscles bulge, ready to strike—but then freezes mid-swing as the distinctive *du-du-du-du du dun-dun* "That's It" ringtone of Liam's Nokia 3210 cuts through the tension. Liam never saw the need to change the factory ringtone, or the phone for that matter. If his mum ever calls, if she's still alive—she'll call this number. He fumbles for his phone, checks the caller ID —it's not Mum—UNKNOWN NUMBER.

"Liam here, what's the story?"

The bodybuilder glances at the crowd of onlookers, and weighing up an assault charge against the satisfaction of revenge, settles for shoving Liam before storming off. "Pussy-ole," he yells back.

Some might call it cowardice. And many have. But to Liam, well, it's just the way he is.

"Err, who's there?" says Liam through the ancient relic with equal measures of excitement and trepidation. He genuinely can't remember the last person to call this phone.

"Liam, how you doin', nephew?" his uncle's familiar warm Scottish timbre fills the line, completely disarming Liam after his near assault.

"Chidi? Uncle Chidi? Er, good, good. I think. You?" replies Liam.

"Liam, it's about your mum."

Liam takes a deep breath—unsure of where the hell this conversation is about to go.

No words come back from the other side.

"Well, what is it?" Liam says, while holding his breath.

"She's a... she's alive. She's been in con-tact," Chidi stumbles over his words.

And with this bombshell, Liam drops into the worn leather seats of the Golf only to hear "number seven, the *flowers*" through the tannoy system again.

Yeah-yeah, Liam waves to him, reaching for his last few quid hidden in the ashtray.

CHAPTER 2
PATSY

DAY 1

The bass drops like a hammer, sending shockwaves through the club's concrete floor. Inside this "creative space" (read: glorified drug den), the dregs of last night's party scene rage against the dying of the night like moths to a flame. But these aren't your average clubbers—this is your wee hours London crowd: trust fund kids playing at being poor, crypto investors/scammers burning through their real money faster than their youth, faded celebrities, and the odd genuine raver who's been going since the days of acid house.

And then there's Patsy—sweat pouring down her face while her long hair whips bottled water across the dance floor.

If you looked at her—*really looked* at her—you might recognise her from that reality show a few years back. The one with all the posh twats living in Belsize Park. She was shinier then, polished. Now she's worn smooth, the way coins get when they've passed through too many hands. Nobody's *really looking* at her though. They're all too busy *watching* her make a complete tit out of herself, snogging some random while her mascara streaks down her cheeks. She can't remember what the pills were that she took. But whatever they were, they kicked in too long ago, and this girl is coming in to land hard.

Still, she keeps chasing that high with vodka shots anyway, as if drinking enough might somehow fix whatever's broken inside. At least the vodka will help her forget why she's broken, for a time anyway.

The DJ, some bearded hipster who probably has a day job in fintech, starts winding things down. "That's all beautiful people, time to find an afterparty..."

Is it really six in the fucking morning? Patsy just about thinks to herself. Well, it's difficult to think with a pint of vodka inside you, a couple of pills and nothing to eat since... Thursday, maybe? Who knows? This is Patsy, enjoying her 'brat summer', which is every summer, actually. As well as every spring, autumn and winter.

Patsy's not ready to leave. She never is. The music might be stopping, but the movie in her head is still playing at full volume. She's still that girl from the TV show, still somebody, still...

"Time to go, love." The first bouncer's hands are gentle but firm on her shoulders. She tries to shrug him off, stumbles and catches herself on some bloke's shoulder. He steadies her, then recoils at the state of her.

"Don't you know who I am?" she slurs, but even she doesn't believe it anymore. To the bouncers, all they hear is a garbled "Dernt ya bluer ma man am?"

She breaks free, clambers on top of a speaker and declares, "I'm the one and only wild Patsy!" Before launching herself onto the dancefloor for a spot of crowd surfing, playing to an adoring audience.

In reality: she's being carried out by three hench security guards, her Louboutins dangling in the air. The red soles are scuffed to hell—like everything else about her, they've seen better days. She's no threat, her eyes rolling into the back of her skull prove that, but management needs this one to leave and sober up. Fast. The security guards deposit her carefully on the pavement outside, where the harsh dawn breaks her fantasy.

"Get some rest, love. Drink some water," they say. Nice blokes, she thinks. Followed by, where the fuck am I? Somewhere east, she figures, maybe north, definitely not west. Oh shit, maybe south? No. Never south. Where are my friends? Did I come with anyone? Fuck, cobbled stones, with these heels, and a coffee shop selling a fifteen-quid latte. Must be East London.

Patsy tries to fix her dress—some designer number that probably cost a month's rent back when she could afford rent—but her fingers aren't working properly. The streetlights blur and swim as she checks herself while fumbling for her phone: designer dress, designer shoes, all the trappings of success—on the outside anyway. Where's that fucking phone? Oh, it's in my hand.

"Yo, white girl," she hears bellowing from the coffee shop selling the fifteen-quid lattes.

"Yeah, you, white girl, from the TV. Come, you look like you need a pick-me-up."

Always looking for the next buzz, Patsy follows those three magic words like a little kid following the Pied Piper. "Pick me up?" she asks.

"Yeah, come on!" says the voice.

The coffee shop glows like a mirage in the harsh dawn light, all exposed brick and artisanal temptation. Patsy stumbles inside and takes a seat at one of the circle tables near the door, not sure if this is another hallucination, and ready to make a quick escape just in case.

Don't sweat it, you're just paranoid, she thinks to herself. Trying to maintain a modicum of normality—but nothing is normal about this situation, and she knows it. Where is she, who convinced her to come in here? Is this even a coffee shop? Is it really fifteen-quid for a latte?

Inside, time seems to move differently, like one of those Dali paintings they made her study for her art A-Level. Patsy can't quite tell if she's awake or dreaming—the edges of reality have gone soft and blurry, the way they do when you've been up for too many hours chasing too many highs.

That's when a steaming hot latte lands on her table. How did it get here? Did it magic from thin air?

No, of course not Patsy—you're just tripping. It was left on the table by the owner of this fine establishment, Macy, a 30-something daughter of African immigrants now selling fifteen-quid lattes to stoned hipsters and out-of-their-face ravers. But this one's on the house. Because, though she gets a lot of celebs in her establishment, she genuinely feels sorry for what happened to Patsy.

"This a fifteen-quid latte?" Patsy asks, looking up to see Macy sitting opposite.

"The one and only. Try it," Macy offers.

"This better be a fucking good latte, for fifteen fucking quid."

Macy sits back, confident in her barista skills.

Though she'd rather have a bucket of ice to suck on right now, Patsy takes a sip of the holy grail of East End coffees. Velvety, delicious, with just the right balance of sweet sweet sugar to bitter Kenyan coffee beans hinting at aromas of... what the fuck is that? Vetiver? Cedarwood? No, it's bergamot. She pretty much gulps the whole thing down in one.

"Careful, you'll scald yourself," worries Macy.

But it falls on deaf ears as Patsy lets out a refreshing "aaaah". She sits back and rubs her tummy. Is this the most fulfilling meal she's had all week? Probably, she depressingly thinks to herself.

"You need to be careful out there, state you're in, good-looking girl like you."

"Yeah well, I'm sober now. Where can I pay?" she pushes back, not ready for another lecture from another rando. She's had enough of those in her life.

"Patsy, it's on the house, you take care," Macy says as she gets up to assist a couple of ravers who have wandered in. Macy moves through her domain like a high priestess in her temple of caffeine, dispensing wisdom and perfectly frothed milk with equal grace. In Patsy's drug-addled state, she seems to shimmer at the edges, as if she might disappear at any moment—guardian angel or hallucination? It's impossible to tell.

"Wait," Patsy says, standing up to face Macy. Patsy, who at a statuesque five feet ten in heels, towers over all five feet of the diminutive coffee shop owner.

"Are you real? Is this a dream?" Patsy asks.

"Maybe I am. Maybe I am not. But it's a memory now, so use it wisely."

And with that, Patsy finds herself stumbling down the cobbled street, looking for her next fix, unsure if what she just experienced was something poignant and life-changing, or if she was on some drug-influenced trip. Either way. Macy was nice. She thought.

𝄞

The vodka cabinet behind the counter calls to her like an old friend. "Russian Standard or Stoli?" she asks the bleary-eyed shopkeeper, who grabs a bottle of Stoli and points to the card machine without so much as a glance away from the international news section of his newspaper. Fifteen quid. Bargain, Patsy reasons.

Outside, the bottle's already open, burning her throat but steadying her hands. That's when she spots them—a group of bright young things, probably students, definitely on something better than vodka. They're huddled around a phone, comparing screenshots of coordinates or addresses or whatever passes for party intel these days.

Maybe they're going on to somewhere cool? Patsy questions. Do people still use the word cool? Maybe not, probably epic or legendary, something their generation desperately wants to own. But let's face it, it always reverts back to being cool—everyone ages—and everyone reverts back to using "cool." Why does one of them keep repeating "gas"—oh maybe they can get some drugs.

Come on Patsy, these kids are gassed up on fifteen-pound coffees. They're off to the gym at midday. Because everyone knows that dancing all night is good cardio, but sculpting your biceps and glutes is what really gets the likes rolling in.

From a safe distance, she follows through the very gentrified East End alleys, trying her best to avoid being spotted. Until she drops her vodka bottle after falling into some steel bins. This is getting desperate.

That's when the tallest one, some lanky boy in a neon vest, notices her first. "Oi," he whispers to his mates, "that woman's following us."

"Woman?" Patsy thinks, clutching her bottle tighter, trying to upright herself. When did that happen? She was their age, like, what, five minutes ago?

"Nah bruv," says another, "Don't get shook, she's just some sus cheugy."

"Probably a stan of mine," says the alpha female, who's just taken a selfie with Patsy in the background. Not quite realising she'll probably be Patsy in just a few years' time. So long as she doesn't hit the booze. But life has a way of throwing shit at you, no matter what your poison is. Till then, cheers, Patsy thinks as she shoulders past them, head high with her heels clicking against the cobblestones. She hears their snickers fade behind her, but it doesn't matter, she already caught the words "warehouse" and "secret location." That's all our Pats needs, cos this girl can find recreational drugs better than any sniffer dog.

The entrance, when she finds it, is almost too perfect—like something from her reality TV days. A nondescript metal door in a wall of graffiti. No bouncer, no queue, just the distant thrum of bass bleeding through cracks in the steel. For a moment, she hesitates… before polishing off her bottle of vodka.

Then she yanks the door open and plunges into the darkness.

This place is a proper wonderland—where green laser lights cut through artificial smoke, and where bodies move like one organism to relentless beats. This isn't some mimosas-and-avocado-on-toast crowd. These people never stopped; they're the real deal.

Time doesn't exist here. Sanity doesn't exist here.

This is where I feel most at home.

On the dance floor.

Alone.

Patsy cuts a lonely figure, in a lonely place, at a lonely time.

Is that? It can't be, she thinks. A six-foot light-skinned mixed-race man in a blue tracksuit raving on the stairs. Liam? No. Just another hallucination—is it? She toddles over to get a closer look, and places her hand on the man's shoulder. He turns around and smiles. It's not him. It's not Liam. It doesn't even look like Liam, and he's wearing a silver dress. She doesn't even know where Liam lives anymore. Probably still in that council flat, waiting for their mum to come home. But she knows. <u>She's dead</u>. Probably jumped. She was definitely more of a jumper than a "leave a pretty corpse" type. Same as me, Patsy thinks to herself. Jumping has a certain je ne sais quoi to it. To leave nothing behind, just disappear in a flash, sucked into the ocean or a mighty river—to let nature take its course. Then it's not really suicide, right? It's a natural death.

At least I've moved on. At least I've made something of myself. At least...

Everything stops. The world tilts sideways. And Patsy, who hasn't thrown up from drinking since uni, promptly empties her stomach all over her scuffed to shit Louboutins... and the Gen Z alpha female who recoils in disgust... "Not cool," the alpha female says.

~ 1996 ~

The world thrums outside the window of the family house with that '90s energy that you can't quite describe—but if you could bottle it, you'd probably get fifteen quid a cup for it today. Little Patsy sits behind the sofa with Little Liam, their hands clasped tight. She's trying to be brave, like her mum always tells her to be, but the shouting has got worse recently.

"You're mental, you know that?" Daddy's voice booms from upstairs. "Absolutely mental. Holding on to the past and never moving forwards. This is why... It's your fault."

Something smashes. Mummy's crying. She's always throwing things, especially when she's angry—like right now. Little Patsy squeezes Little Liam's hand tighter—even though he's older, he's always been the one who's afraid of the dark. Afraid to go alone to the shops for a pint of milk, afraid to go to school every day. But she's not —she breezes through life with an air of confidence unmatched by most. She could never understand it—how they grew up in the same house, with the same mum, but LeeLee moved through the world like he was trying not to be noticed, while she faced it head-on, ready to take on anyone who looked at her, or him, wrong.

Little Liam reaches around the sofa and discreetly pulls his precious new CD Discman from next to the stereo stack system. He carefully places the headphones over Little Patsy's ears, gives her that gentle smile that always makes everything better. The music starts— something about "Common People" by Pulp and the old singer's story about playing pool always made her laugh.

More crashes from upstairs. Daddy's voice gets louder: "Your drinking, your moods, your obsession with that bloody urn..."

The special jar. The one Mummy keeps on the mantelpiece. The one nobody's allowed to touch, ever. Little Patsy doesn't understand why, just knows it's something to do with LeeLee's real daddy, Noel.

Suddenly, Mummy's running down the stairs, tears stream down her face, leaving long black streaks, she snatches the special jar and grabs a photo from the wall—the one of Liam and Noel, the one Daddy hates.

"Kids, we're leaving. Now."

She drags them by their hands to the front door and throws their jackets on, which Little Patsy thought was strange, given it's 30 degrees outside.

Little Patsy looks at her daddy at the top of the stairs, his face red with anger—but temporarily softened as he forces through a smile to his little girl. Then she looks at Mummy, wild-eyed and desperate, an uncaged beast. She's seen this look before, the last time Mummy took her and LeeLee to Uncle Chidi's for a weekend "break." That wasn't much fun either as Mummy spent the whole time crying.

"She's my daughter, you don't touch her!" Richard screams as he runs down the stairs two at a time. Little Liam pulls her back behind the sofa, and all she can remember is the old singer in the song saying he wants to live with common people over and over, as Mummy and Daddy fight behind them.

Just then, her hand is grabbed, she's pulled out of her sanctuary behind the sofa, and they're running down the street. Past the neighbours looking from their doorsteps, past the kids playing had, it, tick, touch, king—or whatever you called it in your area.

They're sprinting for the car. Sally's sobbing, clutching both kids' hands with only the urn under her arm, her purse in her jacket pocket and the car keys to their green car. Richard gives chase, and all Little Patsy wants to do is run back to him and tell him it's going to be okay.

"You can't hold on to the past, he's never coming back!" She remembers him screaming.

Sally starts the car and drives away in first gear. Richard catches up and tries to open the door, but Sally quickly locks them—so he violently bangs on the window. Blood streams down his face from where she must have hit him, and now Little Patsy's not sure who to be more scared of. His palm leaves a bloody print on the glass as he pleads:

"Stop the car. Give her to me."

"I won't let you split them up," Sally says through gritted teeth.

"When you get back. She's coming with me. You understand?"

That's when Little Patsy tries to open the door, only for Sally to forcibly push her back into the seat with such force it leaves a bruise on her shoulder.

"You'll be back. You always come back..."

Sally hits second gear and speeds away, leaving Richard standing in the middle of the road, blood on his face, looking more hurt than angry as his little girl stares back at him from the back window with tears running down her face, screaming:

"DADDY!"

"DADDY!"

"DADDY!"

Little Liam turns up the volume to his new CD Discman, desperately willing Damon Albarn's melancholy words to block out the violence through Blur's bittersweet "To The End."

And all Little Patsy can think is: *Why does Mummy always have to ruin everything?*

DAY 1

Patsy finds herself grinding against some random bloke, then another.

Then the bass drops and she recognises those haunting synths immediately—"Born Slippy". The one from that film about those Scottish junkies, the one Liam played obsessively that summer. She always thought it wasn't meant to be played through his tinny headphones, but could never quite work out where the song best belonged. Now she gets it—the way those ethereal vocals float over the crowd like a prayer in this cathedral of sound, the synthesisers building to something religious. Though, that could be the last of the ecstasy coursing through her veins. Who really knows?

Then those drums kick in, and nothing else matters.

Her mascara streaks down her cheeks, but she doesn't care. The men try to step away politely—they can smell the desperation on her—but she's got them cornered. Through the strobing lights, their faces blur into Richard's, into Liam's, into every man who's ever left her.

"Wait—I recognise you..." one of them says, squinting through the darkness. "You're that bird off the TV, Belsize something..."

She doesn't hear the rest. Doesn't want to. But then hands are grabbing her, yanking her backwards. Female hands, manicured nails digging into her skin.

"Get off our boyfriends, you slag."

Patsy tries to focus on the women's faces, but the room won't stop spinning. She catches fragments—designer outfits, professionally done makeup—everything she used to be. One of them slaps the guy she was dancing with.

"We haven't done anything," he protests. "She was all over us..."

The women drag her by her hair towards the exit. She should fight back. The old Patsy would have. But what's the point? They're right about her. They're all right.

"Fuck, that light is bright," Patsy thinks, shielding her eyes. She turns to try and get back inside, but hears "Fuck off, Belsize bitch" followed by—

THE PUSH.

She's falling backwards down the steep metal steps. In Patsy's mind, this all happens in slow motion, a cocktail of booze, drugs and a reckless streak will do that to a girl. Maybe this was the push Patsy needed? Maybe it's the push that will get her back to winning ways?

CRUNCH.

CRUNCH.

CRUNCH.

That definitely wasn't slow motion. And something definitely broke. The heel on her left Louboutin for one, and maybe a few fingers. Hard to tell when you're this wasted. Best give it a day or two.

Something's ringing. Is it my phone? she thinks. Maybe that's just the ringing in her head from where it hit the concrete. Patsy opens one eye, cheek pressed into the gutter, tasting blood and vodka.

"Patsy? Patsy?"

The Scottish accent is vaguely familiar. "Ewan... McGregor? Is that you?" she asks, not really caring if it's another hallucination or not.

"Patsy? Are you okay? Shit, are you fucked up again?" says Chidi.

"Uncle Chidi?" she mumbles in response.

There's something about a specific set of words that can make a person sober up in a heartbeat:

Social Services are here.
We've seen the video.
Your mother's most likely dead.

Or—

It's about your mother. Sally. She's been in contact.

Patsy's suddenly standing. Suddenly sober for the first time in a long time. Also suddenly lost for words.

All she can muster is an imperceptible sigh.

When suddenly—WHACK—her left Louboutin hits her on the head, chucked by one of the angry girlfriends. Followed by "Slut!"

Today is Saturday. And Patsy doesn't know it yet, but today will be the last day of the life that she has come to take for granted.

𝄞

The Uber driver doesn't seem fazed by Patsy's head lolling out the window gasping for air like Heath Ledger's Joker. South London on a Saturday morning in this heat would make anyone pant. Though the hangover and comedown probably aren't helping. He's prepared, seats covered in plastic, because in London, you never know who you may pick up or who may throw up. He's keeping an eye on his rider, because he knows the signs. Dry retching being the main one.

"Lawyer can't fix that, you know?" he says, eyeing her through the rearview mirror.

"Excuse me?"

"Your face. Looks nasty. Want me to go to the hospital?"

Patsy catches her reflection in the mirror—mascara war paint, split lip, the beginning of what will be a spectacular black eye. She shrugs. She's looked worse. A few years ago, when they held that makeshift memorial for Sally at Uncle Chidi's, for example. Funny how you can have a wake without a body. Just an empty coffin full of memories and a daughter's certainty that her mother had finally done what she'd always threatened. Liam hadn't come, of course. Still paying the bills on that council flat, still waiting on that footstool in the middle of the living room watching the door. Still believing that their mum will come back. Idiot. She used to think.

But all that's in the past. For now, Patsy cannot get past the fact that her mother, after nearly fifteen years of radio silence, in which they assumed she was dead—is alive.

"What's the time?" she asks, desperate to change the subject in her own head.

"You're wearing a watch."

She is. Sally's old Timex. The only nice thing her mum ever bought herself (from John Lewis, using a one-off bonus from the supermarket job she had at the time).

"It's stopped." And a long time ago, Patsy thought to herself.

The Uber driver, completely missing the mood, cranks up the stereo as "Connection" by Elastica comes on. Those first sharp, unforgiving guitar chords rip through the taxi. "Ohhh classic," he reminisces, already nodding along. "Do you remember when this came out? Maybe you're too young?"

I'm not too young, you patronising prick. Justine Frischmann's about to start spitting the word "whore" over and over, cleverly hidden behind that iconic opening guitar riff. Just what I need right now—another woman calling me names.

"Can you turn it down. I hate the '90s," she says.

"What?" the driver replies.

"FUCKING TURN IT OFF," she abruptly screams.

The driver turns it right down. But it's too late. Something about this song has brought up thirty years of pain, fifteen years of not knowing, ten hours of excess and thirty minutes since she found out her mum is alive. She sticks her head back out to the window for some of that fresh South London air, but instead of air getting in, she expels the contents of her stomach down the side of the car.

The driver's just grateful she had the courtesy to do it outside.

Well, at least I won't need my stomach pumped again, Patsy thinks, channelling some of that positive energy her big brother always used to spout. Those forward-thinking positive vibes that always used to make her sick. Like now.

That's the last of it, she thinks, as she spits out the final strings of mucus and bile before hauling herself back inside.

"Give me them sunglasses you're wearing," she demands to the driver.

"Excuse me. I will not."

"Give me them glasses or I'll give you one star and say you made me feel 'uncomfortable'," she says, using air quotes.

"What? You wouldn't?" He figures she wouldn't. He hopes she wouldn't.

That's when Patsy shows him the one-star rating on the phone, not yet confirmed, and demands: "Let me out here, we're done."

"No wait. Here. Take them," he says as he hands over the (fake) Ray-Bans he picked up at some holiday kiosk for thirty quid. Patsy looks them over, clearly spotting their fakery, but considering the shiner on her eye, opts to forego the stigma that may come her way.

That's when she gets a call from David@Catston's—her boss. Fuck. It's a Saturday, and reality TV doesn't pay the bills anymore. Not that it ever really did, but at least 'Belsize Beaus' gave her what she craved —thousands of strangers telling her she mattered. Where premium people lived premium lives, and every sideways glance meant another week of trending. God, she'd have done anything back then for those likes, those follows, that validation she never got at home. But her time as a reality TV star is long over. No amount of Insta posts about M&S hampers or picnicking in a park on a Saturday can fill that void for her. She's over it. She thinks. Reality TV stars are fucking everywhere—infesting her TV, her social media, her billboards. At least when she was faking it, there was some art to it. Now these premium people with their premium lives spam her feed with carefully curated perfection—one sponsored post at a time, telling you how to live your life better. George Orwell couldn't make this shit up, she once mused. Figuring if you dangle enough golden carrots in the world, we'd all stay on our hamster wheels long enough in the hope that one day, just one day, we'll get our chance. She had her chance. The only satisfaction she gets these days comes from watching these desperados debase themselves on whatever godforsaken challenge show is trending, sucking down bull semen for gold stars which can be swapped for meals and contracts with multinationals selling gym wear, swimwear, menswear or whatever type of "wear." If you can't be them, wear them. That might just make you feel a tad better about your soul-crushing irrelevance to society.

Though, deep down... Patsy would love to be known for sucking down bull semen instead of... we'll get to that later.

So like everyone else, Patsy works. She sells houses for Catston's Estate Agents—*Where Premium People Buy Premium Homes*. Perfect role really, helping people hide from reality in overpriced floor space. Just like she does. Pretending to be something you're not is the one skill reality TV taught her that actually pays dividends IRL (to any ancient beings over the age of 35, that means *In Real Life*).

The phone feels heavy in her hand. David. Always David. Always demanding. The only David she puts on her work voice for.

"David. I shall not be in today." That's the truth.

"No, not feeling myself." That's also the truth.

"High fever. Nausea. Headache." She's on a roll. This is all true.

And like most pathological liars with narcissistic tendencies, she just can't help blurting out a lie that slides out smooth as silk—"I'm in bed." He'll believe her. They always do. Why wouldn't they? She's perfected the art of being exactly what people expect—damaged, but functional. Unreliable, but just reliable enough.

She doesn't want to engage with the truth. Not today. Not after everything. The truth of her mother. The truth of her life. The truth of her spectacular unravelling.

"Have Janine take my viewings, ya? I've got a big one on Primrose Hill Road at eleven. The clients are coming in from New York. And tell her not to fuck it up."

"Peachy," she says. Before hanging up.

Suddenly, the world tilts and the last hour comes crashing down around her—the vodka, the drugs, the fight, the phone call about her mother, David@fuckingCatston's—it all converges at once as she loses consciousness.

Actually, it's something a lot more scientific—the calories I need to survive are splattered across the side of this taxi. My internal resources, like my emotional well-being, are well and truly utterly depleted.

And then, darkness.

Wake me up before you go-go. Please. Or just let me sleep, either/or, don't mind.

CHAPTER 3
WHAT'S IN THE BOX?

DAY 1

Patsy's Uber pulls up outside a nondescript office on Peckham High Street just as Liam's orange Golf claims the "parking space" across the big white zig zags outside. The Uber driver, having endured quite enough of his now fully unconscious passenger, decides that the easiest way to avoid being embroiled in a celebrity groping scandal is to drag Patsy out by her ankles. He then helps himself to a five-star rating and a fifty-pound tip on her phone, muttering "for the glasses," before repeatedly hammering the office doorbell.

Liam climbs out of his Golf, assessing the scene—his sister laid out on the pavement, the exasperated Uber driver, the passing crowds of casual rubberneckers. Seemingly nonplussed, he steps over Patsy's prone body and reaches for the intercom by the door.

"Yeah, who's there?" says Chidi.

"Uncle Chidi, it's Liam. And Patsy, I think," he says, lifting up her new Ray-Bans.

"You don't know what your little sister looks like?"

"It's been a while," says Liam. The weight of this phrase carries heavily on him. He should know. He's her big brother. And here she is, passed out on Peckham High Street at midday in a pair of broken high heels and a designer dress. How did it get to this? He thinks. Before the obscene BZZZZZZZZZ of Chidi's ancient door unlocking system lets them in.

He throws Patsy over his shoulder, and as he carries her drunk ass inside he stops at the threshold. This is it. This is where we find out what happened to Mum.

𝄞

Inside, Chidi's office is exactly what you'd expect from a high street lawyer—fluorescent lighting buzzing overhead, wood veneer desks, carpet so threadbare you can see the concrete underneath—all the furnishings afforded by a lawyer who plies his trade bailing out drunks on a Friday night guilty of GBH. "No" and "comment" are his two favourite words. He even has them enshrined on a giant plaque on the wall above his desk. But this day is different; this day, he can finally put his law degree to good use. Helping his dead brother's family is the least he can do. Family is important, he thinks to himself as he scrutinises the estranged siblings sitting in his office.

Liam sits bolt upright in his chair, fiddling with his CD player, reading the manufacturer's label on the back. The one he's read a million times before during times of stress. The one he can recall in his sleep.

"Class one laser product. Battery supply one v times two," he mumbles in a surprised tone, like it's the first time he's read it.

Patsy slouches low, hiding behind her stolen sunglasses and what's developing into an impressive black eye. She squeezes herself tighter into a ball as Liam reminds everyone that this Sony Discman was —"Made in Japan. Fancy that."

"So, how long is it since you last saw your mother?" Chidi interrupts, looking between the siblings and cutting between their awkwardness.

"Fifteen years... maybe. Nearly sixteen," Liam offers. "Before she, you know, left the reservation."

Chidi shifts his attention to Patsy. She gives a noncommittal shrug. "Yeah. Fifteen, sixteen years."

"Nineteen and counting," Liam corrects. "For her."

"Well whatever." Patsy waves her hand dismissively before Liam addresses the elephant in the room. "She's not dead?" he asks.

"Correct."

"I knew it." Liam quietly fist pumps, not really reading the seriousness of the situation.

"Look, dead or alive, why am I south the river? On a Saturday?" Patsy changes the subject.

"Now that's the million-dollar question," Chidi beams. And to this remark, Patsy slides down her sunglasses and gives Chidi that cold, hard stare that reminds him of Sally when she was not having one of her better days.

In response, Chidi indicates an ornate steel Indian style trunk sitting on his desk. About the size of a vintage suitcase, its heavy padlock gleams in the artificial light.

"This came for you. Both of you. From your mother." He pauses as Liam leans forward while Patsy slumps further into her chair. "And it came with a letter."

Chidi slides a letter across his desk. Liam reaches for it with the eagerness of a little kid at Christmas, still keeping hope, still positive that he'll get that upgrade from the Sega Master System to the Megadrive. Patsy rolls her eyes from behind her shades and tuts. She never desired any upgrades—they just happened.

"Sally wants to see you. Both of you," Chidi says, watching their reactions carefully. "She knows it's been a terribly long time, but it seems she wants to make amends. Reconcile." He pauses for dramatic effect. "It also appears Sal won the lottery."

Patsy, who's been examining her cuticles with feigned disinterest, suddenly sits up straighter. Liam, meanwhile, maintains his best poker face—which, given his usual demeanour, isn't saying much.

"Scratch card," Chidi adds.

Patsy slumps back down.

"One million."

The sunglasses come off, and Patsy's good eye widens.

"One million?"

Chidi produces a photo like a magician pulling out his ace. It shows Sally, looking frazzled and distinctly unhappy, holding one of those massive novelty cheques. The date stamp reads 2010.

"She wants you both to share it."

"What's the catch?" Patsy's seen enough reality TV to know there's always a catch. "There's always a catch with that insufferable woman. She's probably dying."

"Well, that's better than dead," Liam pipes up. "I figured she chucked herself in the Thames." Then he registers the date on the photo. "Wait—2010? That's when she walked out. All this time she's let me suffer, and she's been a millionaire?"

"Suffer?" Patsy scoffs. "You haven't worked a day in your life. Got your council flat though, haven't you? For life, no less. Do you know what kind of security that brings?"

Liam's blank expression answers that question. He assumes Patsy doesn't know about the eviction notice. Or the new development replacing his home. So, rather than confronting the issue which would prove him right and make her look a tit, he keeps schtum.

"Didn't think so," Patsy mutters.

"Your mission, should you choose to accept it-" Chidi starts, immediately regretting his attempt at humour as both siblings stare at him. "Right. Well. She wants you to deliver this box to her. Further instructions are in the letter. But there's one strict condition—you must not open the box before you see her. She'll give you the key then."

"Fuck that. Probably drugs inside," Patsy dryly declares.

"Could be the money," Liam suggests, as he lifts the box, giving it an experimental shake. "Oof, heavy. Maybe it's in gold bars? Diamonds and jewels?"

"Or a gold egg-shitting goose?" Patsy offers.

Liam's already grabbed a letter opener and is eyeing the lock speculatively when Chidi intervenes: "Your mother specifically said the box contains the total sum of her estate. And if it's forced open, everything goes to Shelter."

The letter opener clatters back onto the desk. Patsy rolls her eyes so hard they might get stuck.

"I am sensing tension," Chidi ventures. "When was the last time you both spoke?"

They both answer simultaneously.

"Five years," says Patsy. "Ten years," says Liam.

"The wake. But then, you weren't really there, were you?" Liam reminds her.

"I was there," decries Patsy.

"Yeah physically, not mentally," Liam mumbles.

Patsy yields to Liam's version with a theatrical sigh, rising from her chair. "Ten years. Well, time flies when you're having fun."

"What if you're not?" Liam enquires.

"Well, then it flies like this bird—out the door." She adjusts her designer dress. "You tell ol' Sal, if she wants to see me, then she can see me; all she has to do is show up. Uncle Chidi. Liam. Adieu. See you in... like another ten years or something, whatever."

Patsy storms out into Peckham High Street, and having given up on her broken Louboutins, she opts to go barefoot. Liam chases her, with the ornate trunk banging against his legs with each stride, and his bucket hat barely clinging to his head.

"Patsy. Pats. Listen up."

"I already have enough money. I haven't the inclination for a wild goose chase." Though the tremor in her voice suggests her circumstances, financial or other, might tell a different story.

"Everyone needs a share of a million quid. What with this economy."

Patsy keeps walking, which is quite the feat given her hangover and the state of Peckham High Street at lunchtime. Liam keeps up the chase, dodging the morning shoppers, delivery drivers and traders.

"Don't you have any questions? I do. We deserve answers."

Patsy stops so abruptly that Liam nearly crashes into her. "ARRRGGGHHH. Fuck. I don't have time for this in my life. The woman abandoned us Liam, left us with nothing but a head full of bad memories and trauma. And now what—we're supposed to come running because she's got money? Liam. Wake up."

"Just do this one thing and that's it, we'll never talk again."

"Well, I don't have a car. Or a license."

"Well, today's your lucky day." Liam points to his bright orange Golf, parked squarely on the zig zags, where a parking warden has just finished slapping a ticket on the windscreen.

"Ta-da. Your chariot awaits," Liam demonstrates with pride.

Patsy rolls her eyes as Liam rips off the ticket—another one for his growing collection.

"Nope. Can't do it. Forwards. Forwards. Always move forwards, never backwards."

"Alright," Liam says, resigning himself to defeat all too soon again. "At least let me drop you to the station. Peckham's not safe for North Londoners. Apparently."

Patsy yields—though whether it's the hangover or the thought of navigating South London's public transport barefoot that does it, only she knows.

The Golf's doors slam like gunshots. The engine roars to life, and the dump valve hisses as "Nancy Boy" by Placebo explodes from Liam's expensive subwoofer speakers. Patsy covers her ears, but there's no escaping that heavy opening riff combined with Brian Molko's sharp pointed lyrics in this tiny little car.

That's when the strangest thing happens. Against type, Liam executes a textbook U-turn, slow and polite, thanking the bus driver who he's blocked as he spins his Golf around, and parks literally thirty metres behind where they started—outside Queen's Road Peckham station. The music cuts off just as abruptly as it began, leaving an awkward silence…

"Why walk when you can drive, in style?"

He centrally locks the doors. Patsy frantically tries the handle—locked. Liam unfolds Sally's letter while Patsy's stomach feels like it's still at the rave she left hours ago. She puts her head between her legs and hyperventilates.

"Liam, open the doors. Open the doors, I'm gonna be sick."

"I can live with that," he replies, not fully believing himself, but willing to tell a white lie to keep her in the car.

"Forwards, always forwards. Never backwards," she mumbles.

Liam looks at his sister, pleading more than anything. He will read this letter anyway; he's waited fifteen years for a sign. But he wants, no, needs to read it with Patsy, his sister. Who he hasn't spoken to in ten years. And he figures that she needs this just as much as he does.

Then, without looking up, Patsy mutters: "Read it."

CHAPTER 4
SALLY

The harsh fluorescent light flickers overhead, casting a sickly yellow pallor across the sparsely furnished room. Sally sinks back into her pillows, the starched white linen sheets rustling beneath her as she attempts in vain to untangle the spaghetti of wires connected to her frail body. She's vaguely aware of white coats filing out of the room, their hushed voices fading to whispers as the door clicks shut. Only the steady, metronomic beep of monitors and the whirring of her fan to keep the heat at bay breaks the oppressive silence.

Sally, now in her sixties, wears the map of her tumultuous life etched into every line on her face. Deep creases fan out from the corners of her eyes, her once smooth forehead now a canvas of furrows, each one a story of worry, of joy, of regret. But amid the silver strands of her hair, vibrant streaks of pink peek out defiantly—a reminder that beneath the weight of years and illness, the wild spirit that once defined her still flickers, refusing to be extinguished.

Her fingers, worn and lined with age and sickness, clutch a creased Polaroid. She traces the edges, lost in a frozen moment of happier times. Two children's faces beam up at her, their grins wide and carefree. A lifetime ago, it seems. Memories. Bad memories she needs to make good.

"Missus Digsby?" Jagdeesh's gentle voice pulls her back to the present. "Sally? Do you understand what the doctors said?"

She blinks, focusing on her young nurse's concerned face. Jagdeesh has been a constant for so long now, his calm, supportive presence providing the balance she always needed.

"Oh. Yes. Yes, I understand," Sally murmurs, her voice rougher than she remembers.

Jagdeesh moves a warm and reassuring hand to hers. She grabs it tight, each word a struggle against her failing strength, "When you get to my age, promise you won't hold on to your regrets before you leave this fair world."

Jagdeesh takes the opportunity to pass on some wisdom he's learned during his considerably fewer years on the planet compared to Sally. Still, he thinks, even our elders need a reminder at times. He leans in closely, with his warm hand tightening around hers.

"The crane perches on the riverbank," he begins, his accent lilting with the rhythm of the old proverb. "She plays joyfully and frolics with her babies."

Sally's eyebrow arches. "Oh, I don't have time for one of your silly proverbs," cutting him short. I'm old and wise enough, she thinks to herself.

Jagdeesh's eyebrows arch back. "Isn't that why you requested me to be your humble attaché at the end?"

"Continue," Sally sighs, resigned. "The crane, go on..."

"So, this crane, she perches on the riverbank. She plays joyfully with her babies. Then, when her babies are not looking," Jagdeesh uses a swooping movement with his hands, "the Hawk of God snatches her away, never to be of this world again."

"Playful sport is forgotten, in its place, silence," he solemnly says.

"I'm too tired to read between that one," she says as she watches the fan whirr left, right... left... right... momentarily hypnotising her.

"If the mother crane knew the Hawk was going to kill her, she would not have played with her babies one final time with such joyful abandon. The final memory for her babies would be a very different one."

And to this, Sally looks at the Polaroid photo.

Sally, not sure if she should laugh or cry, drifts her gaze to the window. Whatever the view is beyond it, it's obscured by half-drawn blinds right now.

"Can I fetch anything for you?" Jagdeesh asks softly.

"A new body."

"I am sorry Sally. I can only pray for the light to shine on you."

That's when Sally's eyes light up with a sudden determination she hasn't felt in a long time. "Some good writing paper. Envelopes. A pen, not a crappy ballpoint. A nice one... a fountain pen, if you can muster it," she pauses, considering her next words, "And a solid box. A large one, steel. There's a shop near the market that makes them."

Jagdeesh nods, making mental notes.

"Oh, and some tea," Sally adds as an afterthought.

"No problem. Though, no sugar with the tea," Jagdeesh cautions.

Sally eyeballs him. "I'm bloody well dying, Jagdeesh. A little sugar. Or you're fired."

As Jagdeesh leaves to fetch her requests, Sally eases herself out of bed and shuffles to the small desk by the window, clearing its surface with trembling hands. The Polaroid finds a new home propped against the wall, those smiling faces a silent witness to what she is about to do.

As Sally traces the edge of the photo, she cracks just the faintest hint of a smile. Those were the days, weren't they? Before it all went tits up. Her gaze lingers on the photo, her mind drifting uncomfortably to the past. Liam, her sweet boy—has he found himself someone and settled down, or is he waiting for the stars to align? And Patsy, her fierce girl—has life softened her sharp edges, or sharpened her soft edges? Not a day has passed without them occupying her thoughts, their absence a constant ache she's carried through the years. She wonders if Liam still loses himself in music, if Patsy's still chasing that elusive validation. Are they happy? Safe? Do they hate her? Love her? Have they found their way in a world that never made it easy for them? Questions that have haunted her every waking moment, fueling both her regret and her resolve.

Yet in fifteen years, she has never reached out to them, to tell them she is okay, to ease their suffering. She understands this contradiction more than most. But time is running out to quantify her choices, to make them understand that sometimes love means walking away, even if it tears you apart.

With a deep breath, Sally pulls herself back to the task at hand. It's time to bridge the gap, to explain the inexplicable. To ask for forgiveness she's not sure she deserves.

She needs them to remember too—not just the good bits, but all of it. The whole messy, complicated tangle of love and hurt and family.

Right, then. Time to set things straight. Starting with that trip in '96.

~ 1996 ~

The summer of '96 hits Scarborough beachfront like England's just won the World Cup. The promenade thrums with life, a sea of neon swimwear and sun-reddened skin stretching as far as the eye can see. It's "Three Lions" on repeat, St George's flags draped from every balcony, and the intoxicating belief that football might actually be coming home. No sunscreen here—just the reckless abandon of children, tins of lager in the shade, love handles proudly on display, and old geezers sporting the timeless socks-and-sandals combo whilst wearing string vests and demolishing pork pies. Meanwhile, seagulls wage high-stakes smash-and-grab raids, snatching chips and sarnies straight from unsuspecting beachgoers' hands.

Little Liam stands transfixed, his new Sony Discman clutched tight. As he hits play on his CD Discman, the opening chords of Oasis' "Champagne Supernova" spill from his headphones. He sways gently, lost in the music, oblivious to the chaos about to erupt. This is the seaside he dreamed about. It's everything he imagined and more.

Little Patsy emerges from Itsy Bitsy ice cream parlour, a vision in pigtails and focused concentration. She's clutching two ice creams, way too oversized for hands as small as hers, teetering dangerously with each step. But nothing stops our Pats; she breezes through the crowds with grace and speed, eager to ensure nothing melts before she gets back to LeeLee with his cone.

That's when Sally bursts out of a red telephone box, hastily wiping tears from her eyes. Whatever just happened in that phone box, she's determined to leave it there. She pastes on a smile before dramatically calling out, "Heyyyy, what's the story baby girl?" whilst comically shooting Little Patsy from the hip with her imagined gunslinger pistols. "Ooo, ice cream. Mmmm, giz a bit," she says, taking a generous lick from Little Patsy's cone. Little Patsy giggles, momentarily forgetting the Herculean task of balancing her cones.

Sally fumbles with her Polaroid camera, corralling the kids for a selfie. She squints into the tiny mirror on the front, angling for the perfect shot. "Say cheese!" she chirps. CLICK—FLASH—WHIRR. The familiar Polaroid ritual unfolds—a memory captured in an instant. It's the camera she'd found buried in the boot of the car, forgotten until now. Today, she's determined to finally put it to good use.

"I want to wave it," Little Patsy demands, reaching for the developing photo.

"No, I want to wave it," Little Liam counters, his headphones now dangling around his neck. Liam Gallagher's voice drifts from the tiny speakers, repeating "why" over and over, before giving way to Noel's melodic solo. The distinctive sound of his 1967 Epiphone guitar floats on the sea breeze, in stark contrast to the family drama unfolding.

As Sally tries in vain to keep the photo out of reach from both of her squabbling kids, the worst fucking thing in the world that could happen to a kid happens. Patsy's ice cream plummets to the ground with a sad plop.

We've all been there, haven't we? Waiting for that moment, after the beat where time stood still. Then...

"ARRGGGHHHH!" Little Patsy's scream could wake the dead, or at least send nearby seagulls scattering. "It's your fault!" she wails, pointing an accusing finger at Little Liam. "Mum, Liam knocked over my ice cream!"

"It wasn't my fault, I was just..." Little Liam starts, but his protest is drowned out by Patsy's increasing hysterics. Who knew such a small package could detonate such pandemonium?

And all the while Liam Gallagher keeps singing through those tinny little headphones, his voice a surreal soundtrack to the unfolding chaos. And then, just when you thought it couldn't get any better, Paul Weller kicks in with his epic guest solo, upping the ante on whatever his meaning of a Champagne Supernova is. The music swells, oblivious to the family drama it's scoring, oblivious to Little Patsy's accompanying wail.

Holidaymakers give the family a wide berth, shooting sympathetic glances at Sally. But even so, Sally just stands there, frozen, as if she's watching the scene unfold between some other family, and from a great distance. Why me? She thinks. Why now?

Little Patsy, fuelled by sugar, rage and the heat of the afternoon, makes a grab for Little Liam's braids. Little Liam, ever the pacifist, doesn't fight back. He just tries to push away, his face a mask of confusion and hurt.

"Muuuuuum," he pleads, as Little Patsy yanks out a handful of his hair.

In a final act of sibling warfare, Little Patsy grabs the squirty sauce from a nearby table and unleashes a red stream all over Little Liam's t-shirt.

Sally watches it all unfold, her mind racing. Fight? Flight? As the chaos escalates, every instinct screams at her to run, to escape. But she's rooted to the spot, the joyful sounds of the seaside fading away, replaced by the thundering of her heartbeat.

Trying to hold back a wail, Little Liam throws his headphones back on, just in time to hear Oasis bring the song to a close. That gorgeous harmonica carries on the wind, drifting out to sea. Which is exactly where Sally wishes she could be right now. The melody mingles with Little Liam's cries, the screams of Little Patsy and the distant laughter of holidaymakers, a bittersweet symphony to an unforgettable memory unravelling before their eyes.

As the last notes fade, Little Liam sees Sally adrift in a sea of chaos, clinging to a smile that feels more like a grimace. The sunny day suddenly seems too bright, too loud, too much for her. She takes a deep breath, steeling herself for whatever comes next.

All she wanted was a fucking Polaroid. "Kids," she sighs. That single word hung heavy through the decades to come.

Now, staring at that same Polaroid years later, Sally hears the sound of playful kids rising over street traffic through her second-floor window. The weight of her next decisions press heavily, but she has made her choice. She knows what to do. Making her way back to the humble wooden desk, her fingers absently trace the scratches on its surface as she fixates on that infamous Polaroid from Scarborough '96. "Kids," she thinks to herself. No longer a lament. Now a painful memory she is determined to change.

The fan whirs overhead, fighting a losing battle against the summer heat wave.

Jagdeesh enters, precariously balancing writing paper and tea atop an ornate trunk—the same trunk delivered to her brother-in-law Chidi's office. The metal catches the harsh fluorescent light, its intricate patterns casting elaborate shadows across the oppressive white walls of her hospital suite.

"My goodness, could you not have got something so... " Sally starts, eyeing the trunk's ostentatious decorations.

"Indian?" Jagdeesh's eyes widen with amusement almost as much as his mouth; he's still not used to Sally's sharp honesty, even after all these years. "I think it's nice."

He arranges each item on the desk with the careful precision of someone who's spent years making patients comfortable. The paper—embossed proper writing paper, not that cheap thin 70gsm hospital letterhead crap—sits in a neat stack next to the matching envelopes. And with the flourish of a magician delivering his prestige, he produces a beautiful ornate fountain pen.

Sally raises her eyebrows imperceptibly, nonplussed. The pen gleams like it's just come from the shop window of some fancy Bond Street stationer's. "That will do," she says.

"*That* will do? Yes, *that* will do—I had to take two buses to find *that*." His mock indignation barely masks his pride.

"What?! It will do. It's fine." She runs her finger along the pen's smooth barrel.

All the while, the tea steams invitingly. "Nothing in England can be achieved without a good cuppa tea first," she says, taking a sip.

Jagdeesh straightens his already immaculate uniform. "Well, if that is all, my shift is nearly over."

Sally gives an imperceptible shrug, the kind she's spent decades perfecting to hide her true feelings. As Jagdeesh turns to leave, she calls after him: "Oh Jagdeesh?"

"Yes Sally?"

He pauses deliberately. He thinks he knows what's coming. Some gratitude…

"The sugar?" she demands.

Well, maybe not. Jagdeesh had expected thanks—but he knows this woman, he knows she is grateful. She has hidden it well. He knows the pain of losing a mother, so he can only imagine what pain Sally is going through, having to say goodbye to her children.

He returns, placing a single serving sachet on her desk with exaggerated ceremony. The white paper packet sits there momentarily until Sally rips it in half and pours it into her tea.

"Shall I turn the light off?"

Sally shakes her head no, but Jagdeesh flips the switch anyway. "Goodnight Sally," he says. His chuckles heard on his way down the stairs.

She sits in darkness for a long moment, letting her eyes adjust. The silence wraps around her like a suffocating blanket—no beeping monitors, no squeaking trolley wheels, no nurses chattering in the corridor. Just the soft whir of the fan and the weight of fifteen years' worth of unsaid words.

Then, with fingers that only slightly tremble, she switches on the desk lamp. The fountain pen feels heavy in her hand, like it knows the gravity of what she's about to write. The nib touches paper, its black ink flows smoothly on the embossed surface:

To Liam and Patsy,

I'd like to say to my dear children but I'm pretty sure you both hate my guts so I'll keep it all quite restrained, for now, so as to avoid insulting your intelligence.

If you are reading this letter, then your uncle Chidi has filled you in on the major details.

That's when the memory hits her. That night in 2010, the fluorescent lights of the corner shop made everything look sickly and unreal...

The scratch card had been an afterthought, bought with the loose change from the bottle of vodka she'd never drink. She remembers the last of her coppers sliding across the counter, the sympathetic look from the shopkeeper who'd watched her decline these past months. As he tears it, he half knows the result—he's seen this scenario play out a million times with his other customers. All going through their own version of Hell.

If it's a winner. No river tonight. I'll start again and give it all to the kids. Her bargain with the universe. Her fragile mind searching for signs in the mundane, desperate for direction. And then it happened.

Three matching numbers. One. Million. Pounds. What? It can't be. The shopkeeper's jubilation seemed unreal, like it was happening to someone else entirely. Someone more deserving.

They'd made her pose with one of those giant novelty cheques, her smile as cardboard as the prop itself. A million quid in her hands and she couldn't feel a thing except the weight of Liam's disappointment, the echo of Patsy's absence. She never went public. Just cashed the cheque, kept the photo, and disappeared—letting the universe that had dealt her this hand guide her next move. To the rational person this might seem odd, but it's important to know that Sally wasn't thinking rationally; she was trapped in a doom cycle... And we'll get to that. But for now...

Her pen hovers over the paper, then continues:

I did indeed win the lottery. It was the day I walked out on you, Liam.

A twist of fate in my favour? Or an ironic message from the universe delivered to royally screw me up?

Divine intervention or cosmic joke? A mother's escape fund or the universe's cruellest prank? These questions have haunted her ever since. She keeps writing, the words flowing now:

But it's important for you to both know that I haven't spent a penny of the winnings.

That money is for you.

If you both want it.

The fan whirs on as Sally's reconciliation stalls. The heavy fountain pen leaves a tiny pool of ink on the paper. The words somehow now feel inadequate. How do you explain fifteen years of absence and a lifetime of being a bad mother? How do you tell your children that sometimes running away is the only way you can stay alive? That being a shit mum, but loving her kids more than anything in the world is just one of those irrational dualities that mystify us as a species. Not that Sally would put it like that—she's more likely to say she needed "space" or "time to think." The classic excuses. We all know them, don't we? We've all used them. Though usually we don't let these excuses last this long. But then, time; it's a motherfucker that runs differently for one person than it does for another.

Then comes the challenge, the demand:

Inside the steel box is the total sum of my estate—only I have the key and you will get it when I see you both...

Together.

At Marston's Caravan Park in Great Yarmouth.

How dare she? How fucking dare she make demands?!

Because even though time passes and it can be a healer, I knew you both wouldn't come to see me together. The rift too wide, the memories too painful, the emotions too raw—so this is precisely why I am insisting that you do.

In the car on Peckham High Street, Liam absorbs these words with his usual placid demeanor. *Oh, makes sense,* he thinks.

No matter how long, the first step of every journey is always the hardest. Please find it in your hearts to come and see me.

One last time.

And then comes the hammer blow. Back in her hospital room, Sally's hand trembles more violently now. These next words cost her more than all the rest combined.

I'm dying you see...

"She's dying," Liam chokes out, though it hardly needs saying. Beside him, Patsy remains frozen, head buried between her legs, listening like it's happening to someone else.

Is she still hallucinating? She wonders.

... and I want to make amends before I shuffle off this mortal coil.

But you must come to see me, together.

Easy right?

Sally.

No. Patsy knows she's not hallucinating. Only Ol' Sal would pass off the best and worst news in such a callous detached way, whilst also ignoring the hypocrisy of her own advice.

"She's joking right?" Liam utters, his voice small in the confined space of the Golf. She always found humour and positivity in most situations—first she says she's alive, but then tells us she's dying. This has to be another one of her wind-ups. It must be. Right? But even his relentless optimism falters at the finality of those words on the page.

"Let me out, let me out." Patsy claws at the locked door, smashing her palm against the window whilst hyperventilating. Unlike her gullible brother, she believes every word of the letter. Every spiteful syllable, consonant and vowel, while coming to the conclusion that if her own mother couldn't be bothered to follow her own advice of "taking the first steps" to say all this to their faces, then why the fuck should she? Fifteen years of believing she is dead, reversed by a fucking letter asking them to ungrieve her... and begin to worry about her instead. Bitch.

"Open the door, OPEN THE DOOR!" The Banshee within her is now fully awake, fully sober and fully raging. Liam fumbles with the central locking, and Patsy launches herself onto Peckham High Street, barefoot and wild-eyed. Walking, running, anywhere—she just has to get away from this space. This time. This truth.

Liam sighs and hops out, nearly getting himself flattened by a red double-decker bus. The 363 to Crystal Palace blares its horn as it swerves around him, the driver's explicit hand gestures lost to Liam's wide-eyed shock.

"Patsy. Pats. PATSY!" he shouts, half-heartedly jogging after her through the Saturday morning crowds. The market traders pause mid-pitch, watching this little drama unfold. Liam can't process his own emotions yet, but some deeply buried big brother instinct drives him to follow his volatile sister anyway.

That's when she spins around, "DON'T YOU FUCKING FOLLOW ME!" Her scream brings half of Peckham High Street to a complete standstill.

"YEAH, WELL GET FUCKED. I DON'T NEED THE MONEY EITHER!" he shouts after her as she disappears into the throng of startled onlookers and Saturday shoppers. It's a lie of course—if anyone needs the money, it's Liam—but not half as much as he needs his mum. He stands alone on the pavement, surrounded by strangers trying very hard not to stare at the bloke in the sky blue tracksuit and bucket hat who's just been publicly lambasted by a barefoot girl in a designer dress after receiving the worst news he could possibly hear.

That's when his Nokia phone alarm goes off, that familiar and unmistakable "That's It" ringtone reminding him of his own stasis—trapped in the past. A time before TikTok-ing teens and Instagram-ing mums, when phones were phones and not portable dopamine dispensers. But they still had the housing department back then, same as now, who incidentally Liam is late to an appointment with about his mum's council flat. The one they think his mum still lives in. The one they're bulldozing in thirty days' time.

He hops back into the Golf and calmly, but not carefully, pulls out from the illegal parking space on the zigzags, directly into a speeding cyclist who slides across the tarmac with a painful-looking skid. The bloke's probably wearing five hundred quids' worth of bright Lycra that's now in shreds. But Liam keeps driving, catatonic to the world around him, ignoring the cyclist's pleas for him to stop. Still, like Liam, no one gives a shit about London cyclists, so we'll quietly remind ourselves of 1996, when the average age of a London cyclist was 12 and they rode BMXs with a flattened Coke can squeezed in between the back wheel arch and the tyre—proper bikes, that made proper noises—BRRRRRRR.

Some things are worth holding onto, even if the rest of the world's moved on.

CHAPTER 5
THE MASTERPLAN

DAY 1

Liam floors his Golf, with a loud BRRRRRRR, but unlike his 12-year-old self, he's going nowhere fast in this midday weekend traffic as he stops at the lights.

That's when the heady toxic mix of happy nostalgia and pain hits him—that unmistakable combination of CK One and Marlboro Lights that defined his mum in the '90s. She said no one wants a who's who of B-sides, he remembers, the words echoing across the decades. A seemingly flippant remark at the time, but one that Liam has always railed against, nay lived his life by.

He slides his beloved mixtape from his Discman into the Golf's CD player. He handles it like it's the Holy Grail itself, inspecting the surface for scratches with near OCD precision. The handwriting on the label is faded now, barely legible, but he knows every curve of those letters by heart.

Track three: "The Masterplan". The B-side of all B-sides. She was wrong about that, so she could be wrong about dying too—he clings to this thought as the deeply sombre acoustic guitar intro builds, that beautiful violin weaving through Noel's electric guitar like a prayer. If no one wants a who's who of B-sides, then they clearly hadn't heard

Oasis at their peak. Sally had, he thought, or maybe she just wore the t-shirt, another lie that makes him question whether he ever really knew his mother.

As Liam loses himself in Noel's lyrics about being part of some kind of master plan, he absentmindedly pulls up outside the crusty old concrete council offices. Shit, if they can't even home themselves somewhere nice, what chance have I got, thinks Liam uncharacteristically to himself. He shakes off those negative thoughts, slaps on a smile and, leaving his Golf on the yellow DON'T PARK HERE box outside the building, bounds inside.

𝄞

Is it the heatwave and lack of air conditioning, or is he just sweating buckets because he's ninety per cent through his game of Snake on his Nokia? His thumb taps up-right-down-right rhythmically in some kind of Buddha-like trance, willing that digital serpent to eat every pixelated dot and finally consume its own tail. He's done it once—and though no one believed him, he knows he can do it again. The snake goes up-right/down-right/up-right/down-right/up-right over and over and over.

"Next please. Sir? Yes, sir." A voice booms across the waiting room, not subtle, clearly heard by everyone.

But not Liam, who's still chasing those dots with his snake. This could be a metaphor for life within the capitalist machine, though Liam wouldn't know anything about that. He's never really chased anything or anyone—not even his own mum when she left him, or his emotionally broken little sister down the high street when she found out her mum was dying. Liam just chases those dots. The same way Insta-mum chases those hearts.

The housing officer, Julie or June or something, gives up and beckons over the young family sitting opposite Liam, their lives stuffed in bin bags, kids balanced on hips. "Next please." They eagerly get up to learn where they'll be sleeping tonight.

That's when Liam finally looks up, scans the situation and awkwardly shuffles over to Joanna or Jocelyn's desk. His snake's at

98% complete—but it's GAME OVER. Dead. Kaput. Like his chances of getting a new home in 2025 London. But he doesn't know it yet, because, he's Liam—the eternal optimist. Even so, as he sits down at Janet or Jacinder's desk, but for the first time in like forever, he begins to properly sweat about his future.

𝄞

Across town, Patsy sits at the white Steinway piano in her Belsize Park flat. Yes, Steinway—like who has one of those in their flat in 2025? Someone who can play, hopefully, and Patsy can. Play that is. Her fingers trace the chords of the final few bars of "The Masterplan". There's no violin, no guitar, no bass, drums or singing—but she replicates it all harmoniously, her soul resonating with the power of some northern council estate bloke's music. Until that final deep chord that ends it all, and she rests her head on the piano keys with a discordant clang.

That's when she hears voices upstairs.

"I love it, I looooooove it."

She looks up, hallucinating? Everything's still in its proper place—the carefully curated art on the walls, the white carpets with that red wine stain she paid a grand to get out, the ostentatiously expensive decor and furnishings. A life built on borrowed luxury.

Is that Minnie she can hear, invading her apartment on a fucking Saturday, on her day off? Only this isn't Patsy's apartment—she's a tenant of her step-mother's, and she should be at work.

"I like to think of it as a high-functioning apartment suited for high-functioning people. Please, back into the living room."

And that's when they enter. The parasites. The cockroaches. The rats. A couple of prospective tenants invading HER HOME before she's even had a chance to check Zoopla for the next place she can't afford.

Minnie—an elegant snob now in her sixties but dressing like she's in her thirties, with enough Botox in her face to give Isaac Newton pause for thought about his law of gravity—spots her and falters, "Oh darling, shouldn't you be at work?"

"You didn't hear the piano?" Patsy asks.

"I thought it was the radio darling. Some awful classical covers program on Radio 3."

Patsy pours herself a stiff vodka from the kitchen.

"I was just showing around our prospective tenants."

"I'll drink to that," Patsy says, gulping down her version of 'day wine'."

"Now Patsy, darling, it's barely the afternoon. Rather early to be on the sauce, don't you think?" Minnie's whispered admonishment barely registers as the married couple fawn over some expensive Italian lampshade whose designer Patsy will never remember, or be able to afford.

"May I ask—fully furnished? Does that include this lampshade... and the piano?" asks the young wife.

"It does," replies Minnie, without hesitation or consultation. Why should she? She bought it. Yes, Patsy loves it, but ownership is black and white—the person who paid for it owns it. Right? Sadly for Patsy, she knows this to be true, both legally and morally.

And for the first time, Patsy has no retort. Maybe it's the possible loss of her beloved piano that's the final straw. This was the one place where she could drop her guard and play her heart out. What she couldn't express through words, she could always find through other people's songs. Songs she plays with muscle memory but also reflexively rejects when she hears them on the radio—painful memories better left buried.

"You no longer play?" the young wife asks, genuinely interested and not at all understanding the nuance of this awkward situation.

"Oh, she still plays," insists Minnie.

"No, I was never really any good. Fat fingers, apparently." She holds up her long, slender and elegant fingers.

"Yes, like Elton John," says Minnie, trying to pull the tenants away from the kitchen where her yappy little dog itches beside the overflowing sink of dirty dishes.

And that's when the young wife, a complete stranger until now, recognises Patsy. Her older husband wouldn't. He doesn't watch TV—well only the rugger and occasionally the cricket—but she does. She watches these shows endlessly because watching "aspirational types" make tits of themselves is a sure-fire way to validate one's own privileged existence. At twenty-two, she's got it all mapped out: law degree, old money husband, and soon-to-be Belsize apartment. Yes, she's renting, but only to "get a vibe" of where she wants her future children to be born. Here or Hampstead—one must try before one buys, after all.

"Patsy? Patsy isn't it? I thought I recognised the apartment, and you from all the pictures on the wall, of course, but I didn't want to be crass. 'Belsize Beaus'?" Her husband's blank expression confirms he's never watched a minute of reality TV in his life. But Patsy has lived it. And Minnie, quietly imploding as she fusses with her dog, hasn't forgotten Patsy's recent past either.

"'Belsize Beaus' darling. Reality TV show. Come on, you know? Patsy here, let me see if I remember correctly... Patsy here—"

That's when Minnie intervenes, not to save Patsy's fragile state of mind, but to spare herself the embarrassment. "Is now a successful prime real estate agent in her own right. Always moving forwards, right Patricia?"

"Right. From prime time to prime estate," Patsy spits out the well-polished line that's got her out of trouble countless times before.

"So, your verdict?" Minnie smoothly changes the subject.

"I love it. The star factor really will add to the je ne sais quoi of my dinner parties. Especially when I tell my guests that the master bedroom was the one used–"

Minnie's heart jumps into her mouth as Patsy grabs the vodka bottle, guzzling it like she's found the last water source in the Sahara.

"Oh, I thought I recognised the bedroom," the husband suddenly interrupts. Much to his wife's confusion as to how he recognises the bedroom, but not Patsy.

"Do you play?" Patsy interjects desperately.

"Pardon?"

"The piano. Do you play?"

And with this, the young woman tells us everything we need to know about her: "Oh no. But I'm thinking—serving table for canapes and champers. Am I right? Am I riiight?"

"Oh marvellous idea, simply maaarvellous!" Minnie claps like a performing seal.

"Argghhhh. It's a Stein-way, you fuck-ing cretin," Patsy screams while storming out. Their voices fade down the corridor behind her as she swigs from the vodka bottle.

"What can I say, still the diva. So, nine thousand per month okay?"

The young woman doesn't even bat an eyelid, whilst her husband tries to stroke Minnie's dog, "Oh no, don't touch my dog darling, fleas," Minnie tells him as he recoils.

"Oh my god, Patsy Fortescue-Smythe just called me a cretin," the young woman giggles.

𝄞

Liam sits in front of the housing officer, barely registering her words. His mind's still processing the details he's just shared—yes, his mum hasn't lived there for fifteen years, but the housing benefit's still going in, and he's kept up with all the bills. Everything's above board, sort of. Besides, she's coming back now, isn't she? They'll need somewhere to live. These fuckers owe him and his sick mum a house. He's entitled to that much, isn't he?

"You've ignored every letter and phone call. Your tower block has been earmarked for demolition. We need the stock," she says casually, condescending him whilst also remaining earnest—in that way only a local government worker knows how to do.

"It's not stock. It's my home, and my mum's when she returns."

"The property was allocated to your mother. Your mother, who, by your own admission, hasn't lived there since 2010. That's fraud, Mr Digsby."

"But we've always paid—"

"Mr Digsby? Liam, do you understand what you need to do? The council has to prioritise women, children and refugees. You're of working age, physically fit, have no dependents—you can get a job and privately rent," she says this barely batting an eyelid.

"So you're taking my home away from me, just like that?" he replies.

"Liam? Do you understand what you need to do? You have twenty-four hours to gather your things and vacate."

Imperceptibly, Liam sighs. They're not seeing it. This is just temporary, just until Mum comes home. Everything will make sense then.

The Nokia's "That's it" ringtone cuts through the tension.

"Yep. Tomorrow, got it—Jacqui," he mumbles to the housing officer, already reaching for his phone as he skulks past the family with the bin bags. "It's Brenda," she mumbles to herself.

"Looks like they've finally run out," he says to the desperate family as his Nokia's ringtone chimes in again, this time with a sense of comical finality: *du-du-du-du du <u>dun-dun</u>*.

"What's the story?" Liam answers.

Two siblings, two lives falling apart in perfect synchronisation. A convergence that nobody saw coming. While Liam stands catatonic in the housing office as Brenda reaches for her phone to arrange tomorrow's repossession of his entire life, Patsy slumps on the stoop of her former apartment block, having dialled her brother's phone number—that she's never forgotten—with the knowledge that her life for rent is probably over.

"Can't believe you still have the same number." She says.

"If it ain't broke." He says.

"We need to talk." She says.

And as both hang up their phones, both sigh—ever so imperceptibly.

𝄞

The concrete towers of Liam's estate loom against the bright blue sky like ancient monoliths. Once a place of countless hopes, dreams, desires and memories, now sealed with steel shutters and resignation. Patsy, still wearing last night's designer dress and stolen Ray-Bans, walks barefoot through a gauntlet of discarded demolition notices and eviction warnings.

The click-click-click of a distant wrecking ball marks time like a metronome. Soon, time here will stop completely, and give rise to new hopes, dreams, desires and memories. But not today. Today is just the depressing bit in between.

Muscle memory guides her to Liam's block. She slumps down on the curb, her whole body aching from hangover and hunger. How many hours since she'd eaten? The vodka had kept her going, but now... her hands shake as she checks her iPhone: -£19,999 overdrawn.

Christ. Really? All those fifteen-quid lattes she supposes. Wait, that was a dream right? Where did all my money go? She thinks.

The gambling app icon pulses invitingly. £100 credit. One good win could turn it all around. That's all she needs—one win. Her last chance to claw back some control.

Her finger hovers over the roulette wheel. 26 RED. Her birthday. It has to mean something, right?

Spin... spin... spin...

2 BLACK. GAME OVER. CREDIT £0.

A sound escapes her throat—something between a laugh and a sob. Then David @Catston's calls.

"Patsy, love..." His voice drips with false sympathy. "About Primrose Hill Road..."

"Fucking Janine."

"Look, it's not all your fault, but... well, it's kind of all your fault. Catston's requires winners Patsy, and when your mum and I agreed for you..."

"She ain't my mum."

She doesn't even let him finish. The screen blurs as tears well up behind her stolen sunglasses. Everything she's built, her carefully constructed facade, is crumbling like the condemned tower blocks around her. Her life, the life that she knew. Is dead.

With a scream of pure frustration, she hurls the iPhone across the carpark. And just as the orange Golf comes cruising around the corner, the phone hits a pothole and rests on the road, cracked but working, a bit like its owner. Well at least she can sell the phone. Cracked or not, a brand-new iPhone is worth something to someone. And that's when it disappears under Liam's front wheel with a definitive crunch.

Kaput.

"What's the story?" Liam calls out the window, casual as anything

—as if the Peckham barney never happened—as if their mum wasn't dying of cancer—as if they both weren't facing eviction.

Patsy can't decide whether to laugh or cry. But then, that's always been the effect Liam has on her.

Liam bounds up the concrete stairs two at a time, leaving Patsy to follow at her own pace. The stairwell smells of stale piss, which Patsy hops over every third step or so. Every touch of the cold concrete on her bare feet reminds her of her spectacular fall from grace.

His flat feels just as cold and empty when they enter—void of real life, like a museum piece preserving a moment in time that's long since passed.

"Haven't stepped foot in here since I was..." Patsy trails off, taking in the unchanged furniture, the walls still plastered with the same peeling wallpaper and family photos of happier times.

"Fifteen," Liam finishes, already throwing effects into a bag—underwear, a spare identical blue tracksuit, a spare Scotland football shirt. His dad's urn comes last, wrapped carefully in the tracksuit jacket.

"I just got fired," Patsy offers in the silence. "Minnie's gonna be pissed. Bloody hated it anyway."

"What was it?"

"Estate agents—was just a stopgap really, whilst I figured out how to get back on TV."

Liam pauses mid-pack. "You were on TV?"

His millions of DVDs clutter the flat, reminding Patsy that this guy is strictly offline. One of the things she actually admires about him.

A small nod from Patsy.

"What kind of show was it?"

"'Structured reality'."

Liam grabs a photo of his mum and dad from happier times, studies it like he's seeing it for the first time. "What kinda nonsense is 'structured reality'?"

"Well, it's like a soap opera—only real lives."

"Oh what, like, um... "Real World: Seattle", "New York"? Any good?"

"Some people found it entertaining."

"Haven't been able to get a proper signal since they switched to digital. I only watch DVDs." He glances at her hopefully. "You on DVD?"

"Internet," Patsy sighs, ever so imperceptibly, whilst absentmindedly chewing a nail.

Liam gauges the mood and changes tack.

"I'll share it. If you come."

"Forget the money, you can keep it all. I don't want it." Patsy sinks onto the ancient sofa, feeling a sense of warmth and familiarity she hasn't felt in many many years.

"But you are right. I do have questions. And number one…"

"Why?" they say together, their voices overlapping in the empty flat.

Liam picks up a Polaroid from '96—him, Mum, and Patsy at the beach. Three smiling faces frozen in time, before everything went wrong. Before time stopped. Maybe this is what the universe had been building to all along—both of them losing everything on the same day, forced back together by circumstances beyond their control. Like some cosmic joke where the punchline takes fifteen years to land.

CHAPTER 6
"GREAT" FUCKING YARMOUTH

DAY 1

The Golf crawls along the motorway's slow lane like a pensioner out for a Sunday drive. Fifty miles per hour. Not forty-nine. Not fifty-one. Just a steady, deliberate fifty that's driving everyone else up the wall. A green Škoda Favorit, one of those boxy Eastern European jobs designed with nothing but pure communist efficiency, pulls alongside.

HONK HONK.

Behind the wheel, a little old lady who can barely see over the dashboard gesticulates wildly at Liam to get a move on. Her blue rinse visible even through his tinted glass.

"WHAT'S THE STORY?" Liam shouts through his closed window. "WHAT YOU IN SUCH A RUSH FOR? DON'T WANNA GET A SPEEDING TICKET LOVE."

He turns to Patsy, genuinely puzzled. "What's she in such a rush for?"

"She's got a point," Patsy mutters, slumped in the passenger seat, slowly dying on the inside, dehydrated molecule by dehydrated molecule.

"Nah, why burn petrol and waste money on a speeding ticket?"

"Where's your satnav?" Patsy asks.

Liam responds by chucking his ancient Nokia at her. This thing may survive a nuclear war, but it certainly doesn't have Google Maps.

"Don't do Google. They're listening to everything," he says, meaning every word.

"Fuck." She says

"Where's yours?" He says.

She holds up her thoroughly mangled iPhone. Complete carnage, no chance of survival.

"Oh. How'd that happen?"

"Forget 'bout it. How we gonna get to, where is it? Great fucking Yarmouth?"

Liam pops open the glove box with a flourish, unleashing an avalanche of dog-eared road maps onto Patsy's lap.

"Analogue baby."

Patsy buries herself in the maps with the kind of frustrated resignation usually reserved for tax returns and IKEA furniture assembly. "It's got to be easier than this."

"Look." Liam flashes her his eternally optimistic smile. "The fuel tank's half full. I'm going fifty miles per hour and we got maps to where we need to be... what's your beef?"

"My beef? Your fuel tank's half empty. You're doing fifty. And we're using actual paper fucking maps!"

While Patsy wrestles with the oversized pages, Liam turns the volume knob with the reverence of a priest performing communion. The opening chords of Suede's "The Beautiful Ones" fill the car—Brett Anderson's falsetto soaring over those signature guitars.

Liam's already lost in it, miming along with passionate abandon while Patsy shields her ears like she's being subjected to torture. Her eyes dart from stereo to window, calculating how to stop her head from physically exploding. Without warning, she winds down the window, hits eject, and launches the CD out into the slipstream.

"WHAAAAAAAAAAAAAAAAAAAAAAAAAATTTTTTT?"
Liam's scream echoes across three lanes of traffic as he watches his precious CD spin through the air.

"Can't do Blur or Oasis... got any R&B?" Patsy asks with feigned innocence.

The Golf's brakes squeal as Liam brings it to an abrupt halt—right there in the slow lane. A chorus of horns erupts behind them as he brings the motorway to a complete and utter standstill.

"It's Suede," he says through gritted teeth, already unbuckling his seatbelt.

"Are you out of your tiny little mind? Get back in the car!" she demands.

But Liam's already marching down the hard shoulder, shoulders hunched against the backdraft of passing cars. The CD lies there like a fallen star, its silver surface now bearing the battle scars of being in Patsy's company for about twenty minutes. He scoops it up, examining the damage—one perfect arc of a scratch across the surface. To the modern-day Gen Zs reading, this type of scratch is like having your Spotify premium account cancelled. Utter devastation.

The walk back feels longer, past a growing queue of irate drivers whacking their horns. As he reaches for the door handle, a massive lorry thunders past inches from his nose, the displacement of air strong enough to send his bucket hat sailing over the car and back onto the hard shoulder.

Back in the car, Liam sits in stunned silence, counting to ten on his fingers like he's done since childhood. Up, then down. A coping technique that's served him well over the years. Patsy watches him—his badly maintained braids now exposed, his precious CD ruined, those fingers still counting—but then, something shifts in her expression.

With a sigh, she opens her door.

"Where are you going?" Liam shouts. But she's already stalking down the hard shoulder in her bare feet, retrieving his hat from where it landed.

"Get a fuckin' wiggle on babe," calls an irate sexist driver from the car behind.

Patsy freezes mid-step, turns, and walks to the wanker's window with deliberate calm and practised catwalk elegance. The SLAP that follows echoes across three lanes of traffic, and Patsy finishes it off with a catlike hiss.

Back in the Golf, she hands Liam his hat along with the closest thing he will ever get to an apology from her: "Shall we?"

She slides the scratched CD into the player and turns up the volume—a peace offering of sorts. The famous intro to "The Riverboat Song" starts up, der de du du duu, and Liam cracks a smile before—d d d d d—stutters and skips like a broken record. To any Gen Zs reading, a broken record is like... oh forget it. Just know that Liam is no longer smiling.

"Oh..." Patsy wrinkles her nose. "You should put your hat back on. When was the last time you washed your hair?" She leaves the question hanging, realising she has now crossed a line.

Liam scrunches his nose, and in response, he floors it. The Golf lurches from 10 mph to 30, 60, 88—still in the slow lane. Up ahead, the blue-rinsed old girl in the green Škoda comes back into view.

"AHHHHHHHHHHHHHHH!" Liam screams.

"AHHHHHHHHHHHHHHH!" Patsy joins in.

"AHHHHHHHHHHHHHHH!" The little old lady's face appears in her rearview mirror, eyes wide with terror.

The Golf swerves across three lanes just in time to avoid rear-ending the Škoda, as well as the truck that nearly flattened Liam. And just as they take over, the gantry's speed camera catches them with a decisive FLASH.

A solemn quiet settles over them as the Golf slows down to 50 mph again. Not only because of the stress they just caused one another. But because there's something about this stretch of motorway that feels really fucking familiar. Like muscle memory, but for trauma.

They have both been on this road together before, their unbelted frames sliding around in the back seat of their mum's Golf—the green one. Sally at the wheel, her knuckles white against the black leather steering wheel. Her voice cracking as she mutters reassurances to herself.

Over the sound of their adrenaline-fueled heartbeats, her voice drifts in from the past—younger, filled with a different kind of desperation:

"It's gonna be okay. It's gonna all be fine. I should have done more. More. Wanker."

~ 1996 ~

The tatty green Golf swerves dangerously through the three-lane motorway, sending Little Patsy sliding across the vinyl-covered back seat into Little Liam.

"I need a wee. Mum, I need a wee." But getting nothing from Sally, who seems to have regressed into her own world, she looks to her brother.

"LeeLee, I need a wee."

"Yeah, just hold it. We'll be there in a minute." Of course he has no idea where they are going or when they will get there, but he won't tell Pats that. Because he does not want to sit in piss. He's also a good big brother, and he doesn't want to worry her.

The green Golf takes the Great Yarmouth exit at the last possible second, its tyres screech across the white lines, sending Little Patsy sliding once again into her brother.

Finally, Marston's Caravan Park materialises through the summer haze like some bargain-basement mirage. Not the kind of place anyone chooses to go—more the kind you end up at because your parents got a stay two nights free voucher in 'The Sun'. A proper chintzy British holiday camp, all faded signage and peeling paint, over-promising on "family entertainment", "luxury accommodation", and a "heated pool".

"Here look, we're here. We're here. Bloody Nora." Sally's manic energy shifts gear as she pulls into a space, the Golf's engine whirrs in protest over the hot weather and ragged driving style. Overwhelmed by the thirty-degree heat, Sally's out of the car and heading straight for the bar before the dust settles. "Kids, stay here. Mum's gasping. We can't check in for a few hours, so entertain yourselves for a bit."

"Liiiiiaaaam," Little Patsy's voice has taken on a new urgency after holding her wee in for fifty miles.

"Okay Pats. One second." Little Liam spots salvation—a toilet block across the site.

"Over there." Little Patsy takes off like an Olympic sprinter, her little legs carrying her towards sweet relief while their mum disappears into the social club.

The playground buzzes with summer holiday energy—wild raucous kids are engaged in water fights, tag, and footy. Game Boys beep and Tamagotchis chirp, desperate for attention. If you're twelve or under in Marston's Caravan Park in the summer of 1996, then this is THE place to be right now. If you're Little Liam, wearing his prized Sony Discman headphones, it's just another place to try to blend in and avoid eye contact.

"Alright" by Supergrass fills his ears. The perfect summer song he thinks, as he makes his way to the merry-go-round, keeping himself to himself gently humming along. But even through Gaz Coombes' uber-cheerful vocals about being young and having fun, he feels *them* watching. Three local kids, led by a pudgy thirteen-year-old, nudge each other and point. Remember: this is 1996 in northernmost Norfolk. Little Liam is perhaps the only Black person they've ever seen, apart from Will Smith and Lenny Henry on the TV. But unlike them, he's not welcome here—and he can feel it.

His Spidey sense tingles, but it's too late. They're on him and before he can react, the pudgy leader rips his headphones off.

"'Ay, jungle bunny. What yer doing with that little girl? You kidnap 'er?" The pudgy kid's Norfolk accent is loaded with menace.

"She's ma sister," Little Liam's voice comes out smaller than he means it to.

The pudgy kid's face contorts in exaggerated confusion. "Whaaattt?"

The silence that follows could fill the Royal Albert Hall. You may as well have told the little git you were Jesus and your dad was Buddha.

"Yah see, that ain't possible coz, see, whites don't come out o' Blacks... an' Blacks don't come out o' whites. It's not scientifically possible."

"Yes they can," Little Liam's voice wavers between defiance and fear as he backs away.

That's when the oldest kid grabs his bucket hat, exposing his unkempt braids. The bullies recoil with performative disgust, pulling faces and waving hands in front of their noses like they've caught a whiff of something rotten.

"Smelly nigger."

The words land like knife wounds slashed deep into his heart. His entire world—who he is, where he belongs, his very right to exist—collapses into that single moment of hatred.

Little Liam reaches for his hat, but they're already tossing it between them like it might poison them if they hold it too long, complete with exaggerated *eerrrs* and *yukkks*.

He's heard this word before—not on the streets of South London, mind, but on some of the CDs his mum listened to when they made his mixtape together. Every time she heard it, she'd take the CD out of the player and quietly bury it deep in the pile to return to the library. He knew the word, but its meaning had always felt distant, abstract—something that belonged to the worlds of the Wu-Tang Clan or Public Enemy rather than his inner-city London life with his white mum and white sister. Until now. Until these kids turned it into a weapon, forcing him to see himself through their eyes. They just spat it out like they were giving someone the time, but it changes everything. It hurts. It hurts in ways he doesn't even have words for yet. And probably never will.

Little Liam reaches for his hat, a further humiliation as they toss it about and laugh. Giving up, he walks away, with their taunts following him across the playground.

"Go 'ome nigger. Go 'ome nigger. Go 'ome nigger."

He grits his teeth and looks back in anger, but keeps his feet moving away from the taunts and humiliation. That's when Little Patsy emerges from the loo, spotting her big brother's retreat as she breezes out into the fresh air, now with an empty bladder.

"Lee, LeeLee. Oh thank Christ. Where ya goin'?"

Little Liam desperately wipes his eyes, choking back words that won't come, "Anywhere but here."

"What's 'appened?" she questions, perplexed at his tears. She's never seen him cry—he's always been the stoic, sensible one who never got into trouble or told off.

But Little Liam just keeps walking. Little Patsy stops, and on hearing the bullies' laughter and horrific chants at her brother's expense, something hardens in her face. She turns and heads towards the bullies. And anyone who knows Little Patsy, knows what's coming next.

The pudgy kid spots her approaching, his cocksure grin spreads across his stupid fucking face. "Yeh, wot you gonna do..."

SCRAAATCH. Without hesitation, Little Patsy's long nails rake across his left cheek, drawing blood, leaving deep caverns in his face.

"AHHHHHHHH!" he screams as he grabs his face, not comprehending how someone so small could cause so much pain.

The playground falls silent. Everyone backs away as Little Patsy snatches her brother's bucket hat back. She faces down the group of boys, and something in her eyes makes them all take another step back. Even the older kids.

She gives her loudest and most fearsome hiss. This is not a cat you want to get on the wrong side of. This is Little Pats. Four feet and five inches of South London warrior. Some things will never, and should never, change.

The bathroom door slams shut with the force of Little Liam's frustration. His scream of anguish echoes off the grimy tiles, raw and primal. Inside, the fluorescent light flickers, casting harsh shadows as he hunches over the sink.

The ancient taps squeak as he turns them, sending tepid water splashing over his hands. The dispenser above the sink spits out a glob of thin pink soap—the cheap institutional kind that smells of artificial flowers and does absolutely nothing. Still, he scrubs at his scalp desperately, as if he could wash away more than just playground dirt.

Then a creak, followed by, "LeeLee, you okay?"

"Go away," he mutters when he hears the door, not looking up to see his sister's reflection in the filthy stained mirror where she stands, hands on her hips, quietly raging.

DING-A-LING goes the shop door. In the site's small corner-shop-come-gift-shop-come-pharmacy, Little Patsy moves with the casual confidence of someone who knows exactly what they're doing—even if what they're doing isn't strictly legal. The shopkeeper barely glances up from her magazine as this tiny girl in pigtails browses the hair care aisle with suspicious intensity.

"Just waiting for my mum," Little Patsy shouts over, whilst something disappears under her t-shirt. After about five seconds of waiting... "Guess she ain't coming," she shouts as she breezes out the door.

When she returns to the toilet, she pauses in the doorway. No words this time—just the soft thud of whatever she stole as she tosses it to her brother. Little Liam catches it reflexively and turns it over in his hands—a green bottle of afro shampoo.

A moment of understanding passes between them, worth more than any number of stolen bottles, scratched bullies or words. Unfortunately, that's more than we can say for Sally's handling of the situation, as she is presently, where the fuck is she? Oh yeah, she's down the pub.

Enchantment. The ironically named social club at Marston's Caravan Park reeks of stale cigarettes and alcohol, all dark wood and sticky carpets straight out of 1983. The place heaves with stout men clutching cheap pints and fags, as their collective mutterings drown out the fruit machines. Through the speakers, "Mustang Sally" by The Commitments drones on endlessly, repeated for the umpteenth time today.

But in the corner, by the payphone, Sally exists in her own bubble of quiet desperation. She cradles the receiver like it's the only thing keeping her upright. A neat stack of 20p pieces sits beside two vodka shots on the phone's metal shelf—ammunition for what's to come.

She cuts a lonely figure, in a lonely place, at a lonely time.

Richard's voice crackles through the line, fighting against the pub's chaos: "Sally, you need to return—we can work through this, but you have to come home." This last bit is said more as a demand than a polite request.

"They need each other," her voice barely carries above a whisper.

"Minnie says I should call the police. She's worried about..."

Sally cuts him off. "Call the bloody police, tell 'em they're on holiday with their mother," she spits.

A beat hangs between them as Richard queues up his next line of questioning: "Don't be like that Sally. Minnie loves Patsy."

Those three words cut through Sally's defences so deeply that for a moment she has nothing to say. Nothing to come back with. Not that she needs to. But in the years that follow, she will relive this conversation a thousand times over, and each time come up with what she thinks will be the perfect reply. But for now… she just slams the receiver down, her hands shaking as she knocks back the first vodka shot. The second follows immediately. And on the way to the exit, she grabs someone's freshly poured pint, downing it in one fluid motion.

Some bucket hat-wearing teen rebelliously switches the mood at the jukebox to Oasis' summer anthem "Don't Look Back In Anger". An epic song with hymn-like qualities about buried memories and moving forwards without regret. Right now it's playing to a room full of people too drunk to notice, apart from the solitary rebellious teenager —and Sally, who finds herself oddly transfixed by the familiar opening chords. Something in the melody cuts through her alcohol haze, making her pause just long enough to listen.

As she exits, she shields her eyes from the hazy glow of the bright afternoon sun as Noel Gallagher's vocals echo through her cranium, telling her not to look back in anger. Advice that would take thirty years for her to put into practice.

Old braid bands lay scattered across the dirty floor. The stolen green bottle of afro shampoo sits on the sink edge.

Little Patsy perches on an upturned bin pulled close to the sink, her small hands working with surprising gentleness as she massages shampoo through her brother's hair. She gently hums "Wonderwall" by Oasis, the melody drifting through the cramped space like a lullaby. She knows it's his favourite song of all time. She knows he plays it when he's stressed the most about school, friends or Mum, usually more about Mum than the other things.

The door suddenly creaks open—the pudgy kid from earlier peers in with a blue tissue paper held to his bloody face. Before he can react, Little Patsy lets out a feral hiss that sends him scrambling backwards. The door swings shut and she returns to her humming, to their moment of quiet healing.

In the dirty mirror, Little Liam studies his reflection. His afro hair, though needing a bit of a trim, has never looked better. Little Patsy watches on, a broad smile drawing across her face, happy with her handiwork. But something in Little Liam's eyes remains haunted as he curls his top lip and jams the bucket hat back on his head.

The door bangs open again. This time it's Sally, stumbling past her children without really seeing them. She lurches into a cubicle, the door slamming behind her.

"Everything alright kids?" she asks. The kids just look at each other.

The sound of Sally peeing fills the awkward silence, followed by her slurred attempt at a song. She sings about starting *some kind of evolution, losing her brains into her head, summertime's-to-bloom...* that's when Liam clocks the attempt, it's "Don't Look Back In Anger". That summer's epic stadium anthem blasted from every car stereo, mechanic's, office and cafe across the land. He doesn't correct her; instead she corrects herself and begins again.

This time, she gets the words right.

Her voice echoes off the tile walls, transforming Noel Gallagher's anthem into something more haunting... and desperate. The kids stand frozen, listening to their mother sing about *revolution from her bed, about brains going to heads, about summertime in bloom.*

Sally attempts to vocalise the iconic guitar solo—and nails it. The best solos don't need shredding, just feeling. That's why they linger, why they burrow into your soul.

LeeLee and Pats exchange a look heavy with understanding beyond their years. They wrap their arms around each other's shoulders and head for the exit.

"Come on kids," Sally calls out. "Sing with me?" her voice now full of joy.

But the silence that answers her is deafening.

"Kids?"

The sound of retching follows the kids out the door, but they don't look back. They can't. Some moments are better left behind in grimy caravan park bathrooms, even if they never really leave you.

DAY 1

Liam's orange Golf pulls into Marston's Caravan Park like a time machine arriving in some grotty parallel universe. Everything's different, yet somehow exactly the same—just more depressing. The welcome sign is new, plasticky and cheap—but still hangs crooked, its promises of "family entertainment" and "heated pool" now replaced with "Costa Coffee" and "hot tubs." The neat flower beds from '96 have been replaced by tarmac with weeds pushing through the cracks. And for some reason, dog shit is fucking everywhere.

Liam guides the Golf into the exact same space where Sally parked all those years ago. Muscle memory, though he doesn't realise it.

"This place feels depressingly familiar," Patsy mutters, surveying the scene through her stolen Ray-Bans.

"Was waiting for you to realise where we were." Liam watches her face carefully.

"You remember this dump?"

"You don't?"

But Patsy just shakes her head. "Probably deleted the memories," she says flatly.

Liam nods, understanding more than he lets on. He climbs out while Patsy heads toward the corner-shop-come-gift-shop-come-pharmacy, muttering something about needing cigarettes and alcohol. Though mostly alcohol, let's be honest, she's gagging for a vodka tonic, with or without the tonic.

The playground's still there, though the equipment's different now—all bright plastic and safety surfaces instead of the metal death traps they used to have. A handful of kids halfheartedly kick a football around, but it's nothing like the wild energy of '96. No Game Boys beeping, no Tamagotchis demanding attention, just the occasional ping of a phone notification breaking the summer stillness.

Liam tentatively makes his way to where the old merry-go-round used to be. His feet know the way, even if his heart's trying to forget why. On his way, he nods to some kids sitting idly under a tree. He wonders if they've just finished smoking a joint, such is their docility. He's wrong. They've just had their spirits crushed by modern-day life, which admittedly, is rubbish. Damon Albarn was right about that.

𝄞

DING-A-LING goes the shop door, as Patsy skulks in.

The shop's largely the same as '96, complete with the same shopkeeper—now older, and greyer, but still manning her post. The shelves have moved with the times though—protein powders and vape supplies replace the Polaroid film and disposable cameras, while phone cases and chargers replace the buckets and spades. Patsy slaps a packet of Alka Seltzer on the counter, her hands slightly trembling.

"You want water with that?" the shopkeeper asks, not looking up from her phone.

"Why?"

"How you going to take it?"

"Maybe I'll sniff it," Patsy deadpans. "Don't happen to sell cigarettes?"

The shopkeeper just gives her a look—no.

Patsy fumbles in her concealed pocket, fiddling with her last tenner and some loose change. She counts the coins—just enough for the overpriced packet of Alka-Seltzer. She then really considers the shopkeeper's advice of buying an overpriced bottle of water with her tenner, but quickly dismisses that idea and screws the note up in her hand, saving it for more pressing matters—like numbing the growing realisation that she's back in this godforsaken place after all these years and that soon she'll be having a showdown with her estranged mum. Ol' Sal who stopped bothering to see her when she turned fifteen. Ol' Sal who pretended to be dead for the last fifteen years. Ol' fucking Sal, she thinks.

On her way out, something catches her eye that makes her stop dead in her tracks. There on the shelf, at eye level—afro shampoo. The exact same green bottle brand she nicked in '96. Guess they don't get many Black guests at this park, she thinks to herself. Wonder why? And with a shake of the head, she quickly exits.

Patsy staggers out of the shop, letting the big metal door hit her on the way out, and that's when she sees it. The bar. Still there, still called Enchantment, though there's STILL nothing enchanting about this "Great" Yarmouth drinking hole. Not that she's judging. The screwed up tenner burns in her palm and this seems as good a place as anywhere to spend it. Who needs an overpriced bottle of water when an underpriced vodka tonic will do?!

Her reflection in the grimy window doesn't lie—barefoot, hungover, in last night's designer dress. But the hair of the dog is calling. Just one, she thinks. To take the edge off before... before what? Before she has to face the woman who abandoned her? Before she has to explain to Sally how her life went so spectacularly wrong?

She stops at the threshold as a red-faced punter stumbles out, letting a blast of "Tubthumping" by Chumbawamba escape with him. He's getting knocked down, but he's getting up again—good for him, she thinks. Is this the universe's idea of a joke? Or is it a metaphor for never giving up that she should pay closer attention to? One never can tell with music this sophisticated.

Even so, as she ponders the merits of the songwriting skills of those Chumbawamba musical geniuses, the ten-pound note is still clutched in her hand.

One more drink, she figures. *Otherwise, I really will have to sniff this Alka Seltzer.*

𝄞

Liam notices a sizable figure approaching from the caravan park's reception. Even at this distance, there's something unnervingly familiar about the man's gait. His doughy face is distinguished by deep scars along his left cheek. The scars are silvered by time, and a patchy beard makes a pitiful attempt to hide them, but it's unmistakably him —the same pudgy kid from that horrible day in the summer 1996.

Since that summer in '96, he's perfected his story—"Got them in a fight with a dog," he tells anyone who asks. Simple, believable. He's repeated the lie so many times he almost believes it himself. Almost. But some truths can't stay buried forever, no matter how deep you try to hide them.

Now, at six-feet tall, Liam towers over the pudgy man, but as usual he'd never use this height advantage to intimidate. Instead, he slouches and makes himself smaller, just like he's done his whole life.

"Digsby? Yer Liam Digsby?" The pudgy man's Norfolk accent hasn't changed either.

Liam's throat tightens. He can't get any words out.

"I said you Liam Digsby?"

Liam barks back his response which takes the pudgy man by surprise, "Yeah, what's the story?"

"Oh no, I meant nuffin' by it. I gotta description of a man matchin' you'll likely visit 'round this time. Along with his, yer, sister." He glances at his notebook. "A Patsy is it?"

Liam nods, wary.

"As I say, I mean nowt by it. It's jus' our office received a letter, from your mam, Sally, is it? With a cashier's cheque for five hundred notes if we give this letter to ya... if y'turn up. Thought it were a practical joke, be honest with ya. The names Wayne, nice t'meet ya." Wayne pauses, waiting for Liam to shake his extended hand back. But Liam's head is spinning, and his stomach is twisted into knots, as the penny finally drops.

Sally's not here.

"You are 'im aren't ya? Your mam said: probaly wear a blue bucket hat, probaly drive an orange Golf, blue tracksuit and be... ya know..."

Liam looks at him blankly.

"Be a tall handsome fella with an afro. Like yerself is. Her words—look—"

Wayne holds out the letter with casual indifference, and as Liam grabs it, he searches Wayne's face for any flicker of recognition, any sign that those taunts had stayed with him the way they'd stayed with Liam all these years. Nothing. Wayne clearly has no idea who he is. "You don't recognise me?" presses Liam.

"No, should I? You been park before? We get a lot of guests."

"You run this place?" Liam realises.

"Oh yer, man an' boy. Raised here, family business..."

And that's when Wayne spots her, over Liam's shoulder—it's Patsy, marching towards them with that same Banshee look from '96, the one that made kids twice her size run for cover. Wayne's eyes lock with Liam's and the colour drains from his face. Oh shit.

"Yoooooouuuuuuuuuuuuuu," growls Patsy, the word stretches out across the park.

"Now her I do reckanise." The penny drops as Wayne looks between brother and sister. "Oh... it's you," Wayne quietly says to Liam.

Wayne cowers as Patsy grabs him by the scruff of his neck, his attempt at maintaining any sense of dignity crumbling in milliseconds.

"Look, I'm sorry, I din't mean owt—we were just stoopid kids."

"Din't mean owt?" Patsy spits back.

"Yeah, look," Wayne gestures to his scarred face. "Every day I'm reminded of that fat little bastard. You taught me a lesson. I've changed—honest."

Patsy thrusts him away like something rotten. "Clear off."

Wayne skulks back a few steps, looking to Liam for forgiveness. "For what it's worth. I am sorry."

"How come you recognised her but not me?" Liam's voice lowers. "Cos all Black people look the same?"

"No mate," Wayne touches his scars. "She gave me these... You din't do owt t'me, did ya?"

Wayne tears the cheque in half and hands the pieces to Liam before heading back to reception. He looks back, once, offering a nod that's equal parts shame and closure.

The silence stretches between the siblings as both come to terms with their individual experiences with Wayne... until Patsy breaks the moment by tossing a green bottle of afro shampoo to Liam.

"Come on, big brother."

𝄞

Old braid bands scatter the bathroom floor again, though this time more cathartic, more like discarded painful memories than angry reactions to a painful incident. The bathroom's had a makeover since '96, if you can call it that—the kind of refurbishment that screams "we spent just enough to keep the health inspector happy". White sinks with squeezy soap dispensers and an air dryer have replaced the crusty yellowing porcelain and mildewed tetanus-infested hand towels of their childhood. The single cubicle's still cramped enough to trigger claustrophobia, and there's still that lingering smell that seems to haunt every UK holiday park bathroom—a potent cocktail of bleach, damp, piss and the whiff of disappointment from not booking that all-inclusive in Spain.

The green bottle of afro shampoo sits atop the metal bin. The tap runs hot, at least, and through the steamy air, Patsy hums "Wonderwall" just like she did back in '96, though she probably doesn't even realise she's doing it as she washes Liam's hair in the sink. Her movements are gentle, practised, as if the twenty-nine years between then and now have dissolved in the warm water. A reflexive action never forgotten.

In the mirror, Liam studies his reflection—a fresh natural afro that makes him look more himself than he has in years. The moment hangs, perfect, and he cracks the faintest smile, until he slaps the blue bucket hat back on, hiding it all away again.

Patsy perches on the closed toilet lid, Sally's second letter trembling slightly in her hands.

"We really worked hard on that, you know," Liam says suddenly.

"What's that?"

"The mixtape, CD."

The memory flashes between them—*Patsy's casual flick of the wrist, the CD sailing out the Golf's window. The deep scratch on the gleaming silver plastic.*

"Mum played it all summer on our last holiday together." He pauses, letting the weight of it sink in. "I've played it every day since."

"Well I mean, all that '90s shoegazing, grunge and introspective navel gazing. Radiohead... Nirvana. Erghh—give me Rick Astley any day of the week." She breaks into an off-key warble of "Never Gonna Give You Up".

Liam's face could freeze over Hell.

"I'll make you a Spotify playlist?" she says earnestly, despite knowing the gesture is half-baked, at best.

"Just... read it," he sighs.

Patsy looks down at the envelope just delivered to them by Wayne, and by way of Ol' Sal. Her fingers tremble as she unfolds the letter, and begins to read:

To my children

Thank you for acquiescing to my request to journey together into the unknown. Well, the forgotten, because if you are reading this, then you have decided to cross that sticky threshold of the past and move forwards together—and ended up in Great Yarmouth.

"I can spot a manipulator from a thousand yards," Patsy interrupts herself. "Don't fall for—"
"Just, please. Read the letter," Liam quietly asks.
"Okay, jeez." She clears her throat.

I never quite knew what was so great about Great Yarmouth. I got two nights free in 'The Sun' newspaper. Sorry for bringing you back to this turgid caravan park of all places, but, we can't change our memories, can we?

I know re-opening the wounds of the past will be difficult for you both, but I wanted you to remember a shared moment in time together that defined who you are and what you mean to each other.

At her desk in her hospital room, Sally reads her letter out loud as she puts pen to paper:

I shall never forget the time you, Patsy, protected your brother and cared for him in his time of need. It wasn't easy for you, you were far too tough for someone of your age.

And for you, Liam, to go through what you did was unspeakable—I'm sorry for bringing you both back.

But most of all—I'm sorry I wasn't there for you both in your hour of need.

Well that's Great Yarmouth done, please come to the place of the infamous ice cream incident of '96.

I'll be there, waiting.

Mum

Sally lays down her pen, hand trembling. Through the window, sunset bleeds into the stark white room, casting a gorgeous deep orange glow over her. She closes her eyes to absorb the warmth of the sun's rays. *Just a few more days like these*, she thinks, and she will be there with her children again.

Jagdeesh enters quietly with her evening tea, but she's already drifting, lost in memories of ice creams and seaside summers.

𝄞

In the grimy holiday park toilet, Patsy folds the letter, resigned to...
"Another goose chase," she exclaims.
"She'll be waiting," he pleads.
"The ice cream incident?" Liam questions.
"The ice cream incident!" Patsy reminds him.
As they each cast their memories far far back to 1996, to what feels like another century, and Christ wasn't it just... both answer at once: "Scarborough."

Liam questions the memory. "You remember that day? Well, I still say it wasn't my fault."

"Oh, come off it," Patsy snaps. "You knocked it right out of my hands."

"Did I? Honestly, I don't remember it that way."

"Well you wouldn't, would you?"

Patsy's already heading out the door, the letter clutched tight. "Come on then, LeeLee. Let's see what other delights Ol' Sal's got planned for us in sunny fucking Scarborough."

CHAPTER 7
TIME FLIES

DAY 1

Night creeps in like time itself—inevitable, unstoppable and unbiased. Somewhere within it, a lairy orange Golf carries Liam and Patsy into a present they've been avoiding for years. Behind them lies everything they've known—ahead, everything they're about to become. If Einstein was right about time being relative, then this Saturday might just have been the longest day of their lives. For Liam, who's sat idly for years, today has been his last day of waiting. For Patsy, who's spent years running forwards at full tilt, this is the day she's finally stopped long enough to start again.

As Liam guides the orange Golf towards a sizeable roundabout, the headlights catch the worn paint of exit signs, none of which seem to point where they need to go.

"Which way?"

Patsy's buried in the map, turning it this way and that as if changing its orientation might magically reveal their route. "Is this even the right map?"

Liam gives her a look that says everything about their current predicament.

"Well how was I supposed to know there'd be more than one

bloody map in your glove box?" She shakes the paper at him. "This one's for Wales! When did you go to Wales?"

"Never," he says.

"Then why do you have its road map?"

"In case I want to go, one day." There's that optimism we all know and love.

"Ever thought about going to East Anglia?" she replies.

"No, where's that?" he says with no sense of irony.

"Urghhhhhh," Patsy growls.

All the while, round and round they go—three full circuits of the roundabout while other drivers blast their horns. Liam white knuckles it shouting sorry, over and over as they go round and round and round as Patsy turns greener and greener.

"Fuck it, turn back." Patsy crumples the map into her lap. "I want to go home."

"Nope. Can't do it. You said it yourself. Forwards never backwards."

"Pleeeaaaase?" she begs.

"No," he demands.

"WHY NOT?" she shouts.

"BECAUSE I HAVEN'T GOT A HOME TO GO TO, I'M BEING EVICTED IN THE MORNING!" he screams.

And to this, Patsy shuts the hell up as she tries to gauge the truth in Liam's outburst. She knew the flats were being demolished, but to be evicted tomorrow? That's news to her. It all makes sense now why he only packed his dad's urn and a few prized possessions.

A road sign flashes past: SCARBOROUGH. Liam takes the exit—the wrong one.

~ 1996 ~

Little Liam sprawls on the carpet playing his Nintendo Game Boy, glancing up at Sally as she rifles through the pile of borrowed CDs.

"Slow jam. Slow jam. Slow jam," she repeats.

CD cases litter the floor, each one rejected for not being quite right. Sally pauses when a particular album finally catches her eye.

"Mum," Little Liam says.

"Yep," she replies.

"What's a slow jam?"

A knowing smile spreads across her face as she holds up the CD to the light streaming in.

"A-ha. Yes," says Sally as she finds what she's looking for.

"Now this," she says, tapping the case with her chipped blue-painted fingernail, "This is what we call a slow jam."

She slides the disc into the CD player and the mechanism whirs to life. "Sometimes, LeeLee, between all the jumping around and guitar solos, you need something to slow your brain down. No mixtape is complete without a slow jam."

The ethereal opening notes of The Cranberries' "Linger" float through the room. Little Liam's eyes widen as Dolores O'Riordan's angelic voice fills the space. Sally closes her eyes, swaying gently, lost in the melody. Then those violins kick in, followed by that drum. Then those lyrics, about being a fool, about being wrapped around someone's finger, about being in so deep.

"This is the one," she whispers, more to herself than to him. "This is a song that makes time stand still."

Little Patsy appears in the doorway, drawn by the music. For once, she's quiet, watching her mum get lost in the moment as the sun beams through the curtains lighting up the discarded CDs, creating a refracted disco ball effect on the room.

The three of them sit there, letting the Limerick band's dream-like sound wash over them, while Dolores' voice connects the space between them. The young family lost in sound, but found in harmony.

The perfect family, in a perfect place, at the perfect time.

DAY 1

The orange Golf purrs along the pitch-black Norfolk country road, its headlights cutting through the night. Tree after tree after fucking tree. Patsy rests her head against the cool glass of the passenger window, fighting the monotonous rhythm of the countryside from sending her to sleep. This is no simple task considering she hasn't slept in thirty-six hours and is surviving on a diet of oxygen and a bottle of tepid water she found in the footwell.

"I'm calling it," she mumbles, her voice heavy with exhaustion. "We're lost and it's getting late. Should we find a hotel?"

"How much cash we got?" Liam asks, squinting at road signs that seem to point to places lost in ancient times—Hag's Pits, Little Snoring, Cucumber Corner and Cabbage Creek. Either he's somehow driven them back several centuries or they've ended up in The Shire from 'The Lord of the Rings', he thinks to himself. Which he watched, on DVD, with Sally.

Patsy empties her concealed pocket. A couple of pound coins fall out and disappear into the gaps of the car seat. "No getting them back, 'bout fifty quid down there," Liam says.

"Spent the last of it on the shampoo and Alka Seltzer," she says, shaking the tablets inside the bottle of tepid water.

"Any credit cards?" Liam asks, assuming she's loaded—from being on TV and all.

"All maxed out..."

She studies the plastic rectangles—her last tenuous connection to her Belsize Park life. AMEX Platinum, Hoare & Co. and Barclays Gold (for emergencies when she has to buy from a less than desirable retailer, you know, like John Lewis). Without ceremony, she winds down the window and tosses them out one by one, watching them disappear into the darkness.

"And accounts closed."

The Golf's brakes screech as Liam brings it to an abrupt halt. Before Patsy can protest, he's out in the road, retrieving the discarded cards from the tarmac.

"They're maxed out and closed," she says incredulously as he climbs back in.

"Yeah, but we shouldn't litter. My window is not a bin," he says, throwing them into the back with his parking tickets. He scans the roadside, and his face lights up as he spots an open gate leading to a field. "I got an idea."

The Golf rumbles through the gate into the field, its orange paintwork almost luminous under the starlight. Patsy practically tumbles out, desperate for fresh air and space. She takes a moment to breathe it all in—the vastness of the Norfolk sky, the whisper of wind through grass, the absolute silence that only exists this far from London. This is Arcadia, a paradise, and a far cry from the Great Yarmouth caravan park and concrete jungle of London they've left behind.

Behind her, Liam wrestles with the Golf's back seats, laying them flat with an awkward clunk. From the boot, he rolls out a mattress that unfolds perfectly into the space, and wouldn't you know it, but he's transformed the car into an impromptu bedroom.

"Wotcha think?" he asks, bright-eyed and bushy-tailed.

"Sleeping in here, with you? Na-a." She flatly rejects him.

"Sleep outside then."

A cow moos nearby, making Patsy jump. "Fuck it. I'll hitchhike. If I get murdered it's your fault."

"Come on—it's not that bad. We can top and tail. I don't snore. And another positive, I won't murder you."

As Patsy walks back—her bare foot sinks deep into a cow pat. "Ewwwww. Yuk. Shit." She finally relents. "Okaaaaay, but I'm at the top end," she demands, while scraping the cow shit off her foot in the grass.

They settle in for the night, Liam with his head towards the boot, long legs reaching over the passenger seat. Patsy sleeps with her head towards the steering wheel, while Sally's ornate trunk rests between them. The silence stretches uncomfortably until Liam lets one RIIIIIIP.

"Oh, disgusting." Patsy recoils, frantically winding down the front window to stick her head outside.

"Not as bad as your feet," he says while they both laugh in hysterics.

While she clambers back into the car, her foot accidentally turns the radio on, and that's when they hear it. They hear her. Delores O'Riordan of The Cranberries. And it suddenly feels like an old friend has joined them in the car. The ethereal opening notes of "Linger" float through the night air catching them both by surprise as they settle back into the bed.

"Remember this?" she asks quietly.

"Mum's slow jam," Liam says.

"This is a song that makes time stand still," Patsy quotes, before catching herself to change the subject. "It's not fair, them taking the flat away."

"Council are knocking them down, building fancy modern apartments," Liam says, as Dolores O'Riordan's voice drifts around them, once again connecting the space between them. "I held on, was pretty much the last man standing... but it's not enough to just pay the bills."

"No job?"

"Got fired a few months back. Job centre offered me a position in KFC—but what's the point, when there's nuffin worth working for?"

"You should have reached out. I work in property, I could have got you a place. Maybe." The words sound hollow even to her.

Liam gives her an incredulous look that says everything.

"I don't want to move," he says quietly.

"No. Right."

"But I knew it was coming," he admits.

"So you did all this?" She gestures at their makeshift bedroom.

"Yeah, spent the last of my salary and benefits on re-modifying. Figured if I can't live in Mum's house, I could live in Mum's old car."

Something dawns on Patsy with that last statement. Mum's old car? Did she hear that right?

"Wait, what? This is Mum's old car—the tatty green Golf?"

"Yeah. Why d'you think I wouldn't drive it over fifty? It's so old it would probably vibrate to death."

"Sounds like a good way to go." Patsy mimes vibrating to death, and you know what? They share their first genuine moment of connection, as The Cranberries' violins swell around them like a memory of better times.

"Where's your gaff then?"

"Think that ship has sailed as well."

"You don't have a house?"

"I never did. I lived rent-free in Minnie's Belsize Park apartment. But she told me..." Patsy trails off, lost in the memory.

𝄞

Patsy's been sitting at her white Steinway, not playing, just existing—vodka in hand, head hanging over the keys, designer sunglasses hiding fresh tears rather than a hangover for once. The apartment felt different that day, as though her own home was already evicting her.

Minnie had glided through the space like someone who'd been planning this moment for months. A heap of designer dresses draped over her arm as she methodically stripped away pieces of Patsy's life. She'd stopped to adjust the already perfectly straight Italian designer lampshade—a power move Patsy had seen her perfect over years of passive-aggressive warfare.

"So Patsy, I'll take these to Oxfam? Hmm?" Minnie's voice was filled with insincerity. "I've checked and they're all size six." Then, that deliberate pause before. "Be a while before you ever get back into them, and why waste? Hmm?"

Patsy had lowered her sunglasses, revealing her red-rimmed eyes. The movement had caught Minnie's attention, but only long enough for her step-mother to register the mascara tracks with a slight smile.

"So Patsy, darling," Minnie had continued, "Maybe it's time for you to straighten up and stand on your own two feet, hmm?" She'd fingered the silk of a Valentino dress that Patsy had bought herself for her last birthday. "You know... you made no mind for my reputation. And that's all we really have, you know. Our reputations..."

"And quite frankly darling," Minnie did that infuriating pause again. "Your father and I are renting out the apartment to pay the lease on a schooner. To sail around the Mediterranean. You understand, don't you Patsy? Time to spread our wings. Time for you to spread yours too. None of us are getting any younger." *That's fucking rich*, Patsy thought, considering the amount of Botox Minnie's had to keep her face looking forty-something for the last twenty years. It's not working, in case you were thinking. It never works. Time is relative, but it's also an arrow—you can't turn back the clocks. But maybe, just maybe, you can start again with just the smallest seed of hope.

𝄞

Back in the car, Patsy stares into the darkness beyond the windscreen. "To sail around the Med," she says flatly, completing the memory. "While I spread my wings." The bitterness in her voice matches the distant moo of a cow somewhere in the field.

"Maybe we should get some sleep?" Liam offers. "Get an early start, wait for Mum in Scarborough, get the key to this." He taps the trunk between them. "Get the lottery winnings and get you a new house."

Patsy shifts restlessly, trying to find comfort on the makeshift bed.

"Liam?" She says.

"Patsy?" He says.

"You got any booze, or ciggies?" She says.

"Nope. But I do have this..." Liam rolls back the little sunroof, revealing a vast blanket of stars above them.

Patsy stares in wonder as a shooting star streaks across the sky. And there it is, the first genuine smile she's cracked all day. Maybe even all year. For now, at least, she's content as Dolores O'Riordan's ethereal voice drifts through the night, a lullaby for two lost souls in an orange Golf in the middle of nowhere, trying to salvage something from the wreckage of their lives.

DAY 2

The first rays of dawn paint the Norfolk sky in watercolour stripes of pink and gold. In the field, the orange Golf sits alone as massive trucks begin rolling through the open gate, their loud engines growling in the morning stillness. One by one they take up position, surrounding the Golf like Tetris blocks, intricately woven onto the field, until Liam's pride and joy is completely hemmed in by a wall of articulated lorries.

Inside the Golf, blissfully unaware, Liam and Patsy sleep in their makeshift bed. Somehow during the night, Liam's big toe has found its way directly into Patsy's left nostril.

Then:

HOOOOOONK.

HOOOOOOOOOOOOOOOOONK.

Patsy jerks awake, her head smacking against the roof. "What the? Who the?" She winds down the window and jams her head outside to squint at the small army of roadies unpacking equipment. "You. You there. Explanation please?"

A Mancunian roadie in a hi-vis and a shit-eating grin leans against their bonnet whilst rolling up a fat one. "Thought you should probably get a groove on. Ahhh, the flowers are bloomin' n' the birds are tweetin'. The morning's glorious."

Patsy growls back, clearly, she's not a morning person.

"We're setting up for a gig. Tonight," he adds helpfully.

Not waiting for Liam to unlock the doors, Patsy wriggles through the window, her designer dress catching on the frame.

"You not part o' the crew?" the roadie asks, watching her less-than-graceful exit.

Instead of answering, Patsy yanks open the boot, causing Liam's head to tumble out like a bowling ball.

"Ah, Parklife," Liam mumbles, still half asleep and still dreaming of his mixtape glory days. Then reality hits. "Wait? What? Pats, what's the story?"

"We're trapped."

Liam quickly assesses their situation—they are indeed very, very trapped. The Golf sits in a metal prison of trucks, staging equipment, and portable toilets.

"Some fucking rock band are playing here?" Patsy's voice rises with each word.

"Ahhh shitting hell." But there's an unmistakable glimmer of excitement in Liam's eyes. "We'll hit the road straight after the gig and drive through the night—she's waiting."

"For how long this time?" Patsy demands, throwing her hands up in exasperation.

"Well it's been fifteen years. She can wait one more night." Liam says, his frankness finally impressing Patsy. But only a little, she's still proper vexed.

"By my calculations it's an hour to Scarborough," Liam says with his usual misplaced confidence.

The Mancunian roadie nearly chokes on the spliff he's smoking. "An hour to Scarborough? Ha... where do you think y'are?"

"Round Lincoln ways?" Liam ventures hopefully.

"Knebston."

"Where's that?" Patsy asks, though her tone suggests she really doesn't want to know.

"A field in the middle of nowhere, about six hours from where you need ta be." The roadie grins. "We just came from Scarbs."

Patsy's carefully maintained composure—already hanging by a thread after sleeping in a car—finally snaps.

"We've gone BACKWARDS?" She rounds on Liam: "Why don't you have a satnav?" She whirls back to the roadie: "And why didn't you wake us earlier?"

She storms off across the field with her bare feet, dodging cow pats as she goes. And her exit would be far more dramatic if she actually had somewhere to go.

The Mancunian roadie watches her retreat with mild amusement. "Here look pal," he says, turning to Liam. "Maybe I could have woke ya's earlier—you just looked so peaceful." He fishes in his hi-vis pocket and produces some crumpled vouchers. "Crew vouchers—for food. Since yer not goin' anywhere anytime soon..."

Liam's eyes light up as he takes the vouchers. "Backstage?"

"Nice try pal." The roadie grins. "'ave a good'un yeah." He heads back to work, leaving Liam standing beside his trapped Golf, vouchers in hand, watching his sister's diminishing figure as she storms toward... well, nowhere really.

𝄞

The breakfast queue at the food station snakes between metal barriers where a mix of sleepy roadies and bustling crew members form an orderly line. Patsy's stomach growls as her eyes lock onto the last remaining croissant—it's probably mass-produced, but right now it might as well be gold flaked from a Parisian boulangerie.

She reaches for it with her trembling fingers, already imagining that first buttery bite. After a night sleeping in a car and days without food, this sad little croissant represents everything good and pure in the world.

"You crew love?" the gruff server asks.

Patsy thinks fast, putting on her best TV smile. "Oh, I'm with the band."

"Groupies don't get crew food." The server's hand demands the croissant back.

"WHAT? Do I look like a groupie?" she says, while standing there in a designer dress and Ray-Bans at 7 am, barefoot in a field, having just said that she's with the band.

And then it happened, the server steals back the croissant, her last salvation, the only thing keeping her from completely losing her shit.

And that's when her tracksuited guardian appears, with his arms loaded with enough food to feed a small army of groupies. Liam dumps a handful of crumpled vouchers on the counter and snags the precious croissant back from the server.

Liam chucks the croissant back to Patsy, and her triumphant smirk quickly transforms into something closer to religious ecstasy as she stuffs the whole thing in her mouth in front of the server, whilst proclaiming "Amm noooot a gwoooppy."

Sometimes the smallest victories taste the sweetest.

𝄞

Liam and Patsy sprawl across the makeshift bed in the Golf, with their crew breakfast spread out between them. Neither speaks at first, too busy stuffing their faces.

"God I'm so marved," Liam manages between mouthfuls.

"Me too."

"What do you think Mum's doing? You think she's travelling to Scarborough or already there?"

"I stopped questioning Ol' Sal's motives and decisions a fair while ago." There's something in Patsy's tone that makes Liam look at her—really look at her—and for once, he understands.

"Come on, eat, eat. Gotta fatten you up," she says, lightening the mood.

That's when Liam gets that glint in his eye—the one that usually means trouble. He grabs Patsy's sunglasses, pulls his bucket hat down low, and tucks a napkin into his collar with exaggerated ceremony.

"We're putting the band back together," he declares with a very bad Chicagoan accent.

"What?"

"The band. Back together." He slurps his orange juice with deliberately awful manners, waggling his eyebrows at her over the sunglasses.

Patsy catches on to his game, and suddenly they're kids again, copying a scene from one of their favourite movies. She links arms with him as they share food across their makeshift picnic.

"Oh waiter, waiter!" She puts on her poshest Belsize Park accent. "I simply must move to another table. These people are frankly offensive—so smelly..." She takes a sniff of her own armpit and recoils. "I mean, they smell absolutely ghastly."

Liam responds by chewing with his mouth open, making exaggerated chomping sounds. Then he tosses a piece of bread across their feast—which Patsy catches in her mouth.

"YEAAHHHHHH!" They both scream in triumph, their laughter echoing through the truck maze.

And for just a moment, the arrow of time moves slowly forwards.

CHAPTER 8
MEMORIES

Another sweltering day brings another grinding whirr of the fan as it soldiers on with its efforts to try and keep Sally as cool as can be during the summer's heatwave. It's still early in the morning, but she's already struggling.

The stark white walls of her hospital room feel particularly oppressive today as she sits at her desk, pen hovering uncertainly over the blank piece of paper staring back at her. The right words seem to have abandoned her for now, leaving a hollow feeling growing inside.

Jagdeesh's arrival with a tray of distinctly unappetising hospital fare provides a welcome distraction. Sally eyes the "food" with barely concealed disdain.

"What's this meant to be then?"

"A cheese toastie, apple, and some Walkers crisps," Jagdeesh announces with mock ceremony.

"Where's the good stuff?" Sally sniffs the air. "I can smell proper food everywhere. How can you deny an old lady a last glorious meal of taste, fat, spice, salt? The good shit."

"Because I'm the one who has to deal with the aftermath—the good shit, as you call it," Jagdeesh replies, though his stern expression can't quite mask his fondness.

Sally waves away his concerns with surprising vigour. "Oh, Jagdeesh. You're so crass. Didn't know you had it in you. Anyway, never mind all that—I'm feeling much better today. Forget that sorry excuse for sustenance. I want to go for a walk, build up my strength." She pats his arm. "I need to be ready to see my children again, don't I?"

"To the gardens?" Jagdeesh offers cautiously.

"To the gardens, my good man."

As Jagdeesh helps her up, linking their arms with absolute care, Sally's eyes sparkle with sudden mischief. "Look at us—we're like that movie, Victoria and Abdul. Have you seen it?"

"No," Jagdeesh plays along. "Which one am I meant to be?"

Sally's laugh turns into a wobble that has Jagdeesh tightening his grip, but she quickly steadies herself. "Come on then. I may have stage 4 cancer that's spreading to my heart, but what's a bit of pressure ever done to anyone?"

"Can't make a diamond without pressure, Sal," says Jagdeesh.

Her gaze drifts to the Polaroid propped on her desk—a snapshot of happiness from decades past. Little Liam and Little Patsy beam at the camera, ice creams clutched in sticky fingers, while Sally stands between them, her smile captured in a moment of time she yearns to experience again, if only for a heartbeat.

"I need this walk." Her voice then softens. "I must see my children again... in Scarborough. They'll be waiting."

~ 1996 ~

The red phone box stands proudly on Scarborough's promenade, its pristine windows gleaming in the summer sun—if there was ever a beacon of everything great and glorious about Blighty, surely it's the red telephone box? Connecting divorced dads to their kids, and prostitutes, throughout the 20th century. Inside every one is a cauldron of countless conversations, hysterical laughter and smiles. But not inside this one right now, it seems, as Sally grips the receiver, tighter than normal. The confined space amplifies every ragged breath, every tremor in her voice.

"It's only been a few days," she pleads, fighting to keep her voice steady. "It's just a little holiday—can you give me that? Give them that?"

Richard's voice crackles through the line, cold and precise. "When?"

"Soon, I'll be back soon." Her composure cracks. "Fucking soon, alright?"

"Tomorrow, Sally."

"Tomorrow? No—that's not enough time." She presses her forehead against the cool glass. "Why are you doing this?"

"So tomorrow then. Yes?" His tone carries that familiar edge, the one that always precedes an ultimatum. "I need to hear you say it."

"No." Her defiance comes out barely above a whisper.

"Sally," Richard's voice softens dangerously. "Say your goodbyes and whatnot. I need Patsy home tomorrow. You understand what happens if you don't bring her back? They'll say you're unstable. Unfit. Think about what that means for both children."

The receiver trembles in her hand. For a moment, she wants to smash it against the phone box window, to scream until her throat bleeds. Instead, she holds it closer, her words coming out with desperate but fearless intensity.

"I'll walk with them off the edge of the world if it stops you breaking them up—you hear me?" Her voice finally breaks. "The edge of the world."

The line goes quiet, but Sally can't let go this time, like she did in the caravan park. She clutches the phone like it's her final anchor to solid ground, tears streaming down her face as each sob echoes through the box. Outside, holiday-makers stroll past, oblivious to the mother whose world is splintering apart inside this bright red emotional cage.

Her fingers trace the cold metal cord, wondering how many others have stood in this exact spot, having conversations that changed their lives forever. What did they say? What did they do? The thought of tomorrow feels impossible right now—it's nothing but a black abyss. Richard's words echo in her head: *unstable, unfit*. One phone call and he could take them both away from her. One moment of weakness and everything she loves could slip away.

Through the smeared glass, she watches her children suspended in a hazy amber light—every gesture precious and fleeting, as if she's already recalling them in a memory. LeeLee, so much like his father it makes her heart ache, so careful and stoic. Then there's Pats, fierce and free, racing ahead without a care. Both innocent of the choice hanging over their mother's head: sacrifice one to save both, or risk losing everything.

This is Sally's earth-shattering choice.

Sally straightens up and wipes her face. She's perfected this move over the years—the art of swallowing grief and painting on a smile. The edge of the world suddenly doesn't seem so far away. But between now and then, there are ice creams to eat and photos to take, memories to capture before they slip away. *One last great day. I'll give them one last great day.*

"Sally, Sally, are you there?" Richard's voice crackles from the dangling receiver until the timing pips finally run out and the line goes dead.

Miles away, in a house that screams old money in Belsize Park—the kind of place Hugh Grant's mum might live in—Richard slowly replaces the receiver. His well-groomed appearance can't quite hide his working-class roots: a few days of stubble shadow his jaw, but it's the injury that draws the eye—a jagged wound running from temple to cheekbone, quickly stitched and still seeping, surrounded by violent purple-black bruising. His left eye is nearly swollen shut, the white of which is a web of burst blood vessels and when he talks or winces, the movement pulls at the stitches. There's still that hint of Cockney that no amount of "mingling" with upper-class types can eradicate. Right now, his words are pronounced with more care due to the swelling, but even still, they come out slurred. His broken jaw is not the kind of damage that comes from a slap or a punch, but from something wielded with desperate force—a brick, a paperweight, something grabbed in blind panic and used to take down a fully grown man.

Minnie hovers by the telephone table, her perfectly manicured hand rests on his shoulder.

"Well?" she asks, though she's heard every word.

Minnie clicks the receiver. Her fingers are already dialling 999.

"Yes, it's my wife. My soon-to-be ex-wife," he clarifies, with his accent weirdly stiffening with faux class. "She's taken my daughter and has... suicidal thoughts. She's already assaulted me, put me in A&E, and mentioned something about walking off the edge of the world."

"Suicidal thoughts, sir?" the operator asks.

"Yes, suicidal. Please. Find my daughter."

Meanwhile, back at the epicentre of what counts for a northern working-class holiday circa the mid-'90s, Scarborough, Sally bursts out of the red phone box, forcing a giddy smile. Little Patsy comes bounding down the street with two massive ice cream cones. "Heyyyy, what's the story? Ooo ice cream. Mm giz a bit." She takes an enthusiastic lick, making Little Patsy giggle.

Sally positions herself between her children, both proudly displaying their ice creams, and the family stands to attention just long enough to take the Polaroid selfie—another memory captured through the iconic CLICK-FLASH-WHIRR rhythm of sounds that defines the Polaroid camera experience.

The photo slowly emerges, as they gather round in anticipation.

"I want to wave it!" Little Patsy reaches for the photo.

"No, I want to wave it!" Little Liam protests, also reaching for the photo.

As Sally pulls the developing photo away from both their grabbing hands, disaster strikes as Little Patsy's ice cream meets the pavement with a decisive splat.

Funny how some moments in time can be remembered differently —crystal clear for one person, misremembered by another, completely forgotten by the next.

This is one such moment. Unlike Patsy's memory of this event— which she swears down to this very day that it was all Liam's fault, Little Liam did not drop Little Patsy's ice cream. It was that rarest of things—a blameless accident.

"ARGGGHHHHHHHHHHH."

Oh dang, accident or not, someone's woken the Banshee.

"It's your fault, that's your fault!" Little Patsy's voice rises to a glass-shattering pitch. "MUM, LIAM MADE ME DROP MY ICE CREAM!"

"It wasn't my fault, I was just—" Little Liam doesn't get to finish as his sister launches herself at him, with her tiny fingers latching onto his braids.

The screaming intensifies as nearby holiday-makers give them a wide berth. Sally stands frozen, catatonic, as Little Liam yields to his sister's assault, trying to push away without fighting back.

A handful of braids come loose in Little Patsy's grip.

"Muuuuuum!" they both scream in unison.

Followed by... the red strawberry sauce... arcing through the air, coating Little Liam in sweet sugary sticky condiment as Little Patsy empties the sauce bottle while screaming bloody murder at the top of her voice, letting out a Banshee of a wail that scares the seagulls away from the fallen ice cream cone.

No amount of "Champagne Supernova" is going to fix this. But Little Liam, ever the optimist, throws on his headphones anyway, hoping those gentle waves and layered guitars will wash this moment away while he quietly counts to ten and back on his fingers.

The ice cream parlour owner—who's been watching this particularly chaotic street performance unfold—finally decides enough is enough. He darts out of his shop and, with the precise timing of someone who's seen his fair share of seaside meltdowns, rescues what's left of his squirty sauce from Little Patsy's death grip.

"Oh mister, I am so sorry," Sally manages, mortified. "Patsy, apologise to the man."

Little Patsy, still in full Banshee mode, plants her feet and crosses her arms.

"Patsy. Apologise."

"No." She stamps her foot and turns around for good measure.

"I'm sorry, sir," Little Liam pipes up, wiping sauce from his chin. "We'll pay for the wasted sauce."

The ice cream man studies the scene before him. This isn't his first summer rodeo on Scarborough's infamous promenade.

"Hey, little one," he says softly, his foreign accent warming the words. "You're on holiday right? Little one?"

Little Patsy maintains her stance, but offers the tiniest of nods.

"Then where's the smiles?" He crouches down to her level. "It's not a holiday if there's no smiles."

"He"—Little Patsy sniffs—"dropped my ice cream."

"Ahhh, Ice cream, shmice cream." He waves his hand dismissively. "I know the owner. What's say we get you a new ice cream? Would that cheer you up?"

Another small nod, this one accompanied by the hint of a smile.

"That okay with you mum?" he asks Sally.

"If it's not any trouble."

"No trouble." He straightens up, gesturing grandly toward his shop. "Come one, come all to my ice cream fun house."

They follow Nikos through Itsy Bitsy Ice Cream Parlour's "always-open" screen doors that look directly out to the beach. Sally feels the soft crunch of sand under her sandals and breathes in the mingled aromas of sweet waffle cones and salty sea air. The sound of happy families enjoying their all-day desserts enthuses with happy screams from the kids rollicking down the Helter Skelter on the beach, the chimes of the arcade next door and the seagull calls overhead.

The place glows with warmth and vitality, everything newly refreshed for the summer season. Cream and brown Oreo cookie tones dominate the freshly painted walls, while the dark leather booths look buffed smooth, no doubt by countless holidaymakers. A pristine Union Jack hangs proudly on the wall, its colours bold and vibrant against the warm tones. The new Mr Whippy machine hums contentedly in the corner, while the gleaming counter displays row upon row of traditional glass jars filled with confectionery for the penny sweet counter. The little paper bags hang ready and waiting for some kid's pocket money, no matter how many pennies they have—this place has a sweet for them.

"Now then, what was it?" Nikos says, absorbing her fury. "One chocolate, one vanilla with strawberry sauce?"

Little Patsy nods, her earlier Banshee rage already melting away at the prospect of a replacement ice cream. But Little Liam spots something on the sun-bleached menu board that draws his gaze—the Mega Deluxe Sundae, a towering confection that looks like something from his wildest dreams.

As Nikos assembles the sundaes, Little Liam produces a 50p piece, placing it carefully on the counter. "Sir, is it okay if I upgrade her ice cream—to the Mega Deluxe Sundae?"

The smile on Nikos' slightly weathered face broadens as he slides the coin back across the polished surface. "Of course. Sit. I'll bring it right over, sir."

The family settles into one of the booths, Sally shaking her head with a mix of exhaustion and fondness. "You kids will be the death of me. So embarrassing."

The children just shrug—whatever—as Nikos approaches with three towering sundaes balanced expertly in his hands. "One for little girl. One for big boy. One for mum."

"Mister, you shouldn't have, I can't accept this," Sally protests, but he waves away her concern.

"Well they are made now, so it would be worse to waste them."

While the kids dive into their sundaes with unbridled enthusiasm, Sally eyes Nikos warily. "If this is just some weird way you chat up mums..."

"I saw you. At the phone—you seemed to be in some distress."

She looks down into her ice cream, cheeks flushing with humiliation. "Oh. Right. No, I mean—"

"It's okay. I don't mean to pry." His voice softens. "It's just, I was always taught that if you can help someone in their hour of need, then you should." He pauses, choosing his words carefully to allow enough space and time to connect between them.

"We don't need to talk about it, we can just exist—in this space—just be here, now, eating ice cream. And when we are done—we can go our separate ways—with smiles."

Tears well in Sally's eyes, catching her by surprise.

"Mum, you're embarrassing us," Little Patsy groans.

"Oh, now I'm embarrassing you, monkey?" Sally manages a little laugh. "These are happy tears."

"Oh good. Happy tears." Nikos brightens. "How about a happy cup of tea? One of my favourite things about this glorious country—tea."

Sally nods, unable to trust her voice, and he heads off toward the serving counter which opens up to the promenade. Little Liam seizes the moment of quiet to pull out his CD Discman, hitting play as the gentle piano intro of Paul Weller's "Broken Stones" fills his headphones. He looks out to the bustling promenade, the beach and the endless sea, thinking to himself that the kids on his street were right, *a holiday to the seaside really is a wonderful thing.* And Paul Weller's voice and words about pebbles and getting home settle him into a place of calm. That and the massive ice cream sundae in front of him.

Through the serving window, Nikos gazes at the busy promenade where happy families stroll past with buckets and spades, kids drag their parents toward the donkey rides and teenagers show off on their BMXs and skateboards. The late afternoon sun casts long shadows across the beach where holiday makers squeeze every last drop from their day at the seaside. It's the height of summer '96—and Britain feels like it's finally waking up from a long slumber.

Between serving customers ice lollies, he notices Sally dabbing at her eyes with a paper napkin, while the kids pretend not to notice. Something about these three tugs at his heart. Maybe it's the way the mother had looked in that phone box, or how quickly the children's squabble had dissolved at the promise of ice cream. *Some pain*, he thinks, *even ice cream can't fix.* But maybe a proper cup of tea might help. This is England after all, there's little a good cuppa cannot fix.

As he waits for the kettle to boil and the tea bag to steep, he watches the siblings sharing their sundaes, their earlier drama now hopefully long forgotten. Perhaps there's a lesson here, he thinks, about what really matters—not the business you build or the dreams you chase, but the simple moments you share with the people you love.

The parlour is everything he'd dreamed of while working those many brutal years in restaurant kitchens around the country—this is his own business, his own piece of British success. Yet watching this little family from the counter, the boy so gentle with his sister despite her temper, he feels the familiar ache of what his ambition has cost him. His own children would be about their age now, growing up without him in Cyprus. Would they be proud of what their father has built, or would they simply see him as a man who chose an ice cream parlour over his family?

The afternoon rush has ebbed away, leaving the parlour in that peculiar quiet where only the gentle whir of freezer units and ever more distant seagull cries can be heard. The sugar rush has finally caught up with Little Patsy, who now lies curled up in the booth, her head heavy in Sally's lap. Across the table, Little Liam bobs gently to whatever's playing through his CD Discman headphones, lost in his own musical journey.

Through the haze of a very heady day, Sally observes Nikos as he works. His movements are practised, methodical—a man who finds comfort in routine but who carries something heavier than his damp cleaning cloth. The counter gleams under his attention, each stroke precise, purposeful. When he finally decides he's cleaned enough, he brings a fresh pot of tea to their booth. The pot's steam rises in delicate wisps from the spout as he pours.

"You have kids?" The question slips out of Sally's mouth before she can properly consider it.

"Two. A boy and a girl." His face softens at their mention, his voice carries a gentle warmth that stops with a slight grimace.

Sally rushes into her next words, tripping over them in her eagerness to keep the conversation flowing. "Your wife work here too? Is it a family business? I know you foreigners like to keep things in the family." She immediately winces at her clumsy assumptions.

But a gentle laugh escapes him, more amused than offended. "Ah, I do love the English language. You have fifty words to say thank you, a hundred words to describe the rain, but just one to describe a non-Englishman."

"I am so sorry," Sally says as she rolls her eyes at her own misstep. How could she, the mother of a half-Nigerian child, be so casually racist? she thinks.

Nikos brushes it off with a laugh to ease her suffering, before his mood shifts again.

"No. My wife, she is back home. In Cyprus."

"Will she be over soon?" Sally asks.

He shakes his head, a gesture so slight it barely disturbs the space between them. "No. We separated. A few years back now."

"I'm so sorry," Sally offers lamely. Another embarrassing misstep.

"It's okay." His fingers now tap an anxious rhythm against his teacup.

"And your kids?" Sally hesitantly asks. Despite her multiple faux pas, everything inside her says that she needs to ask this question, for his sake. He has helped her, and now she thinks: *I can help him.*

"They live with her." His gaze drifts beyond the parlour's steamy windows and out to the open sea. "I haven't seen them in three years."

The admission hits Sally square in the chest, forcing out a breath she didn't know she was holding. "That must be…" But she can't even comprehend, let alone find the right words.

"Brutal? Sad? Impossible? All of it and yet none of it." He attempts a smile that fades before it can fully form. "I try sometimes, to call. But every time I pick up the phone… I get as far as dialling, then the words fail me and I hang up before it connects."

"How come?"

"Shame." The word barely makes it past his lips. "Pride. Sooner or later, the weight of it all…" His hands make a vague gesture in the air, like he's trying to catch something that keeps slipping away. "It begins to drag you under."

Sally nods, understanding coursing through her like an electric current. She glances down at Little Patsy, peaceful in her slumber, then across to Little Liam, now more alert to the conversation happening within this space and time. And it may be as delicate as spun sugar, but like most great moments in time, this one is to be banked as a timeless memory.

"Do they know you love them?" she asks him directly.

Nikos takes a deep breath before answering, "I honestly don't know."

"As long as they know you love them—they'll be okay. Time is one thing, but love transcends, you know? Love transcends."

Nikos wipes a few rogue tears with his napkin. "You look like a good mum. Children need their mums," he says, as he takes a deep breath.

Little Patsy wakes up and stretches her arms, her attention instantly grabbed by the wall-mounted TV above them, where five very different young women in platform trainers bounce around a grand staircase singing about what they really want. The sound is muted, but their exuberant and carefree energy cuts through the emotional heaviness of the ice cream parlour. Sally joins Little Patsy in watching the Spice Girls stamp their feet on those stairs, beginning a cultural earthquake that no one saw coming. Their lives seem a world away from Sally's, but even so, she hopes these five girls will be great role models for her Little Pats. Even if they are just a flash in the pan.

"Not my cup of tea," Nikos says with a gentle smile while referring to the TV screen. "But the kids love them."

"Speaking of tea," Sally says, glancing at the wall clock. "We should probably..."

She fumbles in her bag for her purse, but instead, her Polaroid camera tumbles out onto the table. Nikos' eyes widen at the sight.

"Is that...?" He picks it up carefully, turning it over in his hands. "I've never actually held one of these before."

"It's a Polaroid," Little Liam pipes up, suddenly interested. "The picture comes out straight away—like magic."

Nikos looks around his parlour walls and stops on his brand new unused pinboard. "Would you...?" He gestures with the camera. "Could we maybe...?"

They gather outside, squinting in the late afternoon sun. Little Patsy, still groggy from her nap, leans against Sally while Little Liam positions himself next to Nikos. Sally shows him how to frame the selfie shot using the front mirror.

"Just press this button here," she guides. "And mind your fingers don't cover the flash."

CLICK—FLASH—WHIRR. The photo ejects with that familiar mechanical rhythm, still dark with developing chemicals. Nikos takes it carefully between thumb and forefinger, watching with wonder as four figures gradually emerge against the parlour's facade.

"Let's take another," he says whilst laughing. They all squeeze in tighter before he says:

"No, just of you this time."

And perhaps for the first and last time on this fateful and memorable holiday to the English coast, Sally's little family of three come together in unison as the camera does its thing.

"One for me. One for you." He quickly hands Sally the camera and the second photo before hurrying inside to pin his photo to the pinboard as it continues to develop—the first customer photo in what will become a collection of memories.

Sally marvels at the photo in her hand, of her perfect little trio. The same photo that Liam has kept with him all these years. Safely tucked next to his dad's urn.

A perfect moment captured in time.

𝄞

Just a few exhausted dads packing up their families' things, a bunch of abandoned flip flops, buckets sans spades, and the odd smug surfboarder getting changed out of their wetsuit occupy the near-empty car park as the day winds down. Sally carries Little Patsy's sugar-induced comatose body to the car. And as she straps her in, Little Liam climbs in beside his sister.

"You not sitting up front with me, LeeLee?" Sally asks.

Little Liam shakes his head, preferring to keep Little Patsy company. Nikos closes the door with a gentle click whilst Little Liam cues up the next track on his CD player. "Cast No Shadow" by Oasis seems the perfect come-down track for his first trip to the seaside, he thinks. Now, he would never think of the words "come" and "down" in this context at his age, but you catch the drift. Right?

"She's something, your little one... electric," Nikos says, nodding toward Patsy.

"Yep, my little electric spice," Sally replies, while digging through her bag to find her Marlboro Lights.

"Must be hard to harness all that energy?" he says sympathetically.

Sally nods, too knackered to elaborate, but appreciating the observation nonetheless.

"I wish you... fortitude. Mum."

"Thank you. I hope you see your kids soon."

Before Sally gets in, Little Liam rolls down his window and stretches out his small hand toward Nikos.

"Mister. Here."

Nikos turns his palm over to reveal the 50p that Little Liam tried to pay him with just a few hours before.

Little Liam nods toward the red phone box silhouetted against the fading light of the blue and golden sky, where wisps of scattered cloud drift aimlessly across the vast expanse.

Understanding flickers across Nikos' face.

"You've got the heart of a star," he tells the boy.

Little Liam nods him goodbye as they pull away.

The Golf putters out of the car park and back along the promenade, stopping at the traffic lights. Through the window, Little Liam watches Nikos at the phone box pick up the receiver and slot the 50p in, while through his headphones, Liam Gallagher sings his brother Noel's poignant lyrics about pride and souls and words that are too heavy to say. Words our Liam hears as a child that he won't fully comprehend until years later, when his own life has gathered similar weight.

A moment of serene calm washes over the promenade. Time freezes—the Golf sits stationary, seagulls are suspended mid-flight, the waves pause mid-crash and the blue and orange flame from Sally's lighter dances motionless against the stillness. The setting sun transforms the phone box into something otherworldly, casting a shadow that stretches impossibly long across the promenade.

Inside the phone box, Nikos takes a deep breath.

He greets them in Greek first, but the emotion catches him off guard as his voice cracks. "It's Papa."

And then, whatever he hears transforms everything. His face lights up with that genuine, unrestrained joy that can only come from hearing your children's voices after so long apart. And in that moment, even this ordinary red phone box seems to glow in the fading light.

Out on the promenade, time begins again and the world continues. The seagulls swoop down for the last of the fallen chips, and Sally's green Golf gets the green light. She takes a long fulfilling drag of her cigarette as she heads out of Scarborough, happy in the notion that in someone's moment of need, she was able to help—despite perhaps needing more help herself than she'd ever dare admit.

Little Liam watches the phone box recede in the distance, its shadow growing longer as the joyful holiday afternoon gives way to the evening's uncertainties. He wonders if this day can ever be topped... and you know what... to this day, nearly thirty years later, he never could for the life of him recall a better day.

And as soon as Sally stubs her cigarette out in the ashtray, she gently pushes her foot down on the accelerator and leaves Scarborough behind, thinking to herself, *one last great day.*

CHAPTER 9
THIS CHAPTER IS ABOUT A FIELD

DAY 2

If Liam hadn't had a proper good day to remember since the summer of '96, then perhaps—just perhaps—today would be the one to break that streak.

"Do you reckon she's been planning this for a while?" Liam asks as they walk through the high grass, following the distant thrum of bass. "To lead us from one place to the next, like a treasure hunt?"

"Don't know," Patsy replies, focused on navigating the uneven ground in her bare feet. "Fucking stones, fucking sticks. I need to find some shoes or sumink."

"But she must've been, right? Setting up all these letters, the timing of it all."

"Last time I went barefoot I was at Burning Man in '23. Go barefoot, they said. Connect with the earth, they said. Do peyote, they said. Bullshit. All I got was fucking blisters. Left after one day, got some rando-billionaire to drive me to Vegas in his swish RV. Much better."

"How long's she got, do you think?"

"First and last time I ever do peyote."

"Did she say anything to you about—"

"Liam." Patsy stops walking. "I haven't spoken to her any more than you have."

"Yeah but—"

"No buts."

And together they hear the music echoing through the trees dividing the fields.

"Look, there's clearly something going on over there. Let's just... I don't know, enjoy whatever it is for once without picking each other apart?"

They push through a gap in the treeline and emerge into another world. The festival site sprawls before them—food stalls, fairy lights strung between poles, craft beer tents, and the unmistakable energy of thousands of people, young and old, determined to enjoy the summer energy.

Patsy stops dead, suddenly aware of a group of Gen Z girls pointing in her direction and whispering.

"Fans 'ay? What's that like? Nice or weird... must be a bit weird, everyone knowing you. I'd do anything for a quiet life."

"You don't say."

"Alright, point taken. I should get out more."

"My sister the celebrity. Why'd you do it?" Liam asks. "The TV thing?"

Patsy shrugs, but then something shifts in her expression. "Saw an advert in a pub window actually. 'WANTED: Real People, Real Drama'. I was three vodkas deep and thought, fuck it, why not? Turned out I was quite good at being real." She laughs, but there's no humour in her voice. "Too real, probably."

"What does that mean?"

"I mean, people like a lush, don't they? Someone with a loose tongue who says it how it is. Who puts people in their place. And not just for the fun of it, but because they deserve it. I was *different, refreshing* all the online blogs and socials would say. *Real.* Until..."

"Until?"

"Well people don't really want real. They want the idea of real. Packaged real. Safe real." She looks up at the festival crowd ahead.

"You know what's funny? This is the longest I've gone without a drink since... God, I can't even remember."

"Two days, if that," Liam offers.

"Has it only been two fucking days? Feels like two fucking years." She squints at the setting sun through the trees. "Look at us though—both broke, both desperate, both chasing after Mum's mystery box like it's full of gold bars or diamonds. Could be full of dusty old photos for all we know, a lifetime of painful memories."

"Reckon you can make it three days?"

"Don't go all AA counsellor on me, LeeLee." But there's no bite in her voice, just exhaustion. She blows the air from her cheeks. "Come on, let's keep moving. Forwards, always forwards," she forces out, not fully believing her own mantra.

Liam puts his long arm around Patsy's shoulder and together they walk into the festival, towards the setting sun. "Alright, alright, no counselling, no picking each other apart, keep moving... and get you some footwear," he says.

"And no booze," she adds. "Let's make it three days," she promises herself.

𝄞

Voices blur together—laughter, conversations in all kinds of accents, the odd whoop of ecstatic joy or indiscernible drunken scream—all bleeding into each other like an FM radio being tuned from one station to the next. The continuous thump of bass reverberates up through the ground, through Liam's festival-friendly well-worn Converse, through the poseurs' Birkenstock sandals, through the amateur festival goer's flip-flops, through Patsy's bare feet and into everyone's chests.

Thousands of hearts beating to the same one rhythm.

Liam opens his eyes, blinking up at that vast sky that stretches above, letting the sound wash over him. Those same wisps of cloud that he always remembered so vividly about Scarborough drift through the fading light as random festival flags flutter in the evening breeze. Guitar feedback cuts through the chatter, then locks into a rhythm that pulls everything and everyone together. The crowd instinctively shifts and sways in a sea of movement that ripples towards the source of the music.

Up on the stage, the band are sweating buckets, their sound frenetic but polished. Free, but precise. The kind of rock and roll that makes you forget everything for just long enough to feel lost in the moment and alive in the present.

Liam and Patsy stand at the peripherals, properly vibing to the music, and comfortable in each other's company for the first time since... well, since that day in Scarborough.

Drinks are passed beside Patsy, the smell of cheap Danish lager hits her nostrils, driving her to distraction.

"Are those vouchers good for booze?" she asks, as her eyes track the myriad of plastic cups moving through the crowd.

Liam shifts his weight. "Definitely er... maybe. Not."

"You want one?" She's already calculating how to get her hands on a drink.

"Not today, not ever," Liam says with a certainty that catches Patsy off guard.

She studies him. "How do you do it?"

Liam looks back, genuinely confused by the question.

"Abstinence," she clarifies.

"I've never touched the stuff. It's poison." Liam shrugs, like it's the most obvious thing in the world. "So it's like if someone offered you arsenic or cyanide—it's a no—every time. A no."

This simple mental trick hits Patsy like a revelation. Could she have been overthinking it all this time? The simplicity of Liam's approach almost makes her angry—not at him, but at herself, at the years spent battling a complicated enemy with complicated (and expensive) solutions. She files the thought away, not quite ready to admit how much sense it makes.

While lost in thought, Patsy gets jostled by the expanding crowd, nearly losing her footing. The proximity of strangers pressing in makes her skin itch with the need for liquid courage. *Poison*, she thinks to herself.

"Look. Just, stand, here, by me." Liam positions himself beside her.

"And, use your elbows. Bit like a chicken." He demonstrates, pointing his elbows and pushing outwards—naturally creating a pocket of space around them.

The trick works, carving out a small sanctuary in the heaving crowd. But just as Patsy begins to relax again, the Mancunian roadie stumbles over, wrapping his arms around them both.

"Come on friends, let's get backstage and have a paaaaarteeee. The band is gonna love you... Patsy off the teeeveee."

Patsy raises her eyebrows at this particular nugget of knowledge.

"Yeh, I watch TV," the roadie slurs, swaying slightly. "Good TV, shit TV, realiteee teeeeveee. Anything's good with a fat one," he says while dragging from his joint, his grin widening as if he's just shared some profound wisdom.

He guides them through the crowd, feeling its rhythm, finding space where none exists, while Liam beams and Patsy just tries not to get stepped on.

"Errr, excuse me, Mister Roadie? I'm not a groupie by the way," Patsy protests, but follows nonetheless.

They push through the masses toward the backstage area, where the best night of their lives was about to begin.

The roadie leads them through a maze of temporary barriers and taped-off areas, swinging his arms like a bad-ass and casually flashing his laminate at security guards who seem more dubious about the two random tag-alongs. To be fair, one does look like a groupie and the other her minder, so they let 'em through without further scrutiny.

"VIP area's just through here," he announces, gesturing toward a collection of makeshift tents with fairy lights strung between them. "Green room, catering, press area—the full festival experience my man!"

Liam's eyes widen at this unexpected access. He's never been 'behind the curtain' before, never seen how 'the magic' happens.

"Is that—?" He squints toward a figure in the distance.

"Haven't a clue," Patsy says, following his gaze to the frontwoman of, well to her they just look like a random collective of middle-aged folks in Levi jeans and tight tops, and she'd be right—they are. As the frontwoman chats to her band members, her distinctive blonde bob catches the light. "Your teenage crush, I'm guessing?"

Liam shakes his head. "No, nothing like that. She just... she always reminded me of Mum."

Patsy starts to make another teasing comment, but stops herself, studying her brother's face as he sizes up this random woman. "Really? Mum?"

"Yeah. The attitude, you know? The hair. That way of standing like she owns the room." Liam shrugs, suddenly self-conscious. "Stupid, I suppose."

"No," Patsy says quietly. "No, I see it."

For a moment, they both watch the frontwoman, seeing glimpses of Sally in the way she gestures, the way she throws her head back when she laughs. The cigarette in her hand is now replaced by a vape, but in a way that makes her look even cooler.

"Do you think Mum vapes?" asks Liam.

"What?" she says.

"Do you think Mum vapes?" he repeats.

"I can't hear you," she feigns, as she turns to walk off. But in her haste to escape, she doesn't spot the grizzly technician laden with equipment hurrying to the stage.

"Oi, careful!" he shouts as he rolls over her foot with a trolley.

"Owww, FUCK! Come on Patsy, get it together girl!" she says as she hobbles off.

The backstage area is a hive of activity—roadies pushing flight cases, band members smoking in corners, journalists with lanyards waiting for their five minutes. It's not exactly the BBC's Glastonbury over-glazed coverage with whatsherface in her thousand-pound wellies and whatshisface with the bad haircut, but it's a different world from the one Liam usually inhabits, and a painful reminder of the world Patsy used to. One where you never know what kind of smarmy "industry" prick you might run into. The kind of fella that promises you the world and delivers you a handful of magic fucking beans. That borrows money from you because "he's waiting for a deal to go through and his money's tied up in stocks and shares or some other kind of bullshit. The kind of bullshit most of us with an average bullshit detector can sniff out before the fella's even thought it. But sadly, our Patsy's bullshit detector needed a bit of fine-tuning at the time.

And that's when she sees him and freezes. Her entire body goes rigid. The world slows, sounds becoming muffled as her focus narrows to a single point—an overly dressed twat in a three-piece suit and leather jacket holding a dry Martini.

"Pats? What's wrong?" Liam's voice sounds distant, underwater.

It's Marcus Watson. Executive producer of the hit "structured reality" show 'Belsize Beaus'. The man who took everything from her and left her chewed up and spat out on the scrap heap.

Of all the fucking fields in all the fucking world, this cunt had to turn up in this one, Patsy thinks. For context, this fella's the worst type of "man" 21st-century society has bred. A greasy talent sucking, fame-adjacent, media vampire with a LinkedIn account he posts to every goddamn day, espousing some "the world is your oyster" bullshit when what he's really saying is "look at me look at me I'm an insecure prick". He's everyone's "friend"—for five minutes at least—until he's sucked every penny out of the relationship. The kind of guy that thinks he's humble because he thanks his waiter with eye contact. He's not humble. He's a complete wanker. We all know a 'Marcus Watson'. And we all hate him. Enough context for you?

Patsy's fingers curl into fists. Her jaw tightens. Three steps. That's all it would take. Three steps and she could smash his smug face into that speaker stack.

"Patsy," Liam says again, firmer this time. He doesn't know what's happening, but he recognises the rage in her eyes. "Patsy, what is it?"

"That..." she manages through gritted teeth. "That absolute—"

Before she can finish, Liam grips her arm, not knowing why but sensing she's about to do something she might regret. "Hey. Not worth it, whatever it is."

Her breath comes in shallow bursts, her nostrils flaring... but Liam's voice, with his long arm wrapped around her, provides an anchor.

The Mancunian roadie reappears, oblivious to the tension. "There y'are! Band's about to go back on for their second set. C'mon!"

He drags them toward the stage, unwittingly pulling Patsy away from a confrontation that might have ended with security escorting her off the premises—or worse. They skirt around Marcus, who thankfully remains engrossed in conversation with a young "influencer".

The roadie pushes them toward a side entrance to the stage. "Wait here, I'll get you the best spot," he says as he stumbles past a complicated-looking sound desk, tripping over the cables and hitting the floor with a thud.

The frontman is mid-way through a back and forth with the crowd when he finally shouts through his microphone—

"AND NOW, THE SONG YOU'VE ALL BEEN WAITING FOR—"

The roadie, slightly panicking now and attempting to be helpful, reaches for what he thinks is an important cable and sticks its jack in a random socket. But really, he's stoned and drunk as shit and shouldn't be anywhere near the sound desk.

Liam notices a split second too late. "No, don't touch—"

SCREEEEEECH—then silence. The frontman's voice dies mid-sentence, leaving only the confused murmurs of thousands of people.

"BOOOOOO!" The crowd's mood shifts instantly.

"Oi Dickheads!" shouts the lead singer from the stage. "Where's ma fucking jam?"

Everyone backstage panics, with technicians rushing to identify the problem. What's only about ten seconds feels about ten minutes of excruciating pain.

Liam, acting on instinct, spots the incorrectly connected cable. He grabs the jack, considers it for a moment, and pulls it out of its socket with a loud SCREEEECH that makes everyone wince.

The frontman's voice suddenly blasts through the speakers: "—THE FUCK? ARE WE BACK ON?"

Every head turns toward Liam, standing there with the jack in his hand, breathing a sigh of relief. The band members, the technicians, even the cool frontwoman—are all staring... and nodding in approval.

"Well blow me down wiv a feather, our fucking hero!" the frontman exclaims.

"Get that man a beer!"

Liam shakes his head. "No beer. Thanks."

The frontman's eyebrows shoot up. "Well, what shall we play yer then, mate? Your choice. Come on."

Before Liam can protest, the roadie shoves him onstage. The spotlight blinds him momentarily, thousands of faces a blur beyond it. He considers the crowd and looks back at Patsy before leaning in to whisper to the frontman.

A grin spreads across the singer's face. "Nice one." He points to Patsy beside the stage. "This next one's fer Patsy. Patsy wiv the silver dress."

The frontman instructs his band before launching into their next song, "This Is How It Feels" by Inspiral Carpets. Track number 11 on Liam's CD mixtape he made with Sally. A fitting tribute to their crazy ass road trip, he figured.

Liam finds himself being pushed back toward Patsy by a grateful stage manager.

"That was fucking insane," Patsy says, wide-eyed, the earlier moment of rage now completely forgotten. "WAAAHHH!" She lets out a Banshee scream of unrestrained joy to the thousands of people screaming back in her direction.

"LET'S AVE IT," Liam suddenly bellows.

And then, without a moment's thought to overthink the consequences, she grabs his hand and together they take the leap, embracing the chaos as they stage dive into the crowd. It's a far cry from the East London rave where rough hands carried her drunken ass out into the cold light of day; these loving hands carry Patsy gently, reverently even. For once, she's being carried in triumph, not in disgrace, holding her big brother's hand as she does it.

With hundreds of arms carefully carrying them back to a place of sanctuary in the middle of the crowd, they feel the power of thousands of voices singing Liam's song—the one he requested for his little sister Patsy—engulfing them, making them feel like the nucleus of their own special moment in time, a moment shared with many thousands of people.

As they stand with their arms raised and their spines tingling, not quite sure what just happened, the music washes over them both, creating a bubble where, just for a moment, their past doesn't matter and their future is just a distant concern.

Liam's in his element, proper loving life. Dancing, jumping, singing along like he's been waiting years to let loose. Which, come to think of it, he probably has. He notices Patsy's unease, the way she's now shrinking from the crush of strangers.

"Remember," he shouts over the music, demonstrating his chicken elbows technique again. "Create your own space."

She mirrors his movements, and just like that, a pocket of sanctuary forms around them. The crowd instinctively gives way, and Patsy feels herself begin to relax. To breathe. To move. And she loses herself to the music and to the moment.

The strobe lights paint patterns across her face as sweat drips from her forehead. Her eyes are sharp now, taking everything in—the visuals swimming above the stage, the wall of sound washing over them, her brother absolutely lost to the music. A shiver runs down her spine as pure joy—unfiltered by vodka or fame or pretence—fills her soul.

Some bloke appears at her shoulder, trying and failing to vibe with her movements. He extends a freshly poured pint like a peace offering, and what would have been catnip to Patsy of (literally) yesterday—she doesn't even look at him, just swings her elbows out in a practised arc which knocks his beer back in his face. Message received. He melts back into the crowd without a word.

Liam throws his arms up in victory, and for once, his perpetual optimism doesn't grate. He's been waiting his whole life for a moment like this—in fact, they both have. Funny how one can get lost in a perpetual loop of misery without realising that a good fucking dance can shake the cobwebs from any relationship.

The music swells around them as the crowd moves as one, thousands of voices joining the frontman's lyrics, sung in a twisted irony, as none of the many thousands of people swaying left and right, and bobbing up and down, feel lonely right now.

They're not lonely. Not small. Not nothing. They're the beating heart of something bigger than themselves, carried along by a sea of strangers who, just for tonight, feel like family.

"THIS IS MILES BETTER THAN ANY FUCKING PEYOTE TRIP," Patsy screams.

And though he's never done peyote, or any drugs, or drunk alcohol, Liam understands perfectly… as this day, is easily, the best day he's had since Scarborough '96.

𝄞

A canvas of stars spans the midnight-blue sky above them. Within the Tetris maze of trucks, Liam stretches out across the roof of the orange Golf with his arms folded behind his neck. He's managed to convince Patsy to climb up with him, though she's wisely perched on the edge, gazing upward with genuine wonder at the infinite cosmos.

"Do you know any constellations?" he asks.

"Yeah, that's the Cosmic Donkey—featured in that Radiohead music video, you know the one. And that cluster there is the Great British Bear, best seen from deepest darkest Peru. David Attenborough did a whole special on it."

Liam seems genuinely engaged, hanging on her every word.

"See that lightning bolt formation? That's where J.K. Rowling got the inspiration for Harry Potter's scar. Officially, it's called Zeus's Vengeance, but most astronomers just call it Harry Potter's arse crack. And that nebulous blob over there that looks like an absolute mess? That's called the Blurry Nebula. Little-known fact but Damon Albarn named the band after it."

"Where did you learn all this?" asks Liam.

"Well, that's what they teach at private school. Star constellations, zodiac signs, and how to pronounce quinoa properly."

"Really?" Liam feigns interest.

"No. They teach you how to be a proper cunt by stripping your heart and soul out, then replacing it with networking skills and a superiority complex. Stellar education, really."

Liam points lazily upward. "That one, "Harry Potter's arse crack," is actually Orion's Belt. Three stars in a row. See? And that bright one there, that's the North Star. Sailors use it to navigate. That other bright one right there. It's not even a star. It's Venus."

"Fuck off," says Patsy, genuinely enlightened.

"Nope. And wait…" He takes her finger and they point together. "That's Mars—the slightly reddish one."

"Bull. Shit. Alright smart guy. So what's that cloudy streaky thing?" Patsy points to a faint, misty band stretching across part of the sky.

"That?" Liam sits up slightly, genuinely surprised by her interest. "That's the Milky Way. Our galaxy. You can actually see it out here in Norfolk because there's barely any light pollution. In London you'd never—"

"Wait, that's our actual galaxy? I thought that was just, like, space clouds or something."

"Nah, it's millions of stars all clustered together. We're inside it, like looking out your bedroom window at the city. That's why it looks like a stripe across the sky. You can see another bit from Australia."

"So, like looking out your back window?" she asks.

"Yeah, kind of… we'll make an astronomer of you yet Patsy Digs—Fortescue-Smythe"

"Digsby," she corrects him, rolling her eyes in his direction.

Patsy stares upward, momentarily silent.

"Mad thing is," Liam continues, "most of those stars are so far away that the light we're seeing now left them hundreds, thousands of years ago. Like, that star there might not even exist anymore, but we're only just getting the message."

"So we're looking at the past?"

"Yeah. Proper time travel. Your brain processes it all in like, what, milliseconds? But that light's been travelling for centuries. Time's well weird like that. Stretches and shrinks depending on where you're standing."

"That's deep for someone who hasn't yet adopted the internet age."

"Books, films and music can teach you everything you need to know," Liam says. "Some of the greatest philosophers are musicians... authors... filmmakers. Noel Gallagher taught me more about life than any social media account."

Liam lies back down. "Mad, innit? Makes you feel proper small."

"How'd you know all this?"

"Mum taught me. When I was about sixteen. We went out on the train to somewhere in Surrey or Hertfordshire or somethin', she booked a cheap room above a pub and we went out stargazing. She'd go all philosopher and say things like: 'It may be an infinite cosmos, but always remember you are one of those stars'... or... 'Anytime you're apart from me, just look up and you can bet I'll be looking up too'.

"Sounds nice," Patsy says, with a hint of resentment.

"It was. Until we got back to the pub, then the tears began."

"Oh yeah. The tears."

They fall silent, drinking in the vastness. The festival's sound system has finally gone quiet, allowing the hum of cricket song to fill the air instead.

"Do you think Mum's looking at these same stars right now?" Liam asks.

Patsy shifts uncomfortably. "Maybe. Probably not, though. She's probably tucked up in a hotel waiting for us, one with a bar no doubt."

"Yeah."

"What are you going to say to her? When we see her tomorrow?"

Liam considers this, his face illuminated by starlight. "Dunno. Been thinking about it, but every time I imagine the moment, I just... go blank. Too many questions. Too much to say. What about you?"

Patsy takes her moment to slide down from the edge of the car.

Liam snorts.

"What's that snort for?"

"Nothing. Just that you're still... You know. Walled off."

"I'm standing in a random field after abandoning everything I know. How's that for walled off?"

Liam raises his hands in surrender. "You're right. Sorry."

Another silence stretches between them, but it's not entirely uncomfortable.

"I'm going inside. Getting cold. Still didn't find any fucking shoes," Patsy says.

"Oh, one last thing before you go to sleep," Liam says.

"Come on, out with it, we'll be here all night otherwise."

"Nah, trust me. I've got a good feeling. One sec, let me just compose my thoughts..."

He shifts slightly, and the resulting sound reverberates through the roof of the Golf. A proper, window-rattling trumpet of a fart.

"Oh, you absolute animal, it went down my throat!" she gasps between laughs. "I could do with some shoes, but you definitely need new boxers."

"It's good luck to fart before bed," he manages, wiping tears from his eyes.

"That is absolutely not a thing. See you in the morning." She disappears inside, though Liam can still hear her laughing from under the convertible roof.

"Night Pats."

"Night LeeLee."

As he gazes at the infinite expanse above, something loosens in his chest—a feeling that's been absent for years. Tomorrow they'll find Mum, get answers, maybe even get that lottery money. But somehow, stretched out beneath the Milky Way, none of that seems as important as it did yesterday.

"Can we just live here, forever?" he says to the night sky.

He doesn't mean to fall asleep up there, but the day's been long, and the cosmos feels like the warmest of blankets.

~ 1996 ~

Little Liam sits cross-legged in the middle of the carpet, surrounded by the CD cases that lay scattered around like treasures he found at the beach. The setting sun filters through the net curtains and the Chicken Tonight smell still lingers in the air, though by now it's replaced by the suffocating stench of his mum's Marlboro Lights and the plastic newness of his prized CD Discman. A heady mix for what is the hottest day of 1996.

Sally kneels by the stereo, her electric blue streaks falling across her face as she plays with the thousands of buttons and dials. Her "Definitely Maybe" t-shirt rides up at the back, revealing the small Celtic knot tattoo at the base of her spine.

Little Liam arranges the cases methodically—albums to his left, singles to his right. He's already familiarising himself with each CD sleeve, tracing the artwork with his fingertips, reading the song titles aloud under his breath like incantations.

"What should we put on it?" he asks, already mentally compiling his list. He's too shy to admit he's been planning this since the moment she handed him the Discman, earlier that day.

Sally crawls over, cigarette dangling precariously from her lips, and sits beside him. "Well, we need something that kicks everything off with a bang—gets your heart going, you know?" She rifles through the pile and pulls out an Oasis CD. "Like this."

She shuffles over to the stereo and slides in the disc. The opening chords of "Rock 'N' Roll Star" fill the room, and Sally air-guitars dramatically, making Little Liam giggle.

"Then," she says, pressing pause, "you build, kinda like a good movie. Every good mixtape tells a story. Ups, downs, ebbing and flowing."

"Like a river?" he offers.

"Yeah, like a river. Like life too, Mister Philosopher," she remarks.

For the next two hours, they huddle together in front of the stereo. Little Liam suggests songs; Sally vetoes some with a wrinkled nose and nods enthusiastically at others as she shuttles back and forth to the kitchen drinks cabinet. They argue good-naturedly over who's better, Blur or Oasis (they can't agree either way), and whether Pulp's "Common People" is based on a true story. Sally thinks not, but Little Liam really wants to believe it is. Both agree it's a wicked song.

Sally shows him how to time the recording just right—waiting for one song to stop completely before pressing play of the new song and hitting record.

"Careful with the levels," she warns, adjusting a dial. "Don't want it to sound like it was recorded in a toilet, do you?"

Little Patsy wanders in halfway through, drawn by the music, and Sally pulls her into her lap. Little Liam notices how his sister's dark mood lifts as the three of them bounce along to Supergrass with Sally holding Little Patsy's hands up, dancing them through the air, while Little Liam jumps up and down on the battered old sofa.

As the evening deepens, Patsy falls dead asleep on the armchair, giving Sally's selections a quieter, more reflective feel. "Always include something to dream to," she says, queuing up "Champagne Supernova". As it plays, Liam starfishes on the carpet, soaking in every ounce of the Gallagher's melodic rock symphony, while Sally flips through the remaining CDs. "Now we need a strong closer," she murmurs, picking up a Suede single. "Something that tells your intended what you really mean to them."

As the room grows darker around them, the illuminated stereo meters bounce gently with the rhythm. Little Liam rests his head against his mum's shoulder as the all-important final song they chose together to close their mixtape plays out. Its final chords seemingly hang in the space between them for an eternity.

"Finished?" Sally finally asks.

Little Liam nods, with that electric feeling of anticipation bubbling inside him—a fizzing in his chest that only kids get when something magical is about to happen.

Sally hits eject, and out comes their creation. She takes a marker and writes in her beautiful flowing handwriting:

LeeLee & Sal's Mixtape
Classics & Tunes Only

She hands it to him like it's the first pressing of 'Abbey Road'. Little Liam cradles it, feeling its weight—heavier somehow than it should be, as if all the emotion of the songs has amounted up to some type of physical mass.

He carefully slots the CD mixtape into his new Discman. He presses play, and as the first notes emerge through the headphones, he throws his arms around Sally, burying his face in her CK One-scented neck. She hugs him back fiercely as he slowly drifts off to sleep in her arms, with the poetic lyrics of those seemingly random '90s singers etching themselves into his developing brain, forming neural connections that would shape his identity for years to come.

This moment, this exact point in time, is where Liam Digsby truly begins.

CHAPTER 10
THE OL' GIRL IS M.A.D.

A long-forgotten song plays from the radio in the corner of the room—a gentle jazz cover that drifts through the hospital air. Sally closes her eyes, the melody transporting her back to her Peckham living room floor, Little Liam cross-legged beside her as they mess around with the neighbour's stereo. The way his eyes lit up when she handed him the Sony Discman. Little Patsy dancing to the music. Why did this memory come to the forefront of her mind, she ponders.

"All done for today, Mrs. Digsby," the nurse says, unhooking the IV bag of chemicals that are meant to be saving Sally's life. Or at least prolonging it. But all in all, it's actually making her feel worse. Much worse. The chemo room stands empty now except for her and Jagdeesh, who sits patiently in the corner, waiting to wheel her back to her room.

"I was miles away," Sally says, her voice raspy and wispy. "Decades, actually."

Back in her room, Sally settles at her writing desk while Jagdeesh adjusts the blinds to let in just enough afternoon light. She pulls out her letter-writing paper, uncaps her fountain pen, and begins to write. The words flow until a violent cough erupts from deep within her chest. She covers her mouth with a handkerchief, but can't contain the spray that spatters across the fresh page, tiny flecks of claret bleed into the cream paper.

"Bloody hell," she mutters, screwing up the paper and weakly lobbing it at the bin. It misses by a mile and settles on the floor beside the others.

"Here, drink some water," Jagdeesh moves quickly to her side, but Sally waves him away.

"I'm fine. I have about an hour before the chemicals really hit me. Just... hand me another sheet."

He does so, watching as she smooths it flat on the desk with her trembling hands before trying again. The pen hovers over the paper for what seems an age. Eventually the pen touches paper and the words glide across the page:

To Liam and Patsy,

"May I ask, Sally?" Jagdeesh's voice has a rare tentativeness to it. "How do you know your children will take the bait and find your letters?"

Sally doesn't look up, her concentration fixed on forming each letter perfectly. "Well, if they want what's in the box, their inheritance, then they will have to use their ingenuity and their intuition. Between the pair of them, they'll get there. I know it."

"And if not?"

Now she does look up, the pain evident in her face, but her eyes clear and certain.

"They'll get there."

There's something primal in her conviction, a maternal instinct that transcends the years of separation. "It's hardwired into us, you know," she says, tapping her chest. "This connection. You can run from it, deny it, pretend it doesn't matter. But it's there. Like gravity."

Jagdeesh nods. He can feel it. He's felt it since he saw her on the street that day, all those years ago, feeding the feral cats outside the hostel where he'd been staying. Something in her lost expression mirrored his own, and when she asked if he knew where to find a decent cuppa tea, he dutifully showed her the way. He never expected to become her caretaker, her confidant, something close to a son. Ironic really. But then she found that with a clean slate she could forget herself, forget her past, her children. And she did, for a time. But never really. The regret, the absence, the shame and the guilt metastasised inside her. Like the fucking cancer eating her alive.

Another coughing fit seizes her. This one is much worse. Jagdeesh supports her as her body convulses, and when it finally subsides, she slumps in the chair, exhausted.

"Perhaps we should continue tomorrow," Jagdeesh suggests.

"No time," Sally whispers. "No time left to waste. I've wasted so so many years..."

She turns back to her letter, hand shaking but determined, with a supportive squeeze of her shoulder from Jagdeesh.

Sally knows they will come. It isn't hope or wish-fulfilment. It's certainty. The same certainty that compelled her to set aside every penny of her lottery winnings, placing their inheritance in the ornate trunk they'll receive when they meet her in Scarborough. The same certainty that makes her write these letters now despite the pain, the exhaustion, the bitter taste of blood in her mouth. The same certainty that time's a healer... maybe.

But they <u>will</u> come, and she will finally make things right.

DAY 3

In the pale blue dawn, birdsong gently wakes Liam from his slumber. He blinks awake, momentarily confused by the vastness above him. The roof of the Golf has grown uncomfortable beneath him.

Someone—Patsy, he assumes—has thrown a crocheted patchwork blanket over him at some point in the night.

He sits up, squinting across the field. It takes him several seconds to register what's different. The field is empty. The trucks, the roadies, everyone—all gone, as if they'd imagined the entire festival. Just his orange Golf sitting incongruously in the middle of a wide open space. In the distance, a farmer herds his cows along the perimeter.

Liam stretches, with a smile breaking across his face. Today's the day. Today they'll reach Scarborough, find Mum, get answers.

He shifts, ready to slide down from his rooftop bed. As he twists too quickly, something in his lower back gives with a sickening pop.

"Owwwww oww oww OWWW. Shit." He freezes, as pain radiates down his spine. "Fuck me."

Patsy's head appears through the car window, hair tousled from sleep. "What's the matter?"

"Back's gone," he grunts, trying to find a position that doesn't feel like being stabbed with a hot poker.

"Serves you right for sleeping on top of a car, you prat."

Liam manages to slide down the windscreen with excruciating slowness, landing on his feet with a wince. The doors and boot of the Golf stand open to the morning air.

"You sober?" he asks, grimacing as he straightens.

Patsy rubs her face. "Day three, baby," she says with mock pride.

He sends the keys sailing through the morning light, and she plucks them from the air one-handed.

"You're driving. Go easy on her."

𝄞

Fifteen minutes later, they're back on the road, with Patsy behind the wheel. Liam's attempt at giving directions has already resulted in three wrong turns and a near collision with a milk float.

"Hey, whoa. Whoa. Go easy," Liam says, bracing himself against the dashboard as Patsy swerves around a cyclist.

"What, it's only a cyclist," she says.

"Yeah, but my car. Go easy on the Ol' Girl."

"Well, today's the day," she says, with a manic gleam in her eye. "Finally get to ask Sally why she done what she done, before she gives up the ghost."

"Yeah. But... just slow down." Liam's pale, partly from the back pain, partly from Patsy's driving.

He gives up on the front seat, carefully sliding into the back bed area, easing himself down with a groan.

"Hey, what's the story?" Patsy asks, eyeing him in the rearview mirror.

"That's my line," he mutters. "Sleeping badly on a car roof all night—that's what's the story, right now anyway."

He curls into a ball, pulling a blanket over himself. Patsy rolls her eyes, humming some indistinct tune as she drives.

𝄞

Patsy has the UK map open on the passenger seat, putting her private school education to good use. Year 8 orientation through the Cotswolds, in case you were wondering. Her finger traces the route northward, tapping triumphantly when she finds what she's looking for.

"A47, A47," she repeats to herself like a mantra. "Aha—fuck you, Google!" she crows as she joins the motorway.

In the back, Liam's breathing has settled into soft snores. She catches sight of his sleeping form in the rearview mirror, curled up like a child beneath his blanket. Perfect opportunity to "get a groove on", as some twat had earlier put it.

The countryside blurs as Patsy's foot pushes harder on the accelerator. The speedometer needle creeps steadily upward—50, 60, 70. The Golf starts to make entirely new sounds at 80 mph. By 88, the dashboard is vibrating in a way that suggests either time travel is imminent or a complete mechanical meltdown is upon them.

The engine gives a premonitory shudder, a clear warning that forty-year-old cars were never designed to move at warp speed. "Come on old girl, you're made of tougher stuff. Shut your whining. Forwards you old bitch. Forwards."

Patsy swerves in and out of traffic, threading the needle between lorries and caravans. Her eyes narrow as she spots a gap that would make a London cabbie think twice.

A truck signals and begins pulling out directly in front of her, but rather than slow down like any sane person, she literally floors the accelerator. The Golf's engine screams in protest as she attempts to overtake.

The vibration starts in the steering column, then spreads through the entire chassis until the whole car is shuddering like it's about to shake itself apart.

In the back, Liam jolts awake, his face a picture of panic. "What the fuck—why is the car vibrating?" His voice quickly rises to a shout. "WHY IS THE CAR VIBRATING?"

Patsy keeps her head down and continues to floor it as Liam thrusts himself across to look at the speedometer.

"88 MILES PER HOUR! IT'S NOT A FUCKING TIME MACHINE," Liam screams.

And that's when an almighty BANG comes from somewhere deep within the engine, followed by that sickening sound of grinding metal. Black smoke billows from under the bonnet, quickly filling the car's interior, blocking Patsy's view of the road.

"Oh for fuck's sake," Patsy snarls, momentarily letting go of the wheel to stick her head out the window.

"AHHHHH WE'RE GONNA DIE!" Liam screams as he lunges past Patsy, grabbing the steering wheel.

"BRAKE!" he shouts into the smoke, but Patsy's got her head out the window, hair whipping in the 88 mph wind.

~ 1996 ~

The green Golf races north under the cover of darkness, the monotonous drone of its engine competing with the throbbing bass from the stereo. Sally's fingers drum against the steering wheel, twitching with nervous energy. She fiddles with the CD player, skipping from song to song, searching for something to match her mood.

"This Is How It Feels" by Inspiral Carpets fades out abruptly as she jabs at the forward button. "Alright" by Cast doesn't last three seconds before being dismissed with another impatient press. "Good Enough" by Dodgy suffers the same fate.

Then she stops. The opening chords of "A Design for Life" by Manic Street Preachers fill the car. Her shoulders drop slightly as some of the invisible tension coursing through her body relents.

James Dean Bradfield's Welsh vocals echo through her cranium, telling her about the end, telling her that there is some design to this life. *If so,* she thinks, *please someone give me a heads up on what's coming next.*

In the rearview mirror, Sally's eyes flick to the back seat. The children are huddled together like the last two puppies of the litter seeking warmth in a cardboard box. Little Liam holds Little Patsy's tiny hand, her head nestled against his shoulder. The strawberry sauce stain on his t-shirt is now a sticky patch, the memory of their earlier ice cream catastrophe already fading into just another moment of this strange, impulsive journey.

"No one's gonna take my babies," Sally whispers.

Little Liam isn't quite asleep. He watches his mum through half-closed eyes, trying to understand what's happening. Adults were strange and unpredictable at the best of times. He often kept his distance, but Mum's been especially odd since they left home. One minute laughing, the next crying, then silent for miles on end.

Sally's voice rises above the music, surprisingly sweet as she sings along to the chorus. Her fingers tap out the rhythm on the steering wheel.

Little Liam catches a word here and there: a wish, a bottle, someone who wants to get drunk designing a life. *Who'd want a drunk designing their life,* he thinks.

Her voice catches. Little Liam watches a tear slide down her cheek, glistening in the dim intermittent yellow light from the overhead lampposts.

The car accelerates. Sally's foot presses harder on the pedal, the speedometer needle climbs as she belts out A—DESIGN—FOR—LIFE with increasing desperation, as if the words might save her if she just sings them loud enough. 70—75—80—88 mph—top speed.

Little Patsy stirs beside him, her fingers tightening around his. Little Liam squeezes back, shielding her from whatever storm is brewing in the front seat.

The Golf flies past a motorway police layby, shaking the police rover sitting idle. The Golf's tatty green paint job briefly illuminated in the orange glow of the motorway lights.

Inside the police rover, a young officer, Rookie, blinks away sleep, her eyes suddenly alert as she spots the green Golf speeding past. She checks her clipboard, nudging her dozing colleague with a sharp elbow.

"'old up a sec." Her Yorkshire accent sharpens with urgency. "Green Golf '84 plate. That description fits the missing child APB." She reads the number plate aloud, "A829 M A D." A small smile tugs at her mouth. "MAD indeed. Come on Nightrider, let's hit it."

Her superior, a veteran cop with thirty-odd years on the force, snaps to attention. Without a word, Nightrider fires up the engine and slams his foot on the accelerator; the car surges onto the motorway in hot pursuit.

Little Liam watches his mum's eyes in the rearview mirror. They're wide, too bright. She looks back at him, her expression softening for just a moment.

"I wish I could turn those back seats into a bed for ya both," she says, her voice cracking. "Just live forever, in here. The three of us."

Something catches in the mirror—a flash of blue light. Sally's face changes in an instant, fear replacing the momentary tenderness.

"No, no, no," she mutters, glancing repeatedly at the mirror. "Not now."

Little Liam twists around to look through the back window. Police lights throb in the darkness behind them, getting closer. The wail of a siren cuts through the night, drowning out the music.

"Mummy?" he whispers.

Sally doesn't answer. Her attention is fixed on the rearview mirror, watching the police car gaining on them.

Little Liam pulls his little sister closer and clips his seatbelt around her, protecting her even in sleep from whatever is happening. The blue lights flash faster now, painting the inside of the car in rhythmic pulses of colour. He has an inkling of why they're running—the fight, the shouting, the blood, everything that went wrong. But why does he feel like it's somehow all his fault? The fear radiating from his mother only makes this feeling worse.

The Golf continues to bomb along the motorway as Sally keeps her foot firmly pressed on the accelerator. Whatever she's running from, she's not slowing down.

"Think we've got runners?" Nightrider asks in the police rover, eyes fixed on the green car ahead. By now, both cops can see a set of terrified little eyes, Little Liam's, looking back at them from the back seat.

"Not sure. Looks like kids in the back, though. Go easy."

The police rover's lights bathe the motorway in blue pulses as they close the gap on the fast lane of the A1(M) heading north to Scotland.

Rookie gets on the radio, "Control, this is Unit 547. Heading north on A1. Suspected link to missing child alert. In pursuit of a green Golf, registration Alpha 829 Mike Alpha Delta. Over."

Some moments burn themselves into memory so deeply that you can always feel the leather seats, always smell the fear, always hear your mum's frenetic breathing like it just happened yesterday. Liam has never forgotten that night—the police lights in the rear-view mirror, the way Sally's hands shook on the steering wheel, the weight of not understanding but still feeling that everything was all your fault.

Now, decades later, it's his turn behind the wheel when everything goes bat shit crazy.

DAY 3

"BRAKE—BRAKE—BRAKE!" Liam screams repeatedly.

Liam's orange pride and joy, now complete with thick black smoke pouring from under the bonnet, lurches violently on the motorway, swerving left and right as both siblings scream. As the car lets out its own dirty mechanical scream, Liam wrestles with the wheel, steering the car onto the relative safety of the hard shoulder, whilst Patsy frantically pumps the brakes, causing the car to skid violently, grinding to a halt with a pathetic wheeze. The siblings sit in silence, shaking from their near-death experience, unable to look at each other. The Golf's engine makes one final death rattle before flames begin to lick up from beneath the bonnet.

"OUT! OUT!" Liam shouts, already fumbling with his door handle. They tumble from the car in a panicked rush, coughing and spluttering as acrid smoke engulfs them.

"Oh shit," screams Liam. He quickly leans back in through the car window, and as the car properly goes up in flames, Liam yanks the ornate trunk and his satchel out.

For a moment, they just stand there on the hard shoulder, watching the car burn. A few rubberneckers slow to gawp at the spectacle, but otherwise the traffic rumbles indifferently past this human suffering.

Liam's face contorts with grief, genuine grief, as his pride and joy, and hopes and dreams all go up in smoke. The orange paint bubbles and peels along with flecks of the original tatty green paintwork, together they flutter and dance in the air. There won't be any cliché last words from Patsy stating "well it could be worse" followed by some Hollywood explosion. No, this is more depressing than that. More real. To Liam, this is the end of an era, an end to his last connection to his mother. Everything slowly burning to a crisp in front of his very eyes. And that's when Patsy blurts out: "Well it could be—"

"WHERE AM I GONNA LIVE NOW?" he explodes, rounding on Patsy, his voice croaking with genuine desperation.

She blinks at him, baffled by his outburst. "LIVE? You can't live in a car. It's a stupid idea, Liam. It's a fucking CAR!"

"Just tell me you have roadside recovery?" Patsy finally asks, her voice quieter but cold as ice.

"Just tell me you didn't drive her over fifty?" Liam counters, equally cold.

By now they are squaring up to each other, nose to nose, with Patsy genuinely looking like she could have him.

"She never goes over fifty. It's a rule," he says.

"It's a stupid rule," hisses back Patsy.

"Clearly. NOT," Liam spits.

The silence that follows is as toxic as the smoke billowing between them.

"You know if you spent more time looking after your relationships than you did on that shitbox… you'd be a lot happier," snipes Patsy. The irony completely lost on her that she's describing her own life strategy, where instead of shitbox we could literally use any other word—vodka, fame, gambling, violent aggression. In any case, her protective steel wall has already lifted around her, wrapping her in its cold embrace once again, ensuring 100% protection from any mug, bitch, dick or twat who tries to hurt her. Not her father. Not her mother. Not her brother. Not today. Not tomorrow. Not ever. Fort Knox ain't got nothing on Patsy's emotional fortifications.

Before Liam can reply, they hear the BLOOP BLOOP of a police siren cutting over the passing motorway traffic.

A motorway police car pulls to a smooth stop behind them, its blue lights painting the smoke in strange warped pulses. A fresh out of the academy PC jumps out and rushes toward the burning car with a fire extinguisher battling valiantly to push back the flames, while a more senior officer approaches the siblings with the measured pace of someone who's seen it all before, but still genuinely loves to help.

There's something familiar about her—wiser around the eyes, her hair shorter than it once was, a little bit rounder across the middle, but unmistakably this is the same officer, Rookie, who had pursued their mother all those years ago just a few miles north of this motorway stretch.

"Go on Jenkins, you go an' put out that fire and whatnot. You got it, yeah?" Rookie says rather unconvincingly to her eager PC. But Jenkins does not "got it". In fact, the fire is getting worse.

"So what's all this about then?" Rookie rounds on the siblings, surveying the scene with professional detachment.

"She killed my car," Liam replies, his voice hollow.

"Ah right, well I better arrest her for murder." The officer's Yorkshire accent wraps around the words with a dry humour that neither sibling appreciates. She studies the smouldering wreck, squinting at the number plate. "Victim: VW Golf, plate number A829 M A D." A flicker of recognition crosses her face. "MAD indeed."

Rookie shakes her head slightly. "Nah. Can't be." She then looks at Liam, and for a split second, a memory surfaces—*terrified little eyes staring back at her from the rear window of a similar Golf, from many moons passed*. The image dissolves as quickly as it appeared.

"Or maybe it could. If I'm honest wi' ya, I'm surprised it's still on t'road.

"I've looked after her well," Liam says defensively.

She places a warm supportive hand on his shoulder.

"That you 'ave, son. That you 'ave."

Rookie nods to Jenkins, who has by now managed to extinguish most of the flames and is looking pretty damn proud of herself. "Call us a tow, babes," Rookie tells her.

"We don't have any money," Liam interjects, avoiding Patsy's eyes.

"Don't sweat it. Happens quite a lot. He'll tow you t'nearest garage."

Liam looks at the steaming, blackened remains of his car. The trusty old Golf—Liam's sanctuary—is gone. "Scrapyard might be better."

The officer nods, understanding perfectly. "Where ya headed?"

At exactly the same time, each sibling responds with:

"Scarborough."

"London."

Brother and sister exchange a look that could freeze the black smoke between them.

Patsy's mouth tightens into a thin line as she looks away from him. Her body language makes it clear that the fragile connection they'd begun to rebuild, this journey, of reconciliation, of reconnection, of hope—is about to snap.

"Sunny Scarbados it is," Rookie cheerily declares, deliberately ignoring the tension between them.

𝄞

The police car follows the tow truck at a respectful distance. Liam and Patsy sit in the back, the ornate trunk wedged awkwardly between them. Neither makes any attempt to shift it, both seeming to prefer the barrier it creates. The countryside begins to change as they veer off the motorway, civilisation thinning out with each passing mile as they head deeper inland.

Fields stretch out on either side, with an occasional farmhouse dotting the landscape. The road narrows, hemmed in by hedgerows thick with mid-summer growth. Yet despite the beautiful Arcadia-esque surroundings of 'God's own country', Yorkshire, neither sibling speaks. They might as well be in different vehicles altogether.

Rookie glances at them in the rearview mirror, breaking the silence.

"Quite a distinct car, ay?" she says.

Liam, staring out the window, doesn't even turn his head. "Can't beat the classics," he replies, his voice subdued and distant. Even he can't find the positive in this scenario.

"Aye, I know that," Rookie says. "You's are talkin' to one." She pauses, then adds, "You two ever been t'Scotland?"

Patsy screws up her face at the random question. Liam doesn't answer immediately. Through the window, he can see Patsy's still fuming reflection superimposed over the passing countryside of wild flower meadows, dry stone walls, and the occasional rogue sheep separate from the pack.

That's when the vague unwarranted interjection of a painful memory hits him. *They're on the edge of a cliff, Sally holds her two young children in each hand. The bottom is so far away, rocks, certain death. Fuck. No way. He grabs Little Patsy's hand and pulls her away from the edge.* And he snaps back to the car.

"Yeah maybe. Once, a long, long time ago. I forget."

That's when he catches Patsy looking at him. Did she just have the same recollection, he wonders. But she sneers, rolls her eyes and looks back out the window.

"You've never been to Scotland. You've barely left South London."

"That's t'thing about forgotten memories," Rookie says, filling the silence. "They're never really forgotten. Just stored deep down, you know? So take care of 'em, cos you cannot relive 'em."

The words hover in the air between them, unacknowledged but heard.

𝄞

The scrapyard appears suddenly around a bend—a bleak oasis of twisted metal containing countless miles of memories. Every car here once carried someone to somewhere that mattered: seasides with the windows down and the music blaring, awkward first dates, the school run, those middle-of-the-night dashes to the hospital. For that drum kit in West London you bought on eBay, that wardrobe from Ikea you couldn't fit into your car without the boot remaining half open, but it's okay 'cos you "safely" tied it closed with a plastic carrier bag. To your parents' house for Sunday dinner, your firstborn's wedding, your secondborn's graduation or your thirdborn's first football match. Your step-kid's piano recital, your uncle's sex-change announcement, or that trip to the palliative unit and then to the funeral home. Or whatever mundane thing you thought you were doing at the time, when really, you were making precious memories. The Batmobile, The Mummobile, The Shagmobile, Betsy, Bessie, Ruby, Baby, Dad's Taxi, The Beast, The Partywagon, The Tank or Dave—whatever pet name was whispered to the dashboard when the clutch gave out on the motorway, or when some dickhead in a BMW (or equally an Audi) cut you off at the roundabout. First cars, family cars, midlife crisis cars, funeral cars—they all ended up in places like this. Metal might be crushed and melted down, but the memories within remain welded to our souls long after the logbook is shredded.

Sadly, for Liam, after 30+ years of faithful service to the Digsby family, today is the day Ol' Girl takes her last bow. The burnt-up orangey green Golf sits forlornly under a towering mechanical claw, looking small and vulnerable. Already, the alloy wheels have been removed and stacked up and a pair of scrapyard workers are extracting what remains of the expensive sound system from the rear boot.

Liam stands with the scrapyard owner, for argument's sake we will call him—Scrappie—a man who embodies every cliché of his profession. Sweaty and overweight, he sports a badly fitted toupee and a T-shirt declaring: 'I'M #1 SO WHY TRY HARDER'. His meaty hand counts out notes onto Liam's outstretched palm.

"...nine-hundred, nine-fifty, a grand," Scrappie concludes.

Liam's jaw clenches as he accepts the money. When he turns, his eyes find Patsy. His gaze hardens into a death stare, raw and accusatory. She's trapped, with nowhere to hide, laden down with the ornate trunk and Liam's satchel.

For a moment, Liam turns away from Patsy, back to the car. He runs his fingers along the contours of what's left of the Golf's door, a farewell caress.

Rookie approaches Patsy, watching the scene unfold.

"Real fond of it then, ay?" she asks.

"Mm-hmm," Patsy murmurs, watching her brother.

"Where did he come by it—t'car?"

Patsy hesitates before answering. "She's always been part of the family."

"Shame..." Rookie says. "To say goodbye to it."

Liam strokes the car one last time, his fingers lingering on the paintwork as if committing its texture to memory.

"Well, time has come for you to leave me too, Ol' Girl," he says softly. "Thanks for the memories."

In this moment, there's something more than just a boy saying goodbye to his cherished vehicle. There's history being crushed, layers of meaning that Patsy is only just beginning to glimpse.

"You ready, son?" Scrappie asks.

Liam leans into the car one final time, sliding the mixtape CD out from the stereo. He hands it to Scrappie, then steps back with a slight nod. Ready.

A memory flashes through his mind: his mother's face looking directly at him, words from long ago on a roasting hot day in Peckham echoing: *"A weepy one couldn't hurt..."*

Scrappie inserts the mixtape CD into a boombox, hits track eight and raises it high over his head. The wistful and melancholic opening guitar notes of "Walkaway" by Cast fill the scrapyard, incongruously beautiful against the backdrop of industrial decay. Each note seems to hang in the air during the Golf's final moments—as Liam stands there, grief-stricken.

The mechanical claw whirs to life. It descends, grasps the Golf, and hoists it skyward. For a moment, the orange car hangs suspended, a bright splash of colour against the sky.

Scrappie, Rookie, and Jenkins all remove their hats in an impromptu show of respect. It's absurd and touching all at once—a funeral for a car.

Patsy watches her brother's face, seeing for the first time the depth of his connection to their mother's car. She'd never understood before this moment. The car wasn't just transport; it was continuity, a thread connecting present to past.

The crusher comes to life with a hydraulic groan. Metal screams against metal—CRUSH, CLANG, SCREECH—until there's nothing left but a compact orange cube, dropped unceremoniously into the yard.

Liam's face mirrors the car's fate—crushed. A lifetime of memories compressed into that small metal cube. Without a word, he walks toward it, bends down, and wrenches the VW and GTI badges from the wreckage.

He clutches them to his chest.

Patsy steps forward and tentatively raises a hand to his shoulder in an awkward attempt to comfort him. And that's when the song, blaring from the raised boombox, just as it reaches its soaring finale, begins skipping—rather unfortunately on the words *walkaway, walkaway, walkaway*. Patsy forces through a smile, but despite knowing she has royally fucked up many, many times before, she figures that killing Ol' Girl may be her biggest fuck up yet.

Liam shrugs her hand off and walks away, his grief transforming to anger with each and every step.

CHAPTER 11
SUNNY SCARBADOS

Liam marches down the empty back road, with his Converse scuffing against the tarmac. His face is screwed up, but the tears tell another story. There's purpose in his stride, an urgent momentum, but his eyes scan the horizon with growing panic.

The emotion that's been building since his car erupted in flames finally erupts from somewhere deep down in his chest.

"ARGGGHHHHHHHHH!"

His scream tears through the quiet countryside, scattering a few nearby birds from a hedgerow. It hangs in the air for a strangely long moment before dissipating into the breeze, leaving him emptier and more alone than ever.

Behind him, the blue lights of the police car flicker as it pulls up beside him. Through the back window, Patsy watches him, her face unreadable behind her sunglasses.

Despite marching with purpose, this is a man with nowhere to go. Story of his fucking life, he thinks, as he gets into the car.

Inside Rookie's police rover, the siblings sit as far apart as the back seat allows. The atmosphere between them is thick with unspoken blame. Liam's breathing is still ragged from his outburst, his jaw clenched tightly. Patsy has drawn her knees up to her chest, her bare feet tucked beneath her on the seat, grimy toes curled over the edge.

Each stares determinedly out of their respective window, watching meditatively as hedgerow after hedgerow, cottage after cottage, wall after wall gives way to garages, shops, blocks of flats and eventually the unmistakable seafront panorama of the great and mighty Scarborough promenade.

Ahead through the windscreen, the light changes as they approach the coast—brighter, more open. The summer sun catches on the sea, a bright shimmering sheet of blue stretching to the horizon. Neither sibling acknowledges the view, but both know they've arrived when the salt-laden air infiltrates the car, that distinctive seaside perfume of seaweed, deep-fried doughnuts and a childhood summer each has never forgotten. The scent presses against them, demanding a reconciliation with their memories that neither wants to face.

Somehow, they've made it to Scarborough after all. Not how they planned, not in the Digsby's faithful four-wheeled servant, but they're here—still together, hanging on by the finest of threads. And if that's not the perfect metaphor for family connection before we continue our tale, then quite frankly, I don't know what is.

𝄞

The police car pulls away from the kerb, leaving Liam and Patsy standing on Scarborough's promenade. Liam, looking completely deflated in his sky blue Adidas tracksuit and bucket hat, and Patsy, still barefoot and still in her silver dress, are not exactly dressed for the hottest day of the year at one of Britain's busiest beach resorts.

Rookie winds down her window and leans out to the pair as she drives past.

"Remember, take care of your memories—it's all we really have."

"Goodbye, philofficer," Patsy dryly calls after her, with a faint smile creeping from the corner of her mouth. She thought it was a funny joke, but only she, as Liam stares daggers at her.

The seaside resort is in full swing. It's hot, it's sandy and summer has found its stride, transforming Scarborough into a heaving, vibrant tribute to British holidaying at its iconic best. Somewhere nearby, the unmistakable chorus of "Wannabe" by the Spice Girls blares from a teenager's phone as a gaggle of tweens perform choreographed dance routines seeking false validation from schoolfriends, strangers, Russian bots and pedos (read: social media). Children slide down the Helter Skelter with plastic trays under their bums, while bored overworked donkeys plod along the beach with perplexed-looking children on their backs wondering if this is really the experience their parents hyped it up to be. It's Scarborough at the height of summer—could it be any more British? Oh wait, over there in the full heat of the sun by the bucket and spade concession selling overpriced plastic tat destined to break before teatime and eventually join the Great Pacific Garbage Patch as another statistic in Greenpeace's annual sea waste report, there's an old-geezer in a Union Jack string vest wearing socks with sandals, eating a pork pie while reading 'The Sun'—unaware of the dastardly seagull shitting on the roof of his Volvo estate while calculating its latest smash and grab mission—to grab his pork pie.

Liam tries to drink it all in, but the loss of his car has left him empty. After a moment, he sets his jaw with steely determination. "Right. Ice cream. Ice cream," he mutters, more to himself than to Patsy.

He starts walking, his pace quick and deliberate enough that maybe, just maybe, Patsy will get lost in the crowd. But Patsy hurries to catch up, her bare feet slapping against the pavement. By now she doesn't even feel the itchy sand, the dropped ice cream or whatever that shit is between her toes. She just strides through it all, every step seemingly a step closer to liberation or redemption… or whatever the fuck is in the big heavy trunk she's carrying.

"Where are you going?" she shouts.

"Ice cream," he calls back.

Liam's eyes scan each shopfront as they pass, looking for something in this familiar but changed landscape. Patsy trails behind, aware of the stares her dishevelled appearance attracts.

"What's to say it's even here anymore?" she asks, doubt creeping into her voice.

Liam doesn't slow down. "I can't. But mum will be."

"Look, Liam. Wait a sec. Wait." Patsy grabs his arm, forcing him to stop.

He turns to her impatiently. "What is it? We're already late."

Patsy shifts uncomfortably, focused more on trying to keep the box from slipping than to look him in his eyes. "Look. After this—no matter what happens. I'm going home. Back to London."

"Well yeah, obviously," Liam replies with a shrug.

"No." She looks up, her expression hardening. "I'm going back alone. This has all been… I'll get a train south. When you get the money. I'm not good for much, but I'm good for my word on this. I'll beg Minnie and Richard to bail me out… again." The last words hang between them, rather depressingly. For all their bickering and emotional baggage, he hadn't considered they'd actually part ways again, and the realisation that Patsy returning to her previous life would probably be tantamount to a death sentence dawns on him with terrifying clarity.

His mouth opens slightly, then closes again.

"Yep. Sure. No, yeah. For me too," he manages finally, rather anti-climactically.

Liam's already searching—the sky, the sea, the land—as if the answers to his questions might be written somewhere in the Scarborough landscape. His gaze settles on the red phone box about thirty metres away. It barely resembles the pristine memory he carries from 1996; now it looks more like a public toilet with its smashed windows, graffiti-covered surfaces and call-girl postcards scattered underfoot. A once proud and iconic obelisk, now a monument of decline and neglect.

Then his eyes shift just beyond it, and something changes in his expression.

"Oh look—we're here."

And indeed, despite everything, Liam has somehow navigated them directly to Itsy Bitsy Ice Cream Parlour. It's been upgraded over the years with a fresh coat of blue and white paint and a modern plasticky sign, but there's no mistaking it. It's the same place their mother bought them two gigantic sundaes all those years ago, where their joint childhood memories were frozen in time, much like the delicious ice cream they'd eaten that day. The place where their mother promised she would be waiting.

The charming wooden veranda doors that once welcomed the sea breeze and wafts of salt and vinegar are gone, replaced by fortress-like white uPVC double glazing. The bell above the door is gone too, replaced by an intrusive CCTV camera. Liam and Patsy scan the room, with hope fighting really fucking hard against the abject disappointment. The parlour that lives in their memory is barely recognisable. The once-vibrant mecca of ice cream has faded, like its Union Jack, hanging dog-eared in the corner next to some Black Friday bargain basement TV, mounted where the trusty old Sony once stood.

Liam gravitates toward a booth, the same one Patsy realises with some bemusement, where they sat in '96. Her fury over the dropped ice cream momentarily forgotten as their mother and the kind parlour owner chatted. The vinyl seats are cracked now, patched up with black gaffer tape, and the laminated menus signify the restaurant is now part of a chain.

"You remember this place?" Liam asks, sliding onto the bench.

Patsy snorts, settling across from him. "I remember you dropping my ice cream."

"And you covering me in squirty sauce. And ripping out my braids," he adds, rubbing his scalp at the phantom memory.

"God, I was such a Hellcat."

"Was?" Liam raises an eyebrow.

Patsy accepts the jibe with a wry smile. She glances around the shop, her expression growing serious again.

"So what now?"

Liam pats his pocket, feeling the thick wad of cash from the car sale. "Well, I have a thousand quid—so... sundaes?"

Before Patsy can respond, he's on his feet, making his way to the counter where a woman about his age dutifully wipes down the counters. Like the original owner, she's also of Greek heritage, but unlike the original owner, her accent is pure Scarborough.

"Good afternoon sir, what can I get ya?" she asks, wiping her hands on a tea towel.

Liam leans against the counter, studying the menu but stealing glances at her face and name tag. "Times change, huh, So-fia?" he says, before immediately regretting how vague that ice breaker sounds.

"Something not on the menu since yer last visit?" she replies with a half-smile that makes him stand a little straighter.

"What, from 1996?" he says with a cheeky smile, attempting to recover. "Place looks a bit different from my memory."

"Oh, yeah, parlour got bought by GlacierCo about twenty year ago, along wit' all other independents from Whitby down t'Skeggy." She shrugs slightly, her eyes lingering on his for a moment longer than necessary. "Well, used to be a family business but... they let me stay on," she admits, with equal parts sadness and pride.

Liam nods and shifts awkwardly on the counter, trying to look as casual as possible. Suddenly, he's aware of Patsy watching from the booth with her eyebrows raised.

Is he flirting with her? Patsy thinks, while internally cracking up as Liam dies of embarrassment.

"Well that's... Sundaes, sundaes, sundaes," he mutters, avoiding going any deeper. His fingers now drumming nervously on the counter.

Sofia points to the menu board hanging above them. Beneath it, Liam notices, is a wall covered in Polaroid photos—hundreds of them, customers spanning what looks like decades. Each one a perfect moment for a family at this former palace of joy. And there, front and centre, faded but unmistakable, is a familiar image that makes his heart skip more than looking into the piercing green eyes of the woman standing in front of him: Little Liam, Little Patsy, and Sally with Nikos from '96.

"That's me..." Liam blurts out, his finger hovering near the photo.

Sofia tilts her head. "What's a bit o' you then? Chocolate and Vanilla? Raspberry and—"

"No," Liam interrupts, pointing directly at the photo. "That's me. And my mum and sister, her over there."

Patsy awkwardly waves. *Hi-ya.*

Sofia turns to look at the wall. "Ahhh," she says, her voice dropping to a gentler register. "You're my mystery guests."

"Scuse me?"

Instead of answering, Sofia opens the till and carefully removes an envelope, which she hands to Liam. "This were dropped off, with a cheque for five hundred quid and instructions t'give t'couple, who look like—well, you both."

She pauses, studying Liam's face. "It was addressed to me dad. But he died some years ago. So I just popped it in t'till for safekeeping." She brushes a strand of curly hair from her face. "It obviously meant something important to someone, and well, I were always taught that if you can help—"

"—someone in their hour of need, then you should," Liam finishes her sentence, an echo from decades past.

"Exactly." Sofia smiles, with a hint of surprise in her eyes.

"I remember your dad," Liam says quietly.

Sofia's face broadens to a smile. She reaches up and carefully removes the Polaroid photo from the wall. The faded colours somehow add to the warm nostalgia of the image—four figures frozen in a moment of unexpected joy.

"He'd never let us take it down," she says, running her thumb over the edge. "He took so many photos of patrons over t'years, but this one always stayed front and centre. He said it were his first photo."

"I guess you always remember your first," Liam offers.

Sofia shakes her head. "No... it meant something more. That day changed his life." Her fingers trace the outline of her father's face in the photo. "He never explained t'details—he were good at that, Dad. Just stuck to the positives."

Liam looks around the shop, suddenly alert. "The person who gave this to you, where is she?"

"Oh no," Sofia replies, "it came by Royal Mail, hun."

Liam's shoulders slump, the hope visibly draining from his face. Suddenly he can't hear or see anything as his head begins swimming with incalculable questions. Well just one really—*where the fuck is she?*

"Hun? You okay hun?" Sofia frowns with concern. "Why don't you go sit down with your sis and I'll bring your sundaes over."

Liam manages a nod and walks back to Patsy, the envelope clutched tightly in his hand.

He tosses it onto the table, landing inches from Patsy's fingers.

"She's not bloody here," he says. "She's not bloody here."

Liam sinks into the booth, looking utterly deflated. Patsy, for her part, seems less surprised.

"Psssht. Why are you surprised?" she asks, eyeing the envelope but not touching it.

Liam looks up at her, his expression hardening. "Because. Because Patsy—I choose to see the wonder in life... instead of—"

"Instead of what?" she snipes back.

"A wall," he says solemnly.

And with that, he snatches up the envelope, tears it open, and pulls out the letter. His face remains carefully blank as he reads, eyes darting back and forth across the page.

"Read it out," Patsy demands. "What does it say?"

Liam's upper lip curls. He crumples the letter in his fist, rises from the booth, and hurries toward the door, rushing past Sofia who stands with two enormous sundaes balanced on a tray.

It's safe to say that times do indeed change. And with it so do memories, for this is not the same Itsy Bitsy they remembered and this is certainly not the reunion they expected.

Liam bolts out onto the promenade, his feet pounding against the worn concrete. This time, fighting every urge to stay put and bury her head in her hands... Patsy does the unthinkable—she chases after him.

"Liam! LIAM!" she shouts, but her voice is lost by the squawking seagulls and obnoxious rings and dings of the arcade next door.

Liam's chest heaves as he runs down the middle of the road, a reckless attempt at avoiding the throng of tourists by darting in and out of the moving cars. He runs faster and faster, his lungs burning. The sound of the arcade machines, children's laughter, and seagull cries all fade into a dull roar.

He sprints down Vincent Pier, past the fishermen, past the tourists, past the lighthouse and as the salt spray of the North Sea hits his face, he realises he has reached the end—there's nowhere left to run.

Liam doubles over, hands on his knees. The realisation crashes over him like the waves below: he's been chasing a phantom, this has been another goose chase. "She's not coming," he says over and over.

The remnants of his hope—the last thread connecting him to his mother—snaps.

His stomach lurches. He vomits violently over the edge of the pier, his body physically rejecting the bitter disappointment. His mixtape, his car, his home—all gone. And now this final blow.

Like the Great Pacific Garbage Patch floating somewhere out there in the ocean, collecting the discarded pieces of people's lives—plastic bottles, fishing nets, lost toys and VW badges—Liam's dreams are swirling together in a concentrated mass of broken promises. Everything he was and hoped to be, reduced to flotsam and jetsam.

Patsy catches up, breathless. She watches him retch again, his body convulsing as he grips the railing for dear life.

When he finally straightens, his face is ashen, eyes red-rimmed. "She's not here," he says, voice empty. "And she's not coming."

"What do you mean, she's not coming?" Patsy asks, with alarm creeping into her voice.

Liam doesn't answer with words. He just thrusts the crumpled letter into her hands and storms away, shoulders hunched against the world.

Patsy stands alone at the end of the pier, with the letter in hand, as the tide continues its relentless cycle beneath her feet. She attempts to read the letter, but like Liam, she can't focus. Instead, she just screams "BOLLOCKS," screws up the letter and shoves it in her pocket before following her brother back down the promenade.

She is still in her silver dress.

She is still barefoot.

She is still raging.

CHAPTER 12
THE REGAL (PART I)

A beautiful sandstone Victorian building, standing ten stories high, overlooks the beach and sea—a remnant of Scarborough's glory days. This is 'The Regal' hotel. Scarborough's finest. Surely a place Liam can't afford, yet he charges towards it anyway.

Fuck it. He thinks.

I'll treat myself. He thinks.

Liam storms in through the revolving doors, where his first glances at the lobby shatter his illusions immediately.

"Shame the inside doesn't look like the outside," he mumbles.

The faded grandeur has been stripped back to utilitarian basics—plastic chairs, a scratched and battered front desk, institutional green paint peeling from the walls. Refugees and homeless people loiter, bored more than anything else—the hotel is clearly an overflow for North Yorkshire's housing department. Patsy barrels in behind him.

"I'm not staying here," Patsy says, scrunching her nose at the musty smell of damp carpet.

"Too many common people for you?" Liam fires back.

"This is less than common."

"You got anywhere else to go?"

She doesn't—and she knows it. She slots in perfectly with the transient, lost and traumatised. Liam already knew this.

At the reception desk, Olivia looks up from her computer screen. Patsy was probably everything this woman aspired to be—expensively highlighted hair, immaculate makeup, designer clothes that don't quite fit the job description (or minimum wage salary). But her eyes are empty, her smile one-dimensional.

"Two rooms please," Liam says, fishing in his pocket for the money roll.

"Sorry sir, we're fully booked," Olivia says, her eyes flicking to Patsy with instant recognition, "but for a twin."

"How much?" Liam asks.

"That will be forty-five pounds, sir."

"Forty-five quid, for a hotel room?" Patsy interjects, unable to stop herself.

"Yes, madam." Olivia's tone cools.

"Where is it—in the kitchen?"

"The basement, madam, next to the kitchen."

Liam slaps a fifty quid note on the counter anyway, but Patsy can't contain her disdain and doubles down on eyeballing the black-mirrored enemy before her. Olivia studies Patsy's face more carefully, and her expression hardens.

"Problem, madam? If you're looking for somewhere with, perhaps, higher production value for your little videos—then the Royal Spa is a short walk away, or The Manor is just outside of town. But it's high season, and they are very nice hotels, so you and your... boyfriend here... may not be so lucky."

Patsy's face drains of colour. She feels like she's just been bitch-slapped. No, something worse. Humiliated. Silenced. Slut-shamed. She slides the key cards off the desk and slinks to the lift, her bare feet barely lifting a centimetre off the grimy floor.

"Enjoy your stay," Olivia calls after Liam with a knowing smirk.

A frosty silence fills the lift. Patsy stares at her warped reflection in the metal doors. The silver dress that cost more than most people's monthly salary now looks cheap and tawdry in the fluorescent light.

"What did she mean—high-end set value for your little videos?" Liam asks.

"I don't know—she must recognise me from 'Belsize Beaus'," Patsy mumbles, examining a chip in her nail polish.

"Well, that's TV—not videos. I've lived in a hole for the last fifteen years, but even I know 'videos' means like YouTube or TikTok or..."

Realisation dawns on his face. All the pieces suddenly fit.

"You didn't?"

She did.

A tear rolls down her cheek, carving a path through what remains of her makeup.

The Great Pacific Garbage Patch of Patsy's life—her digital footprint, her mistakes, her heartbreaks—none of it would ever truly disappear. It would just break down into smaller and smaller pixels, forever floating in that vast electronic ocean, waiting to wash up on some stranger's shore. Like it just did with Olivia. And just like it would in every bar, every club, every shop, every house and every other hotel she'd ever walk into and everywhere she'd ever go—for the rest of her goddamn life.

FUUUUCCCCKKKK IIIITTTT, she screams in her head.

The 'followers' she'd craved so desperately to attract now felt like a swarm of locusts, consuming everything real about her, leaving nothing but an empty husk. She'd sacrificed her dignity for the validation of strangers, chasing mini-dopamine hits while social media emperors in their glass towers turned her desperation for human connection into a commodity. And now, here she stood, next to the last and only real connection she had left in the world, and he was about to realise just how far she'd fallen. The carefully constructed image she'd maintained up till now—the successful reality TV star who'd simply moved on to other ventures—was crumbling around her.

Her stepmum had warned her about her reputation. Her father couldn't even look at her, let alone talk to her. And now Liam would know too. There is no distance left to run, nowhere left to hide.

DING. The lift doors open.

"Whatever," Patsy says, stepping out into the basement corridor, throwing her Ray-Bans on while marching towards the kitchen door, which, as it happens, is just where their shitty hotel room is.

The door swings open to reveal what Olivia had generously termed a "twin" room. And if things couldn't get worse for the siblings, it turns out that the "twin" room is not a twin at all, it's a shitty double with a bed that dips horribly in the middle due to years of hosting drunken one-night stands. The lone window sits high up in the ceiling, splattered with bird shit that filters the semblance of daylight into a grimy haze.

For Liam, this is home for the night and he quickly settles in. But for Patsy, this is the ninth circle of Hell. She quickly surveys the dismal offering and immediately tries to backtrack past Liam.

"I saw a park bench outside with better kerb appeal," she says, her posture stiffening with dismay.

Liam doesn't stop her.

"Suit yourself," he says with a shrug.

There's no judgement in his voice—just the same steady, reliable Liam who's managed to stay in one place all these years, in case they needed him. A human landmark you could set your watch by.

He slides the ornate trunk under the bed with the reverence of someone who understands what it means to preserve something important. His meagre belongings, however, are slung on the side table—his battered sky blue bucket hat, roll of money, the salvaged VW badges and some pocket fluff. His satchel with his dad's urn goes down with particular care. The scattered collection looks desperate on the chipped laminate—all that remains of a life paused for fifteen years.

Liam takes a deliberate sniff of his armpit, then catches Patsy's scent—three days of vodka sweats and something deeper, something more entrenched that he can't quite put his finger on. "I need a good cleansing," he says, heading for the bathroom.

The shower pipes groan to life. Patsy remains poised for escape, but something keeps her rooted. Maybe the knowledge that she truly has nowhere else to go. Maybe something else. She perches tentatively on the edge of the saggy bed, as if afraid it might swallow her whole.

"Least the shower pressure's good," Liam calls out over the rush of water. Then, after a beat: "Did you get paid a lot for them?"

Patsy tenses. "For what?"

"The videos."

"No," she quietly replies, her voice brittle. "I'm not talking about it."

"If not now, then when?"

"Never. And never with you."

The water continues to drum against the shower tiles, a steady rhythm that fills the silence between them.

"Then with who?" Liam's voice is gentle but persistent. "Doesn't look or sound like anyone else gives a shit about your wellbeing." He pauses before, "I mean, I'm a lone wolf—always have been. No surprise that I don't need to check in with anyone. But you—I mean, you're a TV celebrity with a day job—and you haven't felt the need to check in with anyone... or on anyone, for what, three days and counting?"

The truth of it makes Patsy squirm—the posh accent, the designer clothes, the carefully curated disdain—all of it stripped away in a dingy Scarborough hotel room. She's just like him. A lone wolf.

"I was in love," she finally admits. "Least, I thought I was. That's why I done it." Her accent slips to reveal the South London girl beneath. "And in my pursuit, or desperation, to be loved back, I let my guard down and let him film us..." She swallows hard. "It was classy."

The memory flashes in her consciousness—*Her five-star bedroom, tastefully decorated, tastefully lit, a camera set up*. Nothing like this squalid room with its sagging mattress and bird-shit skylight.

"I would have done anything for him to love me back," she continues. "Anything."

"Then what?"

"Then he dumped me and leaked the videos. I heard he got paid well for 'em." She stares at her hands, at her chipped and dirty fingernails.

"He was at the festival thing, the concert."

"Ohhh, that posh twat you were gonna deck."

"Yep."

"You should have told me, I would have decked him."

"Nah, you wouldn't," she says while snorting out a laugh.

"Nah, I wouldn't. But I would have let you deck him."

"Thanks. I think." She grimaces.

"I got fired from the show, lost lucrative contracts, my career died, and now I do the walk of shame everywhere I go."

Several beats of silence pass between them.

"Not with me you won't," he says matter-of-factly.

Patsy's lips twitch with just the hint of a smile.

In the shower, Liam considers that he has never really moved on, never risked anything. While in the bedroom, Patsy realises she has done everything to move forward, only to end up right back where she started.

"Hey, don't forget you're also an alcoholic," Liam adds, not unkindly. The kind of blunt observation that only someone who's known you since childhood can make.

"I prefer the term perma-toasted—wouldn't quite say it's full-blown alcoholism yet. But I do have a gambling problem. Problem is, I'm lousy at winning."

The shower switches off, and Patsy can hear Liam crashing around the tiny cubicle looking for his towel, before hearing the hair dryer turn on.

"Yep—no coming back from that," he says, but there's a lightness to his tone. No condemnation. Just acceptance of who she is, who they both are.

"Indeed." Patsy nods, her eyes distant. "Forwards. Got to keep moving forwards. Never backwards."

Her gaze drops to the crumpled letter clutched tightly in her hand.

Oh, fuck my life, Patsy thinks as she takes a deep breath while smoothing out the screwed up letter. Her mother's elegant handwriting, which she had long forgotten, swims before her eyes for a moment before coming into sharp focus:

To my dear children,

Welcome back to Scarborough. Or Scarbados, as the locals call it.

The postcard says it's stunning - well it is I suppose - with long sandy beaches - they have those - with some of the best family attractions in the country – well that's more of a stretch than the beach is long.

Great ice cream though, right? I trust you dug into a sweet sundae at Itsy Bitsy's?

Sally's voice fills Patsy's head, so vivid it's as if she's sitting right there at the end of the bed, chattering away with that familiar self-conscious humour.

Anyway, enough of the idle chit chat. You're probably wondering where I am right now.

Well, it's not great news.

I have been delayed in my recovery to meet with you in sunny Scarborough. Turns out chemo's a brutal bitch.

Patsy stiffens her shaking hand as she takes another deep breath.

I so wanted to go on this final trip with you, together, as we did in '96. Please forgive me, but you will have to complete the last leg of the journey together, without me.

There is so much I want to tell you and need to explain. But it will have to wait just a little longer.

The next lines hit like a punch to the gut:

Find me at Cape Wrath. The coordinates of which are: 58.62° N, 4.99° W.

A satnav won't find it. And if you get lost, just ask for the 'Edge of the World'.

Patsy's heart sinks. Another delay. Another journey. Another excuse. The familiar cold weight of disappointment settles in her chest. She cannot go on. The letter slips from her fingers and falls to the floor, where it lands face down on the grimy carpet, next to the ornate trunk.

The hotel room door clicks open. Then slams shut with a finality that shakes years of dust from the cheap hotel room light.

With hot shower steam still evaporating from his shoulders, Liam sticks his head out of the bathroom door, his hair now perfectly shaped.

"Patsy?"

Silence. He shrugs, secures his towel and lays on the bed—which promptly gives up whatever structural integrity it was pretending to have. The middle finally collapses, forming a perfect V-shaped valley around him.

"Brilliant," he mutters to himself. But our Liam, ever the optimist, makes the best of it anyway, shutting his eyes for a nap, humming to "Wonderwall" along with the sound of clattering dishes he can hear through the paper-thin walls.

On the side table sits his satchel, his bucket hat, his car badges and the pocket fluff. But the money roll is gone. Along with any hope of making it to Cape Wrath.

𝄞

The door to the basement room clicks shut, but doesn't block out the sound of Liam calling after her. "Patsy?" she hears, followed by the bed finally giving way with a loud clunk as Liam collapses onto it. "Brilliant," she hears him mutter. She leans against the door, her breathing fast and shallow as a wave of claustrophobia washes over her. Through the thin walls, she can hear the kitchen plates clanking and clinging, but then something else catches her attention. Liam's gentle humming of "Wonderwall," slightly off-key but earnest. The tune stops her dead —the same melody she hummed to ease his pain and suffering in that grotty caravan park toilet is still his way of dealing with stress.

For a moment, she almost turns back, almost opens the door to face whatever comes next together. The humming continues, so hopeful, so trusting. She can't bear to be there when that hope inevitably shatters, can't watch his face when they discover the trunk is empty, or worse—filled with nothing but more broken promises.

Time does that thing again—stretching and contracting like a snapped elastic band. The last three days feel like thirty years in reverse. She glances at her watch—forgetting that the bloody thing hasn't worked for years. Another inheritance from Sally that fails to deliver, yet she wears it anyway.

A memory flits through her mind: *she's looking at her mother's watch, fascinated by the second hand's relentless unstoppable march.* "Will mine go as fast as yours one day, Mummy?" *Sally laughs, that genuine hearty motherly laugh that became rarer as the years progressed,* "Yeah baby maybe. Time moves differently for everyone, my love. You'll understand when you're a wee bit older."

Well, now she's much older and feels she understands bugger all. That watch might be broken, but time hasn't stopped moving; it's left her behind. That's our Patsy though. Never able to see the positive, never able to take pride in the smallest of wins. The eternal self-critic.

The lift doors open, and Patsy steps in, jabbing at the button for the ground floor. Her reflection in the mirrored wall is a complete fucking horror show—mascara-smudged eyes, dirty silver dress, and worst of all, still fucking barefoot. If anyone from 'Belsize Beaus' could see her now, she'd never live it down. Or maybe she'd just scratch their putrid little eyeballs out—she's indifferent really because well let's face it, there's not much of a reputation left to protect.

The muffled ding of the lift arriving on the ground floor brings her back into the room. The lobby's faded grandeur—all peeling wallpaper and worn carpet—feels appropriate for her current state. She's hit the bottom before, but this is a new low. No clothes, no makeup, no phone, no shoes, and her only ally in the world is downstairs napping in the country's cheapest and shittiest hotel room.

Patsy spots the lobby toilets and makes a beeline for them. If she's going to think clearly, she needs to at least feel somewhat human again.

The ladies' toilet is mercifully empty. Fluorescent lights flicker and buzz overhead as Patsy surveys herself in the full-length mirror.

Christ, she looks rough. Like she's just stepped off the set of a Prodigy video. The silver dress that had seemed so glamorous in London is filthy now, streaked with dirt and creased beyond hope. Her feet are black with grime.

Oh what I wouldn't do for a fifteen-quid bergamot latte right now, she thinks. Oh wait, did I dream that? Fuck. Where am I? This is a dream... I haven't woken up. I haven't woken up. She tries to convince herself by slapping her cheek, before facing up to reality.

She turns on the tap and tests the water. Lukewarm, but it'll do. She grabs a handful of scratchy green paper towels, dampens them, and begins wiping down her arms and face. She squeezes out a dollop of pink goop from the soap dispenser. It smells vaguely of artificial cherries, but it's better than whatever smells are emanating from her crevices.

Oh this feels good, she thinks.

Then: You dumb filthy bitch, this is only what you deserve.

Lifting one foot into the sink, she winces as the water hits a cut she hadn't noticed before. Blood and dirt swirl down the drain as she scrubs, the physical pain a welcome distraction from the chaos and degrading internal monologue going on in her head.

As she works, she begins to hum, then sing quietly. Her voice echoes off the tiled walls as she works her way through the familiar melody of "Wonderwall." Though this time the moment feels... empty.

The memory ambushes her without warning—*it's her, humming the same tune while washing Little Liam's hair in that grotty caravan park toilet. Him sitting there, trusting her, while she gently untangles his braids.* Before everything went to shit. Before they were torn apart.

Shut up. Shut up. Stupid bitch. Cunt. I hate you. I hate you. You're nothing.

Tears spring to her eyes, and before she can stop it, a sob escapes her throat. Then another. And another, until she's crying properly, one foot still in the sink, shoulders shaking.

The door swings open, and a cleaner—fifties, perpetually exhausted, working herself to a shorter life expectancy—pushes in her cart of supplies. She takes one look at Patsy, barefoot and crying at the sink, and simply sighs.

"Don't mind me, love," she says flatly, giving Patsy a clean white towel from her cart. "Seen worse."

Without another word, she begins mopping the floor around Patsy, the sharp smell of bleach cutting through the air.

"Sorry," Patsy manages between sobs. "I'll be out of your way in a minute."

The cleaner shrugs. "Take your time. Clock's ticking either way."

Patsy uses the fresh towel to wipe her eyes clean, which streaks mascara across her cheek. The cleaner's right though, time marches on whether she's sobbing in a toilet or not.

She finishes washing her feet and dries them with the towel. There's nothing to be done about shoes, but at least the dirt is gone. She splashes water on her face one last time, straightens her silver dress as best she can, and scrapes her clean wet hair into a nice tight bun using a hair bobble found by the sink. And you know what, she looks clean. Fresh. Without the makeup to hide behind, her face is raw, real with a visible black eye and delicate freckles—all the things 'Belsize Beaus' taught her to cover up. For the first time in years, she looks like herself. She hands the towel back to the cleaner, with a fifty-pound note from Liam's cash roll wedged inside, and strides out with as much dignity as a barefoot, puffy-eyed woman in a raggedy designer dress can muster.

Patsy enters the lobby as a new woman—or at least, a cleaner version of the old one. The lift is just across the lobby, a straight shot back to Liam and their unfinished quest. She takes three determined steps toward it before the muffled sounds of music drift from the hotel bar. Just a beat, just enough to catch her ear.

She pauses, her newly cleaned feet feeling every fibre of the worn carpet beneath them.

Just a glass of water, she tells herself. *Just a minute to think.*

The bar is dim and depressing in the way that only sad chain hotel bars can be. Faded photographs of local landmarks line wood-panelled walls. The jukebox in the corner plays something vaguely familiar—one of those '80s songs that everyone knows but no one remembers the name of.

The elderly barman raises an eyebrow at her arrival—don't get many pretty young ladies in here—he quietly thinks to himself, but he says nothing as she slides onto a stool.

"Glass of your finest aqua, please kind sir," she says, her throat still raw from crying.

As he fills a glass from the tap, Patsy surveys the room. Almost empty, save for a couple of businessmen types in the corner, nursing pints and casting occasional leery glances her way.

The barman slides the water across to her.

"You don't happen to know the time of the last train to London?"

"Aye, little miss. Quarter past eight. Station's just round t'corner."

"Thanks," she says, taking a sip. It tastes metallic and warm. Disgusting. No wonder thirty per cent of British people are high-functioning alcoholics. Or is it fifty per cent she thinks.

"Anything else?" he asks, already turning away.

A voice at the back of her head whispers: You've cleaned yourself up. You've made a decision. The train station's just round the corner. You can get the last train out of dodge. Reward yourself. One drink for the road. Just one. You're not an alcoholic, you're just perma-toasted, and you can stop whenever you want. You just choose not to.

The same voice that's been her downfall a hundred times before.

"Actually," Patsy says, setting down the water. "Double vodka, neat."

The barman doesn't even blink as he reaches for a bottle and pours. The clear liquid catches the dim light, drawing her gaze.

"Rough day?" he asks, sliding the drink toward her.

"Rough life," she replies, taking the first sip. The familiar burn is comforting, the warmth spreading through her empty stomach like wildfire.

One drink becomes two.

Two drinks become three.

The clock above the bar reads 8:15—an hour since she'd arrived, an hour of her life dissolved in vodka. The elderly barman has warmed to her, wiping down the same spot on the bar over and over as they chat about nothing in particular.

She downs the rest of her third drink and signals for a fourth.

"Missed yer train then. Last train south's just after ten," he tells her, "but it only goes as far as York. You'd have to stay the night there to catch the London connection in t'morning," he says, before heading into the store cupboard.

Patsy nods, calculating times and distances in her increasingly fuzzy mind. Time seems to be closing in around her, her options narrowing with each tick and tock of the grandfather clock in the corner of the bar.

She discreetly borrows the vodka bottle and free pours herself another drink. And by the time she's halfway through it, the two men from the same corner have migrated closer, taking up stools just one away from hers. Their conversation grows progressively louder, glances in her direction more frequent, emboldened by her increasingly unguarded smiles and the growing pile of empty glasses in front of her.

"I know you," says the bolder of the two, a man in his forties with a wedding ring tan line and a cheap polyester shirt stretched across his belly. "You were on that show, weren't you? Belsize something?"

Patsy studies him through the pleasant haze of vodka. Time seems to move differently now—the clock hands spinning too fast and too slow all at once.

"Might've been," she says, reaching for her glass.

"Yeah, yeah," the man continues, nudging his mate. "'Belsize Beaus'. You were the posh one who..." He trails off, suddenly aware he might be crossing a line.

The second man, much sweatier, emboldened by his friend's recognition, leans closer. "Got any more videos coming out?" he asks with a smirk that makes Patsy's skin crawl.

She notices the sweaty man's packet of cigarettes on the bar in front of him. Without asking, she reaches over and extracts a fag, placing it between her lips. "Got a light?" she asks, her voice dropping to a dangerous octave.

The sweaty guy fumbles with his lighter, eager to please. The flame illuminates Patsy's face momentarily, throwing her features into sharp focus. She inhales deeply, feeling the smoke fill her lungs—a secondary poison to complement the vodka.

The men get caught in a gaze, momentarily hypnotised like a cobra listening to its master's flute. Only, the cobra is the one doing the hypnotising right now.

"So," the rotund man continues, "you really are her then?"

Patsy takes a mouthful of vodka, letting it sit on her tongue for a moment.

"Don't get many celebrities…"

Then, in one swift motion, she sprays her mouthful of vodka into their faces.

"FUCK OFF, NORTHERN MONKEYS," she spits, her voice carrying across the empty bar and through the lobby.

Covered in spat out vodka, the men retreat, muttering swear words and slurs, as Patsy returns to her cigarette, taking another deep drag. The momentary victory feels good—better than the vodka, even. For a second, she's powerful again.

That is, until Olivia from reception appears at her elbow, her resting bitch-face even more disagreeable in the bar's unflattering light. Patsy takes a minute to visually digest her in more detail—mid-twenties with that fierce look of someone who thinks fame and money equals value.

"You can't smoke in here," she says with the satisfaction of a mere mortal catching out a disgraced celebrity.

Patsy looks up to meet her gaze, and a slow smile spreads across her face. In this moment she's the clean strong woman from the bathroom mirror, not the snivelling wreck crying over the sink; she is invincible.

"Oh really?" she musters, clearly annoyed at this lesser being. "Now there's me reasoning that physics says otherwise."

She holds up the cigarette theatrically. "See, I put this here," she demonstrates, placing it between her lips, "I drag," she inhales deeply, the ember glowing bright orange, "and I puff."

The cloud of smoke hits Olivia square in the face, making her sputter and step back.

"What I think you meant to say is," Patsy continues, forcing out her most privileged and condescending accent, "You are not allowed to smoke in here."

Olivia's face reddens, her eyes narrowing. "That's what I meant."

"What you gonna do about it?" Patsy challenges, slipping seamlessly into her South London accent.

Olivia leans in closer, her voice dropping to a whisper. "I watched every episode, you know. I rooted for you. Had the same haircut and everything. Look how you've ended up."

For Patsy, it's like looking into a funhouse mirror—seeing her younger self, the girl who once watched reality TV and confused their world of fame with one of escape, now sneering at what she's become.

Without warning, Patsy grabs Olivia's wrist. She squeezes, twists and pulls her close. "You don't know the first fucking thing about me," Patsy whispers menacingly.

"SECURITY!" Olivia yelps, her voice suddenly shrill. "Get her out of here!"

The opening beats of "Tubthumping" blast from the jukebox—the sweaty bloke's idea of a joke—as two beefy security guards appear, grabbing Patsy under the arms. She wriggles, managing to slide through their grip just long enough to snatch her vodka from the bar and down it in one defiant gulp before they recapture her.

As they drag her toward the exit, that false confidence begins to ebb as reality quickly seeps back in through the cracks of her armour. But despite her untimely ejection from the hotel, swimming around somewhere within the ten measures of vodka and all the false bravado, a decision crystallises with brutal clarity.

Sober Patsy = weak Patsy.

That's it Patsy. Stay positive love.

CHAPTER 13
THE REGAL (PART II)

But that's the problem with our Little Pats, isn't it? She can't stay positive.

The security guards deposit Patsy unceremoniously onto the pavement outside The Regal hotel. She lands with a thud, and what little dignity she had left now remains in the no man's land between the bar and the doorway.

"Consider yourself checked out," Olivia calls after her with smug satisfaction.

Patsy staggers to her feet, the silver dress catching the streetlight as she sways. The fabric clings to her awkwardly while the vodka in her system causes the world to tilt at peculiar angles.

"Goddamn! What's a girl gotta do to get a little action 'round here?" she shouts at no one in particular, the words slurring into one another.

The Scarborough night air hits her like a wet slap. Not the refreshing sort that sometimes sobers one up, but the dizzying kind that makes everything worse. Big blasts of sea air enter her lungs pushing oxygen into her bloodstream enhancing the effects of the alcohol while the cool sea breeze elevates her heart rate only causing the alcohol to expedite its way to her brain. Less scientifically put, she's wasted. She stumbles away from the hotel, each step a negotiation between her addled brain and increasingly uncooperative bare feet.

The cobblestones of Scarborough's old town are beautiful in daylight, quaint even. At night, to a drunk woman without shoes, they're fucking torture. Patsy stumbles along with as much false bravado as she can muster, her bare feet finding every uneven surface, every sharp edge. Then—vwoooom—her world tilts sideways and she's suddenly on her arse, staring up at the night sky, wondering how she got there.

A passerby, some Good Samaritan type in her seventies, bends down to help her up. Her little old hand extends out, and as the old woman pulls Patsy to her feet, Patsy's free fingers close around the baguette peeking out of the old lady's breadbag. Without a word of thanks, she grabs the baguette and legs it, disappearing into the night, leaving the bewildered old girl calling after her—"That's my dinner," she decries.

"Well a girl's gotta eat," Patsy mumbles to herself as she takes a big chomp of the slightly stale, but hearty baguette.

𝄞

Back at The Regal, Liam sleeps soundly, oblivious to the chaos his sister is causing up at street level. The bed, broken beyond repair, cradles his body like a baby in his mother's arms. His face shows the peaceful expression of a man without a care in the world.

That's it Liam, stay put mate. But that's the problem with our LeeLee, isn't it? Waiting eternal for life to happen.

Peace and bliss. Before the door bursts open with the two burly security guards barging in followed by Olivia, her face a mask of righteousness.

Liam wakes with a start, his body jerking upright. "Animal Nitrate," he blurts out, the words of a Suede song tumbling from his lips before his brain can engage what the fuck is going on.

Olivia's eyes widen at the broken bed and at Liam, in only his towel—her worst suspicions confirmed. "Huh, you perverted bastards," she says with disgust. "Grab your things, you're out."

"What the, why? What's going on?" Liam asks, his voice rough with sleep.

"You and your depraved girlfriend are outta here," Olivia sneers.

Reality crashes in on Liam. He shoots a glance around the room, noting Patsy's absence, the open door, the hostile faces. "Ohhhh Patsy!" he groans, putting it all together.

Now frantic, he throws on his clothes, his movements clumsy and rushed. His hand reaches for the cash roll on the bedside table, the small fortune from selling his car, their last ticket to Scotland, their last chance to cash in their inheritance—gone.

"Bugger," he mutters, a word that's woefully inadequate for the magnitude of this disaster. But then this is Liam. A man who never shouts to get his point across, a man who buries everything so deep, it would take a thousand years of boring into his soul to find out his true feelings.

Before he can fully process the implications, the security guards manhandle him toward the door. He struggles against their grip, but it's futile. It's happening again—another eviction, another home lost.

As the door slams shut behind them, the room remains vacant, but for the ornate trunk beneath the broken bed, forgotten in the chaos. Inside it, somewhere within its steel confines, sits their inheritance—and the key to their future.

The security guards drag Liam through the hotel lobby by his tiptoes. The long-term residents—a mix of homeless families placed by the council and asylum seekers waiting on decisions—look up briefly from their mobile phones. Their expressions show a flicker of recognition, not of Liam specifically, but of the situation. Another eviction. They return to their screens, where headlines about climate change, immigration policies, global conflicts, and housing crises reduce their traumas to cheap political talking points.

But Liam's vexed. Not just annoyed or put out, but properly vexed. Maybe for the first time since—well, since he was a child. His usual passive acceptance has given way to something else. Something hotter.

"Bugger. Bugger. Bugger," he repeats, each iteration growing more forceful than the last.

As the guards prepare to deposit him onto the street like yesterday's rubbish, Liam digs in his heels. His crusty old Converse trainers squeak against the polished floor.

"WAIT," he shouts, surprising even himself with the volume. The guards pause, momentarily thrown by this unexpected resistance. "Where would a minor celebrity alcoholic gambler go for a good time round 'ere?" he asks earnestly.

Olivia draws a smirk across her lips. She savours the moment, this tiny power she holds by remaining silent.

"Please, she might hurt herself," Liam begs.

And in that moment, beneath all the jealousy and desperate dreaming, something simpler surfaces. An unexpected kindness. "Flash Bux Casino," she says finally. "Down by the pier."

The guards release him with a final shove, and Liam stumbles onto the pavement. The night air hits him, cool and bracing. He steadies himself, his mind racing. What he needs now is a plan. A proper plan. And a soundtrack to go with it.

From a nearby pub, the unmistakable opening chords of "The Riverboat Song" by Ocean Colour Scene spill out into the street. That distinctive, driving guitar riff that feels like a call to action. Like the start of something important.

Outside the pub, a lad in a souped-up orange Corsa idles at the lights, London-grime music blares from his rolled-down windows. He spots Liam in his dishevelled state and gives him a dismissive once-over. For a second, Liam sees himself reflected in those judgemental eyes—another wasteman, going nowhere, with nothing to show for himself.

But not tonight. Tonight, he's got a sister to find. Money to recover. A journey to save.

The music seems to sync with his heartbeat, with his footsteps as he sets off toward the pier. He lets it fill his head, the soundtrack to his mission: Du du-du, DA-da. Du du-du, DA-da. Du du-du, DA-da. Du du-du, DA-da…

With Ocean Colour Scene in his ears and determination in his veins, Liam Digsby, for once in his life, is moving forwards of his own will, rather than waiting for the world to carry him along.

𝄞

Patsy hunches over the sink in the ladies' toilet, squinting at her reflection in the mirror. The warm soft lighting helps to hide every ring of exhaustion on her clean, fresh and youthful face. She studies herself. She looks thinner, feels thinner. Her silver dress hangs limply on her frame, but in this mood light it comes alive, shimmering like new.

The half-chewed baguette now sticks out from the vacant toilet bowl farthest to the left. A posh-looking woman in her sixties, not too dissimilar looking to her step-mum, Minnie, exits a cubicle and places her designer handbag on the counter. She begins washing her hands while smiling vacantly at Patsy. Patsy's eyes flick to the woman, then back to her own reflection with an equally vacuous smile. When the woman turns away to grab a paper towel, Patsy's hand darts into the open handbag in one fluid motion. She extracts a lipstick, eyeliner and a compact without the woman noticing.

Holding eye contact all the way, the woman leaves with another smile, and Patsy gets to work.

Oooo Dior Rouge, a girl's best friend, she thinks, as she applies the stolen lipstick with surprising precision given her drunken state. As she applies the lippy, the crimson colour takes hold, along with the familiar numbing of indifference. Her mask is slipping back into place, and she welcomes it. Next, she dusts her cheeks with La Mer pressed powder, softening the worst of the last few days' damage and covers as much of her black eye as possible. Then comes the Chanel mascara—each stroke thickening her lashes, each layer hiding her behind another coat of steel.

Than, a glance down at her bare feet.

"Fuck it," she mutters to her reflection while fanning herself with the money roll. I've got this far without them. I don't need shoes to turn this into ten grand.

She stares at her rejuvenated self in the mirror, but she doesn't recognise the reflection of the woman looking back anymore. No matter, she can't have people seeing the desperation behind her eyes. So she shakes out her hair, pulls down her fake Ray-Bans, puffs the air out of her cheeks and saunters through the door to the casino floor—where she thinks, right then at least, is where she belongs.

Flash Bux Casino gleams with an artificial glamour that's truly impressive by Scarborough standards. In the same way that Blackpool Tower is impressive… if you've never seen the Eiffel Tower. This isn't Las Vegas—it's not even Blackpool—but it tries its hardest with the myriad of mirrored surfaces and countless flashing lights.

The clientele match the setting—local glam types flashing smiles with blindingly white "Turkey teeth" while pissing away their wages. The sort who consider themselves proper posh because they holiday in Marbella once a year and know which fork to use with seafood. Well, they are posh, just not Minnie posh. Who's old posh. Real posh.

Patsy, looking reborn, spots "them" as she arrives at the roulette table. Them—the kind of people who'd step over a homeless person, to blow their wages on red or black. She's not sure if she's better or worse than them—she's about to gamble away someone else's money, after all—but at least she knows what she is. She gives her head a small shake. Not the time for social commentary. Not when there's tequila to be had. Which she slams down hard with a wince.

A few tequila shot glasses sit in front of her. Patsy snorts salt off her fist, then slams another shot down, followed by a bite of lime. She's clearly having fun. If she drinks vodka to forget, tequila is what she drinks to feel alive.

A waitress brings over another glass, and Patsy immediately signals for another. The alcohol burns through her veins, a familiar fire that both soothes and excites. This is her natural habitat—the place where consequences can always be put off until tomorrow.

The sound of the roulette wheel clicks to a stop followed by cheers and a loud "YES!"

Patsy throws her arms up as the croupier adds more chips to her already impressive pile. Five grands worth, give or take. The chips form an unstable mountain that she hasn't bothered to organise—well, why would she? Despite being evicted, slut-shamed in front of her brother and rejected by her mum (again), she's five grand up and…

"Mumma's on a roll," she announces to no one in particular, but loud enough for everyone to hear.

Her voice attracts some rizzless Joe, the sort of bloke who still wears jeans with a suit jacket and uses too much hair gel. He slides up beside her, his cheap aftershave announcing his arrival way before he does. On any other day this guy ain't getting a look in, but this ain't any old day, this is Patsy at her best, or worst—depends on your perception I suppose. And Patsy's perception right now, is all kinds of fucked up.

"You know you're drop-dead gorgeous," he says, breathing beer fumes onto her neck.

Patsy turns to assess him. Not her usual type, but it's been a day, and validation is validation, right? "Oh yeah?" she says just before she grabs him by the collar to pull him in for a snog. It's messy, public, and exactly what she needs right now—proof that she still exists, that someone wants her, even if it's just some rizzless Joe with aspirations way beyond his means.

When they break apart, rizzless Joe leans in real close. "Maybe after this we go back to yours and whack out the iPhones?"

The words wash over Patsy in a cold wave of shame. The familiar suggestion—phones, recording, exposure. All the humiliation comes flooding back. She pulls away as if burned. Her face shifts, the drunken playfulness gone, replaced by something harder. Her posture straightens, her mind suddenly crystal clear despite the alcohol.

"Put it all on black," she says to the croupier, her voice steady.

The croupier, a woman in her fifties who's seen it all before, raises an eyebrow. "All of it, madam? Are you sure? You're well up."

Without hesitation, Patsy slides the entire disorganised mountain of chips across the table. Her fingers linger on them for just a moment —not with regret, but with acknowledgement of what she's doing.

"And another round for my friends," she announces, plucking a £200 chip from the pile and handing it to the waitress. "Keep the change," Patsy says, feeling that karma is on her side tonight. The waitress's exhausted face momentarily brightens. She has deep circles under her eyes and a wedding ring that's been twisted anxiously all night. Patsy recognises a kindred spirit when she sees one. The waitress mouths a silent "thank you" before hurrying away, and Patsy feels a flicker of genuine warmth—she believes—it's now or never.

"Okay, all on black. Ready?" says the croupier.

"Actually, what wins me the most money, toots?"

"Any single number, madam. Five thousand will win you a hundred and eighty thousand pounds."

Patsy looks to the heavens, and after a beat, she commands, "Zero."

Gasps ripple around the table, which by now is joined by the casino manager who hovers behind with a couple of his security guys. Standard operating procedure for any high roller. The manager nods his approval to the croupier who picks up the ball.

The pile of chips sit on zero. A point of no return. This is what she wants—to win it all, to prove that Patsy Digs—Fortescue-Smythe can make it on her own. No need for her "inheritance." No need to see Liam again. Just Patsy... and a hundred and eighty thousand big ones.

The wheel awaits.

The croupier spins the wheel elegantly—not too fast, not too slow—just right for maximum tension. This woman's a pro. She knows how to hypnotise the room with her wheel of fortune, or doom, depending on your perspective at the time.

The room holds its breath.

By now, the table is packed with onlookers. Everyone in the casino has momentarily stopped their own selfish pursuits to gawp at the beautiful barefoot girl in the silver dress who's bet it all. Middle managers and weekend warriors hungry for a spectacle that isn't their own dreary lives. Win or lose, they are in for a show and a story to tell.

Patsy now feels the weight of her gamble. A brief moment of clarity cuts through the alcohol haze. She goes to grab a drink, but she's dry, the table is clean, so she grabs rizzless Joe's beer and chugs the bottle, belching loudly as she finishes.

Everyone applauds and she gives them a bow. The Queen of Chaos, taking her curtain call.

𝄞

For Liam, everything happens in fractions.

He bursts through the casino entrance, assaulted by lights and sounds designed to disorient. The place is a labyrinth of noise and flashing colours—a sensory overload meant to separate punters from rational thought.

He notices a crowd gathered at the far end, people standing on their tiptoes, craning their necks.

Time slows.

His heart recognises what's going on before his brain does.

"Patsy," he sighs.

He jumps onto a nearby Blackjack table, ignoring the dealer's protests. From this vantage point, he sees Patsy's moment of bliss, in horrific clarity:

There's Patsy, front and centre, commanding the roulette table, surrounded by leeches and losers.

There's a mountain of chips, all on zero.

There's a roulette wheel, spinning hypnotically.

There's the croupier, who looks Patsy in the eye and lets the ball fly.

"PATSY - NO!"

Every head turns. The dizzying chaos pauses as they take in the sight of a six-foot bloke in a sky blue Adidas tracksuit standing on the Blackjack table, bucket hat askew, eyes wide with panic. The casino manager stops his security from interjecting; the place is too packed and the stakes too high.

For Patsy, everything happens too fast.

The wheel is spinning. The ball is already dancing along the rim. And suddenly, there's Liam, again. *What is it with this guy?*

Then—time speeds up—clickclickclickclickclickclickclick goes the sound of the ball hitting the frets of the wheel.

"NO-WAIT!" Patsy screams at the croupier, the alcohol fog lifting just enough for panic to set in. But it's too late.

"The ball is in play, madam," says the casino manager as he places a firm hand on Patsy's shoulder. Ensuring she stays put to win big or lose everything... no in-between, no stopping, no going back.

For the croupier, she's seen it all before. The desperate bets. The last-minute regrets. The dramatic interventions. Twenty years in Scarborough casinos, and human nature never changes. For her, time is constant. Time helps to pay the mortgage, which she remembers she has extra to pay this month because the Bank of England has whacked up the interest rate. And here's some impossibly beautiful girl in a gorgeous dress worth more than her salary gambling five grand. And it's only Monday. Where's my £200 tip? she quietly thinks.

The wheel spins at its regular pace.

The ball bounces precisely as physics dictates.

The wheel clicks, each sound marking another step toward the inevitable, like the inexorable ticking of a clock that can't be turned back.

Click. Click. Click. Click.

"TELL ME YOU DIDN'T BET IT ALL?" Liam shouts, his voice cracking with desperation.

"I BET IT ALL!" Patsy cries back, no longer able to watch, hands covering her face, fingers splayed just enough that she can peek through if her courage returns.

The ball pings back and forth, defying gravity for what seems like an eternity. Time stretches and compresses all at once. The universe narrows to the size of a roulette wheel.

But if there's one thing our Liam has learned along this journey, it's that time waits for no man.

He sees only one option.

With a primal shout that comes from somewhere deep and previously untapped, Liam launches himself across the room in a desperate dive. His body arcs through the air in perfect slow motion, arms outstretched like a superhero making his last stand. He flies over the crowd with his hand stretched out and crashes onto the roulette table, sending chips flying in a multicoloured explosion.

The ball, still bouncing, still deciding their fate, makes one final ping—

And lands squarely in Liam's palm.

Done it. Over. Saved the day, he thinks.

For one frozen moment, triumph flashes across his face.

He will get to Scotland. He will see his mother before she dies.

Then reality descends in the form of security personnel, who materialise from nowhere and pile onto Liam like rugby players in a scrum. He disappears beneath a mass of black suits and earpieces, his yelps of protest muffled by the weight of professional enforcers.

"Don't hurt him, HE'S MY BROTHER!" Patsy shrieks, suddenly protective, suddenly sober.

The croupier's voice cuts through the chaos, cool and final: "Player forfeits—deliberate obstruction of the ball." She attempts to gather as many of the chips as possible, but Liam and the security team are doing a great job of making this nigh on impossible.

The casino manager, his hand still on Patsy's shoulder, has had quite enough of the Queen of Chaos. "Time to go, miss."

"GET YOUR FILTHY HAND OFF ME, PIG!" Patsy screams at the top of her lungs.

And that's exactly when the chaos explodes. The once-orderly crowd smells opportunity. A chap in a kilt, probably not Scottish, probably on a stag do, lunges for a stack of chips. A woman in pink follows suit, grabbing a handful. Suddenly, everyone's a thief, snatching at the scattered chips as the security team struggles to maintain order while pinning Liam down.

"I'm really sorry, I'm so sorry," Patsy pleads to the casino manager. Her instant change of tack takes him by surprise. Even so, he knows he has a job to do and steers Patsy firmly towards the exit.

"Please, just one more spin! I can win it all back."

"Your brother broke the rules. House policy."

Through the melee, Liam catches a glimpse of Patsy being escorted out, her silver dress flashing in the ceiling mirrors. Security guards pull him to his feet, with his arms twisted behind his back. "Get off me, you don't understand." But his protests are cut short by a jerk of his arms as he is dragged towards the doors. This time though, instead of pleading, he fixates on his true enemy, Patsy—who he can now see through the glass doors crying on the pavement.

Patsy finds herself standing barefoot in the cold. The waitress she'd tipped is leaning against the wall, with a cigarette glowing between her fingers.

"You all right, love?" the waitress asks.

"The chip," Patsy says desperately. "That chip I gave you. I need it back."

The waitress looks at her with tired eyes. "Already cashed it and paid the lecky with it. But here—" She shrugs, a small gesture that speaks volumes. This is routine for a woman who has seen generosity turn on a dime when the stakes get raised. The best thing she can do, without lying, is to actually spend the money before they ever ask for it back. She extends a loose ciggy from the pack. "Least I can do."

Patsy takes one, and the waitress lights it for her. She inhales deeply, the smoke burning her lungs in a familiar, comforting way.

The casino doors burst open, and two security guards throw Liam out onto the pavement. He stumbles, nearly falls, then straightens himself with as much dignity as he can muster. His bag containing his spare clothes and his dad's urn comes next, which he catches, luckily just before it hits the ground.

Blood trickles from his nose and his bucket hat is gone. But it's the look in his eyes that tells Patsy everything—the look of someone who just stepped across a line he never knew was inside him. Patsy knows this look well, she's never seen it in her brother. Well maybe once...

For a moment, they stand there, these two broken pieces of the same puzzle, staring at each other as the neon lights flash around them. The waitress senses the fireworks display that is about to commence. She stubs out her fag, flicks it in the bin and makes herself scarce.

The full weight of failure crushes the siblings as they stand eye to eye. The neon lights that had seemed so inviting to Patsy earlier now cast a harsh, accusatory glow over her. This is a spotlight she really doesn't want to be in right now.

"That was everything we had," Liam says, his voice spitting with a rage he's spent years suppressing. "And now we're both homeless, and this journey is dead. How are we gonna see Mum now?"

And that's when Patsy doubles over, retching tequila shots and chunks of French baguette all over the casino steps. "Go easy on me, bro," she manages between heaves.

And something in Liam—something long dormant—snaps.

"Go easy? Go easy? Why?" the words burst from him like water through a failing dam. "You've done nothing but make this journey... fucking impossible. You complain about everything, wrecked my car and lost our money—not to mention you scratched my CD."

He draws himself up to his full height, blood trickling from his nose, eyes burning. "And 'bro'? You don't get to call me bro. Where have you been in the last fifteen years, when I needed you?"

Patsy straightens up, wiping her mouth with the back of her hand. The alcohol haze is momentarily lifted by indignation. "When you needed me? You're the big brother in this relationship."

"But you had money. And means to help." Liam gestures wildly at her, at her silver dress that even now, dishevelled and stained, screams privilege. "Whilst I was wasting away in a council flat waiting for our mum to come home to us, you were living the high life with your rich pals."

Something vulnerable flickers across Patsy's face, quickly replaced by defensive fury. "I don't have any pals. You know, I went to a forty grand a year school and not one person has kept in touch with me since graduation. Ya wanna know why?"

She moves closer, the smell of tequila and sadness rolling off her in waves. "Because I was a tourist. A fucking tourist. A poor girl, given a leg up—because her dad was shagging some rich slut."

She pauses, swallowing hard. "They knew it and I knew it—I didn't belong there."

Her voice drops, suddenly serious. "You're lucky—you grew up poor, you lived a poor life. No goddamn fakery—you'll never know what it's like not to fit in."

Laim pauses momentarily before, "Apart from every single time I step out of the house."

He gestures to himself, to his skin. "You may look at me and see your brother and think we're equals—but you're in the minority."

Patsy is taken aback by this. *What does he mean?*

"I'm half Black, half white—but no one sees the white—I'm just Black and fully poor." Liam's words come faster now, years of silence giving way to brutal honesty. "You're white and rich, and what have you got to show for it? A squandered life."

Patsy recoils, then rallies with her own venom. "I've never had a life. You took it." She jabs a finger into his chest. "You took my mum when she chose you over me and you pushed her away. And now she's AWOL—AGAIN."

"Well that's not my fault," Liam protests.

"It never is, is it?" Patsy's voice rises to a screech. "Nothing is ever your fault!"

Liam's next words are precisely aimed to inflict maximum pain: "And whose—fault—was it to hit record on your little home videos?" The words flow like time itself—unstoppable, irreversible, cascading through the space between them. Unthinkable and irretrievable. A line crossed that can never be uncrossed.

And Patsy knows this, as she awakens the Banshee inside.

"AAAAGGGGHHHH!"

Patsy's fist connects with Liam's mouth before either of them registers what's happening. A crack of knuckles against teeth is followed by fresh blood which spurts from Liam's split lip to go with his bloody nose.

In the distance, police sirens wail and blue lights flash, approaching fast.

Liam spits a mouthful of blood onto the pavement, and their eyes meet for one last electric moment—where rage, hurt, and something like grief pass between them—before he turns and hastily jogs down the road. He angrily screams as he runs, kicking over a bin, then kicking a shop window—causing its glass to spider web.

"AAAAGGGGHHHH!" he lets out thirty years of pain and anger on the cobbled back streets of Scarborough. Fitting really, as this was the very same town the cracks in the family blew wide open all those years ago.

"SHIT—THE BOX," he cries, realising he has left their mum's steel box in the hotel.

"Liam. LIAM." Patsy's shouts follow him down the street. "I'm done. We're done. This thing, whatever it is—it's dead. You're dead to me. COWARD!"

Somewhere in the dark, a clock tower chimes midnight. Time marches on, indifferent to their pain. Sally had once told Liam, on a night much like this one, when the world felt cruel and incomprehensible, that love was the only thing that transcended time and space. "An enduring love," she'd called it. He never knew at the time what that meant. He doesn't feel it now, and neither does Patsy, who, to be fair, hasn't felt real love for an awfully long time. Too long for any person, of any age, to bear.

Liam and Patsy stand at opposite ends of the street now, separated by more than just cobblestones and distance. The gulf of time and space between them is measured in years, in silence, in ignorance, in shame, in spite, in anger, in all the things they never said to each other or to their mother to put things right. But what happens when the clocks stop? When the watch breaks, when the family fractures, and when the journey ends? Well, you have to get it going again. Sally knows this. Somewhere out there. She knows this as she waits patiently for her children to come to her.

Still tucked away under a broken bed in a dingy hotel room, Sally's final gift waits inside a humble steel box. Patient and timeless. Like a mother's love.

<u>Enduring</u>.

CHAPTER 14
PARK LIFE

The police car moves quietly through Scarborough's empty streets. Patsy sits in the back, pressing her forehead against the cold window as her hangover kicks in. The alcohol haze has lifted, making way for the obligatory migraine that pounds at her temples. The cold glass offers cold comfort.

Though she's been in many scrapes over the years, many slanging matches, many violent and public breakups and many moments brought about by poor decision making—she's never found herself in the back of a police car. It's always been:

"She's no real threat."

"She'll sleep it off."

"Best be getting off with you madam, miss, sweetheart."

Or some other condescending remark that treated her as non-threatening. Patsy never really made any mind of it before, didn't think it was a "thing", she thought it was normal. Now she's in the back of a police car for the first time. And it sucks balls. It means you've hit rock bottom. No matter the reason why. The law only gets involved when you need help, or a kick in the arse. Either way, you're faced with the inevitability that this is gonna be a long night. God, I'd give anything to be back at The Regal on that broken bed, she thinks.

Rookie's eyes flick to the rearview mirror from the front passenger seat, studying her passenger. "Not the finest of situations you two have found y'selves in," she casually lets rip while sipping an extra-strong McDonald's coffee. The steam fogs up the windscreen, causing Jenkins to whack on the fans. "Most people come to Scarbs for a good time, not whatever you two are doing." She pauses, taking another sip while leaning back through the cage. "Long way from London," she adds with a hint of judgement, "more like a married couple than brother and sister."

Patsy doesn't answer. An awkward silence fills the space in the car instead, broken only by the hum of the engine and the occasional crackle of the police radio. It's not that she doesn't have anything to say, it's more that she doesn't know how to respond to someone who is showing genuine concern. It's a new feeling. Especially from a woman. Shame she's been placed in the back of a police car to experience it.

"Hey, how 'bout some music?" Rookie says as she fiddles with the radio, settling on a familiar tune that at first Patsy can't quite make out. A tune she knows but can't quite place. They're halfway through an opening acoustic guitar strumming interlude, in F# minor Patsy discerns, followed by a gravelly-voiced northerner. Then it dawns on her. The acoustic guitar is played by Noel. The voice is unmistakably Liam's. It's "Wonderwall". The song LeeLee uses to hum himself to sleep. The song she hummed while she cared for him in the caravan park loos.

"Ohh classic, 'ay did you get tickets? I didn't," Rookie says to Jenkins as she hums along, followed by an off-key rendition of the chorus, singing about backbeats, and streets, and winding roads asking for someone to maybe save her. She gets the words wrong, she sings off-key. But for Patsy the moment couldn't be more cutting. Couldn't be more personal. It's like the universe has bored into her soul, right here, right now, and is twisting all the broken pieces back into place. Resurrecting Little Pats, in the very same place where it all began to fall apart.

Patsy gently wipes a tear from her eye, before the dam finally and irreversibly breaks. No longer is she crying for her own poor decisions, like she has done so many times before. She's crying because she knows she needs to change.

"Let it out, let it out," Rookie adds meaningfully. They drive past Itsy Bitsy, past the red phone box and away from the resort, the landmarks of her childhood sliding by like a montage of everything she's tried to forget—as the song draws to its eventual close.

"Strong Yorkshire brew will sort you right out," Rookie says. "Or as you Southerners put it," she adds with a theatrical wink, "a nice cuppa tea," delivering this in her worst attempt at a Cockney accent, which Patsy can't help but smile at.

The silence this time is softened by the radio presenter's dulcet tones keeping the truck drivers, late-night shift workers, midwives and emergency service heroes—those who keep the country quietly ticking along—motivated. Patsy listens half-heartedly, suddenly aware of this parallel nighttime Britain she's never really considered. People working while she's been partying, keeping everything running while she's been collapsing. How many times has she been rescued by people like Rookie? How many times has she called an ambulance at 3 am expecting someone to appear like magic because she's fallen into some gutter? The uncomfortable realisation creeps in: her entire lifestyle, her entire existence, depends on these invisible workers that she's never bothered to acknowledge. She's a societal pariah, a sap, a leech.

In year 9 English she was forced to read '1984'. Her teacher said it was to try and learn more about 'the working class' experience. So that they could better understand the people they would one day manage. She finally sees firsthand what Orwell meant now, and how her teacher was trying to manipulate her. The proles—the forgotten masses—keep everything running so that the privileged classes can wallow in their own fabricated dramas. And in her world, she's not Winston Smith questioning the system. She's one of the party members, blind to her own complicity, living off the backs of others while believing her own suffering somehow matters more. Perception and reality do not make good bedfellows.

The truth hits her with nauseating clarity: she's been playing her role perfectly in this upside-down world—consuming, complaining, collapsing, then expecting someone else to clean up the mess. A perfectly packaged product of late-stage capitalism. She imagines Orwell watching her now, notebook in hand, jotting down notes for the sequel to his dystopian masterpiece where the villains don't even realise they're the bad guys. No. In Orwell's 2084, the world is run by vapid social media influencers and reality TV stars who distract the masses while everything crumbles around them... only so that they can fill their pockets.

Oh no.

Oh fuck.

That's her.

That's now.

And she is not in bed with the best society has to offer. She thinks about all the TV execs she's met, the ones who bemoaned "the state of this country" while crafting the next episode of the world's most uncultured TV. The VIPs at Ladies Day who'd lecture her on immigration between betting on Saudi Arabian-owned horses assuming she was of some kind of regal stock while not realising her brother was half Nigerian and wasting away on a council estate. The same people who'd never acknowledge how their own lifestyles depend on the very system they claim to despise. All of them, all of *us*, she thinks, railing against a system we take for granted every single day. Realising that these people aren't as deeply concerned about the country as they say they are, they're only concerned about their own privileged lives within it.

Whatever "buzz" she had is now sprawled out across the steps of Flash Bux Casino, along with the last of her dignity, leaving that hollow clarity that comes with the inevitable backslide into sobriety. Each amber street lamp outside flickers across her face in the back seat of the rover, a strobe-like effect that seems to dissolve her former self frame by frame while the closed pubs and arcades blur past—their darkened windows a reflection of her darkened soul.

And that's when the car rolls into the police station car park, where a harsh glare floods through the windscreen, washing her in bright white light—giving her pause to finally face the music.

𝄞

Liam storms through the empty reception area, past the vacant desk. No sign of Olivia. Just as well. He's not in the mood for another confrontation.

The stairwell door bangs against the wall as he shoves it open, taking the stairs two at a time to the basement level.

The long, dimly lit corridor stretches before him. Green-tinged fluorescent lights flicker overhead, casting eerie shadows on the faded wallpaper. The kitchen is closed right now, but this only makes everything feel even more desolate.

He tries the handle. Locked. Of course it would be.

"Bloody hell," he mutters, stepping back.

Without hesitation, he rams his shoulder against the door. It doesn't budge. Another try, harder this time. The wood splinters around the lock.

One more go and the door flies open with a satisfying CRACK, banging against the wall inside.

The room is exactly as they left it—broken bed sagging in the middle, Liam's towel on the floor. And there, just visible beneath the broken bed frame, is the ornate trunk.

Liam drops to his knees, slides his arm under the bed and pulls the heavy box out, clutching it to his chest for dear life.

For a moment, he sits there on the floor, breathing hard, the trunk held tight against him.

"Got you," he whispers.

A quick glance around the room to see if they've left anything else important, but there's nothing. Just broken furniture. Emptiness.

He rises, trunk tucked firmly under his arm, and disappears into the corridor without looking back.

𝄞

The station buzzes with the grim energy of a busy night in Scarborough during the headiest days of summer. Unforgiving lights paint everyone in the same unflattering shade, but Patsy notices something else—something that makes her gut twist.

A young Black man sits handcuffed to a bench, suit trousers torn at the knee, blood crusting on his lip. Next to him, two South Asian teenagers wait silently, hands cuffed on their laps. A middle-aged woman in a cleaner's uniform—Somali, maybe—argues quietly with a desk sergeant who commands her to keep her voice down. Her accent is loaded with distress, and her attempts at English are more than easy to discern, yet the sergeant rolls his eyes anyway, looking for any way to make things more difficult for this woman, who, like everyone else in here, is at her lowest ebb.

Patsy's never noticed before. Never had to. But tonight, the demographics are unmistakable.

"This way," Rookie says, guiding her past the waiting area.

Patsy spots a woman in her late fifties with badly dyed blonde hair slumped in a plastic chair. Recognition cuts through her. The harsh light of sobriety is starting to shine on everything, and everyone more clearly.

"Is that...?"

"Aye," Rookie nods, her voice dropping. "Mandy Mulligan. Used to be the landlady on 'Village Green'. A regular here now."

The former soap star's head snaps up at her name, her desperate eyes meeting Patsy's. There's a brief flash of embarrassed recognition before Mandy looks away, scratching her forearm. "Give you an autograph for a fiver," Mandy jokes.

"Fame's a right bastard," Rookie adds, steering Patsy toward a small side room. "Seen it happen to a few of you lot."

Patsy notices how Mandy—the only other white woman in the waiting area—sits unrestrained, unchallenged. Just like her.

It's not really a cell—more a holding room with a blue plastic-covered mattress to sit on, a toilet and institutional white walls. There's even a few books by the window. Jenkins enters with a thick blanket and a steaming mug, the scent of strong tea quickly fills the small room.

Patsy wraps the blanket around her shoulders, suddenly aware of the privilege in this simple kindness. "Am I under arrest?"

Rookie sits beside her. "Think of it like drunk tank, in ol' Wild West."

"What about my... brother?" The word feels strange in her mouth. Brother. After years of pretending he didn't exist. "He's out there somewhere... will he be okay?"

The question holds more weight than she intended. Not just about tonight, but about everything. His whole life.

Rookie's expression shifts. "Lost Southerner out there in the Northern wilds at night? We'll find him."

She stands, leaving behind the faint smell of a not too unpleasant floral perfume that Patsy's never smelled before. Why would she? It's from the discount section at Boots. Though they shop in the same stores and walk the same streets, these two women are not navigating the same world.

"Jenkins checked w'hotel, but he's not returned. I'll go look for him myself."

The door closes with a soft click, and Patsy's left alone with her cooling tea, the smell of perfume and her sharpening thoughts. Exactly what a drunk tank was invented for, she thinks. Rather positively. Doesn't everyone get sent off with a slapped wrist and a "don't do it again"?

Then, Liam's words enter her conscience. *Apart from every single time I step out of the house! You may look at me and see your brother and think we're equals, but that's not the same for everyone else, is it?*

How is his world different from mine? Has my entire life been served to me on a silver platter because of my race? Why didn't Minnie and Richard ever see Liam as my equal? My big brother? Why were we separated only for every other weekend together, with Liam staying with Sally, every night, every day? No respite for Sally. No break from or for Liam. No holidays to Spain, Greece, Disneyland Florida or the Maldives for him.

Why? The explanation has always been that Liam wasn't Richard's son. But this logic doesn't quite fit anymore. I knew plenty of stepsiblings from equally broken homes who moved seamlessly between parents, who shared holidays and bedrooms and lives without anyone batting an eyelid. Those families found a way to blend. So why not mine?

The uncomfortable answer hovers at the edge of her consciousness, too raw to fully articulate even now. But she can't unsee it anymore. Not after tonight.

My drinking, my gambling, my reality TV nonsense—was I handed these chances over and over again not only because of my wealth, but because of something as arbitrary as skin colour? Clearly, because here I am in a police station. But I'll probably get away with it. Because I'm a white girl. And white girls don't go to prison for being drunk and disorderly.

Through the small window in the door, she watches as Mandy Mulligan is gently led to another room, walking with the exaggerated care of someone trying desperately to appear sober. Meanwhile, the suited Black man is escorted roughly toward the cells.

"I was mugged. I din't do nuffin'," he pleads with sincerity.

That could be Liam, Patsy thinks. Every night that could be him. No wonder he stays at home, night after night. The realisation settles over her like the police-issue blanket—heavy, scratchy, and impossible to shrug off. Though she tries anyway, throwing it off her shoulders with a sudden movement as something primal breaks loose from deep inside her.

An ARGGHH of anger rips from her throat, the Banshee finally exorcised. Maybe forever this time.

As she falls to her knees, completely exhausted from the night, week, month, year, her whole fucking goddamn mess of a life, she can't help but feel that she cuts a lonely figure, in a lonely place, at a lonely time, and would do anything for a hug right now from someone who loves her. But unfortunately for our Pats, those people are in very short supply.

𝄞

The park sits empty and desolate, save for a few benches occupied by rough sleepers. Each one a lump of blankets under the dim streetlights, with a mangy dog for company by their side. A melancholy song by some American ingénue wafts from a nearby flat—all breathy vocals and electronic beats, the kind NME would call "hauntingly beautiful" or "Americana at its most poignant" but what Liam would call "pretentious shite". Some stoned student has got their window wide open so that EVERYONE knows just how dramatically sad they are right now, at 2 am. The song's mellow notes hang in the cold salty air as she whispers about self-care and validation, those superficial modern mantras that only serve to give the person espousing them permission to be a selfish twat.

Holding the ornate trunk tight and with his satchel wrapped over his shoulder, Liam scoffs as he enters the park. From Britpop's cool optimism to barely audible confessionals about anxiety and therapy. How did we get here? A global financial crash, austerity, and the socio-economic clusterfuck that followed; Brexit, endless wars, housing crises and zero-hour contracts all topped off with a mother fucking pandemic. It all contributed to this dog-eat-dog mentality where everyone is out for themselves. Survival is the most primal of all instincts—and it's showing right now, in this park.

So, is it any wonder artists today sing introspective nonsense about themselves instead of selling the idea of a better tomorrow? No anthems, no swagger, no romance. Just sad boys and girls with synthesisers declaring that "It's okay not to be okay". Fucking hell. At least in the '90s they had the decency to put a beat and a jangly guitar behind their misery without relying on the "context" being learned through a pushy social media post. Whatever happened to nuance and intrigue? Why does everything have to be so on the nose? Liam thinks as he shuffles behind a row of bushes, watching as the blue lights of a police car slide across the landscape. He hunches down instinctively, with his heart thumping against his ribs.

This is what it feels like to be a criminal, he thinks. It's not as cool as in the movies. In fact, it feels horrible.

Inside the car, Rookie and Jenkins scan the park with tired eyes.

"Ain't seen him," says Jenkins, scribbling something in her notebook.

"Keep looking," Rookie replies, her eyes lingering on a shape that might or might not be Liam. "Poor bugger's got nowhere t'go," she says as she lets out a massive yawn.

The patrol car moves on, taking its unsettling blue glow with it. Liam exhales, watching his breath form clouds in the night air. The overly synthesised breathy singer hits a particularly mournful note about her "broken pieces", and something in Liam's chest tightens in response.

"How did I get here?" he mutters to the darkness.

How did he get here? Homeless. Easier than you might think, right? One minute you're watching the carpet slowly being pulled out from under you by the system, next you're sleeping rough in Scarborough of all places, jumping at police lights like you've murdered someone.

That's when he thinks about Patsy. Where is she? Cursing his name and regretting ever agreeing to this wild goose chase, probably. But at least she's somewhere safe and warm, probably. The thought brings him unexpected comfort. She'll be okay, the police will look after her. She can always call her dad.

He gnaws at his lip, anxiety gnawing right back at him. For all their bickering, for all her pointed words, he can't help but worry about her. That's what big brothers do, right? Even when they haven't been proper brothers for decades. Even when they've spent more time apart than together. Some things just stick, like that instinct to check she's alright.

Should he have stayed with her? Another failure to add to his mounting collection, another moment where he didn't stand his ground.

"She's better off without me anyway," he mumbles, trying to convince himself. "Always has been."

He tries the first bench where a rough sleeper, wrapped in a tatty Sports Direct sleeping bag, eyes him warily. A dog lifts its head from beside the man, baring its yellowed teeth.

"Taken," the man growls. "Fuck off."

Liam tries the next bench. A woman this time, her face hidden beneath a woollen hat pulled low, clutching a carrier bag like it contains the Crown Jewels.

"Piss off," she hisses before he can even speak. "Find your own spot."

The same for the next. And the next. All occupied. All hostile. The universal language of the dispossessed—territory is everything when territory is all you've got. It's no different here than it is anywhere else. Only here there's no leaseholder agreements or deeds. It's first-come first first-served and dog-eat-dog.

Liam cuts a lonely figure, in a park full of lonely figures where each 'unperson' guards their small slice of territory at the witching hour—perhaps the loneliest time of the night, when even the drunks have staggered home and the early risers are still hours from their alarms.

The synthesiser trails off mid-verse and the window slams shut with an irritated bang. They've made their point, whoever they are. You're sad, we get it, put it online like everyone else, Liam thinks, as he jumps the fence back into the street. The darkness swallows him whole as he shuffles into an alleyway. Now he's just another 'unperson' in a country full of them, searching for somewhere, anywhere, to rest his head. To feel comfort. To feel part of something bigger than himself. To feel love. To feel home.

𝄞

Patsy lays wide awake. The noise of the police station has settled down, but let's face it, this place is 24/7 noise—doors clanging, radios crackling, drunks shouting for water, for lawyers, or for their mums.

She lays on the hard mattress, so thin she can feel the concrete lumps underneath, and thinks about her comfortable Belsize Park trappings. Her Queen bed with its Egyptian cotton sheets and memory foam mattress topper from Selfridges. All white furnishings, minimalist and tasteful, like something out of a Sunday supplement. Her beloved Steinway. Her kitchen with its island and marble worktops that do everything for the modern home cook, yet she only knows how to operate the air fryer and the wine fridge. All the trappings of a wealthy socialite, but a gilded cage is a cage nonetheless.

She runs her fingers over Sally's broken watch. Wonders where Liam is. Whether he's safe. Whether he's thinking about her too. She wonders what her followers would think if they could see her now. Former reality star, former estate agent, former rich girl, currently lying in a police cell in Scarborough with dirty feet and the taste of tequila and vomit clinging to her teeth. The mighty fallen and all that. Then she realises. People are gonna think what they want and what you want them to think about you, is rarely what they will. That's the thing about perspective, it shifts, bends and warps.

I don't give a fuck what they think about me anymore.

A police officer walks past, peering through the glass before moving on. Patsy doesn't even pretend to be asleep. What's the point? She lays wide awake, full of worry. For herself. For Liam. For all the wasted years between them. And for the first time in her adult life, she wonders what her mother would do.

𝄞

The alleyway smells of piss and discarded kebabs. Liam crouches behind a skip, his breath still forming clouds, but smaller now as he tries to control his breathing. He pulls a flattened cardboard box—for a 65-inch flat screen TV by the looks of it—over his head and shoulders. The cardboard does little against the cold that seeps up from the damp concrete. He curls into himself, hugging the ornate trunk and his bag, trying to conserve heat, trying to think of anything except the fact that he's sleeping rough for the first time in his life. He's shed all his money, his flat, his beloved CD, his bucket hat, his loyal car, and now his sister.

What's left? He considers.

A police siren wails in the distance. Liam flinches beneath his cardboard shield.

"You're a coward," echoes through his mind, over and over. Patsy's voice, but not just hers. It's everyone's voice. It's his own voice. Incessantly calling him a coward. Over and over and over. He instinctively touches his fat lip where Patsy punched him. It's stopped bleeding, but it's also a painful reminder of the gulf between them.

He tries to close his eyes, he tries to sleep, but every shuffle of feet past the alley entrance jerks him awake. He pulls out the crumpled letter from his pocket, squinting at it in the dark. His mother's words blur and shift on the paper. The promise of meeting her at Cape Wrath suddenly seems like a joke. A cruel prank on a man whose life has been a series of false starts and wrong turns. "Fucking stupid," he whispers to himself, letting his head fall back against the brick wall. "Like she was ever coming."

DAY 4

Light slants through the small, high window of the holding room, painting a thin rectangle on the opposite wall. Patsy lies on her side, eyes wide open and bloodshot. She hasn't slept a wink.

She stares at the patch of light as it slowly changes colour from grey to pale yellow. Morning. Another day to face. But this time things feel different. She feels different.

She sits up, wincing at various aches and pains. She pulls out Sally's watch and stares at it, tapping the glass with her finger. Still stopped. Still broken. Like everything else.

Patsy has shed so much, but the greatest thing she has let go of is the notion that she can control what others think of her. That Patsy is dead. The reality TV star Patsy. The ~~sex tape~~ online Patsy. The drunk fool that everyone loves to hate.

All she has is this broken watch. And then she considers for the first time the reason why her mum bought this watch. It's elegant, but not pretentious; it's functional but stylish. It fits pretty much every outfit. And it was bought with a little bonus that Sally worked hard for. It's the only thing on her that feels earned. Shame it's broken. She'll get it fixed when she gets back to London, she thinks. But back to what? The life she had? The thought makes her stomach turn, but the alternative—continuing this wild goose chase with Liam—seems equally impossible. At least in London she can beg for a small loan to get back on her feet again, or a bed for the night.

She turns the broken watch over on her wrist. Lost between past and future, just like its owner.

The first hint of sunrise breaks over the North Sea, painting it in surreal shades of amber and gold. Gulls soar and cry overhead, early risers in search of whatever the rats have forgotten or ignored.

Liam walks slowly along the promenade, arms laden heavy with the trunk and his bag, shoulders hunched against the morning chill. His Converse scuff against the concrete with each step, the only sound besides the crashing waves and the gulls. He looks like he's been dragged through a hedge backwards—hair a mess, clothes damp, dark circles under his eyes. The sea looks so inviting right now, he thinks, maybe go for a swim. Permanently. But he shakes that idea off instantly.

The amusement arcades are shuttered, Itsy Bitsy is closed. Only a few elderly dog walkers are out, subtly ignoring him as they pass, too British to ask if he's okay.

He stops at the railings and stares out to sea. The horizon shimmers with promise, but not for him. He's a man adrift, cut loose from whatever moorings he once had. No flat. No car. No sister. No mother. Nothing but a scratched mixtape and a head full of memories.

He cuts a desolate figure. In a desolate time.

Behind him, the Victorian splendour of The Regal hotel looms large and imposing. People with proper lives and proper jobs will be waking up there, planning their days, moving forwards. Not him. Never him.

Liam's fingers tighten around the railing. Something unfamiliar, but recognisable, bubbles in his chest. Anger. Primal anger.

"You're a coward," he whispers, echoing Patsy's words from the night before. Hearing how they feel in his own mouth. "Coward."

A group of teenagers strut past, eyeing his dishevelled appearance. One of them makes a pointed comment just loud enough for Liam to hear. Something about "wasteman" and the "trunk." Any other day, he would have hunched further, made himself smaller, invisible.

Not today.

"Fuck off. Get a job," Liam barks, his voice steadier than he expects. The lads scoff and move on toward the waiting souped-up orange Corsa, which speeds off with a high-pitched VREE-PSH of the dump valve.

Liam turns back to the sea. The bubbling in his chest hasn't subsided. It's growing, changing into something else. Determination. Or desperation. Hard to tell the difference sometimes with LeeLee.

"Scotland," he says to the waves. "The edge of the world."

The red phone box stands like a lonely sentinel on the promenade. Once an icon of British life, now just another relic—chipped paint, missing glass panels filled in with prostitute flyers, and of course, the unmistakable stench of piss. Like everything else in this country, Liam thinks, left to rot.

Dawn continues to creep across the horizon, illuminating the phone box which calls to Liam like some sort of siren. Liam shakes his tracksuit leg pocket and hears a faint jingle. He drops his last coins into the slot. The metallic clink echoes in the small space.

Who is he gonna call? Patsy? Mum's gone AWOL. Steve-O's probably still asleep, and anyway, what would he say? "Alright, mate, fancy a quick drive to Scotland to find my mum?" Maybe the housing officer to beg for his flat back, or what's left of it.

No.

No one to call.

No one at all.

But he holds the receiver anyway, presses it to his ear tightly. He just needs to hear a voice—any voice—even if it's just the automated operator telling him to please hang up and try again.

He looks at his reflection in the dirty steel of the phone unit. His features distorted and warped. The stubble on his face has grown through his boyish looks, not a cool stylistic choice like George Michael or Prince, but the mark of a man adrift. His eyes are red raw, bloodshot from exhaustion, deep crevices carved beneath them. The small scar above his left eyebrow—from when he fell off his bike at age eight and Mum kissed it better with a Ninja Turtles plaster—stands out pale against his otherwise grimy face.

He barely recognises himself in this tarnished, imperfect mirror. A stranger stares back. He looks at his dirty reflection and can feel the trauma building up to the surface—years of it, decades of it, threatening to crack the foundation he's built his entire identity upon.

"You're a coward," he whispers into the dead phone. "Coward. You're a coward."

The words taste bitter in his mouth, but there's something cleansing about saying them aloud.

~ 1996 ~

The same phone box, but pristine then, the red paint vibrant, the glass clear. Sally holds the receiver for dear life.

"I'll walk with them off the edge of the world if it stops you breaking them up—you hear me? The edge of the world," she hisses into the phone, tears streaming down her face.

Little Liam stands nearby, his Discman's headphones clamped over his ears, the sounds of "Champagne Supernova" drowning out most—but not all—of his mother's anguish. Like always, he's watching everything, while appearing to be in his own little world. And at this moment, he watches her legs give way, with her free hand pressed against the glass for support as she sinks toward the ground.

DAY 4

The phone emits a steady, monotonous dial tone. No one's listening. No one's ever been listening.

Liam clicks the receiver button, the sharp sound echoing in the cramped phone box. His hand lingers on the cold plastic, reluctant to break this final connection to nothing. Patsy was right about so much. About moving forwards, always forwards. About how waiting for something to happen is the wrong approach. About how he's been stuck in place since she left, since Mum left, like a scratched CD permanently stuck on song 2, thirty seconds in—never able to skip forwards.

"I've been waiting for them to come back," he murmurs to himself, the realisation dawning with the sun. "All this time, I've been too much of a coward to fight for them."

It's a circle, he sees now. Sally at that phone box, begging for her children to stay together. Him at the same phone box, with no one to call. Twenty-nine years of standing still, of letting life happen to him, of watching the carpet being pulled from under his feet and doing nothing to stop it.

He's been a coward. Not in how he walks away from fights, not in how he refuses to raise his fists, but in how he's refused to live his life.

"No man is an island," he whispers, a half-remembered line from a movie he's long forgotten about. But he's made himself one. Cut himself off. Drifted away from the mainland until he couldn't see the shore anymore. And with this revelation, he caves, slumping to the grimy pissy floor of the phone box, gripping the receiver for dear life as he sobs uncontrollably.

Rubbing her eyes of the morning grit, Rookie spots Liam falling out of the phone box, she signals to Jenkins who quickly hits the sirens with a short bloop bloop.

Liam's heart sinks as he sees the blue lights flash. But this time, instead of hiding, instead of running, he simply stands there. Lets himself be seen. Rookie's police car pulls up, and she steps out, approaching him with quick, purposeful strides.

Liam drops to his knees, not in surrender but in sheer exhaustion. All the fight, all the running, all the waiting has drained out of him. For a moment, it's just him and the great big endless ocean in front, stretching out like his uncertain future—vast, intimidating, seemingly impossible to face alone.

Until Rookie puts her strong motherly arms around his tense shoulders, the warmth of human contact shocking after the cold night. Her face is a mixture of concern and relief.

"There you are, lad," she says, her voice gentler than he expected, like someone coaxing a frightened animal. "Been looking for you all night."

"Have you?" he says with genuine surprise, his voice small and fragile in the morning air. As if the concept of someone actually searching for him—caring where he's gone—is the most foreign thing in the world.

CHAPTER 15
A BITTERSWEET PROMISE

DAY 4

Patsy sits up as quickly as she can, as Rookie bounds in with a greasy paper bag that emits the unmistakable scent of bacon.

"Morning, bright eyes," she says, dangling the bag in front of Patsy. "Got you some breakfast."

Patsy's stomach lurches at the smell, but before she can respond, Rookie jerks her thumb over her shoulder. "Found your brother too."

Liam shuffles in behind her—laden with the trunk and his satchel—looking rough as fuck. His eyes are bloodshot, his sky blue tracksuit filthy and damp, and his hair needs a good brush. The siblings lock eyes for a moment before Patsy's stomach lurches. She scrambles to the toilet in the corner, retching loudly.

"Charming," Liam mutters, standing awkwardly in the doorway.

Rookie closes the door with a heavy click, trapping the three of them in the confined space. Patsy flushes the toilet and drags herself back to the hard blue plastic mattress, sprawling across it in defeat.

Liam, having nowhere else to go, perches himself on the closed toilet seat on the other side of the room. The siblings have effectively claimed opposite corners, as far from each other as the small room allows.

"Why are you helping us?" Patsy asks, her voice raspy from vomiting. She wipes her mouth with the back of her hand.

Rookie leans against the wall, arms folded. "Apart from being a good cop?"

Patsy reflects on this, *fair enough,* she thinks.

Then her expression softens. "Look. Full disclosure. I met your mother." She pauses, her eyes drifting to some distant memory. "Well, I think I did. Many, many moons ago."

Liam and Patsy both straighten at this, their mutual animosity momentarily forgotten.

"I was a Rookie—and well—it were a different time back then." She smiles wistfully. "Things were a lot less… complicated."

Liam leans forward with sudden interest. "Our mum? You're sure it was her?"

"Green Golf? Plate number A829 M.A.D? MAD indeed." Rookie's gaze drifts between them. "Two little ones in the back. A boy and a girl."

Patsy and Liam exchange glances—not quite warm, but no longer arctic.

"Tell us," Liam says, pulling himself closer. "Please."

Rookie settles against the wall, her police radio crackling softly at her hip, which she turns off. "It were summer, mid-'90s sometime, can't remember exact year, but I remember that car and I remember your mother…"

The room lights seem to dim as Rookie's words transport them back to a dark motorway and a desperate woman at the wheel of a tatty green Golf…

~ 1996 ~

Blue lights continue to flash in Sally's mirror. "Are they for me?" she thinks. "I ain't done nothing wrong," she pleads to whatever Gods are listening. She accelerates faster—78, 79, 80 mph and increasing, swerving it into the slow lane, undertaking a slow-moving lorry. All the time, the whites of Sally's eyes burn through the dark, while Little Liam quickly looks back and forth at the chasing police car. It's not like the movies, he thinks, where the heroes are being chased by a thousand cop cars and always get away. In the movies, the good guys laugh and make jokes during car chases. But Mum's hands are shaking on the steering wheel, and the car's swerving all over the place.

The police rover appears with its blue lights sweeping through the darkness. It veers across the lanes, pulling up in front of the lorry and right alongside her.

Through the passenger window, Rookie jabs her finger towards the hard shoulder, her face contorted into a mask of official authority. Pull over. Now.

Sally shakes her head, tears streaming down her face. She isn't stopping. Not now. Not when she's gotten this far. She risks a glance to the back seat, where Little Patsy still sleeps, oblivious to the chase unfolding around them. Little Liam's eyes are scarily wide, taking it all in. Taking a deep breath, she locks eyes with the policewoman and mouths silently, deliberately: "Please. Don't take my babies."

Inside the rover, Rookie catches the desperate plea. She peers through the darkness at the green Golf's back seat, making out two small forms—one sleeping, one awake and frightened. Children. She glances down at the missing person report in her lap, scanning the details again.

"'old up, Nightrider. We got a couple o' wee ones in the back." She squints through the darkness. "It's dark, she's probably just scared. Maybe we should ease off?"

She chews her bottom lip, already second-guessing herself.

"You know, follow and observe?"

Nightrider shoots her a sideways glance, his weathered face illuminated by the dashboard lights. After a moment's consideration, he nods reluctantly.

"Aye. Rookie."

The blue lights stop flashing, casting the motorway back into darkness punctuated only by the Golf's headlamps and the dull orange glow of the motorway lights.

A momentary wave of relief washes over Sally, quickly replaced by the cold reality of their situation. Her adrenaline finally lowers, leaving her whole body shaking and as her eyes drop to the fuel gauge, she notices the needle is hovering just above empty.

"Bugger," she whispers, scanning the signs for the next services.

Then, salvation appears in the form of a depressing motorway garage.

In the grimy single-person petrol station lavatory, Sally splashes cold water on her face, trying to wash away the panic and exhaustion. The harsh fluorescent light flickers irregularly, casting shadows under her eyes that make her look ten years older. She stares at her reflection, at her wild eyes and dishevelled hair. Who am I? Who have I become? How did I get here? What's next? Questions she doesn't have the answers for.

"Get it together," she whispers.

Her hands are still shaking from the chronic depletion of adrenaline. Some electrolytes and sugars will sort that out, she thinks. Or coffee. Coffee will be fine. Or vodka.

Around her, the walls tell a story of a country in flux. A faded poster for Take That's upcoming tour is pasted on the wall, Robbie's been torn off and someone's drawn over Gary Barlow's head with a spurting penis. Next to the toilet roll holder, someone has daubed: **SEE YOU AT KNEBWORTH AUG '96**, and a massive **OASIS** has been scratched into the door with a car key. Aggressive graffiti competes for attention: **VOTE NEW LABOUR** is painted in red nail polish on the cistern, with **LONDON TORY-MAFIA SCUM OUT!** painted next to it. A more ominous **BNP 4 BRITTAN** with a badly drawn Union Jack dominates part of the filthy wall by the toilet seat. But someone else has written **FASCIST PIGS** underneath, along with **IT'S SPELT BRITAIN, MORON**.

Sally avoids touching the grimy surfaces as much as possible. Everyone seems to have an opinion about where the country should be heading. Nobody seems to give a toss about where she's going, or what she's running from. And it's best if everyone keeps their opinions to themselves, she thinks. This is the best place for it, locked away in a motorway loo. God forbid everyone getting the chance to voice their opinion in public. Imagine the chaos.

She takes one last look at herself in the cracked mirror, where beneath, someone's declared that **BRITPOP IS DEAD** in thick black marker. Not yet it isn't, she thinks. Nothing's dead until it stops breathing.

She yanks a rough paper towel from the dispenser, hastily dries her hands, and takes one long, steadying breath. No time to waste. She buttons up her Levi's 501 jeans, gives herself one last look in the mirror, and hastily exits. Though as she does, her legs wobble through fear of what she will do next.

The police rover cruises into the petrol station, headlights sweeping across the forecourt until they illuminate the familiar green Golf.

"Didn't get far then," Rookie says, with a hint of smugness in her voice as she spots their evaders parked at the pump. Nightrider kills the engine with a grunt and a matter-of-fact, "They never do."

Rookie unbuckles her seatbelt and reaches for the door handle, already mapping out the arrest in her head. "Look after them nippers, Nightrider," she says over her shoulder, all business now.

Nightrider leans back in his seat with a world-weary sigh. "Aye. Rookie," he finally says, as the door slams shut.

Sally emerges from the station, keys clutched tight in her hand. She keeps her head down, eyes fixed on the concrete as she walks briskly toward her car. Just a few more steps. Just get to the car. Just—

She sees the polished black boots blocking her path before she registers the uniform. Rookie stands directly in her way, arms folded across her chest. Sally tries to sidestep around her, but Rookie isn't having any of it. She moves in the same direction, cutting her off. When Sally tries again, Rookie grabs her firmly by the shoulders.

"Please," Sally begs, her voice barely above a whisper. "I have to get going."

"Ay. Look." Rookie's voice is firm but not unkind. "I just wanna talk. You're in no bother till I say you're in bother, okay? And at moment, you're in no bother." She loosens her grip slightly. "I just wanna talk. Can you do that f'me?"

Sally's shoulders slump. There's no running now. She nods in defeat, staring at a discarded cigarette butt on the ground between them. Behind Rookie, the green Golf sits at the pump with her babies still safely buckled in the back seat. So close to escape, yet completely trapped.

The petrol station forecourt glows under harsh sodium lights, creating pools of yellow that barely illuminate the surrounding darkness. Sally sits on a low wall a little way from the shop, shoulders hunched against the night chill. From here, she can keep an eye on her car where Nightrider leans against the bonnet, arms folded, standing guard over her children. Every now and then, he peers through the window, checking they're still okay. She silently thanks him for this small kindness.

The shop door jingles as Rookie emerges with two steaming cups. She crosses the forecourt and hands one of the white polystyrene cups to Sally. Sally takes it gratefully, wrapping her cold fingers around its warmth. She sips—grimaces at the bitter instant coffee taste—but doesn't complain. It's hot, and that's what matters.

For a long moment, nobody speaks. Just the distant hum of traffic from the motorway, the occasional whoosh of cars passing on the slip road. The night feels suspended, a brief respite from the frantic chase that preceded it.

"So," Rookie finally says, blowing on her own coffee. "Where ya headed?"

Sally stares into her cup, watching the steam rise and dissipate. The adrenaline has completely drained from her system now, leaving her slightly dizzy.

"Well by way of London, we were in Great Yarmouth," she starts, words tumbling out too quickly, "and then Scarborough—on holiday with the kids. Taking them somewhere nice, you know. Before. Before..."

Rookie raises a hand, a gentle gesture to stem the flow. "Slow down. I asked where ya headed?"

Sally takes another sip of the bitter coffee, buying herself time.

"North the border," she admits finally.

Rookie leans against the wall beside her, close but not touching. Her presence is oddly comforting despite the uniform.

"Now why would you want to be going to a place like that when the weather's so lovely down 'ere?" The question is casual, conversational, as if they're just two women chatting on a normal night.

Sally traces the rim of her cup with her finger. The cheap polystyrene squeaks softly.

"My husband," she says quietly. "He's from there. Was from there. But. He died."

"I'm very sorry." Rookie's voice holds genuine sympathy. "Recent?"

"Feels like yesterday, but—nearly ten years now." Sally gazes across at the green Golf, at the shadows of her children barely visible through the windows. "I'd just had my first. He was attacked by—because of, well—he was Black."

The confession hangs in the air between them. Rookie nods slowly, looking out at the same night sky Sally is studying.

"Aye. The world's certainly got some growing to do."

A lorry rumbles past on the slip road, its headlights briefly illuminating their faces before passing on.

"So," Rookie continues after a moment. "Do you know why we stopped you?"

Sally forces a weak smile. "On account of my holiday?"

"Well, yes, actually." Rookie turns to face her fully now. "Got a report of a little girl, kidnapped by her mother, matching your description and vehicle."

The words sound like they're echoing through a void. Kidnap. Your vehicle. Mother. Sally sets her coffee cup down on the wall beside her, suddenly needing both hands free as she gulps, before pleading, "Well, it's just me, my kids and me, were, are on holiday." She swallows hard. "I'm trying to get some recovery time in."

With trembling fingers, she lifts the hem of her t-shirt, revealing a pattern of bruises across her torso—fresh purple ones layered over yellowing older marks and faded green patches, a grim calendar of abuse written on her body. The cool night air raises goosebumps on her exposed skin. Rookie's eyes widen slightly, her professional demeanour cracking for just a moment. The bruises speak volumes in the silence that follows.

Some days earlier in Peckham. The stereo stack system topples as Sally pulls herself away from it, while Richard charges across the room towards her. She shuffles backwards, but there's nowhere to go. The coffee table catches her behind the knees and she stumbles.

"Who do you think you're talking to?" Richard's voice is dangerous.

"Please, the kids—"

He's on her before she can finish, his weight pinning her to the floor. The first punch lands on her ribs, exactly where the bruises from last week have just begun to fade, exactly the same rib he broke a year ago that never fully healed. The second punch follows, then a third.

From the doorway, Little Liam watches, frozen in horror. Little Patsy appears behind him, and without a word, he reaches back and pulls his sister close, turning her face into his shoulder.

"Don't look," he whispers, his own eyes unable to tear away from the scene. "Don't look."

Another punch. Sally's gasp of pain catches in her throat.

It seems like a lifetime ago now. She's been through Hell and chose to run, from London to Norfolk to Yorkshire, and now finds herself in some shitty petrol forecourt at a pivotal crossroads where her choices will dictate the rest of their lives.

Sally lowers her shirt, shivering slightly.

"My current husband," she says quietly, "ain't from Scotland."

Rookie's gaze travels from the colourful tapestry of Sally's pain to the green Golf, which is not just a vehicle to 'get from A to B' as many might dismiss this humble car to be, tonight it's Sally's getaway vehicle. Rookie's expression softens further.

"Go on, wake 'em and ask them if you want," Sally insists, nodding toward the car. Her breath catches. The suggestion hangs in the air between them—a test, perhaps, or a genuine offer.

After some consideration, Rookie shakes her head. "Let the angels sleep is what I say," she mutters, almost to herself, "cos when they wake, it's hell."

Sally nods gratefully, relief washing over her face.

"I just want to..."

"Stop," Rookie raises her hand, cutting her off. "Don't say anything else." She glances back at Nightrider, who's wandered a few paces away to smoke. When she turns back to Sally, her voice drops lower.

"You know, we often get false reports from controlling husbands, and they often give inaccurate information."

A meaningful pause hangs between them. "It's also hard making sense of what comes through t'radio too—often write down the wrong number plate. You understand?"

The meaning is clear. Sally swallows hard, fighting back tears.

"I'm a good mum," she whispers, "I'm a good mum."

"Aye," Rookie says with unexpected gentleness. "I have no doubt o'that."

She looks out at the motorway, where headlights stream past in the darkness, each one carrying its own story, heading to its own destination. Each journey, a much bigger decision than the driver ever imagined.

"Life's a complex symphony," Rookie adds quietly. "Gotta keep on, love, gotta keep on."

Sally closes her eyes, letting the words sink in as a tear rolls down her cheek. When she opens them again, there's new resolve.

From the car, Little Liam watches through half-closed eyes, taking it all in, but pretending to be asleep. He sees his mother's shoulders straighten, sees something pass between her and the policewoman. He doesn't understand what's happening, but somehow he knows it's important—one of those moments adults have that changes everything. He continues to peek through the window, he spots Nightrider sitting on the bonnet of their car, bored and smoking. He rubs his eyes, trying to make sense of what's happening. Little Patsy remains fast asleep beside him, her head lolled against the window, breath fogging the glass in a small circle.

Outside, Nightrider stretches and hops off the bonnet, ambling toward the women.

"Ay Rookie, what's t'story?" he calls out.

Rookie turns, her face unreadable in the artificial light. "Come on Nightrider—this ain't vehicle we're looking for. Wrong plate."

A beat passes between them. Understanding dawns on Nightrider's weathered face.

"Aye, wrong plate indeed," he agrees, the corner of his mouth twitching upward. "Lass or not, you'll make a great cop, Rookie."

Rookie walks Sally back toward the green Golf. As they cross paths, Nightrider gives her a solemn nod goodbye, a small gesture that carries the weight of something much larger.

By the time Sally slides into the driver's seat, both Little Liam and Little Patsy are awake, watching her with wide, uncertain eyes. She exhales a long, shuddering breath of relief, as she grips the steering wheel tight.

A tap on the window makes them all jump. Rookie stands there, leaning down to peer inside.

Sally lowers the window cautiously.

"Scotland's about two hours that way," Rookie says, pointing north. "Out of English jurisdiction then."

Sally nods, understanding the gift she's being given.

"Mum, what's going on?" Little Patsy asks, her voice small in the darkness.

Sally turns to face her children, studying their faces as if memorising them.

"Kids. What I'm about to say to you must stay with you till you die. Do you understand?"

They don't, cos they're kids—but they nod anyway, sensing the importance of the moment.

"Life is hard and we won't always get what we want. Things will come between you. People mostly—but you must always remember one thing for me... okay?"

"What is it Mum?" Little Liam asks.

Sally reaches back, placing a hand on each of their knees. "That you love each other. No matter what. And that love is what will keep you bound to each other—no matter what. Do you understand?"

Something in her voice makes them both sit up straighter. They nod, not just agreeing but meaning it. Outside, Rookie watches through the window, discreetly wiping a tear from the corner of her eye.

"Always look after each other," Sally insists, her voice cracking. "Promise me. PROMISE ME."

"We promise," the kids say in unison.

They understand this, even if they don't understand everything else that's happening.

Sally starts the engine. The green Golf rattles into life and pulls away from the forecourt, tires crunching on the loose gravel. In the side mirror, she watches Rookie grow smaller, the policewoman raising a hand in farewell.

Some moments stretch and compress in memory—the frantic drive down the motorway seems to have lasted seconds, while the brief conversation in the forecourt feels suspended in amber, preserved perfectly despite the passing years. Time would march on—governments would change, Britpop would fade (and come back again), mobile phones would shrink and then grow enormous once more, Diana would be mourned, the Millennium Bug would threaten and fizzle, London would become the centre of the world and host the greatest Olympics of all time, skinny jeans would come into fashion, Leicester City would win the Premiership, children would grow, the Queen would celebrate jubilee after jubilee... and then be mourned—but through it all, across recessions and referendums, through rain-soaked festivals and sun-baked beer gardens, through every stupid war, through every stupid prime minister, certain promises remain rooted in the soul, becoming their own kind of forever. Like the quiet dignity of helping a stranger in need at a petrol forecourt. Like the bond between siblings who once made a promise in the back seat of a battered green Golf, racing toward Scotland in the darkness.

Like love.

CHAPTER 16
ROLLING WITH IT

DAY 4

Liam and Patsy sit in the holding room. Though the morning light filters through the reinforced glass window, the room remains decidedly glum. The words from Rookie's story about their shared history hang in the air between them.

"I don't recall any of that," Patsy says, running a hand through her dishevelled hair.

Rookie leans against the door, her face softening. "Aye, ya wouldn't —you were only little." She taps her temple. "I remember cos it were ma first brush with domestic violence. Things were real bad back then," her voice drops, "and you always remember your first."

"I remember," Liam says as he stares at the floor, the fragmented memories fitting together like puzzle pieces. His mother's face in the rearview mirror, panicked. The flash of blue lights. The way she'd clutched his hand so tightly it hurt when they'd finally stopped at that petrol station. Rookie's words of comfort to his mum on the forecourt.

Rookie calmly opens the door. "Come on then, drunk tank's done its job. Time to go."

The morning sun is harsh and unforgiving on their tired faces as they exit the station. They stand awkwardly on the pavement, neither wanting to speak first.

Rookie follows them out. "I'll never forget what your mum said t'ya," she says, her voice unexpectedly loaded with quiet emotion. "Life is hard and we won't always get what we want. People'll probably come between yous—but you must always remember one thing."

Liam shifts his weight, clutching the ornate trunk tighter.

"That you love each other," Rookie continues, "and that love is what will keep you bound to each other—no matter what." She pauses, letting the words sink in. "I told that to my own kids."

And with that, she's gone, disappearing back into the station before either of them can respond.

The memory slams into Liam—his mother's voice from that night in '96, crouched beside them in the car, making them promise to look after each other. The weight of that broken promise sits heavy on his chest, constricting his breathing.

All these years, he'd blamed everyone else. His mother for leaving. Richard for splitting them up. But what had he done? Nothing. He'd let time pass, let the distance grow, never reaching out, never trying to find Patsy. He broke the promise he made.

Liam stares at his sister's profile, seeing for the first time how much she resembles their mother—the same determined set of her jaw, the same vulnerability hiding behind her eyes.

"She might have given up on us, but I'm not giving up on her," he says, his voice a whisper.

Patsy turns to him, her face unreadable, closed off. She opens her mouth as if to speak, then seems to think the better of it.

No more words pass between them. Instead, they stand facing each other for one moment longer—a moment filled with all the things they should say, but don't. And as the sun rises, it casts their shadows on the wall behind, where a poster for an upcoming '90s revival gig featuring bands they once listened to together in the back of their mother's green Golf flutters as a gust of wind rips it from the wall. The memories they've stirred up on this journey scatter like the morning litter, leaving nothing but the harsh reality of the present cold light of day.

Then Patsy turns right, heading south.

And Liam breaks left, heading towards the train station's northbound platform.

They walk away from each other, two lone figures growing smaller in opposite directions, connected by nothing but a shared past they can't escape and a mother who seems just as far away now as she has ever been.

It's over.

𝄞

Jagdeesh stares at the contents of the ornate trunk. "You sure this is all okay? To send?" he asks.

Sally sits at her desk, pen hovering over paper that bears only the words:

To my dearest children, Liam and Patsy,

"That's every penny of my estate," she says without looking up. "You can't take it with you. Chidi, my brother-in-law, will take care of things at the other end."

Jagdeesh can see she's spent, emotionally and physically. "Come on, shall we get you to bed?"

"I need to finish. I need to put into words what I couldn't say after all these years. They deserve that much at least."

"We will finish the job. I promise," Jagdeesh says gently as he lifts her up.

"You'll have to deliver the letters already written," Sally tells him. "We'll send the box ahead tomorrow, but I'll deliver this last letter in person. If it all goes to plan, I can be in Scotland soon and wait for my children to come back to me—together."

"Sally, you may have to accept that you are too sick to get to Scotland..."

"No. I will. I can." The certainty in Sally's voice leaves Jagdeesh shaken.

He nods, gathering the letters she's already completed. He secures the ornate trunk with a decisive click of the lock, then places the key in Sally's palm, closing her fingers around it.

"You can give this to them yourself," he says, trying to believe it.

"When they bring the box to me, together, we will open it, together —that's a promise I intend to keep," she affirms, as she lays on the bed fiddling with her little digital radio.

Jagdeesh plants a kiss on her forehead, tucks her in and heads for the door. As he steps out, music follows him from Sally's radio into the main ward—Paul Weller's "Changingman" now blasts out in a show of defiance to Death himself.

Sally lets the music in like an old friend, one who's seen her through the best and worst, and who will stay until the very end.

The corridor stretches before Jagdeesh, its walls a dingy shade that might once have been white. He passes through the main ward where patients, all Indian, lie on beds arranged too close together. They all watch him with mild curiosity as he exits the big room at the end, the one with the fan, and the window, the one with the British music coming from it, and the white woman in it.

The music follows him, threading between beds and bouncing off walls—defiant, out of place. Patients tap fingers against sheets, nod heads imperceptibly. The song is from some distant land, but the pulse and raucous energy of it speaks to everyone.

The stairs are concrete, worn smooth in the centre from years of use. The windows in the stairwell are cracked, patched over with yellowing tape, and the air grows thicker as he descends. Indian porters in light blue uniforms pass him, nodding respectfully.

When Jagdeesh pushes through the double doors at street level, the full sensory assault of Jodhpur hits him at once. India's "Blue City" throbs with life—tuk-tuks and trucks honking incessantly, street vendors calling out their wares, the smell of spices and exhaust fumes mingling in the air. And everywhere, people. Moving, shouting, bargaining. Cows wander freely between vehicles, treated with more deference than pedestrians. Music coming from cars, from cafes, from stalls, from people singing—a cacophony of sight, smell and sound.

He steps out into the chaotic street, momentarily dazed by the transition from the hospital's relative peace. Through the sea of colourful saris and kurtas, he spots his destination across the road: the unmistakable red and yellow sign of India Post.

Clutching Sally's letters to his chest, Jagdeesh takes a deep breath and plunges into the current of humanity, carrying her words—and her hopes—toward her estranged children, who have no idea of her ill health or whereabouts. Which is India. As it happens. Only four and a half thousand miles away.

𝄞

Scarborough. Scarbados. Scarbs. Whatever you want to call it, like most British towns it has a train station. This one, like The Regal hotel, is a relic of Victorian grandeur... now reduced to bland functional utility. Two parallel platforms face each other across the tracks, their once-ornate iron work and decorative canopies now weathered by decades of sea salt and neglect and clumsily covered in plastic signage.

Liam walks along Platform B heading north. His worn satchel is hunched over his shoulder and the heavy ornate trunk, which came all the way from India, pulls at his arm muscles. His head's down, counting the cracks in the concrete beneath his well-worn trainers.

Across the tracks on Platform A heading south, Patsy moves in the opposite direction. She walks gingerly in her bare feet. Her face is drawn and eyes heavy from a night spent worried in a police cell. She wonders how it's only been four days since she left the sanctuary of Belsize Park. Four days that seem a lifetime. Four days where you've looked into your soul and worked out where the rest of your life will go. Well, wherever her life's heading, it won't be anywhere in Scarborough, as she is determined to get on the next train. Ticket or not, she's getting out of Dodge. And that's when she spots him, looking across from Platform B, the tracks between them might as well be the Himalayas. *This guy!* She thinks.

"Where you headed?" Liam calls across the divide.

"Where you headed?" Patsy echoes back at the same time.

"North." He says, shaking the trunk.

"South." She says, shaking her bare right foot.

They stare at each other, the finality of their divergent paths settling between them like the metal tracks.

"Alright then," Patsy says, with forced nonchalance.

"Yeah, alright then," Liam answers, already turning his back on his sister, determined to finish this whole mad quest to find their mother without her.

But he stops. Something inside him—the part that remembers holding Little Patsy's hand on road trips, the part that Sally had nurtured to be decent, the part that Sally made them make a promise to—won't let it end like this.

"For what it's worth," he calls, turning back, "I'm sorry. For what I said last night."

Patsy's shoulders tense. She mumbles something inaudible.

"What?" he says.

"I SAID OKAY," she shouts, then adds, "I'm sorry too."

Liam cups his ear with a small smile. "What?"

The last vestiges of Patsy's pride crumbles. She squeezes her fists, and then releases them. "I SAID I'M SORRY TOO. For wrecking your car. For gambling away your money."

Liam considers this. "OKAY. And what about my CD?"

The memory flickers across Patsy's face: *the casual flick of her wrist, the pristine mixtape sailing out of the Golf's window, the look on Liam's face as he was scrabbling along the hard shoulder to retrieve it. Not anger, but fear, no— loss.*

"Yes," she admits with a grimace, her voice carrying the weight of genuine contrition. "Yup, I'm sorry for that too. Your window is not a bin."

Liam nods solemnly. No, it is not.

"I guess this is goodbye," Patsy says, and a small part of her—the part that remembers being seven and having her big brother protect her—hopes he'll protest.

"Yep. Goodbye, Patsy."

"Goodbye, Liam."

But something flickers behind Liam's eyes. He digs into his jacket pocket and pulls out Sally's crumpled letter. The creases are deep, the paper worn from being read over and over. He holds it up like a talisman.

"It's not too late," he calls across the tracks.

"What's not too late?" Patsy asks, but her words are swallowed by the shriek of brakes and the hiss of hydraulics as their trains, one going north, one going south, arrive in perfect synchronicity, blocking their view of each other.

Through the rush of commuters and daytrippers, Liam's voice carries across: "TO CHANGE YOUR MIND."

Patsy stands frozen as the doors slide open. People jostle past her with travel suitcases and prams bumping against her legs. She watches Liam step onto his northbound train without a moment's hesitation.

She looks south toward London. Toward the only future she's programmed herself to consider. Forwards, always forwards. Never back.

Her hand goes to her wrist, to Sally's broken watch. It sits there, staring back at her. Time standing still. Like this train. If only for a moment, as this beast is about to get going.

A station guard gives her a pointed look and blows his whistle. She hesitates, one bare foot raised to the carriage step, one foot on the platform.

"Miss, make your decision. On or off," says the station guard.

Beep, beep, beep go the closing doors.

𝄞

Inside the northbound train, Liam makes a beeline through the carriage, hustling past a pensioner with shopping bags and a young mum at her wits' end, trying, and failing, to calm a screaming toddler. He spots the vacant toilet at the end of the carriage and darts inside, locking the door behind him with a satisfying click.

The toilet is about as pleasant as you'd expect on a British Rail train—a cramped cubicle filled with suspicious smells and strangely stained surfaces that definitely harbour more bacteria than you'd care to imagine. Liam gives the toilet seat a perfunctory wipe with some ragged paper-thin toilet tissue before perching on it, the Indian trunk balanced precariously on his knees. This fifth-class private compartment will be his ticket-free sanctuary for as long as he can manage it.

"All aboard!" comes the conductor's voice, muffled through the walls as the train lurches forward, its wheels screeching against metal as it pulls away from the platform.

Patsy stands in the aisle watching the other train depart. Her chest heaves. Her hair is wild. She looks like she's just escaped from a mental institution. A middle-aged woman with a blonde bob clutches her M&S handbag closer to her chest while a businessman in a suit reading the cricket section of The Telegraph draws scorn on her. A group of teenagers snigger behind their phones, already filming her for their TikTok followers. Patsy ignores them all, scanning the carriage with determination. Near the far end, she spots what she's looking for—the universal sign for the toilet. She's halfway down the aisle when she notices the ticket inspector working his way through the next carriage, methodically checking tickets.

"Bollox," she whispers.

She picks up her pace, but stops inadvertently to pick up a fallen ticket for a struggling elderly gent... and hands it back to him with a broad smile, which he duly returns, before she makes a beeline for the loo.

The toilet is just ahead, but the door is closed with the red OCCUPIED sign staring back at her.

She hammers on the door with her fist. "Hello?"

No answer.

"Bollox," she says, much louder this time.

The ticket inspector is just about to make his way through the carriage partition doors, with his ticket machine at the ready.

"Oi!" Patsy hisses, knocking harder. "Whoever's in there, hurry up! I'm pregnant and I need a..."

The lock slides open, and the door swings inward to reveal Liam, his expression a mixture of surprise and confusion.

"You're pregnant?" he asks, eyes darting to her flat stomach. "I'm gonna be an uncle?" he says, gleefully.

Patsy rolls her eyes. "What, with the amount I drink?! I was just..." She pauses, taking a breath. "You're right. We're all we have, and Mum said we had to look out for each other. She was right and I'm holding up my end of the bargain."

Before Liam can respond, she squeezes into the tiny cubicle, pressing him back against the wall.

"Quick, the inspector's coming," she whispers, pulling the door closed behind her and turning the lock with a satisfying clunk.

The space is impossibly small for two adults. Patsy hoists herself up onto the edge of the sink, her legs dangling uncomfortably near Liam's face as he perches back on the toilet seat. The Indian trunk sits wedged between them, an ever-present reminder of their mission to meet their mum at Cape Wrath or the 'Edge of the World'—wherever that may be. 480 miles from Scarborough by train, as it goes.

Liam begins to hum under his breath—that familiar indie riff that's been stuck in his head since the '90s.

"Please don't," Patsy groans, "not Oasis again."

"Roll With It," Liam says with a hint of pride, "the B-side to—"

"I know what it is," she interrupts, shifting uncomfortably on the sink edge. "You used to play it on repeat in your room until Da... Richard threatened to throw the CD player out the window."

"Still got it," Liam says, tapping his temple. "Every note, from every song of my mixtape stored up here. And "Roll With It" was song number ten."

He resumes humming, a bit louder now, adding in some of the lyrics under his breath. Patsy rolls her eyes but doesn't tell him to stop again. There's something almost comforting about this annoying habit of his—a constant that's survived their many years of separation.

"Right," she says, catching her breath. "How much cash you got?"

"Nudda," Liam replies, patting his empty pockets. "You?"

"Nudda," she echoes. "So we have to get to the edge of Scotland to meet Mum. We've no food, no cash, and no car."

Liam's eyes drop to her feet. Patsy's feet are filthy—the soles black with grime, the cut on her foot now crusted with dried blood.

"And you're not wearing shoes."

"And I'm not wearing any shoes," she agrees, wiggling her toes self-consciously. "So what's the plan, Batman?"

Liam shrugs, the movement barely perceptible in the confined space. "Well, Patsy, sister, I tried making a plan, and it backfired spectacularly. We got stuck in a field, lost the car, lost all our money and spent the night in a police station. I'll get us to Scotland, but as for plans, nah. I'm just gonna roll with it..."

"Roll with it? That's your plan?" Patsy's voice rises incredulously.

"Yep," Liam says. His voice then takes on that philosophical tone that always used to drive her mad as a teenager, and which clearly still does, "One to another, Sis. At some point, you have to accept that there is no plan and that the world is wide and that we are really small. And take comfort in that."

He turns to look pensively out the tiny window, watching as the urban sprawl of Scarborough gives way to the lush green fields of the North Yorkshire countryside, while humming along to "Roll With It."

Patsy stares at him, her brow furrowed. "Wait. What?"

"Keep the faith," Liam says simply, then adds with a small smile, "You know, like the song."

A knock at the door makes them both freeze.

"Tickets, please," comes the muffled voice of the inspector.

Their eyes meet sharply. SHIT!

"Oh, my wife's in there, chap," calls a quavering voice from outside. "She's got a bad stomach and, well, doesn't travel well. She may be in there some time."

It's the elderly gentleman Patsy helped earlier, returning her kindness with a lifesaving intervention.

"Righty-ho," the ticket inspector says while exhaling, highlighting his disinterest, as they hear the electronic buzz of his ticket machine and his clunky footsteps moving up the carriage.

They breathe a collective sigh of relief. Liam starts quietly humming again, drumming his fingers lightly on the Indian trunk. Patsy notices his lips moving with words she can't quite make out.

"Well," he says, catching her look, "we are gonna be in here for a looooooooong time, so we'll just have to make our own entertainment."

Patsy rolls her eyes, but this time she actually listens to his quiet singing, and the words take on a new meaning as she commits fully to finding their mum at the edge of the world. They may be running late, but after this many years, she figures their mum can wait... just a little longer.

503, 502, 501 miles and counting. As the train's wheels churn along the tracks, it becomes the rhythm section to the siblings' journey north as they belt out "Roll With It" while drumming on the Indian trunk, and splashing water on each other from the tap.

YORK STATION

The siblings shoot across the platform just as the final boarding announcement drones from the speakers. Liam grabs Patsy's elbow, pulling her through the closing doors of the Edinburgh-bound train.

"This way," he whispers, checking both directions along the carriage before ducking into the toilet.

The lock clicks. OCCUPIED. Sanctuary, for now.

Patsy immediately commandeers the tiny sink, scooping handfuls of water over her head. "God, I feel disgusting," she mutters as she rinses her hair.

Liam digs deep into his satchel and produces the afro shampoo bottle she bought him back in Great Yarmouth.

With a quick 'why not?' she lathers up and instantly feels better.

The countryside blurs outside as miles tick by. Fields melt into towns then back to fields again. Through the tiny toilet window, Liam watches England slip away beneath wheels that never stop turning. Beside him, Patsy studies her reflection in the glass, water dripping from her freshly washed hair. For the first time in years, a flutter of anticipation sparks in her chest. Somewhere in the far north, her mother is waiting. After everything, after all this time—she's actually going to see her again. The thought both terrifies and exhilarates her.

491, 490, 489 miles to go and counting.

EDINBURGH WAVERLEY

The siblings casually sneak through the station squinting under the harsh train station lighting. A sea of Scots ebb and flow around the departure board that flickers with destinations and times. The obligatory bagpipe busker blares out a rendition of some classic tune. No one's quite sure if he's doing it justice, or flat-out murdering it.

While Patsy finds her way to the large network map mounted on the wall, Liam ducks into the overpriced Boots. He casually picks up a hairbrush, gives his hair a few quick strokes until it forms a nice shape, then discreetly places the brush back on the shelf.

Rejoining his sister, he spots her finger tracing their path forward—a thin red line stretching northward.

"Edinburgh to Inverness," she murmurs, followed by, "then Inverness to Thurso."

Liam's finger continues from where hers stops.

"And then west," he says, tracing the coastal route to Cape Wrath. "To the edge of the world."

Their eyes meet. No words needed. Just a nod between them—they're committed now.

Patsy feels a strange mix of dread and hope flutter in her stomach as she stares at their final destination. After all these years, what would she even say to her?

While waiting for their next train, Liam rummages through a Biffa bin near the emergency exit. He emerges triumphant, holding aloft a pair of women's flip-flops, one with a broken strap.

"Jackpot," he grins.

"You've got to be joking," Patsy says, but she takes them anyway.

"Better than nothing, innit?" he replies.

On the Inverness-bound train, they settle back into their preferred positions in the toilet—Liam perched on the closed lid, Patsy on the edge of the sink, cleaning her crusty feet. She examines the broken flip-flop, and without hesitation, she grabs the hem of her designer dress—the last relic of her Belsize Park life—and tears a strip clean off. The sound of ripping fabric echoes in the tiny cubicle.

"Hold this," she instructs Liam, handing him the flip-flop while she tears another strip from the dress.

She threads the first piece of cloth through the broken flip-flip, fashioning an unexpectedly elegant repair. Then, after gathering her still-damp hair, she hands Liam the second strip of fabric.

"Make yourself useful," she says. "Tie it tight."

"How tight?" Liam asks.

"Like you're angry with it," Patsy replies, and for a moment, they both smile.

Liam secures her hair into a neat ponytail, pulling it tight as instructed, and Patsy nods her approval.

"Not bad," she says, admiring both repairs.

Liam digs through his backpack and pulls out his spare sky blue tracksuit. "A bit on the big side, but..."

"You've had that all along?" she remarks, incredulously.

"Well yeah, but I had Dad wrapped in it." Referring to his dad's urn, who he has unwittingly taken on this journey with them.

Something in Patsy's expression softens as she looks at her brother, and for a moment, she sees him not as the annoying man-child she's been stuck with, but as someone who's been carrying his grief—literally—all this time.

She takes the tracksuit with a gentle nod, then looks down at her now-ruined designer dress, the tear having opened up the seam all the way to her hip.

"Oh this will help with that," Liam says, whipping out his spare Scotland football shirt, which he tosses to her.

Patsy catches it, her face twisting in horror. "Hell no."

But somewhere in her mind, Sally's voice cuts through: *Throw in a few surprises...*

With a resigned sigh, she pulls the baggy football shirt over her head. Then, with surprising dexterity in the cramped space, she shimmies out of her dress and moves towards the small window, ready to finally purge her old life, once and for all.

But something stops her. She turns to Liam.

"Your window's not a bin, right?" she says while smiling.

Liam smiles back and nods with approval as Patsy crumples the dress and stuffs it into the actual bin. The last remnant of Belsize Patsy, gone.

279, 278, 277 miles to go, and counting.

THURSO (THE END OF THE LINE)

They emerge into the late afternoon light in perfect sync. Liam and Patsy stride out onto the platform wearing matching sky blue tracksuits and Scotland football shirts, finally in step, finally in harmony.

A gentle breeze carries the salt tang of the North Sea. They've come so far, yet the most important part of their journey still lies ahead. Liam considers his sister, seeing not the prickly reality TV star from days ago, but a determined woman ready for whatever comes next. He drapes his arm across her shoulders, and to his surprise, she doesn't shrug it off.

The sign for the **WEST HIGHLANDS** points the way with its oversized arrow, and they follow without hesitation. Every step means a second closer to Sally, every second turns to a minute, every minute an hour. The rhythm of their journey ticks on like a watch that's finally been wound. In just a few short hours, they'll have achieved their mission. They'll see their mother again. Why didn't you fight for us? Why did you leave? Was I just too much trouble? Did you truly love me, us? Why wait till you're dying to return? All the questions that have haunted them for years will finally have answers.

Liam glances at Patsy as they follow the sign. Her face has lost that permanent scowl, replaced by something softer, more hopeful. Maybe it's getting her as far away from London as possible and seeing the glorious Highlands that has softened her? Whatever it is, he feels it too—a lightness he hasn't experienced in years. The weight of the past seems to lift with every mile marker they pass.

Whatever awaits them at Cape Wrath—at the 'Edge of the World'—they're ready for it now. Together.

71, 70, 69 miles to go and counting.

CHAPTER 17
IF TIME IS CONSTANT, BUT OUR MEMORIES WERE MADE IN THE PAST, THEN THE PAST IS ALWAYS PRESENT.

~ 1996 ~

The green Golf GTI Mk 2 rattles into Lyndhurst Grove and pulls up just down the road from Sally's terraced home. The car's ancient now—bought near new from some dodgy bloke in Camden Town in the 80s. No air conditioning, black smoke belching from the exhaust, over 100,000 miles on the clock, but she's never once let Sally down. Noel had insisted on checking every nook and cranny before they handed over the cash, much to the seller's obvious irritation who looked like he had an acid house party to get to. Together they'd fixed her up, resprayed the mismatched panels and replaced the cigarette-burned seat covers. This was the car that Noel drove Sally to the hospital in, and the car he drove all three of them home after they welcomed baby Liam into the world.

"Cheers, Ol' Girl," Sally whispers, patting the roof as she locks up. It's become a ritual—her little thank you to the motor that keeps her world turning.

The heat hits her the moment she steps onto the pavement. She quickly steps aside as a bunch of BMX bandits zoom past, the Coke cans clipped to their spokes make that classic BRRRRRRM sound.

"Oi, mind out," she warns cheerily.

"Sorry Sally, can Liam and Patsy come out later?"

"We got plans," she calls after them, but they're already bombing down the road.

Somewhere down the street, kids are having a kickabout, and "Three Lions" blares from a passing Ford Escort. This makes her grin, despite finding the whole football obsession completely mental. Then, a massive BARKING rottweiler bounds toward the garden gate. But Sally doesn't break stride, it's only her neighbour's dog—all slobber with no bite.

"Afternoon, Jarvis. Alright, Mr. Barrett?"

Her elderly Rastafarian neighbour emerges from behind his prize roses, mopping his brow with a tea towel. "Bless up, Sally. This heat's somethin' else, innit?"

"Love it. Better than the rain," she replies.

"Left Jamaica for the rain, y'know," he chuckles, scratching Jarvis behind the ears.

"Hang on—you left paradise for this?"

"Paradise is too hot, Sal. Give me a nice bit o'drizzle any day. Keeps the roses happy, innit?

"But… Peckham?" she questions, a little too incredulously.

"This place got energy, Sal. No beaches, granted, but it's jus' as alive—and it rains—can't beat that temperate climate love."

Sally laughs as she makes her move to the front door, "Speaking of energy, better get inside before my two destroy the house."

"Bless," he says, while chuckling. "Kids, am I right?"

Sally bounces through her front door, glancing at her watch: 3:31. Result. That Friday afternoon feeling floods through her—two whole days of freedom stretching ahead, no work, no customers, no stress. She dumps her handbag on the hallway table, kicks off her sandals, and sighs as her bare feet connect with the cool wooden floor.

Bliss.

"LeeLee? Pats? Mumma's home," she calls out, shrugging off her cardigan.

The muffled sounds of television laughter drift from the living room. Sally pokes her head around the doorframe to find LeeLee and Pats sprawled on the carpet, surrounded by snacks, with their faces illuminated by the blue glow of the telly. They're watching that scene from 'The Blues Brothers'—the one where Jake and Elwood make absolute chaos in the fancy restaurant. Pats giggles as John Belushi stuffs his face and LeeLee mimics the movements, pretending to chew with his mouth wide open.

She spots the envelope on the side table—MARSTON'S CARAVAN PARK. She tears it open, scans quickly, and grins. Reservation confirmed for this weekend. Perfect timing.

"Hello, my little monsters," Sally says, with her voice carrying a lightness—maybe because of the weekend plans she's got brewing. A proper little break: two nights free at some caravan park in East Anglia, thanks to 'The Sun' newspaper.

"Have you been good for Daddy?"

Their heads swivel in unison, momentarily distracted from the antics on screen.

"Richard said we could watch TV," Little Liam says quietly.

"That's fine, LeeLee," Sally says, ruffling his braids. Her fingers linger in the soft coils, and suddenly she's back in the upstairs bedroom in the mid-'80s—*Noel's patient hands guide hers, showing her how to oil their baby's scalp, how to be gentle with the delicate growing curls. "Like this, Sal. See? He's beautiful."* Some memories fade, but this one remains crystal clear—Noel's voice, his gentle touch, his pride in their son.

But something feels off. The house is too quiet. Richard's car is in the street, so he must be home, but there's no sign of him. Then she hears it—a stifled giggle from upstairs, followed by the unmistakable creak of bedsprings.

Sally freezes. Her instinct is to run upstairs and confront whatever is happening, but she glances at the children, so innocent, so unaware.

"Where's your dad?" she asks, fighting to keep her voice steady.

"Upstairs, Mumma," Little Patsy says, turning back to the TV. "He's been up there ages."

Another giggle floats down the stairs, followed by a low, masculine chuckle that Sally recognises all too well. Her heart seems to stop in her chest, time collapsing around her as realisation dawns.

She glances at her watch, a habit born of always being on time, of always keeping everything together—but today she got off early. The second hand judders to a stop, a tiny mechanical heart attack in the midst of the impending chaos. She taps the glass face but nothing happens. For Sally Digsby, 3:33 pm on this Friday afternoon will forever be the time when her world stopped turning. But time doesn't stop for Sally. She moves towards the stairs with deliberate calm, each step measured and precise, as if walking through the annals of her memory as she creates it.

"Stay here," she instructs the kids. "Keep watching your film."

Ascending the stairs feels like climbing a mountain. Each step takes her higher towards something she knows will change everything, but she can't stop herself. It's like watching a car crash in slow motion—horrifyingly compelling—and with each step her anger intensifies, each increase taking precious seconds that can never be reclaimed.

At the top of the stairs, she pauses outside the bedroom door. The sounds from within are unmistakable now—the rhythmic creak of the bed frame, breathless moans, and Richard's voice murmuring endearments that he hasn't spoken to Sally in years.

She doesn't knock. Why should she? It's her bloody bedroom, the same room where she'd gazed upon Noel's sleeping face in those early married days, the same room where she'd nursed Little Liam through his first fever, the same room where she'd reluctantly created new memories with Richard after believing she might never move forwards again.

The door swings open to reveal Richard, her husband, the father of her daughter, naked and entangled with another woman. Not just any woman—Minnie, the wealthy divorcee who owns the chain of estate agents. The same Minnie whose office windows Richard has been cleaning every Tuesday morning for the past six months.

Time stands still. Or perhaps it's just Sally's broken watch. In this moment, past, present, and future collapse into a single point of blazing clarity.

Richard's head snaps up, his eyes shocked. "Sally! You're home early."

Minnie, looking infuriatingly calm for someone who's been caught shagging another woman's husband with her kids downstairs, makes a half-hearted attempt to cover herself with the duvet.

"Take a picture, it might last longer," Minnie drawls, attempting to regain some dignity. "It's been going on for six months. Time waits for no woman, Sally dear. You can't expect a man to live in the shadow of a ghost forever."

Something snaps inside Sally—a dam breaking, years of resentment and compromise flooding through her system. She lunges forward and grabs Minnie by her long blonde hair, yanking her from the bed with surprising strength.

"Get out," she hisses, dragging Minnie towards the landing. "GET. OUT."

Richard stumbles after them, putting his y-fronts on backwards. "Sally, calm down. We need to talk—"

But Sally is beyond talking. She's in that place where fury meets clarity, where every slight, every micro-aggression and every disappointment crystallises into perfect, incandescent rage. She drags the 'other woman' down the stairs.

Little Liam and Little Patsy stand with their faces a mask of confusion and fear. Sally barely registers their presence as she hauls Minnie towards the front door.

"Mumma?" Little Patsy whimpers.

"Go back to your film," Sally says, not breaking stride. "Mumma's just taking out the filth."

She flings open the front door and physically propels Minnie onto the pavement outside. The 'other woman', naked save for a pair of knickers, stumbles into the wall—her pale flesh lighting up the street for the gawking neighbours.

"My clothes!" Minnie protests, with her arms crossed over her fake tits, and her face flush with humiliation.

Mr. Barrett looks up from pruning his roses, eyes widening at the spectacle before him. Minnie shrinks under his gaze.

"Lawd 'ave mercy," Mr. Barrett says, shaking his head slowly. He looks past Minnie to Richard, who's now at the doorway. "Sally is good people, y'know. You mash up you life for dis?"

He kisses his teeth in disgust and tugs Jarvis away as it growls at

Richard. "Some man nuh deserve dem good family," he mutters as he enters his front door.

"Well, I need my clothes," Minnie repeats, voice trembling with fury and embarrassment.

"Walk in shame, for the rest of your life. Bitch." Sally slams the door so hard the letterbox rattles, sealing off the immediate past from the imminent future.

She turns to find Richard standing in the hallway, hastily dressed now, his face flushed with defiance, no guilt present. He's not the window cleaner she married anymore; he's someone else, someone she doesn't recognise in this suspended moment between what was and what will be. She notices LeeLee hiding Pats behind the sofa—their usual sanctuary when Richard snaps.

"It's over, Sal," he says, his voice steely with resolve. "I'm leaving, and Patsy's coming with me."

Sally snarls, "You get fucked she is."

"Get used to it, Sal. The family courts look at facts, not feelings. I've got a stable relationship, a good income thanks to Minnie, and a proper house. What've you got when I stop paying the rent here? A council flat with your bastard son?"

Sally steps towards him, her fists clenched. "Over my dead body will she spend her life raised by a thick thug and a dirty slag."

Richard's face fills with rage. "I've never been good enough. You hold on to him in the past like he's some kind of god."

"You're not half the man he was."

"Yeah! YEAH!"

That's the snap that Richard was waiting for, as his control shatters completely. He storms into the living room, towards the mantelpiece where a simple urn sits beside a framed photo of Noel in his Scotland football shirt. Liam's father. Sally's first husband. A moment captured from 1986, preserved in time to forever remain in Sally and Liam's present.

"Don't you dare—" Sally begins, but it's too late.

Richard snatches up the urn in one hand and the photo in the other. With a savage grunt, he hurls the framed photo against the wall. The glass shatters, with fragile shards exploding across the carpet.

Little Patsy screams. The image of Noel—smiling, alive, frozen in time—lies exposed among the broken glass.

"Stop it!" Little Liam yells, with tears streaming down his face.

"Shut it, niglet," Richard says, storming towards the downstairs toilet, the urn clutched in his iron grip. He shoulders the door open, twisting the lid off the urn.

"No!" Sally screams, her voice raw with desperation. "NO!"

Despite her bruises, despite his size and despite his hard wiring for violence and abuse, she launches herself at Richard's back, clawing scratching fighting with the feral intensity of a woman who after many years has just woken up to recognise her value. He's focused on upending the urn into the toilet, trying to scatter the grey ashes of Noel into the water. The physical remains of a man long dead but eternally present within this household. But she won't let him, she keeps the urn upright with all her strength.

"Stop!" Sally's voice breaks on the word. She punches, kicks, anything to make him stop, but Richard is bigger, stronger, fueled by jealous rage. Her nails rake down his face, drawing blood, and he turns, shoving her away with brutal force. Sally slams against the wall, the breath knocked from her lungs, but the urn is now safely out of his hands. Richard advances on her, his face contorted with a fury she's never seen before. He hits her—once, twice—fists pounding into her ribs, her stomach, thighs, places no one will see.

"You think you're so much better than me?" Richard snarls, spittle mixed with blood flying from his lips. "Saint Sally and her perfect dead husband. This is the real world, Sally. The past is the past. Move the fuck on."

Sally instinctively curls into herself, protecting her vital organs. Through tear-blurred vision, she sees the urn on the floor. She lunges for it, grasping it to her chest. Seeing her movement, Richard reaches down and wrenches the urn from her grip.

His rage peaks; he raises his arms, the urn clutched in his hands, preparing to bring it crashing down on Sally's head.

That's when Little Liam moves.

Something in the ten-year-old snaps.

This quiet, gentle boy who has never raised a hand in anger, who walks away from playground conflicts, who turns the other cheek to racial taunts, launches himself at Richard with a primal scream.

"GET OFF MY MUM!"

Little Liam jumps on Richard's back, small fists pummeling, legs kicking. In his hand, somehow, he's grabbed Sally's crystal ashtray from the coffee table. Before he can think, before he can stop himself, he brings it down hard on Richard's temple, splitting the ashtray into two jagged pieces.

Blood spurts and Richard howls, dropping the urn to clutch at his head. He staggers, momentarily stunned, then turns on Little Liam with murderous intent.

"You little—"

But Sally is on her feet now, scooping up the urn, pushing herself between Richard and her son, who she takes the broken ashtray from. In her eyes, past, present, and future collide—the woman who lost her first husband now defends the son who bears his features.

"Touch him and I'll kill you," she says, her voice deadly quiet as she holds the jagged ashtray to his jugular.

The moment hangs in the balance—Richard, bleeding and enraged; Sally, bruised but unbowed; Little Liam, shocked at his own violence, staring at the blood on his hands with horror dawning in his eyes. In these suspended seconds, he makes a vow to himself that will echo through the decades: never again. Never again will he raise his hand in violence, no matter the provocation.

Little Patsy stands in the doorway, trembling, tears streaming down her face. "Mumma?"

Something in Sally's expression shifts. A decision crystallises. She grabs Little Liam's hand, noting with horror the blood on his small knuckles. Then she hits Richard on the head with the blunt side of the ashtray piece, knocking him down with cold determination and relinquishing whatever fear she had of him.

"Let's go," she says, her voice strangely calm. "Let's go."

She scoops up Little Patsy with her free arm and, still clutching the urn, herds the children towards the front door. Richard, dazed from the fresh blow, struggles to follow, blood streaming down his face and eyes.

"Sally!" he roars, as his hands slip around in his own blood. "Don't you fucking dare take my daughter!"

But Sally's already out the door and past Minnie, who's shouting obscenities from the pavement. She bundles the children into the green Golf, hands shaking so badly she struggles to get the key in the ignition.

The engine sputters to life. First gear. Richard is at the driver's window now, pounding on the glass with bloodied fists.

"Stop the car! Give her to me!"

The central locking clicks, just before Richard yanks futilely at the door handle.

"I won't let you split them up," Sally shouts through the glass.

Richard's expression turns murderous. "When you get back, she's coming with me. You understand?"

Sally slams the car into second gear and the Golf lurches away. In the rear-view mirror, she sees Richard standing in the middle of the road, blood streaming down his face, mouth open in a silent howl of rage. The image burns itself into her memory, a horrid snapshot that will resurface in her dreams for years to come.

Little Liam and Little Patsy huddle together in the back seat, shell-shocked and silent. Little Patsy looks back at her dad with worry and a child's confusion in her eyes as she tries to make sense of what she's witnessed. Little Liam stares at his hands, at the blood drying in the creases of his knuckles. Something has changed inside of him too, a fundamental shift in his understanding of the world and his place in it. He puts his headphones over his ears and presses play on his Sony Discman.

Sally drives blindly, without direction, just away—away from the broken home, away from the violence, away from the shattered remnants of their family life. Her watch has stopped at 3:33, but the car's digital clock reads 3.45. Time continues its relentless march and this 12-minute moment will stretch to fill the years and decades ahead to become the genesis point where their family story, unceremoniously, split into three.

Sally winces in pain as she shifts her trusty green Golf into fourth gear and hits the dual carriageway. She doesn't know where they're going. She doesn't know what will happen next. All she knows is that she won't go back. Not today. Not tomorrow. Maybe not ever.

In the boot, nestled among jumpers and emergency supplies, the urn sits secure, wrapped in one of Sally's cardigans. Noel's presence, constant and comforting despite the years, despite the distance, despite death itself. Past and present, memory and reality, all flowing together in a continuum that defies the tidy boundaries of linear time.

CHAPTER 18
ENDURING

JODPHUR PART I
2025

Sunset in India. The evening rays of the dusky orange sun cast long golden shadows across Sally's hospital room, bathing the white walls in warmth while burning her thin elongated shadow onto the wall where it dances with her every pained movement. She sits by the open window, watching Jodhpur, India's gorgeous blue city, come alive with the evening bustle far below.

Trucks and tuk-tuks weave between cows and pedestrians in that uniquely Indian choreography of organised chaos. It's a miracle no one is killed, but from her high vantage point, she sees the magic of Indian traffic in all its glory, which she considers briefly is a microcosm of humanity itself—millions of micro-decisions made in milliseconds to avoid catastrophic collision. People yield and advance in a dance of survival and progress that makes no logical sense, yet works with startling efficiency. A complex symphony, she remembers someone once describing it as. Everyone has a place to be, and everyone wants to get there safely.

Just like when she made the decision, within a millisecond, to leave Richard that fateful day during the height of the summer of '96. A snap judgement that altered three lives forever.

To many, 1996 was THE year. Euro '96 had the whole country singing 'Football's Coming Home', and even if it didn't end thirty years of hurt it didn't matter, because the country was riding the crest of a wave that was 'Cool Britannia'. Trainspotting's skagheads told us to 'choose life', and Damien Hirst was slicing various animals in half and calling it 'art'. Everyone was doing the Macarena, Britpop reached its zenith before its inevitable crash and burn, and the Spice Girls zigazig-ahd their way into the global consciousness with Union Jack dresses, platform trainers and 'Girl Power'. Oasis played Knebworth and a quarter of the population of Britain used fucking landline telephones to try and buy tickets to watch Noel thrash his guitar and Liam thrash his voice during the height of their powers. Sally had been there through it all, making a mixtape CD with Liam and dancing along to it with Patsy, oblivious to the fact that these ordinary moments would one day become extraordinary memories.

She muses that her memory has since become a time machine, a vault where her children exist in playful abandon. Stored away are all the moments she took for granted then, but now wishes she had years longer to relive. *'Remember, take care of your memories—it's all we really have'*. A wise Northerner told her that once. A distant, almost-forgotten memory that has suddenly snapped back into sharp focus.

The sweet smell of jasmine from the gardens mingles with the pungent spices from the street food vendors below, teasing her nostrils. Fifteen years she's been here. Fifteen years since she'd stepped off the plane with nothing but a suitcase and a determination to start anew. The weight of that million quid had felt so heavy then, so fraught with possibility and guilt. She'd spent none of it on herself —not one penny. Instead, it had gone to the street kids, to the school and to Jagdeesh's education. To a future for Liam and Patsy that they didn't know existed. As she sat there on the plane to New Delhi, which Sally only chose as her destination because it was the very next plane out of Heathrow after her cab dropped her off, she promised herself that she would get her life together and work her way through her issues. With no one to rely on, and no one relying on her, it came to her easier than expected.

Sally tucks the last unfinished letter into her journal. She'll finish it on the plane.

"Packet of Salt & Vinegar Walkers, a cup of PG Tips, and a proper chippy tea," she whispers to herself, listing the small home comforts she'd missed most over the years. Not that the food here isn't magnificent—it is—but there were some tastes of home that just can't be replicated, just as there are some holes in the heart that can't be filled from five thousand miles away.

The clock on the wall shows 6 pm and like clockwork, a hospital orderly wheels in her evening meal with a nod and a smile: the same bland rice and dry toast she's been served every evening since her fatal diagnosis. She pushes it away without a second glance.

"No pakora tonight then?" she jokes weakly, more to herself than to the non-English speaking porter.

The doctor had been clear this morning—two weeks at most. But what did doctors know? They'd told Noel he had six hours after he was assaulted, and he'd lived for three days—the best and worst three days of her life were those spent making final memories with him and Liam. They'd told her mum she had months, but she was gone in a fortnight before Sally could even move on from denial. Life doesn't run to schedule, especially when you're dying.

A child's laughter echoes from somewhere down the corridor, reminding her of Jagdeesh's parable about the Crane Mother and her chicks.

"The Hawk of God snatches the Crane Mother away, never to be of this world again," she murmurs. "Playful sport is forgotten, in its place, silence."

She understands it better now, but not as Jagdeesh intended, which was that if she went silently into the night it would ease her children's pain. For Sally, the Crane Mother was robbed of the chance to say goodbye—to make those final moments count—to explain. And her children were left with only silence, just as Sally had left Liam and Patsy. Just as her own mother had left her. The endless, maddening silence of someone there one minute and gone the next, with a lifetime of questions that can never be answered.

No. She won't be that crane. Her children deserve more than silence. They deserve an explanation, a goodbye, a chance to ask their questions. They deserve the truth, even if it hurts. Even if it means she has to drag her failing cancer-filled body across continents to deliver it.

The last rays of the orange sun disappear, calling time on today—as it has done for the 1.6 trillion days that have come before it. In zeros, this looks like:

0 0 0 0 0 0 0 0 0 0 0 0

Each and every day of every single living creature, plant or organism that has ever lived—humans with our fleeting 26,298 days on average, or the humble mayfly who completes its entire life cycle in just 1, or Methusala the Great Basin bristlecone pine tree in California, who's experienced 1,772,558 days and counting—are tucked into one of those zeros. A blink in cosmic time, yet we exist, all of us, within every single one of those beautiful infinity loops—forever. Including Sally, whose time on this physical plane has almost reached its final few ticks and tocks.

TickTockTickTockTickTockTickTockTickTockTickTock...

Sally rises from her chair. With quiet stealth learned from years of midnight escapes from Richard, she opens her drawer and pulls out the clothes she'd laid aside—her best Levi jeans, a baggy T-shirt, and a cardigan for the English chill she'd no doubt receive at Heathrow arrivals. She dresses as quickly as she can, wincing as the fabric catches on the IV port in her hand. She yanks it out without ceremony.

"I'm done with dying," she says.

Her bag is already packed. She's been ready for days—passport, medications, the trunk, the key, her Polaroid photo, her fountain pen and her final letter, incomplete though it is. The words will come. They have to. They will come.

Footsteps approach from outside the door. She freezes, like when she was a schoolgirl caught smoking with her best mates Jenna and Sophie behind the school's science block in the seventies... but Jagdeesh's familiar shuffle disarms her and she casually sits at her desk.

Through the open door, white coats blur in the doorway as the doctors finish their evening rounds. They nod perfunctorily in her direction before leaving. None of them can see that she's fully dressed beneath her hospital gown.

As soon as they're gone, Sally grabs her bag. She moves slowly but with determination—each step calculated, each breath measured. She's halfway to the door when Jagdeesh enters.

His eyes narrow. "What are you doing? Get back to bed."

"No," Sally says, straightening her spine. "And you can't make me."

He scans the room, sees the suitcase and the trunk and instinctively knows what she is up to.

"Well, you haven't finished your letter yet," Jagdeesh argues, "and it will be the middle of the night before you get to the airport. And you'll have to pray for a plane at that time to London."

Sally lashes his words back at him. "Then pray for me. I'll finish the letter on the flight."

Jagdeesh backs off, crestfallen. "Sally. No. You can't go. It's not right to..."

"What? Die?" her words freeze the air between them. "I'm either going to die alone here, die alone on a plane trying to see my children, or die having seen my children, one last time." She takes a breath, steadying herself. "So you just try and stop me, or step aside, because I'm not staying."

Jagdeesh looks at her—really looks at her—and recognises the steel beneath the frailty. He steps aside, shoulders slumping in resignation.

"I don't want you to die without me," he says, suddenly realising that he may lose the closest thing to a mother he's had since his own passed away when he was a child. To this, she hugs him tenderly and kisses his cheek with a solemn smile that says she has to leave.

"Look. Just meet me at the bottom of the stairs," he says. "I'll take your bags and try to buy you some time. We can catch the next flight, whenever it is."

A smile breaks across Sally's face. "Okay, I'll meet you downstairs."

She slips past him into the corridor. The stairwell door creaks as she pushes it open, revealing the long concrete steps spiralling downward. Freedom is just thirty steps away. Twenty-nine. Twenty-eight. Twenty-seven… and counting.

Jagdeesh arranges pillows under the blanket, creating the age-old illusion of a sleeping patient and switches off the machines. He places Sally's suitcase and the steel trunk by the door, ready for a quick escape. As he exits, he takes one last glance at the mock-up of Sally in the bed. It won't fool anyone for long, but perhaps long enough for them to board a plane.

He bounds down the stairs, taking them two at a time. His heart races with a mixture of fear and hope—fear that they'll be caught, hope that somehow, against all odds, Sally might get her wish to see her children one last time.

When he reaches the bottom floor, his racing heart stops dead.

Sally lies across the steps, motionless, her body twisted at an unnatural angle.

He throws the suitcase and trunk to the floor with a loud thud that echoes in the stairwell and drops to his knees beside her.

"Help," he calls. Then louder: "HELP! SOMEBODY HELP!"

As voices and footsteps approach rapidly from above and below, Jagdeesh takes Sally's hand. Her fingers are still warm and she gives his hand the faintest of squeezes.

Perhaps the Hawk came early to collect.

THE EDGE OF THE WORLD
DAY 4

The Highlands stretch before them, vast and ancient and full of its own memories of historic battles, wandering Kings, beheaded Queens and lost groomsmen on stag dos gone awry. It's making a new memory now, one of Liam and Patsy walking side by side along a deserted road, dwarfed by sweeping mountains to either side. Heather carpets the landscape in a vivid palette of purples interwoven with greens. Wild goats, sure-footed and curious, scramble on rocky outcrops before disappearing over ridges. Compared to the field in Norfolk, where Liam and Patsy danced the night away at the festival, this is a true Arcadia. A place so majestic, so undeniably beautiful, where God (whichever one you believe in) chose to crown their masterpiece. There's likely no better place for Liam and Patsy to make new memories as they edge closer to seeing their mum.

Liam draws a deep breath, filling his lungs with the crisp Highland air. It feels different up here, cleaner, clearer.

"This place is so..." he begins, searching for the right word.

"Scottish?" Patsy offers with a wry smile.

He shakes his head. "Peaceful." His voice drops to a whisper. "I feel at home."

They continue in silence, their footsteps crunching on stone and gravel. For the first time since they embarked on this journey, the silence between them isn't loaded with resentment or years of unspoken grievances. It simply exists, a shared moment of something approaching peace.

From a distance, the siblings appear tiny against the dramatic landscape, minuscule in fact. They reach a bend in the road and stick out their thumbs as the distant rumble of an engine breaks the silence. After what seems like an age, a battered white and blue pick-up truck slows and stops just ahead of them, its wheels kicking up dust.

Liam steps forward, clutching Sally's letters. He suddenly becomes conscious of his sky blue Adidas tracksuit, matching with Patsy's—but enough of his Scotland shirt is showing to give him the confidence to lean into the cab window. He considers the driver, a farmer-come-hiker type and his passenger, wearing skinny jeans, a pair of Ray-Bans and an Annie Lennox T-shirt.

"Wherey'headedladdie?" the driver's voice is so rich with Highland life that Liam barely understood a word he just said. So he makes a calculated guess.

"These coordinates," Liam begins, sorting through the papers, "um... 58.6—"

The driver waves away the numbers and speaks a little slower for the towny traveller. "Nay laddie... where ya headed?"

Liam straightens up. "The edge of the world?"

The driver and his navigator both nod, as if this makes perfect sense. Liam signals to Patsy, who clambers up onto the truck bed. Before he joins her, he leans back through the window, "Cool T-shirt by the way."

"You too," she says back.

Liam follows Patsy up onto the truck bed, settling beside her, crammed between the hay bales and tools. After a moment's hesitation, Liam puts his arm around Patsy. She doesn't pull away, instead she leans in and rests her head on his shoulder.

Inside the cab, the driver exchanges a knowing look with his passenger. The radio crackles to life, and the unmistakable opening folky guitar chords of "Caledonia" fill the truck before the poignant opening lyrics of missing home bring this stretch of the Highlands to life. The driver turns up the volume and sings along, as his passenger joins in with the chorus, both giving it their all, the way any Scotsperson does in any stadium, pub, truck cabin, their home or wherever they may be in the world when this song comes on.

The delicate guitar and vocal harmony floats back to Liam and Patsy. Liam, with his arm around Patsy and the Indian trunk between them, taps his fingers in time with the music against his dad's urn which sits in his lap—he closes his eyes and feels the vibrations of the music flow through him, through his sister, through his dad's urn and through his mum's Indian trunk. Despite being on the road, and in the middle of nowhere—he can't help but feel more intrinsically bound to this place, and to his family, than he has ever been.

As the truck winds its way along the Highland road, carrying them closer to their destination, Patsy looks up to see her big brother with his eyes closed, and at peace. A lyric about losing friends that needed to be lost feels epically poignant to her right now. She has one friend. And for her that's more than enough to build a future with.

The truck rounds another bend, and the majestic sweeping land seems to give way to the endless sky ahead. The edge of the world comes into view, its boundary between earth and heaven no longer just a metaphor.

60 miles and counting. They'll be there by sunset.

THE EDGE OF THE WORLD
~ 1996 ~

Sally stands at the cliff edge, clutching her children's hands where the land meets the sea as the sea meets the sky. Cape Wrath stretches before them, wild and magnificent, the edge of the world, the bridge between the land and the vast endless loop of the ocean that connects us all.

The wind whips her hair, mirroring the turmoil inside her. Mascara streaks down her face as she looks out over the Atlantic, its waves crashing violently against the rocks below. The air tastes of equal parts salt and freedom. Seabirds wheel overhead, their calls barely audible over the constant roar of the sea and the incessant doom spiralling thoughts in her head.

These cliffs have stood witness to a million stories—Viking raids, shipwrecks, lovers' promises, desperate prayers. They've weathered storms and sunshine alike with the same stoic indifference. The Highlands don't change, not really. Not like humans do. They remain while empires rise and fall, while hearts break and mend. From nothing to the dinosaurs to right here and right now.

Sally feels minuscule here. A mere speck against the enormity of space and time. The vastness before her offers a terrible invitation. One step. Just one step and it would all be over. All the pain, all the uncertainty, all the bloody unfairness of it all. He won't split them up. She won't let him, not at any cost.

"Maybe we should... walk off the edge of the world, now?"

"Mum." Little Liam's voice pierces through her thoughts. Little Patsy's hand tightens in hers, a silent reverberation of her brother's fear.

Sally's mind slips deeper, into a dark possibility.

"I should do it," she whispers. "Just join him. It would be so much easier."

Little Liam pulls back sharply, his face hardening into something primal. He grabs Little Patsy's hand and yanks her away from Sally, putting himself between his sister and the edge. He bares his teeth to his mother, protecting his sister from the one person who should never be a threat. In this moment, he becomes immovable, like the Scottish headland itself.

The look on his face snaps Sally back to reality. To what she was contemplating. To what her children thought she was contemplating. She pulls them both into a fierce hug, her body trembling. When she speaks again, her voice is steadier.

"No, LeeLee," she says, her voice breaking as she drops to her knees on the rough ground. "Of course not. I'd never hurt my babies. I'm, I'm sorry for scaring you."

A sudden gust of wind blows in from the ocean and envelops them, as if the world itself exhales in relief.

The boot of their faithful green Golf opens, revealing Noel's urn nestled carefully among blankets, a precious cargo that would one day make this same trip again.

"Liam," she says, her voice catching. "I need you to know something. Your daddy once told me..."

GREENWICH DISTRICT HOSPITAL
~ 1987 ~

Post-birth bliss suffuses the otherwise sterile room with warmth. Noel cradles baby Liam in his arms, his face soft with wonder, hope and love—all the pre-programming every human baby comes with.

"Look a' him," Noel says softly, his Glaswegian accent echoing around the room. "Perfect. Ay?"

Sally watches them from the bed, exhausted but content. Noel's large, gentle hands make tiny Liam look even smaller. His dark skin contrasts with the hospital-white blanket.

"He has your nose," Noel says, not looking up. "Thank Christ."

"Shut up," Sally laughs weakly. "Your nose is perfect."

"Aye, but yours is more perfect. Everythin' bout you is more perfect."

An older nurse pokes her head in, and smiles awkwardly at the sight of them. Sally doesn't miss the momentary confusion in her eyes —Black father, white mother, the mixed-race baby.

But the woman's professionalism quickly reasserts itself.

"Everything alright in here?" the nurse asks.

"Everything's… perfect," Noel answers, still not taking his eyes off his son.

When they're alone again, Noel brings Liam to Sally's bedside. He sits at the edge of the mattress, their new family complete in this precious circle of three.

"My pa woulda loved him," Noel says quietly. His own dad had never left Lagos, and had only seen his two Scottish-raised sons a handful of times before passing. "A true shame," he adds softly. "We'll take him there someday," Sally promises. "I'd love to go."

"Ay, let's pack our bags then. What are we waiting for? Get outta bed lazy," he jokes with her. And as she laughs through the pain and tiredness, he lovingly kisses her forehead.

Outside their window, another National Front march proceeds— cars honk, people shout across the divide and young shaved headed men in steel toe capped Doc Marten's with red and white laces and

Union Jack patches swagger along demanding people like Noel and Liam—BLACKS—leave. But here and now, this family is untouchable.

Noel leans down and kisses her lips. His voice drops to a fierce whisper, "I would walk off the edge of the world for you both. If I had to."

"Don't talk like that," she says. "We've got nothing but time." Sally reaches for his hand, squeezing it tight.

"Aye, our love is... enduring."

THE EDGE OF THE WORLD
~ 1996 ~

Sally takes a blanket from the boot and wraps it around her shivering children.

"LeeLee, I brought you here because I want you to know that your father and I have an enduring love. A love that transcends time and space." She studies their small confused faces. "You know what that means? Enduring?"

Both children shake their heads.

"It means forever," she explains. "Like nothing can break it. Ever." Her voice catches again. "I forgot that for a while. But you must never forget that our family's love is enduring. Your love for Patsy and her love for you are enduring."

"Enduring," they echo in unison, the word strange and solemn on their small tongues.

The three small figures form a vivid tableau against the vast pale blue sky, green land and dark blue ocean. Sally opens the urn. Three hands—Sally's, Pats' and LeeLee's—shake and scatter Noel's ashes together. The wind catches the remnants of Noel's physical form, sending a cloud of grey flecks dancing across the surface of the sea before disappearing into the distance.

At one with the earth again.

Enduring.

Afterwards, back at the car, Sally shows Little Liam the urn, still containing a handful of ashes. "These are for you LeeLee," she tells him gently. "To hold on to him."

Little Liam takes the urn carefully, his small hands cradling it close to his chest.

"That's Daddy's heart," she whispers. "It belongs to you."

JODPHUR PT II
2025

In her hospital room, Sally lies on her bed surrounded by doctors. Her breath comes in shallow gasps. Blood stains the hanky she clutches in her hand and her face is noticeably bruised and jaundiced.

"Nurse Jagdeesh, how could you let this happen?" The doctor's voice is sharp with accusation and scorn.

Jagdeesh stands with his head bowed, in utter shame, with utter sorrow. "I am very sorry, Doctor," he offers emphatically.

"Don't be sorry to me. Be sorry to our patient."

Sally, weak as she is, raises her hand in protest. "He owes me no such thing."

She touches Jagdeesh's face softly. "You have been..." A violent bloody cough interrupts her. "I hope that you can come meet them with me."

"I promise, you rest now, Sally."

The doctors exchange solemn glances and quietly exit, leaving Jagdeesh to keep vigil. He tries to maintain his professional composure, despite his tears.

"Hey. No." Sally's voice is barely a whisper now. "You, you don't shed a tear for me. Don't be afraid. I am merely one star... in an... infinite cosmos."

Jagdeesh shakes his head fiercely. "No. No. You are my star."

A smile forms across Sally's pale lips. "I know. I love you, Son."

"I love you too, Mum. All of your children do."

Sally's eyes drift to the door, where row upon row of her former students wait silently. Children she'd taught English to, the only skill she had to give, along with a lifetime's worth of hard-earned wisdom.

Her eyes drift next to the half-finished letter on her bedside table. "I just need a minute. Longer. I have to finish my... forever letter." Her hand trembles as she struggles to lift her pen.

"Okay, let's finish this thing," Jagdeesh says, taking the pen from her.

"And then, I'll rest. And then... I'll be with my babies again," she vows. Hope flickers across her face as she struggles for breath.

"You promise?"

"I promise," he says with absolute surety.

"Shine on Sally. Shine on," he adds.

And she drifts out of consciousness.

THE EDGE OF THE WORLD
DAY 4

The dusty white and blue pick-up truck glides along the mountain road, painting a small moving portrait against the vast Highland panorama. Yellow grass, purple heather, and white snow-capped mountains blur together in an obscenely glorious riot of colour. The horizon arrives, where the Atlantic Ocean shimmers like a promise, a promise the siblings have upheld, through thick and thin, high and dry.

Liam absorbs the moment, soaking in every nuance and detail of the landscape and of this feeling. Hope. Acceptance. Himself. He can't help but think about the final track his mum insisted they put on their mixtape CD. He remembers it vividly, his head on her shoulder as she picks up a random single by a band named Suede, which Liam thought at the time was a very strange name for a band. Not like Oasis or Blur. Though now he thinks about it, Suede was really quite on point for what they were—sleek, sophisticated, over the top—but somehow also really fucking cool.

"You need a strong closer," says Sally, her fingers tracing the edge of the plastic CD as she absorbed the artwork. *"Something that tells your intended, the person you're making this CD for, what you really mean to them, and maybe what you want from them. Other than your opening song, it's perhaps the most important track on a mixtape."*

In the back of the truck, Liam closes his eyes and lets the gentle rocking motion carry him back. He tries to remember the opening to "Stay Together", the ethereal guitar intro flowing into that unmistakable drum beat. Brett Anderson's haunting voice had seemed almost otherworldly to him as a child—a voice that didn't belong to the laddish reality of the other Britpop cohort. He's listened to this song every day on his precious CD, and now the chorus repeats in his head like a mantra, like his scratched CD stuck on its most important message. *Stay Together. Stay Together. Stay Together.*

Patsy watches her brother, his lips moving silently to words only he can hear, wondering what he is singing. She hears a schism of words: hearts, together, skyscrapers, stay, time bombs. She's sure that in Liam's head it's all making sense. When in reality, he's just as lost in the music as she is, surfing a nostalgic fever dream set in Peckham, during the unforgettable summer of 1996 as Bernard Butler wields his 1961 Gibson ES-355 to close the song with his soaring guitar riff. The chords flow, as enigmatically as Bernard himself, through the massive speakers connected to the stereo stack system in the family's front room, while Sally, who has by now thrown on a black leather jacket, sways and sings along playing air guitar. Fully embracing the moment, fully embracing being these kids' mum—and all the memorable moments that come with it.

As Liam opens his eyes, he isn't quite sure if this memory is exactly as he remembers it, or if he is mixing his mum up with Brett Anderson's inimitable style. Fuck it. Both are as cool as each other, he figures. My mum could have been in Suede. He thinks.

The ornate steel Indian trunk that was delivered to Uncle Chidi's office just a few days earlier, still sits between the siblings, silently experiencing every conversation, every argument, every song, every car ride, train ride, all the highs and all the lows of their journey. For the first time since they'd begun this road trip, the trunk doesn't feel like a burden. It feels like what it truly is—their mother's last gift. When she finally sees her mum, and she opens this box, whatever is inside, Patsy figures it's inconsequential compared to the gift of reconnecting with her brother, after so many lost years.

They round a bend in the road, and the full expanse of the North Atlantic opens up before them, endless and ancient. Liam and Patsy exchange a glance. No words are needed now.

1 mile to go.

0 miles to go.

Arrival.

They've reached the edge of the world where Sally surely awaits.

CHAPTER 19
THE FOREVER LETTER

The pickup truck trundles along the bumpy road, its heavy wheels crunching over loose stones as the vast windswept landscape stretches out around them. Liam and Patsy, still pressed together in the back, jolt with each rut and pothole as the truck chases down the gradient, past the towering lighthouse towards the shepherd's cottage. The Indian trunk that was wedged between them starts to slide with each bump, breaking free from the safety of their legs. As it bounces dangerously toward the edge of the truck bed, Liam lunges forward, throwing himself on top of it just before it can vault over the side and down the sheer cliff drop. By now, the weight of the day, and their journey through the country from wherever to right here, has caught up to them. They're running on fumes and determination now, too far to turn back, too close to give up.

They finally pull up to a small stone shepherd's cottage perched on the edge of the cliff. Smoke billows from its chimney, curling up into the rapidly darkening sky. The Scottish Highlands roll away behind them, but ahead—nothing but the endless Atlantic, stretching out to the horizon, no longer a crisp line like it was in Scarborough. Here the lines blur, Patsy notices, like something from a Turner masterpiece—where sea and sky melt into one another seamlessly. The kind of paintings she'd spent hours admiring in the National Gallery during those rare enjoyable day trips that her private school insisted upon. The setting sun hovers just above this threshold, casting a warm glow that transforms everything it touches, creating an almost ethereal, spiritual quality to the landscape.

Patsy giggles at Liam sliding around holding the trunk, and stands up to ride the final twenty metres or so, holding on to the roof bar of the truck—soaking it all in. Her usual critical filter has dissolved somewhere between Scarborough and here. She doesn't try to judge or analyse or find fault, she just absorbs the beauty without restraint. For perhaps the first time since childhood, she allows herself to be genuinely moved by something, her carefully constructed walls dismantled by exhaustion and the raw magnificence before her.

"Last stop—the 'Edge o' the World'," calls the driver, turning back with a nod.

And it truly feels that way to her now—standing at the precipice of something much bigger than herself, or their journey, or even their mission to find Sally. Something ancient and timeless.

The cliff drops away just beyond the cottage, with nothing between them and America but three thousand miles of churning ocean. Windswept mountains cradle the little hut on three sides, sheltering it from the worst of the elements. The air tastes different here compared to Scarborough, Liam thinks. Here it tastes of salt and something else—soil, peat, moss, thistle and heather, the raw essence of Scotland herself.

Liam hops out first, his long legs stiff from the journey. He stands motionless, at first welcoming the scenery, which makes a stark change from the decrepit council estate he left just a few days earlier. But then recognition floods back. This is no stranger's landscape to him. The memories might be faded, distant, but they're here—lurking just beneath the surface of his consciousness.

"Why the hell do I know this place?" Liam mumbles to Patsy.

The siblings wave off the pickup, watching until it disappears around a bend in the track.

"I remember this place," Liam says quietly, his voice nearly carried away by the wind.

Patsy steps beside him, her face solemn. "Me too. The cottage." She gestures toward a flat piece of ground a few yards away. "And Mum parked over... there. And we walked to the edge."

She points toward the cliff, where the land simply vanishes. That cliff edge—still the same after all these years. Still dangerous. Still final.

"I thought she was going to kill us," Liam says.

"Blimey," Patsy whispers, the recognition of what could have been, but what wasn't, passing like a shadow across her face.

"It's where we spread Dad's ashes."

Patsy steps closer, putting her arm over his shoulder, pulling him into a sideways hug. The gesture comes more naturally now than it would have even a day ago. "Do you remember him? Noel?"

"Bits and pieces. Hugs. Laughter."

Liam's mind flickers back to a moment in time so distant he can't be sure if the memory is real or constructed: *Noel, his face bright with joy, lifting three-year-old Liam high above his head, their laughter mingling in the sunny afternoon.*

Liam walks to the precipice, his body now tense against the chilly coastal wind. He stands in the exact same spot where, as a child, he'd watched his mother scatter his father's ashes. The ocean, so far, far below, looks the same—eternal. In another twenty-nine years, it will still be here, unmoved by whatever other human dramas play out on its shores.

"You think Mum's in there?" Patsy asks, nodding toward the shepherd's cottage, where a warm light glows from behind the tartan curtains. She notices the hint of a shadow moving around inside.

The cottage looks cosy, inviting even—a beacon of warmth against the rapidly cooling evening. And as the sun sets on their epic journey, it casts long shadows of the siblings while painting the sky in streaks of amber and violet.

Inside the hut, someone watches through the window as Liam and Patsy approach. The figure coughs violently, the sound hidden by the thick stone walls.

The wooden door to the shepherd's cottage slowly creaks open, silhouetting a figure against the warm light from within. The person's face is obscured, shrouded in the shadows between the indoor light and growing evening darkness.

Liam's heart leaps into his throat. "Mum," he calls, breaking into a run. "MUM! It's Mum! Mum, we've got so much to tell you…"

Patsy runs too, her face alight with a mixture of excitement and trepidation. So many years, so many things to say and ask… which she can do now with her brother beside her.

As they get closer, the figure resolves into a distinctly different shape. Taller, broader-shouldered, Indian. Jagdeesh emerges from the hut, with Sally's final letter clutched in his hand, his expression sombre, his bottom lip quivering.

The setting sun catches the trio perfectly as they converge. The light is golden, almost ethereal, as if blessing this moment of reunion. But there's something wrong with the picture—only Jagdeesh casts a shadow across the rocky ground. The siblings' shadows, which had slowly returned throughout their journey as they found their way back to themselves, have vanished again.

Jagdeesh speaks quietly, his words carried away by the wind. "Your mother, Sally," he begins, his voice heavy, "she wanted so desperately to be here. To see you both. But—"

Liam drops to his knees as the truth slams into him. The journey, the letters, the trunk—all of it orchestrated by a woman who knew she would never see the end of the story. The realisation crushes something inside him, the hope that had been building throughout their journey.

Beside him, Patsy crumples to the ground, her legs giving out beneath her as she processes Jagdeesh's words. Her face twists with grief, freshly realised and raw. The hope and positivity that's been so hard for her to achieve, so hard for her to earn, evaporates in a mere millisecond. After years of cynicism, she'd finally allowed herself to believe in something—to envision a reunion, a reconciliation, a path forward. And now that fragile belief is as diminished as the shadow she no longer casts.

"I'm so very sorry," Jagdeesh says, extending the letter toward them, his eyes glistening with emotion and his face fraught with pain.

"She fought so hard to be here. Her last wish was for both of you to complete this journey—together."

The sun sinks lower on its path—creating another beautiful infinity loop, continuing its cosmic cycle that will continue regardless of the countless human tragedies that have happened this day. Yet for Liam and Patsy, time once again stands painfully still.

𝄞

A pot of chai bubbles on the open stove, infusing the shepherd's hut with its warm, spicy aroma. Despite the tragedy hanging in the air, Jagdeesh has managed to create something resembling a home in this remote outpost. Universal skills learned from years of making people comfortable when they are at their lowest. The tea suddenly boils over, hissing as it hits the hot surface.

"Oh bugger," Jagdeesh mutters, rushing to move the pot.

Patsy and Liam sit at the wooden table, faces drawn with grief. Their eyes are red-rimmed, and they periodically dab at tears with their sleeves. The ornate Indian trunk rests between them, its brass fittings catching the firelight.

Jagdeesh coughs violently into his elbow, then wipes his nose with a handkerchief.

"One week in the Scottish summer and I get my first ever cold," he says, attempting to lighten the mood.

Patsy looks up at him with disbelief crossing her features. "You've waited for a week? Alone?"

"What did you do?" Liam adds, his voice empty of feeling.

Jagdeesh pours three cups of chai, the steam rising in light wisps. "I'd like to say meditate—but to be honest, I just reflected on the time we had together." He hands them each a cup. "I was a street kid, and, well, she took a lot of us in. She paid for my nurse training. So it was only proper that I waited..." He gazes out the window at the endless Scottish darkness. "Forever, if I had to."

The wind moans around the cottage, infiltrating through the cracks and crevices of the walls and roof creating an eerie and haunting accompaniment to their collective grief.

"What if we had never come?" Patsy asks, her voice barely above a whisper.

Jagdeesh's eyes soften. "Sally knew you would."

He slides the envelope across the worn wooden table. The movement is gentle, almost ceremonial.

"In every fibre of her being, she knew you would come. Even though she knew she wouldn't be able to come herself."

Liam reaches for the letter, then hesitates, his hand trembling above the envelope. The paper is cream-coloured and expensive—the kind Sally would have chosen for something important. Patsy places her hand over Liam's, and together they open it, unfolding the pages within to reveal Sally's elegant handwriting.

To my dear children,

Liam begins reading, his voice unsteady,

Whom I love more than life itself.

The words lift from the page as Sally's voice seems to come in with the wind to fill the room:

So, you have reached the end of my little treasure hunt and presumably Jagdeesh has told you the news that I am no more.

If not, surprise.

In her private room in India, Sally sits propped against pillows, her writing paper sits squarely on her tray table. Her bruised face is now more gaunt than ever, her once vibrant skin now paper-thin and yellow—but her eyes remain bright, for now at least, as she delays the morphine. The pen moves slowly across the page, each word carefully considered, each movement of her hand deliberate and painful, like trying to chisel her legacy into stone, with each word written, harder and more painful to write than the last.

I am sorry not to deliver these words in person.

She writes, the scratching of her fountain pen provides a gentle counterpoint to the fan's steadfast rotation.

My hope was that by re-treading our anguish-filled footsteps together, you would replace them with happy memories and let go of any malice in your hearts about shitty Great Yarmouth caravan parks, dropped ice creams in Scarborough or being chased by the police through the north of England.

A violent cough rips through her body, and a drop of blood spatters the page. She stares at it for a moment, then continues writing beside it.

Back in the shepherd's cottage, Liam and Patsy huddle closer together over the letter.

The paper quivers in Liam's hands as he reads.

I owe you both an explanation, and an apology.

Sally's voice seems to emanate from the pages:

I didn't want to slide away from this world only to find that I've lived just the length of it. I wanted to have lived the width as well.

And I did.

But I had to let you both go, for all our sakes.
Because I was a runaway train heading into the abyss.

Sally closes her eyes as she writes, recalling her journey: *She stares at a handful of prescription pills in her palm, contemplating oblivion. She walks away from the council flat, her shoulders hunched against the guilt. The winning lottery numbers reveal themselves as she scratches—she can't believe her luck.*

Dazed but determined, she walks through the departure gates at Heathrow, then steps off a plane into the wall of heat that is Jodhpur, ready to start again.

So I got lost.
I lived.
I breathed.
And then I found myself.

Sally remembers herself writing on a chalkboard, teaching English to a classroom of eager children. Outside, she embraces street kids with the same fierce protectiveness she once showed her own children. And in her quiet moments, she sits alone, tracing the outline of Liam and Patsy's faces in her Scarborough Polaroid, her most treasured possession.

And I looked back, not in anger, but in happiness.

Sally's voice continues.

I remembered the good and forgot the bad.

Her words pause, before:

Patsy, your fortitude...

Liam passes the letter to Patsy, their fingers brushing. Layers of Patsy's fringe fall in front of her face, while the gentle firelight catches in her tears as she reads.

Patsy, your fortitude to do the right thing has always been your greatest strength.

No matter what, you always come around fighting for those who need you.

Like in Great Yarmouth in '96...

Patsy's suddenly back in Great Yarmouth '96: *Her small hand rips open Wayne's face as she defends her brother. Her eyes ablaze with righteous fury. A fury that often got in the way of her thought process as she got older, but which has also protected her every day since. She recalls washing Liam's hair throughout the years. An act so intimate and tender on the surface, but loaded with fierce protection within.*

Sally's voice resumes from her deathbed as she struggles to keep the fountain pen upright:

...and this fortitude is why you are here, with him now.

As you blossomed into a smart, headstrong teen, I became ashamed of my living situation in comparison to what your father offered.

When I should have taken you under my wing, I made up excuses not to see you. In doing so, I would have realised that you were just growing into your honest and tenacious self.

These are traits that I lack, and I am so immensely proud of you, and of the Banshee inside of you.

I regret suppressing my inner Banshee. I allowed your father to take too much of me.

Ultimately, it led to our family breaking down, and this was my fault.

Patsy reads the last couple of lines aloud, the words resonating through her as though Sally is in the room, reading along with her:

You should have been raised in a loving home, by your loving mother, and for this I am sorry.

I am so sorry to leave you, my beautiful baby girl.

Patsy's body shakes uncontrollably with sobs until she goes limp, with exhaustion and utter dejection. Liam wraps his arm around her shoulders, pulling her close. She hands him back the letter, unable to continue, so Liam picks up where she left off reading aloud:

Liam, your compassion to quickly forgive could be perceived as cowardice.

The world is downright mean and those who aren't cut-throat seem to get beaten.

It's not fair.

But you never bemoaned your situation and walked away from every attack, fight and jibe with your head held high.

The memories flood in for Liam: *His younger self walking away from Wayne and his mob, his dignity intact despite the taunts. He turns away from the bodybuilder in the petrol station, rather than escalating the confrontation. He sees the sneering face of the Tesla bro as he drives away in his orange Golf, content with his own station in life, content with Ol' Girl.*

He gathers his strength and continues reading Sally's forever letter:

Despite the nature of your father's passing...

Liam succumbs to a brutal flash memory: *Noel surrounded by racist thugs, trying to protect himself as steel-toe-capped boots connect with his body, over and over. The sickening crack of bones breaking, along with Noel's cries are only amplified by the silence in the alley as passersby run and hide, rather than help.*

Despite the nature of your father's passing... you have never raised a fist in anger, and for this I am so immensely proud of you.

So, no, your compassion is no weakness, it is your greatest strength.

When Patsy was taken, it was just you and me. Me and you. Together. Everywhere. You latched on and wouldn't let go.
You became my shadow.
I perceived this as suffocating...

The image is sharp and painful: *Sally storms out of their flat, vodka bottle clutched in her hand, her face contorted with frustration as she shouts: "You're suffocating me."*

The letter trembles in Liam's hands as he reads by the firelight of the cottage. His tears fall onto the paper, blurring the ink.

I perceived this as suffocating...
...when I should have perceived this as love.

He continues reading, but this time his voice breaks.

That was my mistake.
When I should have listened, I shouted.
When I should have pulled you closer, I pushed you away.
When you needed me most, I left.

This memory perhaps cuts the deepest of all: *The front door stands open, with Liam sitting alone in the middle of their flat, on the footstool, with devastation written across his young face as he realises his mother may never come back. For Liam, time stops, and this broken moment in his timeline becomes* his stasis for the next fifteen years, waiting to continue, only when his mum returns.

Liam wipes the tears from his eyes, as Sally reads from her deathbed, her voice timelessly joining Liam's across the divide of space and time:

I am so sorry to leave you,
my beautiful baby boy.

In her room in India, the light has dimmed to a soft glow. Through the half-open door, the children from her school wait silently, their worried faces illuminated by the tealight candles used to mark the doctor's pathway between them. Inside, Sally struggles to finish the letter, her breathing laboured, each word now a gargantuan effort. Jagdeesh sits beside her, his hand steady as he takes the pen.

"Let me," he whispers.

Sally nods and speaks the words, each syllable a precious expenditure of her waning strength.

Never forget,

She says,

I bore both of you in the same womb.
Though separate, we are one and our love is enduring...
forever.

Jagdeesh writes these words, carefully and deliberately. The most important words he has ever had to write.

Please don't look back in anger at our time together,

Sally continues.

But I don't make this a demand from beyond the grave.

All I ask for, is your forgiveness.

Her voice grows fainter, but her eyes remain clear and determined.

Thank you for taking me on this final journey with you.

I'm sorry if I was ever a burden.

She pauses, gathering her remaining strength.

I love you, forever.

Mummy XX

Sally closes her eyes, and a peaceful expression finally settles over her face. She draws her last breath, holds it for a moment, and then, she lets go—making a gentle, almost imperceptible sigh. She passes into time. This has been her last day. But even when this day ends, her time within today's infinity loop—remains eternal. As it does for us all, when our time comes.

Outside, in the still and quiet ward, the rows upon rows of Sally's students—young and old, all Sally's children—light their individual candles one by one. The small flames spread until the ward and corridors are aglow with their quiet vigil.

In the silence that follows, the only sound that resonates through are the gentle weeps of Jagdeesh, as he lets go of his mum.

The fire in the shepherd's cottage makes a loud crackle, waking Jagdeesh from reminiscing about his own painful recent past. Patsy's raw cries fill the space between the cottage walls while she sobs into Liam's shoulder, her body convulsing with the primal grief that only losing a mother can unleash. It's a pain so visceral and all-consuming that it defies articulation.

The hut feels smaller now, the walls closing in as they huddle together on the rough wooden floor. The crackling fire offers neither warmth nor comfort, just dancing shadows.

Jagdeesh moves quietly, almost reverently, across the room. He slides a simple steel key toward Liam. Their eyes meet in a silent exchange of permission, of passing responsibility.

With trembling fingers, Liam reaches for the key. He turns to the Indian trunk that has been their constant companion throughout this journey. Whatever is inside was the reason they came together in the first place, the reason they undertook this mad road trip from one end of one country to the other end of another. A unification of two very different countries, a unification of two very different siblings. But as different as they may look, all are bound by an unshakable and enduring love. Whatever is inside this Indian steel trunk is their mum's last surprise, *the total sum of my estate,* as she told them in her very first letter.

The padlock clicks open with surprising ease.

Inside the trunk—the vessel they've carried for miles, argued over, protected—sits three items:

The Scarborough Polaroid, of the three of them.

An ornate iron key, its intricate design catches in the firelight.

And a square urn, with a sleeping lioness adorning its lid.

"Sally's ashes," Jagdeesh says softly.

The simple words detonate in the room. The finality of it. The absolute, irrevocable truth that Sally is gone forever—reduced to dust in an ornate container.

"No... no... NOOOOO!"

Patsy's wail isn't the controlled Banshee scream Liam has grown accustomed to. This is something deeper, more guttural, torn from somewhere primal. She lunges forward, snatching the urn before anyone can react, and bolts for the door.

The cold night air hits Liam's face as he scrambles after her. The wind has picked up, carrying the salt of the sea and the Atlantic rain in with it.

Patsy stands at the cliff edge, her silhouette stark against the backdrop of the endless black ocean. Her scream carries over the waves—not performative or theatrical, not like Patsy of old, this time it's a howl of pure anguish that seems to come from the deepest darkest part of her. She holds the urn tightly against her chest, not a mother cradling a child, but a child cradling her mother.

Then, for a heart-stopping moment, she leans forward, toes inching over the precipice.

Liam rushes forward, Jagdeesh close behind.

"It's not fair and it's too hard," Patsy sobs, her words whipped up by the wind into an echo.

Liam inches closer, hand outstretched. "I know."

Patsy spins around, eyes flashing with sudden fury through her tears. "No—you don't. You had time with her. And nobody came for me."

"She knew that—" Liam starts.

"But what about you?" Patsy's words crash over him. "I had no one growing up. A violent father and a horrible, fucking horrible, stepmum. Patsy, don't eat this, don't do that, wear this. Wear that. Think of our reputation—" Her voice rises to a scream. "WELL FUCK YOUR REPUTATION!"

She struggles to breathe as her chest heaves with every hitched intake of cold oceanic air. "I have no happy memories of her, just this stupid broken watch."

With her hands shaking, she rips Sally's watch from her wrist. For a moment, it dangles from her fingers, suspended over the abyss below. But even as her arm extends, her fingers tighten around it, refusing to let go of this last tangible connection to her mother.

Then—a movement that stops Liam's heart—Patsy steps one foot over the edge. Below is the abyss of the Atlantic, one slip, one gentle push from the wind and it will mean certain death. Liam's seen the look in Patsy's eyes before, in their mother, on this same precipice in 1996.

"Patsy, please." Liam's voice breaks. "Please."

The wind whips his pleas away, but he continues, drawing closer. "You're right. I could have done more—I should have done more." The truth spills from him now, no filters, no pride. "You're right. I had Mum and time passed. And more time passed, and more, and it felt okay cos Mum was there."

His voice grows stronger as he moves toward her, inch by inch—hand still outstretched. "And I clung to her for dear life. So no wonder she upped and left."

The confession burns his throat on its way out. "I squandered my time with her. And then she wasn't—there."

Patsy's eyes lock with his, the fury within her slightly ebbing, making room for something else—recognition.

"And no wonder—I reminded her every day of that moment with my refusal to move forwards."

His voice cracks again, but he pushes on. "It broke her, and it's my fault she walked away," he confesses.

"I'm sorry."

The words hang in the air between them, inadequate but cathartic.

"I just stopped."

"I just couldn't get past you leaving."

Patsy braces against the strong wind, which whips around them.

"But I promise from this day, minute, second, moment forward, I will never leave you alone."

A beat passes between them, suspended like Patsy's foot over the edge.

Then slowly, achingly slowly, she steps back onto solid ground.

Liam extends his hand, palm up—it's more than a simple gesture, it is an invitation. A promise. For a better life ahead.

She wobbles slightly, clutching the urn and watch tightly in one hand as she reaches for him with the other. Their fingers touch, then clasp, and he pulls her into an embrace.

They stand there, holding each other facing the howling wind, silhouetted against the vast expanse of sea and sky. Two broken pieces, finally fitting together.

Time seems to stop around them—a perfect, crystallised moment of connection.

Tick. Tock. Tick. Tock.

The sound of time, which has haunted them both since childhood, seems to surround them, growing louder. As if the Universe itself is now spinning around them and only them, circling, observing this pivotal moment from every conceivable angle.

Times a funny thing, ain't it?

This single thought echoes simultaneously through both their synchronised minds.

Sometimes, the clock stops for all of us and getting it going again... well, that's the hard part.

Their embrace tightens.

But you got to. Get it going again.

Still clutched tightly in Patsy's hand, Sally's broken watch—frozen in time at 3.33 since 1996—flickers back into life. The second hand twitches once, then continues its steady march forward.

Time resumes its course.

Tick tock tick tock...

CHAPTER 20
GENESIS

SALLY '96

The Golf rattles through the morning traffic of the Old Kent Road. Sally's hands shake at the wheel, her knuckles as pale as her complexion. A nearly empty vodka bottle rolls across the passenger footwell, clinking against empty Coke cans. The tremors in her hands have nothing to do with the drink, though. They come from somewhere deeper. An end. An end to a priceless and unforgettable final holiday. An end to her family—the only thing she had. The only thing she thought she was ever good at.

On the radio, the familiar piano chords of the summer's biggest hit, "Don't Look Back In Anger", drift through the car's speakers. For a moment, Sally remembers singing along to it just days ago, windows down on the Scottish highways, the kids laughing in the back and shouting *SALLY* as loud as they could. Now the melody feels unfamiliar. She slams the radio off with the side of her fist. She hasn't got time for this song. Not with her new reality pressing down.

The rearview mirror reveals the equally drained little faces of her children. The new silence in the car is hauntingly oppressive, broken only by the rattling engine, Sally's staccato breathing and the shouts of the traders and shoppers on the busy street—where life goes on, no matter the weather, the family dramas or the political situation of the world.

Tell them it's going to be okay. Tell them you'll fix this. But the words don't come.

Richard's voice intrudes instead: *You're not capable, Sal. You're unravelling. Everyone can see it. She's better with me.*

Yesterday, in the Highlands, she'd nearly walked off a cliff with her children. Had it not been for LeeLee, her brave little boy, pulling Pats back... the thought makes her stomach wretch. *Could I do it again?*

"Mum?" Little Liam's small voice calls from the back seat.

"Not now, LeeLee," she says, softer than she means it to be.

The familiar terraced houses of Lyndhurst Grove appear, and Sally feels the weight of inevitability pressing down on her chest. The Social Services car is already parked outside their home. Two officers stand on the pavement, clipboards in hand. Richard's silver Audi gleams beside them, and just behind it, Minnie's green BMW Z3. *She even outdoes me in the car department.* Sally thinks. Despite it being a warm and pleasant morning, a cold sweat comes over her.

Sally pulls up, kills the engine, and sits still. She can feel their judgement through the windscreen. Every morning school run she's missed. Every parent's evening she's arrived at smelling of vodka. The time she made a show of herself at the kids Christmas play two years ago. Every time the neighbours heard her screaming at 3 am. Letting her son hit her husband with an ashtray. It all tallies up in their eyes: she's not a fit mother. *Maybe they're right.*

Before opening the car door, Sally turns around to face her children. Her eyes settle on Little Patsy, taking in every detail of her daughter's face. She unclasps the watch from her wrist—the silver Timex she bought years ago as a special treat to herself.

"Pats," she says, her voice cracking slightly. "Baby girl, I want you to have this. You always like playing with it, don't ya? Right? Tell me?"

The watch face is slightly cracked, the hands frozen in place. Time stopped at 3.33.

Little Patsy stares at it, confused. "But it's broken."

"I know, my love. It stopped working, but maybe..." Sally doesn't finish the thought. *Maybe one day you'll fix it. Maybe one day I'll fix us.*

She places it in Little Patsy's small palm and closes her fingers around it.

"Come on, we're here," she says, the words feeling empty in her mouth, coming out more on autopilot than with any genuine feeling. She opens the driver door, but hesitates, before sucking up whatever dignity she has left and lets the kids out.

The walk up the garden path takes a lifetime. Every step feels like time running backwards, undoing years of their life together. The older Social Services officer offers a tight, professional smile. Richard stands in the doorway, his face wrapped with additional bandages to really oversell his injuries. Minnie hovers behind him, not quite daring to step forward.

"Sally," says the Social Services officer. "Thank you for bringing Patricia back as arranged."

As arranged. Like this is some scheduled playdate.

"I have the court order here," she continues, passing her a document that Sally makes no move to take. "Mr Smith has been granted temporary sole custody, with a view to making arrangements permanent."

There he is, with the smuggiest fucking face I've ever seen him have, whatever did I see in him?! Desperation I guess, the same thing he probably saw in me.

Richard takes the opportunity to correct the woman, "It's Smythe, with an e, not Smith."

To this, the woman raises an eyebrow, she's heard it all before, but she's just a power broker for the state here, personal opinions are irrelevant.

"Come on, Patsy girl," he says, voice gentle in that way that makes Sally's skin crawl. "Let's get you settled."

Little Patsy looks up at Sally, her eyes questioning. *Tell them no. Fight for me. Please.* But Sally knows what happens when she fights. The bruises under her clothes serve as a warning—it will all only be held against her character anyway.

"You be good, Pats," Sally says, voice scarcely a whisper. She wants to kneel down, to hold her daughter one last time, but her body refuses to move.

Little Patsy hesitates, then takes Richard's outstretched hand. As they turn to go inside, Sally feels something inside irreparably tear.

"We'll need to make arrangements for your son as well," The woman says. "The council has a temporary—"

"No," Sally cuts in, finding her voice at last. "Liam stays with me."

The woman nods. "You'll need to register with housing immediately. Your tenancy agreement—"

"I know, we have until five o'clock," Sally says. "Come on, LeeLee."

She takes Little Liam's hand and turns away, unable to look back at the house that was once their home, at the daughter she's leaving behind.

Then, suddenly brightening, Sally picks up the pace. "Righty-ho, if we hurry, we can get a new flat before tea time, get you Maccy D's, yeah?" she says, dragging Little Liam faster than his little legs can manage.

Sally doesn't look back.

She can't.

Time has fractured for her, and all she can do is move forward, with the shattered pieces of her past falling away with each step.

PATSY '96

The car journey home feels like it's taking forever. Little Patsy sits beside her brother, who hasn't spoken since they left Scotland. Mum keeps glancing in the rearview mirror, her eyes wild and desperate.

They're going home, but it doesn't feel like going home. It feels like heading toward something terrible.

Patsy remembers the cliff, how the wind had whipped her hair into her eyes, how Mum had stood too close to the edge, talking about Liam's dad in that weird faraway voice. She remembers how LeeLee had pulled her back when Mum's eyes had gone strange and distant. It had been scary, but then Mum snapped out of it, and they'd spread LeeLee's daddy's ashes, and it had been beautiful, in a way.

Now, nothing is beautiful.

The Golf lurches to a stop outside their house. Patsy spots her dad's silver car and Minnie's cool green sports car and feels a weird twist in her stomach—relief and dread, tangled together like how LeeLee's headphone wires sometimes get. At least with Dad, there's no standing at the edge of cliffs. No long drives where no one knows where they're going. No Mum drinking from bottles that smell gross and that make her voice change.

And there's Minnie. And Minnie likes me, at least I think she does. She's always treating me, so long as I never mentioned her to Mum.

Sally turns off the engine, and silence fills the car. Her shoulders slump forward like she's carrying something very heavy. Then she turns around, her face no longer someone that Little Patsy recognises.

"Pats," Mum says, her voice strange and crackly. "I want you to have this. You always liked playing around with it, yeah?"

She holds out her silver watch—the one Patsy has always been told never to touch. The watch face is cracked, the hands frozen.

"But it's broken, Mum," Little Patsy says, not understanding.

"I know, love. It stopped working. But maybe..." Mum doesn't finish, she just places the broken watch in my hand, and I close my fingers around it.

It feels important.

Maybe Mum will explain later.

"Come on, we're here," Mum says, turning away.

They walk up the path like they're in slow motion. Dad stands in the doorway, his face half-covered in a big white bandage. Behind him, Minnie peers out, looking afraid of something before hiding back behind the door.

Two strangers with clipboards wait on the path. One of them, a woman with her hair pulled back so tight it looks painful, is talking to Mum, but I can't really hear what they're saying. "Court order, custody, time apart," and other grown-up words that make no sense.

Richard steps forward with a massive smile. "Come on, Patsy girl," he says, holding out his hand. "Let's get you settled." Patsy looks up at Mum, waiting for her to say something, to explain that this is just temporary, that they'll all be together again soon. But Mum's face has gone blank, like the telly does when the signal cuts out.

"You be good, Pats," Mummy whispers, not looking me in the eye.

Patsy hesitates, then takes her Daddy's hand.

It feels wrong, like sleeping in a bed that's not yours. I want to pull away, to run back to Mummy and LeeLee, but Daddy's grip is tight, and Mummy isn't even looking at me anymore.

The watch weighs heavy in her palm, she wonders if she's supposed to give it to Daddy or keep it a secret. She decides to hide it in her pocket. It's the one piece of her Mumma she has left.

As Richard leads her into the house, Patsy turns back. Liam is staring at her, his face screwed up in a way she's never seen before. It's my fault, she thinks suddenly. All of it. The fighting, the running away, everything. If I hadn't been so difficult, if I hadn't screamed so much, if I hadn't scratched that boy's face, she'd take me as well.

Inside, Minnie's concern doesn't quite reach her eyes. "You poor thing," she says, but it sounds rehearsed. "You must be exhausted after your... adventure."

"Holiday," Patsy corrects her as she moves to the window to see her mum and brother walking away. Mum's hand pulls LeeLee along a little too hard, he looks back, his eyes meet hers through the glass. He looks angry, no—more than angry. He looks like how she feels inside, like something is breaking.

Years later, she'll recognise it as the precise moment when time stopped for both of them. When their shared timeline splintered into two separate existences.

She clutches the broken watch in her pocket, the hands frozen exactly like her life is now. Stuck in place while everything moves on around her.

LIAM '96

Every bump in the road makes Little Liam's jaw clench tighter. The Golf crawls through the streets of London, and with each passing mile, the anger inside him grows. It's no longer hot and explosive like it was when Richard had tried to hit Mum a few days ago, when he smashed Richard's face with the ashtray. Now it's turned cold and hard, a block of unmeltable ice wedged deep in his chest.

The houses on their street look smaller than when they left. Shabbier. Or maybe it's just that everything looks different now after their family "holiday". Dad's urn sits between his feet, wrapped in his old Scotland football shirt. He grips it tightly as the car stops.

A black car waits outside my house. Two official officer types stand beside it with clipboards and serious faces. Richard's Audi is there too, gleaming like it's just been washed, and behind it, some green sports car I've never seen on the street before. Mum turns off the engine and sits still for a moment, her fingers tapping against the wheel in that way she does when she's trying not to reach for a bottle. She looks like she might be sick again, like she was when we were at the services earlier that morning.

Then she turns around, and Little Liam feels a flutter of hope. Maybe she's got a plan. Maybe she's going to tell them to run for it. Or she'll floor it again like the other day.

Instead, she takes off her watch—her special watch, the one she's always telling them not to touch—and holds it out to Patsy.

"Pats," Mum says, her voice tired. "I want you to have this. You always loved to play with it, remember?"

Little Liam stares, a fresh wave of anger surging through him. *Why does Patsy get the watch? Why not me? I'm the oldest. I'm the one who's always looked after Mum when she's been drinking. I'm the one who hit Richard with the ashtray to protect Mum. I'm the one who pulled Patsy back from the cliff edge when Mum was acting weird.*

"But it's broken, Mum," Patsy says.

"I know, love. It stopped working. But maybe..." Mum trails off, dropping the watch into Patsy's palm.

What about me? Little Liam wants to shout. *Don't I get anything?* But the words stay locked in his throat, behind the wall of ice. *Best not cause another fight.* He concludes.

Mum says something as she turns back to the front, but Little Liam isn't listening.

They walk up the garden path, each step makes the anger inside Little Liam grow. Richard stands in the doorway, a white bandage covering most of his left cheek. He tries to look concerned, but Little Liam sees the truth in his eyes—he's glad he hit him with the ashtray, in fact he wishes he hit him harder. Behind Richard, the blonde woman Mum beat up in her knickers hides behind the door.

What's she doing in my house again?

One of the officers, a woman in a dark suit, talks to Mum about custody and court orders. I understand more than they think I do. I've heard the neighbours talking, seen the way people look at Mum when she picks me up from school. I'm ten, not stupid. I know she drinks more than other parents. But then other parents didn't have their husbands beaten to death in an alleyway. I also know that.

"Come on, Patsy girl," Richard says, reaching out. "Let's get you settled."

Patsy looks up at Sally, waiting. Little Liam waits too, still believing, even now, that his mum will fix this. That she'll stand up straight, pull them both close, and tell everyone to get out of their house.

But Sally doesn't move. She just whispers, "You be good, Pats," and then looks away, like she doesn't care what happens next.

Little Patsy hesitates, then takes Richard's hand. As they turn toward the house, Little Liam feels something fundamental shift inside him. The world slows down. He hears his own heartbeat, loud in his ears, his nostrils flare, his lips purse, his pupils dilate.

He looks back at Pats, and their eyes meet. All his rage, all his hurt, all his confusion pours into that look. Not at her—never at her—but at everyone else. At Richard with his ugly face and his new car. At that cowardly woman hiding behind the door with her evil stepmother look and slitty judging eyes. At the officers with their clipboards and their rules. At Mum for giving up. At myself for not fighting harder.

Through the front door, he can see into the living room. The stereo system sits silent in the corner. The CD collection—meticulously organised by band, then album, then release date—stands untouched on the shelf. The curtains are fully open now, casting the room in bright sunlight. No blood on the floor anymore. Everything wiped clean. Everything in its place, pristine and still, so different from the warm, homely, messy space where he and Sally had made their mixtape together. Where all three of them had danced on the rug.

"We'll need to make arrangements for your son as well," the officer woman says. "The council has a temporary—"

"No," Mum cuts in, her voice suddenly firm. "Liam stays with me."

It's the only fight she has left in her, and she's using it for me. It should make me feel better, but it doesn't. Not after seeing Pats disappear into the house with Richard's hand on her shoulder.

"We have until five," Mum replies to something the woman says. "Come on, LeeLee. Let's get you a Happy Meal."

She takes his hand and pulls him away. But his head is already turned back, with his eyes fixed on the house, on the window where Patsy's face appears, small and pale behind the glass. He burns the image into his mind: his sister, watching him leave. In that moment, time stops for Liam Digsby. The internal clock in his head, in his heart, the thing that makes everything move forward, freezes. Everything that comes after—the council flat, the years passing by, Mum leaving—it all happens in a kind of suspended animation.

Static.

Unmoving.

He's looking back, not just at Patsy, but at everything—at their home, at their family, at the life they could have had... should have had, and this feeling will stay with him for decades to come.

Young Liam Digsby looks back in anger—and the clock stops ticking—waiting patiently for its moment to begin again.

CHAPTER 21
A COSMIC JOKE

DAY 5

The Scottish morning brings a stillness to the cottage that feels both sacred and heavy. Outside, a pale dawn breaks over Cape Wrath, washing the landscape in muted gold and cobalt blue. Inside, warmth returns to the space—the fire crackles in the hearth and a pot of aromatic chai simmers on the stove.

Sally's trunk sits open on the table between them. Its mysteries now revealed: the faded Scarborough polaroid, the ornate iron key that seems to promise something more, and of course, Sally's urn—with a sleeping lioness perched atop it. Just like Sally to choose something both understatedly elegant yet quietly fierce.

Liam carefully removes the lid of the urn. Then, reaching into his satchel, he pulls out Noel's urn. Without a word, he tips the last of his dad's ashes in with Sally's. "Look after each other," he whispers.

Jagdeesh moves around the tiny kitchen with the ease of someone who's lived here for years. His tall frame ducks instinctively under the low wooden beams as he reaches for three small glasses and a paper bag from a cupboard, revealing a bottle of Old Pulteney 18 Years Single Malt —'The Maritime Malt'—as proudly stated on its label, purchased from the distillery itself on his own epic journey through a country he's quickly fallen in love with.

"A toast?" he says, holding up the bottle. "For Sally."

Liam looks at the amber liquid with a moment's consideration, then gives an almost imperceptible but awkward shake of his head. "No, thank you," he quietly says.

"I'm an alcoholic, that's poison to me," Patsy says simply. No drama. No fanfare. Just the truth, stated aloud perhaps for the first time.

Something in the way she says it makes both men pause. It isn't an apology or a confession—it's a statement of fact. A truth she's ready to own. The first step toward fixing whatever was broken inside.

"But I'll have another chai," she says with a small smile.

Jagdeesh nods, returning the Scotch to the cupboard and reaching instead for the pot of chai that's been brewing. The rich scent of cardamom and ginger fills the small space as he pours three cups. "I don't drink either, was going to be my first, so… a waste of a hundred and fifty quids. I should have bought the 12-year."

They raise their mugs in silence, the steam rising between them.

"To Sally," Jagdeesh says softly.

"To Mum," echo Liam and Patsy together.

The tea is sweet and spicy, warming them from inside out.

Outside, the wind picks up, whistling around the nooks and crannies of the small cottage as if someone or something is calling to them.

It's cold at the cliff edge, where the wind whips at their hair and clothes, but somehow it feels right, natural. The vast expanse of ocean stretches before them, steel blue under the early light, whitecaps dancing across its surface all the way to the horizon. Morning puffins dart out over the water, hunting for their breakfast, while a golden eagle suddenly swoops over the trio's heads—causing the siblings to duck in alarm while Jagdeesh smiles, taking it as a sign that Sally is truly with them.

This really is the edge of the world, or at least, it feels that way.

Liam holds the urn carefully, its weight surprisingly substantial in his hands. Patsy stands beside him, her eyes red-rimmed but dry now.

They've cried their fill through the night and this moment calls for something else.

They look at each other and then back at Jagdeesh, who stands at a respectful distance away. With a slight nod, Patsy beckons him forward. This is his loss too.

"You should be with us, bro," Liam says. "She'd want that."

Jagdeesh steps forward, completing their small circle at the edge of the cliff.

Liam carefully removes the lid of the urn. For a moment, they all stare down at the grey ashes—the physical remains of the woman who brought them into the world, tore them apart, and ultimately reunited them as part of her final swan song.

Then, three hands reach forward and each takes a handful of ash.

As Liam's fingers close around the soft grey powder, a memory washes over him—standing in this exact spot nearly thirty years ago, the wind just as fierce, the ocean just as vast. Dad's ashes had felt different. Coarser. Or maybe that was because his hand had been so much smaller then, tucked between his mum's warm palm and Patsy's sticky fingers. He remembers looking up at Sally's face, the tears streaming sideways in the wind, and how she'd crouched down to their level after they'd scattered the ashes.

The words "enduring" and "love" echo in his mind like a mantra. He returns to the present as the wind carries Sally's ashes over the water, dancing and swirling before disappearing into the enormity of the sea and sky.

"An enduring love," Liam whispers.

"That transcends space and time," Patsy adds softly.

Their words hang in the air.

And for a moment, it's as if Sally's voice joins theirs, the same gentle collection of words from all those years ago, connecting past and present in a way that wraps around all three of them standing at the cliff's edge.

Back in the cottage, the once roaring fire has surrendered to ash. Patsy and Jagdeesh have already vacated the cottage and last to leave is Liam, who says goodbye and thank you to the ancient dwelling—his story in this place, has come to an end, for now. He gives a scrap piece of paper, which they all just wrote together, a final read. To make sure it's as perfect as can be.

It's perfect, so he leaves it by the bottle of Scotch on the table. A small gift for the lonely shepherd or lost sibling, who might next seek refuge in this remotest of outposts.

The door closes behind him, leaving just the unopened bottle of Scotch and a sense of finality hanging in the air.

The note reads:

> Please toast me to Sally.
> A beloved mother.
> From, her loving children

Some say, you may have to go all the way to the edge of the world in order to find yourself. Well, if you're looking, there's an ancient shepherd's cottage at the northernmost tip of Scotland where three lost souls once found themselves—and each other. The bottle waits, patient as time itself, for the next wanderer.

Jagdeesh's rental car, a black VW Golf, pulls away down the narrow track, growing smaller against the vast landscape until it's just a speck, then nothing.

Scotland's wilderness stretches in every direction—wind-stripped mountains meeting cloud-etched skies in a symphony of eternal permanence and constant change.

Ahead of the siblings lies whatever comes next. Behind them, the ghosts of who they've been. But now, unlike before, time moves forward for both of them.

𝄞

The warmth of the cottage fades behind them as they settle into Jagdeesh's rental car. The heater blasts against the Highland chill, but none of them speaks as the car pulls away from Cape Wrath.

Jagdeesh drums his fingers against the wheel before breaking the silence.

"Where to now?" he mutters to the satnav as he punches a postcode in, squinting at the display.

"God, these things make life so easy," he says.

Liam nods as he glances at Patsy in the passenger seat. "Yeah, better than a paper map, I s'pose." Both siblings chuckle at the inside joke.

Jagdeesh catches their shared moment. "So, I never asked, how was your trip here? Go smoothly?"

And to this, the siblings burst out laughing in hysterics—the kind of uncontrollable laughter that comes when the absurdity of everything finally hits home. Patsy wipes tears from her eyes, while Liam clutches his sides, half-recalling something that happened along the way.

Jagdeesh looks confused but smiles anyway, understanding that some jokes don't need to be shared to be healing.

"Mate, have we got a story for you..." Liam begins, catching his breath. "So it all began in Peckham, three, four—"

"Five," Patsy interjects, suddenly the authority on their shared timeline.

"Five days ago," Liam continues, settling back into his seat as the Scottish countryside rolls by. "Uncle Chidi calls us both, right, and..."

Their voices overlap as they take turns telling fragments of their journey, talking over each other, correcting details, arguing about who was at fault for what—the soundtrack of siblings who have finally remembered how to be a family.

𝄞

Staring out at the passing landscape, the countryside rolls by in a blur of greens and purples, the heather shifting in waves. The rhythmic motion of the road lulls them into a contemplative quiet.

Patsy's attention drifts to the trunk nestled between her feet. She runs her fingers across its surface before pulling it onto her lap. After a moment's hesitation, she opens it again, reaching for the iron key they'd discovered alongside Sally's urn.

She holds it up to the light streaming through the window. The key is heavy, ornate—older than anything mass-produced today.

"Jagdeesh," she says, breaking the silence. "What's this key for?"

He glances at her beside him, then back to the road.

"I honestly don't know. She wouldn't tell me. Sorry."

Liam catches Jagdeesh's eye in the mirror.

"That she kept entirely to herself."

The radio suddenly crackles to life—a distant signal from a radio tower—and the unmistakable saxophone intro of Blur's "Country House" fills the car. The sound of Britpop feels jarring after the solemnity of the morning, yet somehow appropriate too. Like time, life continues its constant march.

After about fifteen seconds of music, Jagdeesh pulls up to an imposing Scottish manor and cuts the engine mid-chorus.

"That's enough of that rubbish," he mutters, switching off the ignition.

"I was enjoying that," Liam protests, leaning forward between the seats. "Why are we stopping here? You'll be late for your flight, mate."

Outside the window stands a proper Scottish estate. The house is classy and old—weathered grey stone walls are draped with climbing ivy, tall windows reflect the clouds, and the slate roof has withstood well over a hundred Scottish winters. This place has history in every crevice. In other words, it's a proper nice gaff.

They step out onto the gravel drive, shoes crunching beneath them. The air smells different here—less wild than Cape Wrath, but still fresh.

A figure emerges from a parked car, and Liam's face breaks into stunned recognition.

"Chidi?"

It is indeed Uncle Chidi, looking every bit the distinguished lawyer in a tweed jacket that seems made for this setting. Liam crosses the distance between them and brings his uncle into a hug, who hugs him back with equal warmth, before yanking Patsy into the embrace.

"Aye son, feels good to come home."

"What are you doing here?" Liam asks.

"One last gift from Sally," Chidi says when they all separate.

Patsy holds up the iron key, glancing questioningly between Chidi and Jagdeesh.

"I was just told to bring you here," Jagdeesh explains, "and to tell Chidi when."

"Sal never touched a penny of the winnings for herself," Chidi says. "She believed that money was a cosmic gift, for the whole family." He gestures toward the front door. "Try it."

With tentative steps, Patsy approaches the heavy white oak door. She slides the key into the lock, and you know bloody what—it fits perfectly.

"When she fell ill," Chidi continues, "she made arrangements with me to buy this place—for you both. With one more condition?"

His words hang in the air for a moment.

"One. More. Condition?" Patsy asks. Her voice rises with each word, as her hand freezes on the key.

Liam's face tightens. The siblings exchange the same look of apprehension they gave each other back in Peckham when Chidi last told them that Sally had "one condition," which led to their epic road trip and eventual coming together.

"Your mission, should you choose to…"

Chidi's expression remains serious for a moment, then breaks into a huge grin.

"…nah, I'm only jokin'—no more conditions."

Relief washes over both their faces and Patsy turns the key with a chuckle.

The heavy door swings open.

As they cross the threshold together, the siblings realise, in their own way of course, that family isn't necessarily found in the places you might expect—not in childhood homes, council flats or swanky apartments, but in the journey with, and indeed, back to each other. This old house, with its history etched in stone, offers them something entirely new: a chance to start again.

Family.

CHAPTER 22
LIAM (REPRISAL)

A dull silver CD with fresh handwriting clicks into a Sony Discman D-99, circa mid-'90s, but it could well be older.

My CD Discman. You remember that right? You know, the one I told you about way back when? The one my mum got me in the summer of '96. Sony. Jet black. An absolute beast. A technological marvel. Well even so, it skips as I rake the last of the autumn leaves so I've upgraded to the fanciest new "thang"—an iPod. I do not know how this thing passed me by, but wow, 40,000 songs, it's rechargeable and has anti-shock protection. Whatever will they think of next? No more CDs though. Shame. But sometimes, well y'cant beat a classic can you? So sometimes I just come out here and listen to my new mixtape. The one I made with Mum is dead, as you well know, but Patsy showed me how to make a new mixtape on her laptop. Took like ten minutes, and there was like zero joy in making it—apart from that we made it together.

I hum a lot. I sing a lot. Not in the right key. Not the right words. But no one's listening... except the birds... and maybe Mrs McPherson from the other property who's always checking in on us like we're running some kind of illegal operation. Townies, she calls us.

From here, I can see the entire back garden of The Country House. That's what we call it: The Country House—with capital letters and everything. Like we're characters in some posh BBC drama. The garden stretches out, all neat hedgerows and flower beds that bloom in summer—it's hard work maintaining it, and expensive, but that's no problem these days, it's the least we can do for Mum. There's a swimming pool we rarely use—because it's fucking Scotland—and we're not as crazy as the average Scot. But it's ours.

There's only one thing missing, well not a thing, a person. But she's here with us. With me. In the wind. In the water. In the trees and in the soil. In my memories and therefore in whatever my version of eternity is. So long as I'm here, so is she.

Let me take you inside for a sec. The walls are covered with wicked framed photos of us on our journeys—each one a shared memory captured in time. That's why they're so special by the way—cos they were shared. We have one rule about what goes up—no selfies. There's baby me with Dad in his Scotland shirt—the proper vintage '80s one, which I've still got. Mum's ice cream Polaroid from Scarborough. The VW and GTI badges I rescued from the scrappie crusher, mounted on a plaque. I miss her, Ol' Girl, but life moves on. Here's one of me and Sofia, from Itsy Bitsy. I went back and… well, finally got to eat my sundae. And in the middle of it all, inside its cream envelope, Mum's Forever Letter, in a nice oak frame. We spent ages finding the right one. None of that IKEA rubbish. A proper, solid frame that'll outlast both of us.

I've got a job now. Nothing fancy, just the local record shop in town. Pay's shit, but I get first dibs on the vinyl that comes in. I've started collecting original Britpop pressings. The owner, Roy, says I know more about '90s music than anyone he's ever met. Like a walking fucking encyclopedia, he says. I take it as a compliment. I'm considering exploring the mid-late noughties rock era next, or Merseybeat or psychedelic prog-rock. Modern music is shit. I'll never get on board that wagon, there's too much fool's gold out there and if you give it time, you don't need to dig so hard for the good stuff. Although, I'm really getting into my Afrobeat.

The scratched mixtape CD sits framed like a platinum record on top of Patsy's new piano.

Though Patsy's made a nice addition to the title:

LeeLee, Patsy, & Sal's Mixtape
Classics & Tunes Only

Fair enough really. There was a time I'd have thrown a proper paddy about that, but that feels like another lifetime.

Patsy learned the sheet music to every song on the mixtape by the way. She's sitting there now, going through her pre-play routine. She does a quick meditation before hitting the keys... and it's the unmistakable opening piano of "Don't Look Back In Anger". I wish I could play the guitar to join in, or any instrument for that matter. But the magical language of music is still a mystery to me. And I kind of wanna keep it that way. So I just drum with my fingers on every bit of furniture and play air guitar. And as Noel sings about Sally not waiting, it makes me remember her, every time. About our time together. About our last and only holiday together through this amazing country. It's not perfect, mind, I can attest to that, but life's like crate digging, isn't it? You've got to sort through all the rubbish to find those rare pressings—the real gold among the fool's gold. And once you know what you're looking for, you don't have to dig so hard.

The music comes to a close as the sun dips low, where I catch my shadow stretching all the way to the edge of the garden. Long and defined against the grass.

And then there's another shadow, stretching alongside mine.

"LeeLee." She says.

"Patsy." I reply as I turn.

We stand there for a moment, our shadows touching on the lawn. Two people. One shadow. Though separate, we are one.

And our love is enduring.

Forever.

CHAPTER 23
PATSY (REPRISAL)

My Hunter's squelch satisfyingly in the mud and leaves as I cross the vast expanse of what some may call a field, but what we call the garden. Two hundred quid for wellies—my old Belsize Park self would've approved of the extravagance, I approve of the practicality. My cashmere jumper—Barbour, naturally—is just the right level of oversized with a cool hole in the corner from where I helped build the shed. My hair's often pulled back in a loose ponytail these days, I've grown out my natural colour and I can no longer be fucked with taking forty-five minutes to apply makeup—nah, these days, I prefer the just "'rolled out of bed glowing look'. Because in this part of the world you do roll out of bed glowing. But, I have never worn a tracksuit since. And I hope I never have to again. Scottish country cool, as Minnie would say. Though she hasn't said anything to me in a long long time. Last I heard, she and Richard were having a splendid time on their schooner in the Med. Good for them. The further away, the better.

From the kitchen window, I watch my big bro rake leaves like some kind of country squire. He's always listening to the iPod I bought him for his birthday. Mind blown was an understatement. Can't wait to teach him about the iPhone. That old Scotland shirt of Noel's hangs framed on the landing now—pride of place. I sometimes find myself staring at it, thinking about the gentle man who held my brother when he was small, whose ashes rest at the edge of the world alongside Mum's.

I often pray they are in good company.

Finally together.

The first month in this ridiculous house was tricky. You know, I measured it in footsteps. Eighty-eight from the front door to the back. Forty-four across the living room alone. Nineteen up each of the staircases—and then the loft. I was looking for the catch, the hidden clause, the trapdoor that would send me tumbling back into my old life. I feel I should have worked harder for it, I feel guilty. I stopped counting after six months, accepted the guilt and channelled it into helping others and sorting my life out so that I could make a home for my bro, who deserves it a lot more than I. It was Mum's wish after all.

A parting gift.

And one I won't spurn.

Ever.

I check my phone, which mercifully, I am always misplacing these days—three missed calls from my producer. The podcast is taking off. We've got a queue of sponsors now. Proper ones, not just generic wellness apps and overpriced organic dog food subscriptions. Last week's episode had over a hundred thousand downloads from all over the world. People call in, share their stories and thank me for making them feel less alone. Me—making people feel less alone. The irony isn't lost, trust, and all I have to be is honest. Turns out that people really do like the truth, it's the context in which one delivers it that matters. And for me, sober as a judge please. Though, every day is a challenge and some days are better than others, and worse. I often get the urge to find the nearest pub, or take a doomdive into social media. But then I pinch myself. I remember Liam's advice that it's poison, and one wouldn't drink arsenic or rub bleach in their eyes. So, with this in mind, it's become easier, and I knit instead. I have a whole basket of blankets, mittens, dog cosies and baby clothes. For, you know, the future.

The newspaper is open on the kitchen table: REVENGE PORN PERV JAILED. PATSY SPEAKS OUT FOR OTHERS. The case took forever, and it was invasive and horrible, but it was worth it. I had to stand in court, look him in the eye, and tell the judge exactly what he'd done. How he'd taken something private and made it public. How he'd tried to reduce me to just a body, just content, just clicks, just monetary gain.

Liam came with me every day. Sat in the gallery. Didn't speak much. Just existed in the space, a physical reminder that I wasn't alone. That I had backup. That if I fell, someone would catch me. We didn't shout when he was sentenced. We held our heads high and watched him skulk into the shadows, where he'll stay for the next few years.

Oh, my favourite part of the house, the living room, where the walls are covered with photos. New ones mixed with the old. Us exploring the Highlands. Us looking terrified on the rollercoaster at Blackpool. Us at Christmas, paper crowns askew, with Jagdeesh, who incidentally is considering coming over here to work for the NHS. In fact that reminds me, I better book us those tickets to see him soon. I can't wait.

And then there's the newest additions—Liam and Sofia, with their matching ice cream moustaches at Itsy Bitsy. I like her. She's good for him, solid. She makes him laugh, challenges him. More importantly, I trust her. Sometimes I catch them just sitting together in comfortable silence—him with his records, her with a book. It's nice. Watching my brother actually living, in his own way, instead of just existing.

Forwards, always forwards. Though sometimes, just sometimes, it's okay to look back. To remember. To use the past as part of an ever-evolving map, rather than as an early chapter in some book we've long forgotten about because we're so fixated on the present. And we're fixed on the present for good reason, it's how we live our lives now that matters.

I have to pass my pride and joy, my new Steinway, to step outside —I often just tinkle the keys in some random order as I pass. It reminds me of Mum. I can feel her in the music, in every note I play. For all our issues, I forgive her and I miss her dreadfully.

Today though, I come to find myself sitting properly at the bench as Liam passes behind me to go outside. As ever, I do my little meditation first—eyes closed, shoulders relaxed, breathing steady. It's become a ritual. Then my fingers find the keys and I play the opening notes of the first song that comes to mind. "Don't Look Back In Anger". I've been practising for months, learning every song on the mixtape. This one's become my favourite. Noel wears his heart unashamedly on his sleeve, it's honest. Pure. Loud and proud. It's a song about letting go of things you can't change—something I've become quite good at lately.

I can hear Liam in the garden, humming away, playing guitar with the rake and air drumming along. He thinks I don't notice, but I do. I always do. It's nice, having someone who sees you. Really sees you. This bliss may not last forever, but it is now—so, I'm gonna soak up every minute till it changes.

The cool autumn air fills my lungs, sharp and clean—better than any cigarette or flavoured vape, I tell ya. My Hunter-clad feet leave perfect imprints in the soft earth, and my shadow stretches across the lawn, meeting his. For a moment they merge, impossible to tell where one ends and the other begins.

"LeeLee." I say.

"Patsy." He replies as he turns.

The sun casts one long shadow across the garden.

One shadow from two people.

Two people both moving forwards.

Our love, like Mum said, is enduring.

Which means forever.

The end.

*To all mums who struggle,
and those we have lost along the way.*

SONGS FROM THE STORY

Street Spirit by Radiohead
Born Slippy by Underworld
Common People by Pulp
To The End by Blur
Connection by Elastica
Nancy Boy by Placebo
Champagne Supernova by Oasis
The Masterplan by Oasis
The Beautiful Ones by Suede
Alright by Supergrass
Tubthumping by Chumbawumba
Wonderwall by Oasis
Linger by The Cranberries
Broken Stones by Paul Weller
This Is How It Feels by Inspiral Carpets
Good Enough by Dodgy
Wannabe by Spice Girls
A Design for Life by Manic Street Preachers
Walkaway by Cast
The Changingman by Paul Weller
The Riverboat Song by Ocean Colour Scene
One to Another by The Charlatans
Roll With It by Oasis
Caledonia by Dougie MacLean
Stay Together by Suede
Country House by Blur
Don't Look Back In Anger by Oasis

ACKNOWLEDGMENTS

This novel celebrates the cultural impact of Britpop and British and Irish indie music of the 1990s. The author gratefully acknowledges the artists and their works referenced throughout this fictional story, including songs and albums by *Oasis, Blur, Pulp, Radiohead, Suede, Elastica, The Charlatans, Supergrass, Ocean Colour Scene, The Cranberries, Placebo, Underworld, Inspiral Carpets, Dodgy, Cast, Manic Street Preachers, Paul Weller* and many others who defined a generation and continue to inspire today.

All musical references are used for cultural commentary and artistic purposes under fair use principles. No lyrics have been reproduced, and all song titles, artist names, and album references are used respectfully to honour the music that forms the emotional backbone of this story.

Special recognition to Noel and Liam Gallagher of *Oasis*, whose sibling dynamic provided creative inspiration for this fictional narrative.

References to '*The Blues Brothers*' (Universal Pictures, 1980) and other films are used under fair use for cultural commentary purposes.

References to George Orwell's '*1984*' and other literary and artistic works are used for cultural commentary purposes.

THANK YOU

Sophie
Amber
Beau
Elliott
Syd
Moses
Italo
Bob
And to every one of my own 'wild' family members (past, present and future) from London to Melbourne, Colombo to Limerick and everywhere in between.
Time is relative.

DON'T LOOK BACK

Printed in Dunstable, United Kingdom